. . . irky and troubled. I cared for them.

—Chris Bohjalian, author of *The Sleepwalker* and *The Guest Room*

"Yoerg spins the story of a family on the brink of collapse—writing with tenderness, grace and truth."

—Randy Susan Meyers, bestselling author of *Accidents of Marriage*

"Beautifully rendered and aching in its portrayal of a mother's slide into mental illness . . . Destined to be a book club favorite."

—Christopher Scotton, author of *The Secret Wisdom of the Earth*

"[A] powerful and haunting . . . novel about betrayal and shame, acceptance and unconditional love. Book clubs will devour it."

—Barbara Claypole White, bestselling author of *Echoes of Family*

"[A] stirring tale of mothers and daughters, their secrets and their strength . . . [A] mesmerizing read."

—Lynda Cohen Loigman, author of *The Two-Family House*

"Gorgeously written . . . and unforgettable, your heart will break and swell in equal measure."

—Kate Moretti, *New York Times* bestselling author of
The Vanishing Year

"[A] powerful story . . . Yoerg's writing keeps us on a high wire of tension as we seek salvation and hope alongside her characters."

—Holly Robinson, author of *Folly Cove*

"With Yoerg's lush and moving prose, the characters are realistic and bold, yet so compassionately portrayed . . . This book will stay with you."   —Amy Sue Nathan, author of *The Good Neighbor*

"A suspenseful and poignant tale . . . Readers will need to be reminded to exhale."

—Amy Impellizzeri, award-winning author of
The Secrets of Worry Dolls

Titles by Sonja Yoerg

HOUSE BROKEN
THE MIDDLE OF SOMEWHERE
ALL THE BEST PEOPLE

All the Best People

SONJA YOERG

BERKLEY
New York

BERKLEY
An imprint of Penguin Random House LLC
375 Hudson Street, New York, New York 10014

Copyright © 2017 by Sonja Yoerg
Excerpt from *The Middle of Somewhere* copyright © 2015 by Sonja Yoerg
Penguin Random House supports copyright. Copyright fuels creativity,
encourages diverse voices, promotes free speech, and creates a vibrant
culture. Thank you for buying an authorized edition of this book and for
complying with copyright laws by not reproducing, scanning, or
distributing any part of it in any form without permission. You are
supporting writers and allowing Penguin Random House to continue to
publish books for every reader.

BERKLEY is a registered trademark and the B colophon is a trademark of
Penguin Random House LLC.

Library of Congress Cataloging-in-Publication Data

Names: Yoerg, Sonja Ingrid, 1959–author.
Title: All the best people / Sonja Yoerg.
Description: First Edition. | New York : Berkley, 2017.
Identifiers: LCCN 2016031060 (print) | LCCN 2016037964 (ebook) | ISBN
9780399583490 (paperback) | ISBN 9780399583506 (ebook)
Subjects: | BISAC: FICTION / Contemporary Women. | FICTION /
Family Life. | FICTION / Historical.
Classification: LCC PS3625.O37 A79 2017 (print) | LCC PS3625.O37 (ebook) |
DDC 813/.6—dc23
LC record available at https://lccn.loc.gov/2016031060

First Edition: May 2017

Printed in the United States of America
1 3 5 7 9 10 8 6 4 2

Cover art: *Sky and leaves* © by Karina Vegas/Arcangel Images;
House © by Sandra Cunningham/Trevillion Images
Cover design by Katie Anderson
Book design by Tiffany Estreicher

This is a work of fiction. Names, characters, places, and incidents either are
the product of the author's imagination or are used fictitiously, and any
resemblance to actual persons, living or dead, business establishments,
events, or locales is entirely coincidental.

To Helga

ACKNOWLEDGMENTS

I'm grateful to my agent, Maria Carvainis, for her unwavering dedication to this book and, as always, to me. I'm also indebted to my editor, Claire Zion, for her insightful direction in helping me realize the full potential of this story. Thanks to Elizabeth Copps and everyone at the Maria Carvainis Agency, and to Jennifer Fisher, Caitlin Valenziano and the entire team at Berkley.

Heartfelt thanks to my readers: to M. M. Finck, for early feedback; to my daughters, Rebecca and Rachel Frank, for their wisdom and patience; to Kate Moretti and Heather Webb for reading with care, more than once, and also for cheering me on, holding my hand and making me laugh. Special thanks to Helga Immerfall for reading, for believing in me and for taking me to Gaynes in 1972 when our mother couldn't accept that I needed a bra. My love goes out to all of you.

I'm not much of a joiner but I'm delighted to say I'm a Tall Poppy Writer. This group celebrates and supports the talent, passion, determination and general badassery of women writers, and I'm lucky to be counted among them.

Finally, I'm grateful beyond words to Richard Gill for loving me despite the fact that I think six impossible things before breakfast. You are honest, loyal and true—one of the best people.

MAD HATTER: Have I gone mad?

ALICE: I'm afraid so. You're entirely bonkers.
But I'll tell you a secret. All the best people are.

—Lewis Carroll, *Alice's Adventures in Wonderland*

Part 1

1

Carole

Carole was ten when her mother was committed to Underhill State Hospital. For a rest, her father had said. By the time Carole was old enough to understand that the truth lay elsewhere, beyond her grasp, her mother had received insulin coma treatment for hysteria, colonics for depression and electroshock just because, and Carole gave up wondering how her mother had lost control of her mind and simply coped with the fact that she had. Recently, Carole overheard the nurses say Solange Gifford was haunted, and although Carole did not, strictly speaking, believe in ghosts, it was as fitting a diagnosis as any.

She arrived at Underhill for her weekly visit a few minutes after nine and signed the register. A vase of lilies crowded the counter, the sweet musky scent mingling with the clinical bite of disinfectant and another smell, mushroomy and dark, that existed only here.

The receptionist greeted her and swiveled to face the switchboard.

"I'll have them send your mother out, Mrs. LaPorte."

"Thank you." Carole felt her cheeks flush. She'd forgotten the woman's name although she'd spoken with her a dozen times. "I'd like to go outside with her, if that's all right."

The woman smiled. If she was insulted at not being called by name, she hid it well. "We'll have to see how she is, but I'll let them know."

Carole nodded and handed a small shopping bag across the counter. "Some blackberries for her. They're coming on fast this year."

She took a seat in the empty waiting area, the same seat she always chose, the left of the two between the ashcan and the magazine rack. Stale cigarette, bad as it was, countered the other odor. She leafed through an issue of *Woman's Day* with Pat Nixon on the cover and suggestions for budget-friendly casseroles. One with tuna and cream of celery soup appealed to her, and her husband, Walt, was fond of celery, but she'd never remember how the recipe went. Someone had torn out a different recipe, ripped the page right down the middle, but Carole wouldn't dream of doing such a thing. Even if she could bring herself to destroy public property, she'd never enjoy the meal.

An orderly came through the double door dividing the reception area from the wards and propped it open with his foot. "Mrs. LaPorte."

She slid the magazine into the rack and stood, her legs heavy, her stomach queasy. She made her way down the corridor and glanced at the windows, set high, out of reach, and thought of the years, the thick stack of years her mother had been locked up here. Thirty-four years inside these brick walls, or barely outside them. Institutionalized. That word said it all. Long and cold and slammed shut at the end like a thick steel door.

The orderly escorted her into a lounge overlooking a slate patio beyond which lay a vast carpet of lawn. Solange stood beside the patio doors expectantly, reminding Carole of how her daughter's cat waited by the back door to be let out. Her mother noticed her and smiled. Perhaps she was having one of her better days.

"Mama." Carole rested her hand on Solange's narrow shoulder and kissed her cheek. She led her mother to the patio and breathed deeply once they were outside. They set off by habit along the perimeter of the grounds.

They were not easy to pair as mother and daughter. Carole took after her father, lanky and square-shouldered, with dark blonde hair and eyes the color and shape of almonds. Her mother was petite and fair-skinned, and her eyes shifted from gray to green depending on the light and her mood. Solange's hair was the color of concrete, but Carole easily remembered the deep red it had once been because she saw it every day on her daughter, Alison. "Red as an October maple," her husband called it.

Solange walked slowly and with a hitch in her gait, as if she didn't trust the ground, making her seem far older than sixty-five. Carole stayed close, her shoulder grazing her mother's, in case she stumbled. It was better to visit this way instead of face-to-face, where Carole could be overrun with a hot sweet tide of pity, and if she looked at her mother directly, the way her eyes shifted out of focus rattled Carole. No, it wasn't so much loss of focus as loss of presence. Solange's eyes would film over, like those of a fish left gasping on the shore, and Carole would be uncertain where she had gone. "Inside herself" wasn't accurate; the bottom had dropped out of whatever remained of her mother's self. This loss, although temporary, was more acutely painful than the long-term loss of her. Carole was accustomed to her mother's institutionalization, but she would never become accustomed to the idea that one day her mother might abandon reality entirely and never return.

They rounded the corner of the main building. Her mother asked, "How's the baby?"

Carole answered the usual questions about her sister. "Janine's fine. School starts in three weeks so it'll be back to work for her."

Solange hesitated. "Back to work?"

"Yes, Mama. Janine works in the school office. She's thirty-four."

Her mother shook her head. "Doesn't seem possible. It truly doesn't."

"I know," Carole said softly, as the passage of time frequently caught even the sane off guard. "She's coming to visit soon, I hope."

"Oh, that's wonderful. She's such a lovely baby." Her voice drifted off.

Carole didn't have the heart to correct her. For years she'd tried, insisting her mother work the logic through and accept that Janine was no longer a baby, or even a girl. But Solange would not utter the name Janine, and no amount of reasoning and explaining could alter her conviction that the infant she'd left behind had stayed small and vulnerable all these years. For Solange, time was a twisted landscape riddled with holes, and Janine the baby had fallen straight through.

Carole moved on to firmer ground. "Did you finish the apples I brought last week?"

"Apples? I think I had one recently. A McIntosh."

"I've left some blackberries at the desk for you. They won't last more than a few days, but I know how you like them." Carole was never sure the staff gave Solange the food she brought, but she continued to bring it anyway. That and providing a few outfits a year was all she could do. It seemed so little. "Mama, how's your friend, Maisie?" Manic-depressive, Maisie had been in and out of Underhill for years—mostly in.

"Maisie? She's fine except when they have to lock her up. A lot of the others are leaving."

Carole nodded. "I'm sorry the new medications don't help you."

"That's all right. I never expected them to."

They circled back to the patio and stopped to rest on an ironwork bench. A few other patients wandered nearby or slumped, sedated or catatonic, in wheelchairs.

Solange said, "As long as you and the baby are fine."

Carole took her mother's hand in hers. "We are, Mama. Don't

worry." She didn't pause to query herself before answering because, until recently, she had always been fine. She wouldn't allow the strain to show. Not here.

The patio doors opened and a woman stepped out, holding a girl about one year old dressed in white and wearing a cap tied at the chin. A man, presumably the girl's father, held an older gentleman by the elbow and directed him to a chair beside Carole and her mother. The older man worked his tongue in his mouth and his limbs trembled violently. The father took the adjoining seat and bent his head in conversation. The child began to fuss, stretching her arms toward her father and kicking.

The mother held her tight. "Not now, sweetheart."

Solange's gaze had been drifting across the grounds, but now she studied the mother and daughter with intent.

Carole shifted to face her mother and touched her arm. "Mama?"

Solange continued to stare.

The girl squirmed against her mother's grasp and whimpered. Within moments, the child's frustration bloomed and she began to cry. The mother tried to soothe the girl but her cries only grew louder.

Solange stiffened and leapt from the bench. Carole's arm shot out to stop her but it was too late. Solange grabbed the child by the shoulders. "Come to me, baby! I'm here!"

The woman twisted away in alarm, pulling her daughter closer. "Leave her alone!"

The girl's father rose and stepped between his wife and Solange, his jaw set. Carole flew to her mother's side.

The man scanned Carole's face and her mother's, assessing the likelihood both were a threat. He turned toward the building and shouted, "Orderly! Nurse!" The woman hurried inside, tucking the child's head into her shoulder.

Solange's eyes were wild and incredulous and filled with terror, as if no part of her comprehended her actions, much less her emotions.

She held her arms outstretched, reaching after the baby. Her face contorted in a grimace, and she cried out, a long, low wail. Carole wrapped her arms around her, in protection, restraint, solace and fear. Her mother's body was rigid and twitched as if electrified. Carole held on, her heart beating in her throat.

A nurse appeared, with a doctor and a syringe. Carole shook her head. "Please, give us a minute. Please."

She ignored the impatience on the doctor's face and the uncertainty on the nurse's, and tended to her mother, stroking her hair and speaking into her ear in the most ordinary voice she could muster. "There were six deer in the field behind the house last night, Mama, lined up as if someone had arranged them. You could hardly see them, the grass being as high as it is on account of all the rain we've had. Walt's been meaning to cut it but it's been too wet and he's been so busy—almost too busy—in the garage anyhow. And between you and me, I'd prefer to see the goldenrod bloom. Last show of summer, they are, and I'd sure hate to miss it."

Solange's limbs softened as Carole spoke, and her breathing slowed, though it still caught in her chest. A trickle of sweat ran down Carole's back and her mouth was dry. The nurse helped her lower Solange onto the bench. The doctor disappeared. Carole knelt beside her mother and smoothed the damp hair from her forehead and stroked her cheek. Solange's eyes were closed. Carole imagined her mother was knitting together pieces of herself before daring to look upon the world again. Or perhaps she was simply tired.

Several minutes passed. Solange slowly opened her eyes.

"Hello, Mama."

She regarded her daughter. "Carole, dear. Is it visiting day?"

"Yes, it's Sunday."

"Are you making a dinner?"

Carole smiled. "Later, yes. If I can corral everyone."

"Well, don't let me keep you." She looked around, as if seeing the day for the first time. "I'm just going to soak up a little sun."

"All right, Mama. If you're sure." She kissed her cheek. "See you next week."

Carole left Solange with the nurse, thanked the receptionist and returned to her Valiant. She drove through the village of Underhill and took Route 120 toward Adams. The smooth workings of the machine under her control and the changing views steadied her nerves, and she reflected on her mother. Solange hadn't had a good day, but it hadn't been an awful day, either. At least her mother wouldn't spend this beautiful morning sedated and oblivious. It was bad enough they had to medicate Solange every night to stop her wandering in search of her baby. Locking the door was not enough, as she only rattled the handle and wailed. The nurses were probably right. Her mother was haunted by a baby lost in time.

Before Solange Gifford had been committed to Underhill, she had been, quite naturally, the center of Carole's world. Then her mother was gone, leaving Carole confused and bereft. One of her aunts let slip that Solange was not tired but mad, which Carole at first took to mean she was angry. Shortly thereafter she learned the word "madhouse" and the significance of her mother's disappearance swallowed her whole.

Everyone continued to call her sister "the baby" long after she'd been named, but she was nothing like the prim porcelain dolls on Carole's dresser. She was swaddled fire, with powerful lungs and coal-black hair. Carole had promised her mother she would care for her sister and protect her, and although she'd been a child herself at the time, she'd done her best.

The road crested a hill, and Mount Mansfield, proud and solid, loomed before her. The spine along its north slope cast a deep shadow into the wooded valley. Later today the sun would find the valley, and tomorrow it would find it again. Normally, Carole would find honest reassurance in the regular sweep of the sun, the march of the hours, the parade of the seasons. She wasn't the kind of person to pine for spring in January or to sigh when the first yellowed birch leaf fell to the ground. She didn't slow her step to look over her shoulder and she certainly didn't crane her neck around the corner of her future, wishing. But for months now something had shifted out of place, as if the mountains and the waters and the sky had been shaken up in a jar and put back together, but not perfectly. The seams were showing. It made no sense, but still.

Carole arrived at a T-junction and came to a stop. She signaled left and peered down the empty road in each direction. Adams was definitely to the left—she'd been here a thousand times—but a worm of uncertainty burrowed inside her. She looked to the right again, where the road divided pastures dotted with cows. On the far side, an old hay barn with a rusted roof slanted a few degrees toward the hill rising behind it. That way was Waterville, and beyond Waterville, Yardley. She was only confused because she hadn't slept well for several weeks and it was catching up with her. That's why everything seemed a little off. She was exhausted.

She glanced in the rearview mirror, unsure how long she'd been stopped in the road. No one was behind her. But she couldn't afford to dawdle. She had to get home, clean the house, help Lester with his reading, get dinner ready and do a load of laundry so Walt would have a clean shirt to start the week. Oh, and she had to find the source of the error—over five hundred dollars—in the garage accounting. No doubt there were a hundred other things she had to do but was forgetting. A knot throbbed at the base of her skull. She studied the barn a second time, and the road, faded yellow lines down the middle. Pressure built at her temples. Carole let go of the wheel, stretched her fingers and gripped it again. Adams was to the left.

She was certain. Nearly.

2

Alison

Alison slid off the beanbag and flicked off the television. *The Brady Bunch* had been boring as usual, but it was Delaney's favorite, and it was her room and her television. Delaney grabbed her sketchpad and scooted onto her bed with the thirty-seven pillows, shaking her head so her silky brown mane fell perfectly across her shoulders. Alison didn't have to see the sketchpad to know Delaney was drawing a bay mare with black markings, same as she always did. Correction. *Her* bay mare: Calamity Jane. Alison had once made the mistake of calling it brown and Delaney had refused to speak to her for days. Delaney had a way of not speaking that made it feel like a month.

"I guess I'll go," Alison said.

Without looking up, Delaney raised her pencil and waved it an inch.

Mrs. Dalrymple appeared in the doorway. "Don't worry your folks by being late, Alison."

Alison stifled a shrug. "Thanks for having me, Mrs. Dalrymple."

"Suck-up." Delaney said it loud enough to reach Alison, but no farther.

Mrs. Dalrymple smiled. "Our pleasure. Make sure you go straight home."

Grown-ups and their pointless warnings. Where else would she go? After dark, crossing the field between their houses was like swimming the English Channel. She'd seen a show about it. You didn't go halfway then get it in your head to try for Newfoundland. "I will."

She put on her Keds, careful not to break the frayed laces, crossed the kitchen and nudged the Dalrymples' golden retriever from the back door. "Sorry, Mr. Darcy." She stroked his head and he mashed his jowls into her palm, coating it with slobber. "Thanks a lot." Alison wiped it on his neck and slipped outside.

The yellow glow of the porch lights reached halfway across the lawn, where two Adirondack chairs squatted, facing the hills. According to Alison's father, "no self-respecting Vermonter would ever set his backside in one of them chairs." He thought Vermonters were always self-respecting, meaning they had more pride than money, and lots to say about out-of-staters like the Dalrymples, though he made them in private and in a sorry voice, the way you'd talk about an ugly baby. Delaney's family had moved to Adams four years ago, at the start of second grade. Alison used to think being a real Vermonter gave her an edge over Delaney, but she'd grown less sure. She stopped at the far reach of the light and turned to admire the house, its porch wide as a driveway, with chairs you could sink into and a swing and, off to the side, cordwood stacked neat as teeth for fireplaces that made the house cozy, which wasn't quite the same as heating it.

She made a beeline for her house through the middle of the field. She could've taken the road, but it was longer and hugged the woods backing up to Buchanans' farm. She knew those woods, and the river flowing through them, better than anything and was convinced they held an abundance of magic. To tease it out, she left folded notes in crevasses and under rocks, and hid special things in small boxes or folds of fabric tied with kitchen string. She'd wait for as long as she could, then make the rounds, inspecting the places for messages from the hidden world whose existence was as obvious to her as the sticky pine bark and springy mosses. Sometimes she'd find slugs in the creases of the notes, soaked with dew or rain, and sometimes the things inside the boxes disappeared. She didn't know what that meant, but she kept at it. At night, though, the woods were their own kind of black, and none of the magic they held was good.

The moon was up and threw a silver veil from behind thin clouds. She could make out the ridge of hills against the sky. At the bottom sat her house, half of the windows pale yellow. Security lights attached to the body shop shone toward the gas pumps, hidden by the house. A single streetlight, whiter than the others, lit up the auto graveyard. Alison had crossed the field a million times. She could do it blindfolded, and had. Using a flashlight felt like a betrayal of a place that had always welcomed her. Even as a toddler, when her brothers were supposed to be watching her and she chased after a butterfly or a toad from backyard to field, nothing bad had happened. Her bedroom faced this way, so this four-acre patch was the first thing she saw when she woke and the last thing in her mind's eye when she lay down at the end of the day.

The wind picked up, sending the smell of sun-warmed earth to her. It had been hot today, but there wouldn't be many more days like it. Earlier she'd noticed a bitter taste at the back of her throat, like she'd swallowed a bug. The faint strawberry sweetness was gone. Summer was down to the last lick of ice cream before the cone collapsed.

Alison felt uneasy and didn't know why.

She stopped, now in the dead center of the field, and stared at the sky. The clouds moved faster, streaking in front of the moon, their edges burning white for a second, then rushing past, leaving the moon uncovered, like an eye. Alison spun in a circle, head tipped back, and traced the shadows as they flew by, her heart fluttering. A curl escaped her headband and stuck on her mouth. She blew it away.

The wind swept from below as she started again toward home. If only she could fly! She stretched out her arms and leaned forward into a warm breath of air, equally soft and sturdy, pressing against her chest. Her legs became lighter, and she walked faster and faster without effort. The sharp edges of the grasses nicked her shins. Ahead, the maple in her backyard, its crown as large as the house, stood bold against the changing sky. In her dreams she had flown over it and far beyond.

On this night, she did not have the power of her dreams. She had only the wind, the clouds and the peekaboo moonlight. So she ran.

She caught the screen door with her heel before it slammed and followed the sound of the television into the living room.

Her dad slouched in his recliner, two empty cans of Pabst Blue Ribbon on the lampstand. "Hey, sunshine."

"Hi, Daddy." She glanced at his right side, the spot where she used to curl up next to him. Her head would bounce up and down when he laughed at *Green Acres*. She doubted she could squeeze in there now. "Where's Mom?"

"Doing battle with the books. Wish I could help her out, but you know about me and numbers."

Sally, Alison's gray-and-black tabby, slinked against her leg. Alison squatted to stroke her. Sally purred and snaked her tail in the air, then hurried down the hall on other business. "I'm going to get some milk then go upstairs."

"All right. You're not missing anything on the idiot box, that's for sure. Sleep well, sunshine."

"Good night, Daddy."

In the kitchen, a sliver of light lay on the floor from the doorway leading to the office and garage. Her mom should've been done with the books hours ago. *Cha-rumph, cha-rumph, cha-rumph* went the machine, as her mom hit enter again and again to move the paper along. Alison pictured her lifting the curled paper ribbon with a finger, leaning forward to read the faint numbers and scowling. The only other time her mom was in the office this late was Tax Time, a gloomy period that cast a shadow on the pale green of spring. Alison knew better than to interrupt.

She opened the fridge and drank from the milk bottle because it was quieter than bothering with a glass, and because she could. On her way out, she dipped her hand into the cookie jar, expecting to find only crumbs, but coming up with a single Nutter Butter with a corner broken off. Her mother was talking to the books now, and her voice trailed after Alison as she left the kitchen, numbers strung one after another like an incantation.

She went up the steps to the second-floor landing, past her parents' bedroom and the one her brothers shared, the low twanging of a guitar solo seeping into the hall. Alison opened the narrow door leading to the attic stairs, flicked the wall switch and climbed up, stretching her neck to graze her head on the sloped ceiling. Crossing to the center of the room, she yanked the dangling chain. The ceiling fan hummed to life and stirred the stale air.

Only half the attic was hers. The other part was piled to the rafters with junk, separated by an old plaid blanket nailed to a crossbeam. "There," her mother had said after she hammered in the last nail. "You're the only one lucky enough to have a plaid wall." It wasn't true, because Aunt Janine, her mom's sister, had red plaid wallpaper in her bathroom when she'd lived in the big house in Burlington, but Alison didn't say anything. At seven, she'd been nervous about moving to the attic, but glad to get away from her brothers. They were noisy and wild and had started giving off a funny smell, like muddy elephants. She'd never smelled an elephant, not even a clean one, but she was sure that's what it was.

She kicked off her shoes, lay on the bed on her stomach and pulled the dictionary from the pile of books on the nightstand. It was a big dictionary, unabridged, a word she'd looked up. She'd flipped to the front, too, to make sure the meaning of "abridged" wasn't something else. That happened more often than she expected. Years ago, she'd overheard her parents arguing about having too many kids and not enough money. Her father had said, "Two was all we wanted, Carole. All we could afford." Her mom said, "You can't blame me, Walt. It was an accident." Alison knew about accidents from the body shop: broken lights, bashed-in doors, sometimes the whole car squished like a stepped-on soda can. In third grade, Marybeth Colton had an accident in her snow pants during recess. Mrs. Jackman made her stand in the hallway to wait for her mother because she smelled so bad, then told the class accidents like that only happen if you have weakness of character. Character, Alison reasoned at the time, lived in your underpants, in which case it was best not to discuss it.

None of it got Alison any closer to understanding why her mother called her an accident, so she'd grabbed the dictionary from the hallway bookcase and lugged it to her room. It took forever to chase the meaning of the words through the pages because each definition had words she didn't know: "unforeseen," "circumstance," "ignorance." She'd smiled a little when she learned what that last one meant.

Whenever she was bored, she'd open the dictionary and hunt for the meaning of words. She started at the beginning and hadn't finished the As yet, but things would speed up once all the definition words she'd tagged in this game of chase would be waiting for her, familiar. But *Webster's Unabridged* could not solve the original mystery, and Alison had been left with the troubling conclusion that someone—her parents, most likely—had knocked something over without meaning to, and she was the result.

Au gratin . . . augur . . . augural . . . augury . . . august. Alison's eyelids were drooping. She set the dictionary on the floor. Downstairs, the door between the office and the kitchen opened and shut. Her mother ran the faucet, clinked dishes, closed cupboards and talked with Alison's father, their voices hushed.

"Alison?" Her mom was coming up the stairs.

"Yeah?" Alison sat up and peered down the attic stairwell. Her mother had stopped halfway up the main stairs. Her face was slumped, from the books probably. Alison smiled at her and she smiled back.

"You going to sleep soon?"

"Uh-huh. Good night, Mom."

"Good night, dear. Don't forget to brush your teeth."

"I won't."

"Sweet dreams."

Her steps retreated. Someone turned up the television. Alison changed into her pajamas and went down to the bathroom to brush her teeth. After, she knelt on her bed and stared outside. Across the field, a few windows shone yellow at the Dalrymples'. The wind had scattered the clouds to the edges of the sky, and only a few stars—the brightest ones—were out. The shape of the woods along the river was sketched against the night.

Alison climbed in between the sheets and hugged Flopsy, her stuffed rabbit, to her chest. *Augur. Augury.* To predict from signs or omens. *August.* Only nine days left of it. Something was definitely shifting. Alison could feel it—in the air, in her house, inside herself—but couldn't put words to it. The feelings were real and strong and made her restless, but she couldn't figure out whether the change was good or bad. She'd have to trust in the sense of things. She'd have to wait for a sign.

3

Janine

Janine hated meeting with Lane Snelling, the guidance counselor. Even being in the same room with him made her skin crawl. It wasn't just that he was ugly; it was that he seemed to try to be as ugly as possible. Few people were naturally beautiful, and she didn't take one iota of her own good looks for granted. Nearly everyone had to make an effort. Or should. In Lane Snelling's case, basic grooming would be a start. She glanced at his feet, knowing it was a mistake. During the school year they'd be hidden inside tasseled loafers (a questionable fashion choice, but they did serve the purpose) but since classes didn't begin until next week, he'd taken the liberty of showing up in Birkenstocks. The footwear wasn't the issue. It was the toes, long and knuckled and heavily furred. And the toenails. A good half inch too long and deep yellow, with grime encrusted along the edges. One of the big toenails was black and humped in the middle like a talon. When God made summer, these feet were not what he had in mind.

Janine could feel her lip curling and forced a smile to stop it. "What were you saying, Lane, about the senior repeats?" The college-recruiting poster behind him showed an ivy-covered building set on a manicured lawn dotted with students reading, talking and laughing. None had ever hailed from Adams, or likely ever would, but it beat staring at Snelling's unwashed hair and cavernous pores. Was taking a shower really so difficult?

"I was saying they shouldn't be allowed to pad their schedules with electives. And that attendance should be monitored closely. There were too many unfortunate grandparents last year. And mysterious illnesses contagious only among students with a grade average below C minus."

"You'll have to speak with the school nurse about doctors' excuses. I only handle class schedules and attendance." Plus a million other things, for both the middle school and high school. Not that Snelling would notice or care. Janine stood and brushed her skirt straight, calling the meeting to a close. She moved to the door, certain Snelling was staring at her behind, a thought doused equally with pride and disgust. Pausing with her hand on the jamb, she cast another glance at his feet. She couldn't help herself. "Enjoy your last days of freedom."

"Freedom? A rational mind is always free."

Oh, for the love of God. He really was an idiot. But she gave him a sweet smile. She wasn't a bitch.

She collected her purse from her desk drawer, checked to see that the desk she'd straightened before the meeting was still tidy and made her way toward the exit. The door to the principal's office was ajar and she scurried past so he wouldn't call her in for One Last Thing. "One last thing, Janine. It won't take a moment." But it always took several. They didn't pay her enough for her scheduled hours, much less for overtime. Principal Ike Kawolski was a disorganized man. His entire working day was a hodgepodge of One Last Things and she did her best to steer clear of them. Of course, as the secretary, it wasn't simple.

She kept her head down as she passed his door. Out of the corner of her eye, she saw Mrs. Penney, the school office employee with no title, inside Kawolski's office watering a plant. Mrs. Penney had worked for the Adams schools since the depression, a vestigial employee whom no person or administration had had the heart, or the gumption, to dismiss. Janine didn't mind. The woman was her own memorial but did no one any harm. Janine only wondered whose salary was larger.

Her cherry-red convertible Ford LTD was waiting in the parking lot. It had belonged to her husband, Mitch, and she'd worried initially that it was a bit short on femininity. But red was her color (what else with raven hair?), and she'd loved Mitch, at least part of the time, in her own way. She was certainly sorry he was dead, as nothing had been easy for her in the intervening three years. And it had been so sudden. He might have succumbed to something more drawn out than a massive heart attack and given her a chance to position herself better. She might have had time to move some money around so it didn't all go flying out the window the instant his soul left his body. She might, at the very least, have had time to prepare and not be blindsided by the laundry list of requirements for the widow of an almost–state senator. (She might have had her hair done.) Instead, he'd yanked open a trapdoor and she'd fallen straight into the basement—Adams High.

Her anger with him for making her a widow was as fresh as it was irrational. That word: "widow." It made her sound both old and used and, worse, an object of pity. Well, she'd see about that. She might be thirty-four, but she knew for a fact she looked a damn sight younger.

She got behind the wheel and started the car. The LTD was a lot like her, now that she thought about it. It had attractive lines and a no-nonsense engine that growled when you put your foot to the floor.

Ten minutes later, she liked the car a good deal less. Just shy of the turnoff onto River Road, smoke started pouring out from under the hood. She pulled onto the shoulder, shut off the engine and smacked her palm on the steering wheel. With the list of things she had planned the next few days, she could do without a predicament. School started next Tuesday and would mark her reunion with Greg Bayliss and the continuation of her quest to make a husband out of him. If she was going to be irresistible on Tuesday, she had work to do.

She climbed out and started walking toward town. The Fosters were just a little ways, and if they weren't home, the gym teacher, Ruth Singletary, lived next door.

Luckily, Prissy Foster was at the back collecting tomatoes. Not wanting to stain her shoes on the grass, Janine shouted from the stone path, explaining she'd broken down and needed to call Walt. Prissy pouted, no doubt thinking Janine had come around for a visit. Fat chance. But Prissy regained her manners and told her she was welcome. Janine went inside and found the phone on the wall between the kitchen and the den. She dialed the garage. It rang and rang, but eventually Walt came on and said he'd be there presently.

Presently, Janine thought. That was a Walter word if there ever was one.

She waved to Prissy Foster as she rounded the house and, magnanimous now that help was on the way, shouted that her garden was lovely. It truly was. The ordinary vinyl-clad house was surrounded by enormous beds of daisies, lilies and gladiolas, with flagstone paths winding in between. The lawn would have evoked envy in any greenskeeper, and the birches and maples were in precisely the right places. Somehow Prissy had not been compelled to add plastic windmills, gnomes, signs with insipid quotations or, God forbid, a gazing ball, grasping clearly that Vermont was neither a miniature golf course nor Victorian England. Pretty, very pretty. Such a lot of work, though. And in the dirt.

By the time Janine got back to her car, her brother-in-law Walt's tow truck was approaching from the other direction. The truck made a U-turn and pulled in front. The dashboard was buried under a thick layer of papers and trash. Janine clucked at the sight.

How did her sister put up with it? Both cab doors opened and Walt and his son Warren stepped out.

She was struck, as she was every time she saw Walt, how precisely he resembled his twin, her dead husband, Mitch, and yet looked nothing like him. It evoked the most peculiar feeling in her, as if her eyesight or her judgment were off, or both. It was like being drunk.

"Afternoon, Janine." Walt put his fingertips on the fender as if the LTD were a horse in need of reassurance.

"Thanks for coming."

He took off his baseball cap, ruffled his hair and replaced the cap. The differences between the twins unaccounted for by genetics were plain. Walt held himself back a little. Mitch never had. Walt's jawline was leaner, his stomach flatter, while Mitch's love of food and drink had earned him a paunch. And Mitch had sharpened the edges of his vowels while Walt's rolled out like polished stones and betrayed him as a Vermonter with each syllable. But sometimes the brothers' resemblance hit her full-on, as it did now. She stared at Walt and he stared right back, his eyes blue as a swimming pool.

Her fingers moved to her neck and fiddled with the top button of her shirt. Walt's eyes unnerved her; the ghost of her dead husband had climbed inside his twin. But there was more there, in Walt's look. Disapproval? Amusement? She was on her back foot with Walt, always had been, although it made no sense. He was a simple man, with no ambition or power. Still waters run deep, people said, but she'd never seen any evidence of it. And yet here was Walt, looking at her as if she was the one who'd guessed wrong at every turn.

"Hey, Aunt Janine."

She'd forgotten her nephew was there. "Hello, Warren."

The boy popped the hood. "Smoke, you said?"

"A lot."

Walt bent over the engine. "Oil's dripping onto your exhaust."

Janine said, "Is that bad?"

He straightened. "Well, it isn't good." He smiled. Mitch's smile. "Creates a pile of smoke, for starters."

Warren laughed and shook his head.

Janine said, "I meant—"

"I know what you meant," Walt said in his soft, even voice. "I was only pulling your leg. It's an easy fix but I can't get to it until tomorrow." He signaled to Warren to drop the hood. "Warren'll drive it in. You can ride with me. One of us'll deliver you home after the shop closes. In the meantime, you can visit with Carole."

She checked her watch. An hour and a half until closing. She didn't want to spend all that time at Walt and Carole's, but what could she say? "I appreciate it, Walt." She fished the keys from her purse and dangled them over Warren's outstretched palm. She could tell he was fighting to appear nonchalant, but he'd always gotten twisted up around her. Since he'd turned the corner from boy to man, his looks her way had become braver. She winked at him, watched him redden and let go of the keys.

The twins were born when Janine was seventeen and living with Carole as she always had. Walt had called from the hospital to say she had two nephews, but one was "not a hundred percent." Lester had been born second, waiting in the dark with the cord around his neck. Warren's foot was looped in the cord, as if they'd been wrestling in there before Carole's contractions began, ending the contest. With each hard-won inch toward birth, Warren pulled the noose tighter around his brother's neck. Warren emerged red and screaming, his brother blue and silent. By the time they came home, both were screaming nonstop. When Warren was old enough to understand the story of their birth, he felt responsible, no matter what anyone said, and tried to make it up to Lester by protecting him. It was touching, Janine supposed, but the whole mess only underscored her conviction that having children was a crapshoot best avoided.

Other people managed fine but she wasn't other people. When she'd first married Mitch, she'd fancied the idea of children, having not thought it through. Luckily, Mitch had been shooting blanks.

Walt whistled as he drove, then pulled into the garage lot. Lester was polishing the bumper of a Buick and dropped his cloth when he saw Janine climb down from the cab of the tow truck. "Auntie Janine!" He rushed at her and threw his arms around her waist, as he had since he was a toddler. He had to crouch to do it now, tall as he was, and ended up mashing the top of his head into her breast. She would have deflected the move, but he was too fast. She grasped his shoulders firmly and held him at arms' length.

"That's better, Lester. I can see you now."

"And I can see you, Auntie Janine."

He wasn't a bad-looking boy. He had a strong jaw, a straight nose and a charming smile, and his hair was dark blond and wavy like his mother's. But his features, in fact his whole person, didn't hang quite right, as if he weren't screwed together properly. He was easy to like, and harmless, which was lucky. After he finished school next year (graduation was out of the question), he'd work at the garage for his father. And when Walt died, Janine guessed Lester would work for whoever took over—Warren, maybe—or find something else. He'd probably lead a happier life than anyone else in the family. Janine wasn't certain how she felt about that.

"You ready for school next week, Lester? You'll meet Miss Honeycutt. I hear she's got all sorts of fun things planned."

The school district had hired April Honeycutt to begin work this year after the state passed a law requiring special teachers for special kids. Janine hadn't met her but had read her job description. The woman wasn't much more than an educated babysitter, but at least Lester wouldn't be spending all day hanging on to Warren and being shushed by the regular teacher.

Lester's eyes were huge. "Did you see Miss Honeycutt? Is she nice or a meanie?"

"I haven't met her yet, but I'm sure she's very nice." She had to be, didn't she? Nice, patient and unaffected by drooling and shouting. Janine could see her now, a darling smile pasted on a dull face, forced into looking after the slow kids because she didn't have the brains, ambition or looks to do anything better.

In his excitement over his upcoming introduction to Miss Honeycutt, Lester dove at Janine's middle again, forcing her to step back to absorb his momentum, and her ankle crumpled. She caught herself in time but annoyance rose in her. "Hey! Take it easy!" She pushed him away and regarded the damp stains on her blouse.

"Lester!" Walt stuck his head around the opened hood of the car in the garage bay. "You finish up with that Buick. Mr. Stafford will be here before you can say boo."

"Yes, sir, Mr. LaPorte." He insisted on calling his father "Mr. LaPorte" during work. Something he picked up from television. "Boo." Lester peered down the road. "Boo."

Janine felt a pang of guilt for barking at him, but then noticed a smear of black on her skirt. Her guilt evaporated. Really, the boy was like an untrained Saint Bernard.

She arranged her handbag and headed inside. "See you at school, Lester."

"See you at school, Auntie Janine!" He shouted, not a speck of resentment marring his grin.

Janine strode through the office, calling for her sister as she went, regretting more with each step having had this visit forced upon her. The dreariness of the surroundings aggravated her feelings. The gray metal desk could have been ripped from a submarine, and the chair behind it had perhaps once been cordovan but had worn to a sickly pink in the middle. The carpeting was no color at all. Chaotic stacks of file folders and mail teetered on the desk, floor and filing cabinets, along with mismatched coffee cups, Coke bottles and cardboard boxes. She pushed open the door to the kitchen, which was cleaner but no cheerier. Faded gold and green brocade curtains hung lopsided on the windows overlooking the yard. She'd rather do without curtains than have those. Not Carole. If she were married to Aristotle Onassis, she'd still wear Edith Bunker housedresses and put up with those curtains. She didn't seem to notice, or to care, and neither did Walt. But it depressed the hell out of Janine.

She found her sister out back hanging clothes on the line. Janine called to her from the step, but Carole didn't hear, so she slipped off her shoes and walked gingerly across the lawn, watching out for bees and cat shit.

"Carole. Hey, it's me."

Janine was practically on top of her but Carole had her back turned and didn't respond.

"Yoo-hoo! Earth to Carole!"

Carole jumped and spun around, a shirt crushed in her hand. "Good lord! Don't sneak up on people like that!"

"I didn't. You're losing your hearing."

"I doubt it." She clipped the shirt to the line at the shoulders and bent to retrieve another one from the basket. "You at the school today?"

"I sure was. My car broke down on the way home. Walt can't get to it until tomorrow."

"That's too bad. Cars can be a nuisance."

Janine puffed out a short laugh. "I should hope so. It's your bread and butter." She crossed her arms, impatient. "Can we sit, or go inside? You know about me and grass."

Carole glanced at her sister's feet and resumed pegging socks. "I need to finish."

"It won't dry tonight anyhow."

"All the same."

Carole's hair seemed more gray than usual and Janine wondered about suggesting she color it. Blondes, even dark blondes, could get away with some gray, but after a while it looked old on them like it did on everyone else. At forty-four, her sister still had her figure, although her clothes did it no justice. For years, Janine had given her stylish outfits for her birthdays and Christmases (nothing fancy, just from Sears and Penney's), but Carole only thanked her and stuffed them in a drawer. When asked, Carole pointed out she didn't socialize, unless you counted handing invoices across the desk in the garage and an occasional trip to church. Janine would pull herself together even for that, but not her sister. She'd been careless about her looks and reticent in her relationships for as long as Janine could remember, and the shell she'd retreated into only seemed to get thicker. Janine might have enjoyed her sister more if they went out to lunch together or shopping, but Carole was too tied down to the garage, Walt, her kids and their crazy mother, and was not one to indulge besides. Janine had been tempted many times to give up—who could blame her?—but Carole had practically raised her. And although her sister wasn't free with affection or tender words, Carole's love was something Janine had always had, like her name.

"Alison eager for school to start?"

"I expect so."

"Sixth grade next week. Doesn't seem possible."

"Well, I've been through it with the boys."

"But little Alison."

Carole cast a glance at her daughter's attic window and started across the lawn with the empty laundry basket. "I don't worry about her like I do the boys."

"Don't you? I thought you worried about everything."

She paused on the landing but didn't turn around. "Are you coming to see Mama on Sunday?"

"I don't think so. With school starting next week, I'm awfully busy."

Carole faced her sister. "I'm happy to drive."

"The driving's the least of it."

"Well, I just thought—"

"Maybe in October, for her birthday. I'll think about going then."

Carole gave her a tired, resigned look. Janine hated that look. She didn't see why her decision not to visit their mother had to disappoint her sister freshly and thoroughly every time. Carole could visit their mother and Janine could do something worthwhile. What was wrong with that?

Carole stepped inside and Janine followed her, blinded by the relative darkness. Carole left the basket on the stairs and crossed in front of Janine on her way to the kitchen. "I've got iced tea."

"Sounds good."

How odd. Her sister normally made a bigger deal about going to Underhill. She and Carole were their mother's only visitors, but Janine rarely went. The place made her ill, especially the smell of cheap disinfectant sprayed over a miasma of sour hopelessness. There was nothing for Janine there. The woman trapped behind the barred windows and brick walls, trapped in the tangled circuitry of her brain, was her mother—she had no reason to doubt it—but the space between them was empty.

It was different for Carole. She and their mother had ten years together. Carole didn't talk about it and Janine didn't want to know what she had missed, but Carole had to have memories of Solange, and Solange of her, never spoken of but existing nevertheless in their separate minds, like copies of a photo placed in separate albums and locked in drawers in different cities.

Truth be told, Janine doubted she would visit her mother more often even if she had albums full of memories of her. What would be the point? Her mother didn't know who she was. Solange knew Carole, called her by name, but never Janine. Carole claimed their mother loved them both, yearned for them, but couldn't connect Janine the baby with Janine the adult. Fine, Janine had said, I know that. But what she could never say to Carole, or to anyone, was that she couldn't connect Solange, the pleasant, bewildered mad-woman, with the longing for a mother she never had. The longing was so pervasive and so real that it was part of her, terrible and familiar, and unrelated to the woman locked up at Underhill, except both were curses she took pains to ignore, or deny. On her best days, when she was her truest self, Janine didn't have a mother and didn't need one.

4

Alison

Alison shook Frosted Flakes into a bowl and poured on milk until it brimmed, then added more, drop by drop, until she judged it one drop short of overflowing. She touched her lips to the edge and slurped, watching the islands of crinkly flakes emerge. "Low tide," she said to no one, and picked up her spoon.

Her mom came in from the garage wearing the same housedress as yesterday, with a splatter of spaghetti sauce near her waist. Alison was about to point it out—her mom hated stains—when she spoke. "Want to go with me to the store?"

"The grocery store?"

"Yes."

"Sure!" Alison scarfed down her cereal and dumped her bowl in the sink. "I'll get my shoes."

Town was three winding miles to the north. The school was on the far side, but during the summer Alison didn't go into town much. It was too far to walk and her bike was a castoff from her brothers, with a banana seat and ape-hangers that made her feel ridiculous. Plus, the road didn't offer much of a shoulder. Once a car had come too near and she'd swerved into the gravel, ending up at the bottom of the embankment, her knees and palms skinned and one handlebar bent like a frog's leg. So she kept to the woods, the river and Delaney's, when her friend wasn't with her horse.

Her mother pulled into the Grand Union lot and parked in the far corner near the Dumpsters. Alison unbuckled her seatbelt and paused. Her mom wasn't getting out. She had one hand on the keys, still in the ignition, and the other clamped onto the steering wheel.

"Mom, let's go."

Her mom pressed her lips together and, blinking hard, stared at the Dumpsters.

"Mom, what's wrong?"

She shook her head, let go of the keys and dug in her purse. "You go in without me, Alison, all right?"

"Why? I don't want to."

Her mom found the shopping list and looked it over. "Get the cheapest unless I wrote down the brand, okay?"

"I don't see why we can't go together."

She handed over her wallet. "I'm not feeling well, that's why."

Why hadn't she stayed home, then? Her mother glanced out her window, then out Alison's, nervous. Alison twisted around. Mrs. Fischer, who used to live next door but had moved in with her daughter after her husband died, waved from her car.

Alison was totally confused. "I thought we were going together. I thought that was the point."

"Please, Alison." She gripped the wheel like she expected a tornado to yank her out of the car.

Alison sighed and opened the door. Before she stepped out, she said, "Can you take me to Burlington this weekend? I haven't got anything to wear for school."

"You've got plenty to wear." Her mother's voice was nearly a whisper.

"Please, Mom. Nothing fits." Alison's throat shrunk. She hoped she wouldn't have to say anything else because tears had appeared out of nowhere.

"School's not for a while."

"It's next week!"

Her mom stared at her as if this was actually news. "We'll see, okay?"

Alison got out of the car, sniffing back tears, thoughts whirling. "We'll see" used to be one of her mother's hopeful phrases but this time it sounded just like "No." It was as if her mom didn't want to be with her, which was weird. Alison had always been her mother's. Her dad had the twins working for him when they weren't in school and it seemed right: the boys with their father, and she with her mother. Her mom couldn't be like Mrs. Dalrymple, who made Rice Krispies Treats with her daughter on a school night, took her shopping even if it wasn't her birthday or a new school year and arranged for Delaney to have father-daughter nights, something Alison couldn't imagine. Her mom had to work in the garage and do all the washing and cleaning and cooking, and Lester needed extra attention, but she'd spend time with Alison whenever she could. She'd read to her, tell stories and make up rhymes, and let Alison borrow whatever she wanted for dress-up. Her mom wasn't chatty or outgoing, but she'd always been there, where Alison could find her. Now her mom was somewhere else in her head—in places Alison was not invited.

Maybe it wasn't her mom. Maybe Alison was the one changing. She wasn't a baby anymore. Even the word "child" felt pinched, same as her toes inside her Keds. She hadn't shot up the way her brothers had, pulled long like Gumby. But something was stirring. She noticed things. She wondered about people, questioning for the first time whether they had to be the way they were. Her mother might seem different because Alison was turning into someone else, someone for whom silly songs and paper dolls were no longer enough. The thought made her sad and confused. Something was slipping away from Alison before she understood what was taking its place.

And now she was wasting one of the last perfect days of summer buying franks and beans and toilet paper.

She crossed the parking lot, pulled a cart from the rack and wheeled it into the store. Her mother's wallet felt awkward in her hand, like a prop. Just get the stuff and get out of here, she told herself. After lunch, Delaney would be back from the stables. Alison tossed two boxes of blueberry Pop-Tarts into the cart—Lester's one and only breakfast food—and paused at the cookies. Oreos weren't on the list, but she added a package to the pile. Shopping on your own had its perks.

Alison lined up at the checkout and was relieved no one she knew was there to see her grocery shopping by herself. She fiddled with the plastic piece you could flip down to make a seat and remembered sitting there when she was little. Well, maybe she didn't actually remember, but her mother had told her a hundred times about how Alison acted like the cart was her official viewing stand and the customers were her loyal subjects. She'd wave at every single person and give them a smiling nod, her halo of curls bobbing. Everyone told her mom how darling she was. Her mom called her the Red Queen of the Grand Union and called herself the Red Queen's factotum. Alison had no idea what a factotum was (she'd have to look it up), but one thing was for sure: her mother had adored her.

She paid for the groceries, checked the change and pushed the cart outside, thinking how she couldn't wait to turn five, then six, then seven, right up until her eleventh birthday last January. Being older seemed to be the secret to so many things. Time was the wind at her back and she ran headlong in front of it, daring it to race her, or lift her completely off the earth.

But now, she realized, even if you don't run, even if you just stand still, things you want and need, maybe the most important things, get left behind. For the first time in Alison's life, growing up didn't seem like such a hot idea.

After lunch, Alison crossed the field and sat behind the hedge that blocked the view from the Dalrymples'. She reached into her paper sack and placed everything on the grass beside her: a spiral-bound notebook and pen, a cloth bag filled with marbles and allies, a pack of playing cards, the Oreos and, finally, a shoe box labeled "Suggestions" on five sides.

Delaney came around the hedge carrying a tote bag and sat cross-legged opposite Alison. Around her neck was a gold medal attached to a green ribbon. "Hey."

"Hey. How's Janie?"

"Oh, she's good. We practiced alternating canters today."

"Neat! What's in the bag?"

"Stuff. Show you later." Delaney pointed at the Oreos. "Where'd you get those?"

"Made them myself."

Delaney laughed. Alison smiled and thought, as she did every day, how great it would be if they could be friends at school, too. She almost asked Delaney if they could this year, but knew that if you had to ask, it wasn't going to happen. Alison was just Delaney's summer friend—handy. Mrs. Dalrymple drove Delaney back and forth to the stables every day but refused to drive her to see her friends when, as far as she was concerned, a perfectly good playmate lived right next door. They got along, especially if Delaney got her way. And this summer they'd found a whole new world to explore together.

Delaney pulled her mother's scarf out of her bag and spread it between them. A gold sun with a face surrounded by a ring of the zodiac signs. The sun's rays were made up of different colored jewels, and the black background had stars and moons and planets on it. Delaney said it was really expensive and her mom would kill her if she knew she'd borrowed it, but her mom never wore it so they agreed it didn't matter.

"Ready?" Delaney reached for Alison's hands. "Behold the Capricaries and their infinite powers!" Alison was a Capricorn and Delaney was an Aries, so together they were the Capricaries. Alison only got first billing because they agreed Ariescorns was silly. Besides, Delaney got her entire sun sign in the name, so it worked out.

They threw their arms in the air. "Behold!"

"Cool," Alison said. "Want to start with a spell?"

"Sure, but I need to tell you something first."

"Okay."

"Because we're friends." Delaney's serious tone made Alison's stomach twist up. "Oh, don't worry." Delaney sat up very straight and flicked her hair off her shoulder. "It's perfectly normal at our age."

"What? What's normal?"

Delaney raised one finger and lowered it until it pointed at Alison's chest.

Alison glanced down. "Something on my shirt?"

"No, silly. Your headlights are showing." She stared at Alison, her eyebrows raised. "You need a bra."

Alison's face got hot. She pretended her shoelace had come undone.

"I'd offer you one of mine, but intimates are not for sharing. Just tell your mom. She probably already has some for you. Mine did."

"Yeah, probably." Definitely not. What if Alison had shown up at school with headlights and gotten laughed at? She looked up at her friend. "Thanks for telling me."

"Sure."

They shared some Oreos and discussed what spell they should do. Alison flipped to a new page in the notebook and entered the date. "How about Summon the Familiars? We haven't tried that one in a while."

"Okay."

"Last known location and activity?"

"On the porch chewing a sneaker."

"Got it. Sally was in the backyard licking her tummy."

"Geez Louise. It's a whole lot easier being a familiar than a witch."

Alison nodded. They each retrieved their familiars' talismans (an old collar for Mr. Darcy and a catnip mouse for Sally), closed their eyes and thought intensely about their familiars. A fly landed on Alison's knee and she thought twice before brushing it off in case she had summoned it by mistake. She was about to open her eyes and call it quits when a bark startled her.

Delaney's eyes were huge. "He's inside and can't get out!"

They jumped up and ran to the house. As they clambered up the porch, Alison saw a deer leap out of the side garden and realized the dog had probably been barking at it. But she didn't tell Delaney. They gave Mr. Darcy a biscuit for his magical powers, drank some lemonade and headed outside again.

"Ready to go under?" Delaney said, lifting the gold medal over her head.

"Yup. Just gotta write it down." Under the previous entry she wrote: "Hypnosis. Subject: Alison. Post-hypnotic suggestion:—" She left the rest of the line blank and gave the notebook to her friend. Delaney slipped her hand into the Suggestion Box and pulled out a folded piece of paper. The box was Alison's idea, too. She worried Delaney would give her an embarrassing post-hypnotic suggestion, so they agreed on thirty possibilities and put them in the box.

"Get comfy," Delaney said.

"I am."

"Look at the medal and nothing else."

"I am."

"Listen to my voice and nothing else."

"I am."

"Stop saying 'I am.'" She swung the medal gently back and forth, sitting straight as a yardstick, and stared at Alison. "Soon you will feel sleepy. Very sleepy." Delaney's voice was low and even. In the distance, a lawn mower started up and a crow let out a loud caw. "Concentrate on my voice. There is nothing else."

Truth was, Alison didn't need Delaney to go into a trance. She could manage it all on her own by unfocusing all her senses. Lying on her bed, or in the field, or riding along in the car, she'd unhitch her eyes, her ears, her nose, her skin from her mind, one at a time, until she was totally inside herself. She'd first realized what she was doing several months ago after reading about trances in a book, but guessed she'd actually been doing it much longer. Maybe forever.

Her eyes fixed on the gold disc swaying in front of her, Alison relaxed into the sound of Delaney's voice without listening to the words. The gold medal, Delaney's face, the green hedge behind her and the sky beyond squished into the same plane. Warmth spread from her middle out to her limbs. She tingled a little everywhere. She was a feather floating in a glass ball—light, whole, safe.

Delaney ended the session by calling Alison's name a few times in a bossy voice. "Welcome back." She held a pack of cards, but not Alison's red Bicycle cards. These were larger with a gray, blue and white plaid design.

"What are those?"

"Tarot cards. My mom's friend brought them from New York."

"You're supposed to do what the suggestion says."

"I didn't follow it, okay? But don't flip your wig. All I did was shuffle them and ask you when to stop."

"That's it?"

"Yup."

"You sure?"

"Yup."

"'Cause if you're holding out on me, I won't let you hypnotize me anymore."

Delaney squirmed and flicked her hair over her shoulder. "Oh, well, the instructions say the reading has to be about something. I did the first one on the list: Past, Present, Future."

"Great. Nothing serious, then. Just my entire life."

"Ready?"

"Wait a sec. Couldn't we have just done the reading without me being under?"

"I guess. But doesn't it seem like it'll be truer this way?"

She had a point. "Okay. Lay it on me."

Delaney turned over the top card and placed it on the scarf. A guy in medieval clothes carried a hobo stick. The sun was behind him and a little white dog was jumping at his feet. At the bottom it said, "The Fool."

"Very funny, Delaney."

"Don't blame me. You chose it." She read from the instruction booklet. "The Fool is your past. It's facing you, not reversed, so it means new beginnings and innocence, and that anything can happen."

"Makes sense when you're a kid. What's it mean if it's the other way around?"

"That you're a crazy idiot. Ready for the next one?" She didn't wait for an answer. She laid the second card beside the first. A woman in a blue robe sat on a chair in front of a tree with red fruit on it. One foot rested on a golden moon. "The High Priestess represents wisdom and understanding. Supposedly this is your present."

"I guess I'm wise, then."

Delaney rolled her eyes and read on. "She guards your subconscious. You're supposed to listen to your inner voice. Okay, that's boring. Let's check out the last one. Your future."

Alison stared at the top card. Her mouth was dry and she felt a little dizzy. Her inner voice, the one she'd just been told to trust, told her she didn't want to know her future. "This is dumb. For all I know you stacked them."

"You think I did that?"

"No."

Delaney nodded and slowly lowered the card, turning it face up as she did. A wheel, fiery red, floated in a sky with puffy clouds. There were symbols everywhere. In the four corners, resting on the clouds, were an eagle, an angel, a bull and a lion, but the bull and the lion had wings, too. There was also a snake, a sphinx and a creepy pointy-headed red fox thing.

"Wheel of Fortune. A very powerful card," Delaney said.

"That sounds pretty good."

"It can be. It can mean good luck." Delaney was staring at the ground, picking at a scab on her shin.

Alison leaned forward and tried to read her friend's expression. "So that's my future? Good luck?" But Alison knew as soon as she said it, that wasn't it. She looked at the card again. She saw it now, what she'd been afraid of all along.

The Wheel of Fortune was upside down.

5

Carole

Mornings were best. Folks dropping off cars at the garage didn't dawdle, mindful of keeping their rides waiting. It wasn't eight yet, and four customers had already come and gone. Walt was outside fixing something or maybe rummaging for parts in the auto grave-yard, a sprawling heap of damaged and rusting metal, which on rare occasion gave up a part for a living vehicle. The twins were sleeping and would still be sleeping at noon if Walt didn't need them, and if Carole allowed it, as she was inclined to do. Once Warren and Lester were up—ducking through doorways, loud on their feet—they filled the rooms, even ones they weren't in, so unlike Alison, who might appear from nowhere or have been there all along.

Carole had slept a few hours, maybe five, a collection of unin-terrupted time that for months had become the best she could hope for. Lack of sleep left her more muddled than she'd been since Alison was a teething baby. She'd figured it would pass—most things did—and cut back on afternoon coffee. Walt was a heavy sleeper and never knew how her nights went unless she told him. She was reticent to complain. One time she did mention it and Walt told her he'd read that insomniacs get about two hours more sleep than they think they do. "Maybe they're too tired to remember how long they slept," she said. And they'd laughed. In any case, it would likely pass.

Carole rinsed the coffeepot, brushed toast crumbs from the counter into her palm and emptied them into the sink. She stood with her hand resting on one of the ladder-back chairs. Her handbag, car keys and a package that needed mailing lay on the table, patient. Walt had abandoned his glasses on top of the *Burlington Free Press* (both could turn up anywhere, but never apart), and one lens distorted the photo of Henry Kissinger beneath it, stretching his face to frightening proportions. Beside the paper stood the salt-and-pepper set with dolphins on it that Janine had brought back from Florida and the apple-shaped napkin holder Lester had made in woodshop. He'd made a cutting board, too, a silhouette of his head. Carole used it the night he brought it home, but when the knife touched his cheek, she winced and touched her fingertips to the mark. Now the board hung next to the stove above the LaPorte Garage & Auto Body calendar they sent out to customers the Monday after Thanksgiving.

She untied her apron, folded it over the chair and went out the back door to the stoop. Walt crouched over the lawn mower holding a wrench. His hair was thinning on top, but he maneuvered his body and handled his tools with the same broad-shouldered grace that had caught her eye twenty-five years ago. He was a solid man, nothing fussy or sideways about him. Some women, Janine for example, liked men with more sophistication. Carole hadn't had the experience of anyone aside from Walt, but there was little doubt in her mind that when it came to people, uncomplicated was a scarce and wondrous quality.

"I'm going to the bank now," she said, "and I'll mail those parts for you."

Walt straightened, wiped his palm on his trousers and came over to stand on the step below her. They were eye to eye. "I'm obliged." He leaned closer, gave her a slow smile. "How about a kiss?"

She pressed her lips to his and turned to go.

He touched her elbow. "How about another one. One for the road?"

She smiled and kissed him again. "Can I go now?"

"Only because my hands are dirty."

"Not just your hands."

He winked. "You got that right, sweetheart."

"I'll be home before lunch anyway."

"You'd better go, so you can come back to me."

"Oh, Walter." She touched his cheek a moment, then went inside to collect her things.

Carole waited in line at the post office, chastising herself for not coming mid-afternoon, when it was usually deserted, and wishing there was a drive-through, like at the bank. Her palms were sweaty and she shifted the box from the crook of one arm to the other and back again. Waiting didn't bother her. She simply wanted to go home. She could have asked Walt to mail it himself, but it had always been her job. How all the little chores had gotten divvied up the way they did she had no idea, but after so many years of being married, it made no sense to change things. It was only the post office.

A fly was crawling along the collar of the man in front of her. It paused and tilted its head, considering the gap to the man's hair. Its front legs probed the air, testing the distance. Carole's neck tickled. She brought her hand up to scratch it and was alarmed to see her arm move toward the man's collar. She pulled it back and held the box tightly in both hands. The man moved to the counter and the fly flew off.

A couple of minutes later it was her turn. She presented the box to the clerk. "Parcel post, please."

The clerk spoke but someone behind her was talking so loudly she couldn't hear. She bent over the counter. "I'm sorry. I couldn't—"

Her words were drowned out. The customer—a man—was practically shouting. So inappropriate to behave that way in public, but she didn't want to say anything to him, or even turn around. His tone was quite hostile, although she couldn't make out the words. Carole met the gaze of the clerk. Perhaps he would intervene. The clerk's eyebrows were raised, questioning, but he stared at her, not at the man behind her, as if waiting for her to speak. His mouth moved and Carole leaned toward him. She couldn't hear. It was hopeless.

She exhaled in frustration. Walt might have to mail his own packages from now on if the Adams Post Office was attracting patrons as raucous as the ones at the Rusty Bucket on a Saturday night. She twisted slowly so she wouldn't appear angry, not wanting to give this rude person a reason to say anything to her.

An elderly couple stood in front of a tall woman about Carole's age. The old man smiled at her kindly from beneath the bill of his feed-store cap. His wife dug in her purse, extracted a tissue and dabbed her nose. The tall woman nodded in greeting. Did Carole know her from somewhere? The shouting had quieted. She scanned the room. A clean-cut man in a navy Windbreaker walked from the wall of keyed boxes and pushed open the door. It could have been him. It must have been.

"Care to insure it, ma'am?"

Carole spun to face the clerk. "No, thank you." Her voice wavered.

"That'll be two fifty, then."

Her hand trembled as she found her purse, pulled two ones from it and laid the bills on the counter. She clicked open the change compartment, concentrating on the shapes of the coins—the largest, two of the largest—and not on the garbled voice, which had returned. The clerk's palm was outstretched and Carole dropped the quarters into it with a nonchalance she did not possess. One of the coins hit the counter and rolled on its edge away from her. She didn't wait to see where it landed. She snapped her purse shut, muttered her thanks and hastened toward home.

Mornings were best, they really were, but they didn't last long.

Alison rushed at her as soon as she came through the door. "Mom! I need to talk to you."

"Is something wrong?"

"Yes! I mean, sort of." She looked over her shoulder, then at Carole, and dropped her voice. "We need privacy."

Alison's urgency agitated Carole. If only she'd stayed in the car until her nerves had settled over the incident in the post office. She needed quiet, but Alison was distressed about something.

"Mom, please." Alison dragged her into the living room.

Carole sat on the couch, put her handbag to the side and unbuttoned her sweater. It was so hot. She took a deep breath and focused on her daughter.

"Tell me what's wrong, Alison."

"We really need to go shopping. It's important."

Shopping. Stores. People. Her chest constricted. She made herself look at her daughter, see her. "I know you want new clothes for school. I remember you told me you did. But I don't think I can go shopping with you today." There. She said it. Alison would understand. They could go another time, once she had slept, when her thoughts weren't so muddled.

"It's not just that, Mom." She stared at her feet. "I need a bra." She lifted her face to Carole, her cheeks flushed, eyes moist and pleading. "Can we please go buy one?"

Murmuring voices hissed, sinister and low. Carole tried to wall them off, push them away. She concentrated on her daughter's face—that open, trusting face—and her heart lurched. The voices grew louder, demanding. Carole shook her head to dispel them.

"No? Why not, Mom?"

"We'll see, okay?" Tears ran down her daughter's cheeks. Oh God, what had she done? "Don't cry, Alison. We'll see." She brushed away Alison's tears and kissed her cheek.

The murmuring grew louder. The sounds were indistinct but pressed hard, edging to violence. Painful, insistent, piercing. A scream rose in her throat and she choked it off. She pushed herself to standing, left the room and climbed the stairs, holding on to the railing. She shut herself in the bedroom, pulled the curtains closed, sat on the bed and clamped her hands over her ears, rocking, biting her lip so she would not cry out.

6

Alison

Alison listened to her mother hurry upstairs and shut the bedroom door. How could her mother just leave her here? Didn't she care? A hollow opened in Alison's chest, crowding out her lungs. She pulled up her knees, wrapped her arms around them and sobbed. She didn't want to go to school without a bra. If Delaney noticed she needed one, then so would everyone. How come her own mother didn't notice, or even care? Alison had begged her for help and all her mother had done was tell her not to cry. Then she'd walked right out of the room. If you didn't want someone to cry, then you should do something for them. If you cared. If you loved them.

Her father came in from the kitchen holding a sandwich and sat next to her.

"What's wrong, sunshine?"

She wiped her nose on her sleeve. She couldn't tell him about needing a bra. She just couldn't. "I need stuff for school. Clothes. Nothing fits."

He took a bite of his sandwich, his eyes on her. "Sounds like a problem we might be able to handle."

"But Mom won't take me shopping."

"Is that what she said?"

"She said, 'We'll see.' Same thing."

He smiled a little, which annoyed Alison. "Your mother's got a lot on her plate."

"She went to town this morning! Burlington isn't that different. She just doesn't care."

"Now, Alison, you know that's not true." He was quiet a minute. "Tell you what. I'm sending the boys into Burlington tomorrow for parts. They can take you to Gaynes. You pick out a few things."

She didn't want to shop by herself. She wanted her mom. But what choice did she have? She only had a few days left. "Okay. Thanks." Her dad handed her half of his sandwich. She peeked under the top slice. Bologna. Her favorite.

Burlington was an hour away, mostly along Interstate 89, running beside the Winooski River. The river behind Alison's house, Mad River, flowed into the Winooski, so that big, wide river belonged to her, too, in a way. Light rain fell and the branches of the oaks and beeches hung heavy against the sky as if the trees were tired from holding them up all summer.

Her brothers were playing Three Dog Night and The Who way too loud on the cassette player. Every time Lester would sing along, Warren would tell him to shut up, which Lester did, but then he forgot by the time the next song came along. She wasn't used to spending much time with them. Six years younger and she might as well have belonged to a different family. They had played with her when she was little, especially Lester. He liked her stuffed animals, and he took out her Barbie more often than she did until their father put a stop to it. "He might not be a genius, goddamn it, but he's still my boy." He said that a lot. It was sweet.

They pulled into the parking lot of Gaynes Shoppers World. Alison got out and checked her front pocket to make sure she had her money. She looked up and Warren was already driving away.

"Hey!" The brake lights came on and she caught up. Lester had the window down and she held on to the doorframe as if she could stop them from leaving again. "When are you coming to get me?"

Warren peered over the tops of his shades. "When we're ready."

"When's that going to be?"

"You wanted to go shopping, and now you're shopping. Lester and me have got other business."

"Picking up parts," Lester said, nodding. "For Daddy."

"Now, Lester, my man, I thought we agreed you were gonna call him Dad like I do."

Lester put his hand to his mouth and chewed on his first knuckle. It made a horrible sound, like stepping on a frog. "I forgot."

"I know you did. That's why I'm reminding you."

Alison patted Lester on the shoulder. "It's okay. I call him Daddy. He doesn't mind."

Warren gave her a look that said what she did wasn't worth discussing. He straightened up, ready to move on. "Back in a while."

"Crocodile," said Lester as they pulled away.

Alison stepped back with a sigh and hurried into the store.

It seemed bigger than when she'd been there with her family. The air was stale and smelled of plastic and popcorn, and the air-conditioning gave her goose bumps. She felt like she didn't belong. Someone would think she was a lost kid and announce it over the loudspeaker.

She headed for the girls' section, her flip-flops slapping on the tile floor. She found the dresses in her sizes and read the price tags. The cheapest was $13.99. She pulled the money out of her pocket, checking for the third time how much she had. Thirty dollars from her dad and three from selling blackberries. She could get the cheapest dress, a pale blue one with a white tie down the front, and maybe have enough for a couple of shirts and a bra, minus whatever the stupid tax was. How much were bras anyway? Well, it didn't cost anything to try stuff on. She grabbed the dress in the next size up, too, worried the ten might be too short for school, and went to look at shirts.

Two moms and two girls were rifling through one carousel, so Alison crossed to the other one, conscious of being on her own. She went through the shirts and fell in love with a teal green one with big white buttons. She stared at the tag until her eyes swam, hoping the $10.99 would become $5.99. She took it anyway, plus a yellow-and-orange plaid short-sleeve one on sale. It was meant for summer, but she didn't care. And if there was a God, bras would be free.

She found the Intimates at the back of the store. An old lady was digging through underpants in a bin, and picked up a pair so enormous it could've been a flag. Alison hustled past and let out a big breath when she saw the Teens sign. There were bras on hangers and bras in boxes, and all of them had sizes made up of numbers and letters, which made no sense. If only she'd paid attention to Delaney and her magazines. She wished, more than anything, for her mom. Her nose stung with tears. She grabbed three different sizes of the Teenform ones—the girl on the front looked about her age—and practically ran to the dressing room.

Alison scanned the tiny room, nervous about undressing with other people nearby, and heard her mother's voice telling her not to touch anything. How could she avoid the floor? Levitate? She stripped off her shirt. Good thing the first bra seemed like the right size because it took her ten minutes to figure out how to put it on. The size ten dress was a little short and the size twelve was baggy and too long. She went with the twelve, figuring she might fill it out eventually. The shirts were perfect.

The lady at the checkout craned her neck to look past Alison as if she might be hiding her mom under the counter. "That'll be $31.39." Alison handed her the crumpled bills, then picked out a hair clip for ninety-nine cents from the checkout display and put it on the counter. The lady sighed like Alison had asked her to start her life all over again, then rang it up.

"Thanks." Alison took her bag and pocketed the change.

"Thank you for shopping at Gaynes Shoppers World."

Outside, the hot, damp air meant to smother her. She pushed her hair off her forehead and searched the lot for her brothers' black Chevy Nova. Nothing. For a while she leaned against a pole and stared at the parking lot entrance but got tired and plunked herself on the curb. At first she was content to watch the cars and people go by—she had her new clothes!—but after what must have been an hour, a shivery feeling crept up her arms. What if they'd forgotten her?

"You waitin' on someone, red?"

A man stood in front of her jingling his keys. He was old, but younger than her father, with slicked-back hair and pointy shoes. Who wore pointy shoes? She didn't want to talk to him because he was a stranger, but she didn't want to be rude, either. You could get into trouble for either one. She also didn't appreciate being called "red" so she kept it short.

"Uh-huh."

He squinted at her. "You sure you don't need a lift somewhere?"

Her insides were squirming, which she was pretty sure had to do with her inner voice. "I'm sure."

The man studied her a long moment. "Your loss, red." He walked off.

He'd made the curb seem like the wrong place to be, so Alison walked to the kiddie rides on the other side of the entrance and found a seat between the spaceship and the pink horse. A ball of worry and anger set up in her chest and got bigger and tighter by the minute. Kids wanted rides and she had to keep getting up. Some of the parents looked at her sideways, like she was too big to be near something meant for little kids. If her mom had come with her, she wouldn't be feeling like a freak. She wouldn't be stuck here, worried and pretending not to be.

She didn't have a watch but knew she'd been waiting more than two hours, maybe closer to three. She was starving. Sniffing back tears, Alison slumped against the neck of the pink horse and closed her eyes. A word came to her from the dictionary: "aggrieved."

"Hey, squirt! Let's go!" Warren wheeled his arm in a circle to hurry her.

Alison jumped up, relief running fast down her limbs, her eyes flooding. She wiped them away and climbed in. Her thighs stuck to the seat as she tried to scoot across behind Lester. Now that she was safe and on her way home, she was furious.

"Where were you? I've been waiting hours!"

Warren took a slug from a Pepsi can. "Went to see *The Last House on the Left*. At least one of us did."

Lester covered his face. "It was too scary."

"You went to a movie? What about me?"

Warren put the car into gear and headed for the exit. "You wanted to go shopping. Don't be a crybaby."

She sat on her hands to stop herself from smacking the back of his head. Another dictionary word popped into her mind: "asshole." She'd been surprised to find it there between "asserveration," which she gave up on, and "Assur," an Assyrian war god. Asshole, asshole, asshole. She'd never said it out loud.

A paper bag rustled. Warren stuffed French fries into his mouth. They had gone to McDonald's!

"Did you get me anything? I'm starving."

"Here." Warren handed her a milkshake. Chocolate. Her favorite was vanilla.

"Thanks."

"And we got you fries, but Lester forgot they were yours and kinda ate them."

Lester gave her the red paper carton. "Sorry." At the bottom were a few broken fries drowned in ketchup.

She put the carton on the floor and slouched, her knees against the front seat. She pulled the crinkled paper off the straw and took a long sip. The engine growled as they sped down the freeway on-ramp. "Riders on the Storm" started playing on the radio, the spooky chords mixing with the engine noise. Warren turned it up so loud Lester couldn't hear himself singing and stopped.

Thrown into this world. The song had it about right. She let the breeze from the open windows whip her hair across her cheeks, wet with tears.

Warren parked in front of the garage and Alison ran inside, her complaints about her brothers perfectly lined up in her head. A VW wagon was on the lift and her dad was underneath, his forearms up in the guts of it. Hoses, shafts, valves and other parts lay scattered on the concrete floor around him, everything dark and greasy, including his tools—and him. Cars were like animals with grease and oil instead of blood. On the outside they were chrome and glass and shiny paint. On the inside they were ugly and mysterious. She knew they were only machines, but that's what bodies were, too. If she saw inside, deep inside, she might not be able to look away.

Her father didn't like interruptions when he was in the middle of a job, so she went straight past the reception desk, through the office and into the house. She found her mother at the kitchen table trimming green beans.

"Hey, Mom."

She didn't react. The beans reminded Alison how hungry she was. She opened the bread box, talking as she did. "You won't believe what Warren did." She pulled out two slices and took the peanut butter from the upper cabinet, unscrewing the lid on the way. She crossed the room to get a knife and stopped in front of the table. "Mom?"

Her mother nodded slightly, head bent.

"Mom! Aren't you listening?" Her mother, a pro at vegetable trimming and countless other supremely boring jobs, was working like she was half asleep. The hammering anger in Alison's head cooled. She picked a bean off the pile and put it in her mouth. As she chewed, she peered into the bowl of trimmed beans. There were lots of bean ends in there.

"Mom?"

Her mother looked up, but not exactly at Alison. "Did you say something about Warren?"

Alison got the knife and started making a sandwich. "He left me at Gaynes for almost three hours."

"Three hours."

"Yeah. They went to the movies." She sat down across from her mother, who'd started in on the beans again.

"Why were you at Gaynes?"

Maybe her father hadn't told her mother she'd gone to Burlington. "Dad gave me money to get some clothes."

Her mother paused. "Did you get what you wanted?"

"I got a dress and two shirts. And a bra."

"So that's good, then."

Was it? Alison didn't feel close to good.

It was as if no one was seeing her, or they were seeing her and not caring. She was like a ghost, but inside she was so alive with thoughts and feelings and fears. Worse, she couldn't figure out how it'd gotten this way. A year ago her mom would've done something about Warren abandoning her, like she'd done when Alison was nine. Warren was supposed to wait for her after school and help her carry home her science project. Instead, he went into Adams and goofed off with his friends. Their mom went ape and grounded him for a week.

Alison wanted to shout at her mother, be loud enough to matter, or crawl into her lap and get closer, help her come back to the way she'd always been, help her remember how they'd fit together so easily. But she was terrified that if she did crawl into her lap her mother would just stand up and Alison would fall to the floor like a dinner napkin that had been forgotten.

7

Carole

Alison stood in front of her holding a shopping bag, talking about Warren, about money, about movies. She talked about clothes, Gaynes. Pains to stay in the lanes. Alison was upset worried confused angry.

Carole saw her daughter from the bottom of the ocean floor. The weight of the water pressed on her eyes, her lips, her chest. Alison's words were falling stones. Carole reached to grab them, to hold them, to put them in order. It was so hard, the stones so heavy. The words kept coming. Her daughter's face was before her, her lovely, dear face, and she could do nothing to help her. Not now, not while the voices were drowning her out, burying sense and decency and love.

If she could explain it to Alison, she might understand. But there was no explanation. The words didn't line up. They sank. To the bottom. Autumn got 'em. She had to try. Find words for Alison's words.

"So that's good, then." She wasn't sure what she meant. The words reached Alison, and Alison wasn't sure, either. She left with her shopping bag.

Carole was alone in the kitchen. The size and weight of the ocean was unbearable.

A heavy, insistent rain drummed on the metal roof, overrunning the clogged gutters and splattering onto the concrete sidewalk below the open bedroom window. Carole had been awake awhile, listening in the dark for sounds creeping toward her from beyond the quiet of the house, whisperings below the sound of the rain. It could have been the hum of the refrigerator or crickets deep in the woods. Did crickets chirp in the rain? It was nonsense, she told herself, to strain to hear something so quiet, so far off, as if hearing would draw them nearer, out of the dark. As if she even wanted that.

Walt lay facing her, his arm solid and warm across her belly. He'd made love to her when he'd found her awake earlier, slow, careful love, as was his way, and her desire. And a necessity, she supposed, in a small house with children and thin walls. She preferred it simply because that was how it was for them and needed no other reason. Walt wasn't an overly affectionate person, and neither was she; still, they knew what it meant to have each other and to find it right and good. But over the last few months, a gap had opened up between them, because she was tired and couldn't think straight, because the voices pulled her so far inside herself that there was no room for him. Making love helped, but only a little. Lying in his arms, she'd almost told him about what happened in the post office, but when she played the conversation in her mind, there wasn't a version of it that didn't frighten her as much as the event itself. As long as she kept it inside, it might remain small, invisible, unreal.

Insomnia was as much as she would admit to, and she held on to a thread of hope that lack of sleep was all that was wrong. In a week, or maybe two, she might ask her doctor for sleeping pills. But that was as far as she would go. She would not end up like her mother, locked away, and her children would not end up as she had, abandoned, especially Alison, who needed her most. Carole, of all people, knew how that felt. No matter what adults say, what reasons they give, a child always blames herself. And Carole could not bear it if she did that to Alison.

Carole lay listening to the rain, weary but not sleepy. Her thoughts were glass shards. She pulled the coverlet to her neck despite the heat and tried to link up her thinking with Walt's snoring, steady as the rain. Perhaps she dozed.

Roused by sounds, she sat up. Someone had left the television on. How could that have happened? She and Walt had gone to bed after the boys had come home, long after she'd said good night to Alison and switched off the attic light. Maybe one of the boys had gone down later? Warren, it would have been. Once Lester fell asleep, he was out until the morning like his father. Warren could've at least remembered to turn the set off.

Carole got up, pulled on her robe and made her way to the hall and down the stairs, navigating by memory more than by the dim glow from the bathroom nightlight. The last three steps were blind. She paused at the bottom and peered into the living room. It was dark inside but the voices from the television were clear. She reached around the corner, turned on the floor lamp and walked over to the set. The screen was black. Something wrong with the picture, then. She twisted the on-off button to the left to turn it off but it wouldn't go. Confused, she turned it the other way. The screen flickered and buzzed as it warmed up. She switched it off, her fingers trembling, and backed away from the set.

The voices grew louder, as if her realization that they weren't coming from the television had given them power, made them bolder. Carole put her hands over her ears and pressed hard, heart pounding. She strode across the room and into the kitchen, circled the table and entered the living room again, crossing to the couch, hands clamped to her head, fear and dread and confusion tying up her muscles, legs stiff shoulders in knots skin stretched tight across her arms tingling. She paced back to the kitchen around the table to shut out the voices but there was no escape. She paused at the back door outside there was space to run away from them. Them. How many? Several dozen speaking at a distance softer and louder but never more distinct. They didn't want her to hear. They were talking about her. She couldn't hear the words the accusations but she knew. They'd gathered because of her. Of what she was.

She'd heard them for weeks now, maybe longer, and dismissed them, telling herself they were from a car radio in the garage, or the boys' stereo. They weren't actually voices, only ringing in her ears because she was exhausted. Since spring she'd only slept a few hours most nights. A little ringing was understandable. She'd tried not to dwell on it, forgetting how often it had actually happened. She'd denied the reality of the intrusive voices and thoughts winding like twine around themselves, cinched tight in a binding knot. It had happened seldom enough that she could pretend it hadn't happened at all. The incident in the post office was the hardest to explain.

Now the voices were no longer muttering but louder closer definitely inside her head. Left of center near the back. She placed a finger on the indentation at the base of her skull half expecting to find a hole.

Until recently, she'd never questioned that the workings of her mind were different from anyone else's. She had assumed she was sane. Isn't that what everyone thought? She was awkward perhaps. Shy always shy. But sane. Her mind judged the time, held the memories, weighed the befores and afters. It contained her experiences, serving them up as lessons vignettes parables, some shining in the light some hiding in the shadows. It held the peaks and troughs of her emotional seas, all of it hers and hers alone, except what she chose to share. She was a wife a mother a sister a woman a daughter, full of the stories the birthdays the anniversaries the tragedies the betrayals the joys the kindnesses. All of it was there. Somewhere.

But now something else was there, too, intruding inspecting unearthing unraveling. Her mind's walls had been breached. She had become inhabited and could not control what she knew, or what she chose to know, the larger danger. Terror rose in concert with the voices inside her, a vicious thunder rumbling from edge to edge to edge back and forth rolling swelling crashing bigger louder stronger worse and worse and worse.

She found herself in the living room standing over the coffee table, her breath coming in gasps, her skin so tight over her flesh that she clutched at her forearms to pull it off. She fought the urge to scream to overcome the voices shout them down, as frightened of disclosing her crumbling sanity to her family as she was of the voices themselves. Lowering herself onto the couch, Carole strove to even out her breathing. She hummed a single note, quietly, as she had done to calm her children as babies, forced the humming into her head into her mind's crevasses her tongue thick against the back of her teeth her throat an engine of the hum.

She hummed who knows how long. Her heartbeat slowed and the mumbling voices retreated a little. She pulled her nightgown over her knees and tucked her hands under her legs. She rocked and hummed, rocked and hummed. Her inner voice, the familiar one, rose unsteadily. She rocked and hummed.

There'd be no more sleep for her tonight. She would wait here for morning and keep the voices at bay by humming and rocking, and by thinking of her family asleep in the rooms above, and, of course, of her mother, who might be awake this night as well, humming and rocking within the hard walls or lost in a sedative fog, unaware of what she might have bequeathed to her daughter.

Her mother. Her mother was inside her. Her father, too. Dormant for so long, now coursing, bathing every cell in the loathsome certainty that despite her strongest hope and best intention she would forsake all she loved.

8

Solange

Solange sat in the chair in her room. Late afternoon sun spilled
through barred windows onto the wall behind the bed, shapes
pulled long from one corner, the lowest ones seeking the floor. Light
pooled and stretched along the planes surrounding her. Time
stretched, too, but not evenly. Not in here. In this room time was
so insubstantial it gaped, like a pie dough rolled too thin, with
drooping holes that could not be closed, days falling through,
weeks, months, years. Memory was supposed to be a line that
traced a waning but orderly past. First one thing, then the next,
building on itself, like a train track, each minute a solid wood tie laid
down, secured, then the next hammered into place. You were supposed to be able to look back on it and witness the inexorable reach
of your life, each moment growing smaller in the distance, inching
away hour by hour, day by day, tie by tie, to the vanishing point
of your own consciousness. You couldn't remember everything,
Solange thought; nobody could, but for most people the track was
there, and it obeyed the march of the days you had lived. But she
had no time track and her memories had floated off, as ephemeral
as pollen on the wind.

She had great big gaping holes in her recollections, years and years misplaced or shuffled, many more forgotten than remembered. Her past was so riddled with holes, and so frail, she could not examine it without more holes appearing. This made her desperate, and profoundly sad, for she sensed her life had been so important to her once—brimming with passion, hope and love—and now she was terrified to lift it by the edges and peek underneath, lest she fall into the timeless black and disappear altogether.

On rare occasions, a cherished memory came to her, sudden and complete, and evoked such pure feeling that she accepted the memory as real. Her heart was a balloon, filled to bursting, and she wept with gratitude. These few, sweet memories pinned her to this earth. And so, too, did the painful ones. Those, it seemed, would never leave her. They would be there when she'd forgotten her own name.

Solange dove from a granite boulder, slipping under the skin of the lake like a knife opening a letter. She swam from the shore, keeping her legs high in the water to avoid the layer of mush at the bottom. Her strokes were long and unrushed, slicing through still water as if she'd been born to it, which, in a sense, she had. Soon she was not a girl swimming from shore, but of the lake itself, liquid inside liquid. The silted floor fell away beneath her.

Halfway to the island she paused. From the land behind her came the muted sound of axes falling on wood. Her father and her brother spent the fine months scavenging driftwood and felling small trees. They'd stack the wood on the houseboat and carry it to the shore towns to sell, along with whatever else they could find that might be worth something. Years ago, long before Solange was born, the houseboats and barges had carried lumber up to the seaway. But they'd run out of trees, or near enough, so now her family and the other lake dwellers were having a hard time making a living. Her grandmother was an Abenaki healer, and her mother had dabbled in it, too, collecting herbs and roots for potions fewer and fewer folks believed in. The wealthy from New York and Boston were buying up the shores and islands and building huge houses and docks for yachts they visited twice a summer. There was a lot of talk about who could or should do what on the lake, and who mattered more: the people who'd always lived here or the people with all the money. She could see both sides, though she didn't tell her family that. It wasn't anyone's fault the trees didn't grow faster than they could be cut down, and if out-of-staters wanted to buy land and build houses so they could enjoy the beautiful place she called home, well, who could blame them? People argued too much about things they weren't likely to change. Most of the talk buzzed around Solange's head like a bee and flew off.

She treaded water for a time, her face to the sky, the water cool and slippery around her legs and warm and soft on her shoulders, then swam out again toward an island no one had bothered to name.

The parallelograms of sunshine on the walls of her hospital room shifted. Time slipped sideways and another memory thrust into her consciousness. Solange lost herself to it.

Muted evening light fell through the dining room's windows, which stretched from the polished oak floor to the elaborate coffered ceiling. Outside, the sky was a pewter dome. Solange heard the lake groan, complaining of the weight of ice, a mournful sound carrying hope of winter's end. Her restlessness grew, coiled like a snake inside her, whenever she heard it. The ice would break in time, and with violence. This was nothing new to her, Vermont exploding into spring, but this year she longed to experience, rather than observe, the change. The groan of the lake ice was the earth tuning for a song she was desperate to hear. She had no idea what it meant beyond her own feelings, which she both trusted and feared.

She moved from the window to set a table near the entrance to the room, smoothing the white linen before she lowered each plate onto it. The plates would be whisked away when the first course arrived, and washed and dried although never used. She'd been working at the Hotel Vermont for two months and the practice still struck her as wasteful and ridiculous. She pushed the thought aside and concentrated on her work. She lined up the bottom edges of the silver, exchanged two wineglasses with water spots for clean ones and stepped back for one last inspection. Her job depended on getting each detail correct, and her family needed her wages, especially in winter. The work did not bother her. Her senses were keener here, where ambition and ease ran sweet and thick as syrup, and success rarely depended on the weather. She didn't know what she wanted from this part of Burlington—it never seemed a question worth posing—but she was curious to see what there was.

The table setting was in order. She started toward the service pantry to check the coffee. A swish of air brushed against her stockinged legs as the heavy doors to the lobby opened. Two men entered, father and son perhaps, in identical black homburgs. They handed their coats and hats to the attendant. The maître d' appeared (from nowhere, as always), bowed slightly at the waist, and conferred with the older man.

Solange busied herself stacking coffee cups and continued to observe the pair. The younger man—more of a boy, she could see now; late teens like herself—bore sun-bleached hair, strong cheekbones and a confident posture. He turned her way and caught her eye. She'd been trained to avoid customers' gazes, but she could not look away. He held her there, an instant, two, three. A warmth like a flush of fever tingled the skin of her face and neck. And still she did not look away, nor did he. Her heart dropped to her feet and stayed there.

He was handsome in the way people who never suffered often were, but there was something else about him, something both

familiar and utterly new. A smile spread across his face, lighting
it. The older man was moving toward her, escorted by the maître d',
but the young man stayed where he was. He began to fidget and his
Adam's apple bobbed up and down. Solange surmised he was nervous. She hurriedly scanned the room to see what it could be about,
and, spying nothing more worrisome than a few regular customers
and the local bridge club, concluded she must be the cause. She had
unnerved him.

Solange straightened and took a deep breath. Her mother, who
was wise about such things, deeply wise, had told her she would
know. An instinct, she had said, same a dog has for which strangers to trust and a duckling has for paddling after its mother. This
feeling of being lifted out of her shoes, this had to be it, didn't it?
Solange opened her heart to the boy and smiled.

With a few hurried steps, he caught up with the others. The
maître d' passed her, and so did the father, most definitely the father, she could see the resemblance clearly now. And the boy, who
had never taken his eyes off her. He stopped beside her, within
inches. She felt the heat of his body along her hip and leaned toward
it, nearly closing the gap. He smelled clean and vibrant, like a cat
come in from the cold. He put his ear to her mouth. Her heart
fluttered, not in fear, but as if it were a nestling, ruffling its wings,
eager for flight.

"Solange," she whispered.

He smiled. "Solange." His eyes were the slate blue of the lake
in summer.

Solange's finger on the cheek of her baby, sated and asleep. A pulse
of heat running through her, liquid silver, the same heat that ran
through her baby. Her warm milk in the baby's stomach. They
shared their bodies, the air, the world, life.

Carole. A song of happiness.

. .   .

Another baby, another girl. The familiar sense that the inch between them was of no consequence. It melted with each gesture,
every sigh.

But this time, surrounding them both, a cloak of fear. This baby,
born between two worlds, would have no name.

9

Alison

She filled her cereal bowl with milk and slurped it away. She was a giant moon making the tide rush out. Frosted Flake atolls rose from the white sea and the natives cheered.

Her father sat across from her with the *Free Press* and a half-full coffee cup. Alison pulled the Living section closer.

"Hunting for your horoscope, sunshine?"

She shrugged. "Sure. And the comics."

He turned the page, bringing his hands together to do it, like he was playing cootie catchers. "How many people you reckon we got in the world, then?"

"Not sure. Too many, maybe."

He nodded. "Almost four billion, last I heard. And there are twelve—what do you call them?"

"Signs."

"Signs. So today, for instance, how many folks are going to have the same kind of day as you?"

Alison smiled. He wasn't asking her to do a math problem on a Saturday morning. He didn't do that sort of thing. He'd just thought of something and was letting her in on it. "Millions and millions."

"That's right." He sipped his coffee and looked at her over the top of his glasses. "Makes you feel that, whatever your day is like, good or bad, you've got plenty of company."

"If you believe in horoscopes."

"Right. Or maybe either way." He pushed his chair back and headed for the garage.

Alison thought of all the bad days her mother had lately. "Daddy? Is Mom okay?"

He paused at the door, surprised she'd asked. "Sure. Sure she is. Just missing some sleep. She's right as rain."

He left. Alison wondered about the saying, about rain being right. How something could make sense but not be completely true. How words could explain things, and also hide them. All her life, she'd relied on her parents for answers to a million questions, never realizing answers could also be riddles.

Alison dug for earthworms in an old flowerbed and grabbed her fishing pole and wicker creel from the shed. Crossing the field, she skirted the Dalrymples' yard and cut through the woods on a path she had worn with the help of deer. She reached the river's edge. The water was so muddy that she'd have to dip her worms in Day-Glo paint for the fish to spot them. Oh well, she was here. She set down her creel and threaded a worm onto the hook, leaving a wriggling end free. Holding down the line with her forefinger, she flipped the bail and cast upstream.

The rain had clouded the river, but the rest of the world was washed clean and the sky was the color of forget-me-nots. A phoebe sang from an oak on the far shore, the cool, clear notes like lines on a page. Alison stepped from rock to rock, and cast into a shallower stretch. She let the worm sink and rested her finger on the line. After a moment, it twitched. She stared at the current where the line disappeared, sure she had imagined it. The line moved again, a tug this time. She jerked the rod to set the hook and the rod bent sharply. A big one! Alison reeled in, a little at a time, and stepped across the rocks toward the shore, her heart flipping in her chest like the fish. She wound the reel bit by bit until only six feet of line was out, swung the rod to her left, dropped the fish on the ground and stepped on it. It had to be more than a foot long. She picked up a rock with a blunt edge, grabbed the thrashing fish and smacked the rock into its neck. She'd never gotten used to this part. With a small fish, she could just jamb her thumb in its mouth and snap its neck. But this trout had huge teeth, so she had to use a rock. She smashed it four times, her breath coming in gasps, before the fish lay still.

Alison wiped her forehead with her arm and stared at the trout. The red spots on its side faded and its eye grew dull. Her excitement about catching it shifted into sadness. She was sorry the fish was dead. One moment it was nosing up the river, minding its own business, and the next it was suffocating on air and getting its neck smashed. She sighed and rinsed her hands in the river. Not even fishing was simple.

She lined the creel with ferns, placed the fish inside and carried it home, amazed at how heavy the creel felt. She got a knife from the kitchen, knelt by the shed and slit the fish open along the belly, spilling the guts onto the lawn. Sally sat beside her, licking her chops. Alison sliced off the head, scooped up the guts and dumped them a few yards off.

"Here you go, Sallypants."

Alison watched Sally start in on her treat. A gleam of white in the shiny mess caught her eye. She gently pushed the cat from what she thought might be the stomach. Sally snatched up the fish head and moved off a few feet.

The stomach had a gash a quarter inch long. Alison poked at the opening with the tip of the knife. Something round and white appeared, the size of a pea. She made the slit bigger and nudged the object out onto the grass. She picked it up and rubbed it clean. It was smooth, and milky. A pearl? How could a pearl get inside a fish? She stood, lightheaded. She balanced it in her palm. It was like holding a tiny moon.

She pocketed it, a calm settling on her like a storm of bees returning to the hive. She didn't know what it meant, but it was a sign. The pearl was hers, a gift of beauty and mystery from the river.

Alison put the fish in the fridge and washed the slime off her hands. She went to her room and hid the pearl in a small box of blue leaded glass with two mirrors inside: one on the lid and one on the bottom. When she first moved to the attic, she'd searched through the boxes and crates, not discovering anything worth taking to the bedroom side other than the blue box, which had been tucked in a pile of soft, yellowed blankets. Her baby blankets, she guessed, handed down from the twins. She'd shown the box to her mother, who'd said it belonged to Alison's grandmother.

"Can I have it?"

Her mother shrugged. "Of course. It's been up there a long time."

Alison had only met her grandmother once, when she was eight. It'd been Mother's Day and her mom was arguing with Aunt Janine, who didn't want to visit Grandma. Finally, her mom gave up and said, "I'll take Alison, then. At least *I* have a daughter who wants to be with me on Mother's Day." It was true. Alison did want to be with her, pretty much all the time, and especially on Mother's Day.

No matter what day it was, Alison was anxious about meeting her grandmother because it meant going to Underhill. Whenever a kid acted nuts at school, someone would say, "They're gonna send you to Underhill!" Alison imagined a huge room full of people making faces and jumping around.

During the car ride her mom explained that if Grandma was having a bad day, they'd just leave the flowers and the cards and come back another time. Alison knew, though, she was only there because of the fight with Aunt Janine. There wouldn't be another time, so she tried to be brave.

Because it was raining out, they met Grandma in the lounge. Alison sank into her seat at the card table, relieved that her grandmother seemed perfectly normal. More normal than a lot of people actually. For one thing, she didn't ask Alison all sorts of questions about school. For another, she didn't say a word about Alison's freckles or her hair. In fact, Alison was a little mad at her mother for never telling her about Grandma's red hair. It was mostly gray now, but she could tell. If they had that in common, there was probably a whole lot more.

Her grandmother smiled when she read the card Alison made. The writing was almost straight and the flower petals had come out pretty even considering she'd drawn them in the car. In her grandmother's smiling eyes, Alison could see she belonged to her, like she belonged to her mom. There was something else, though. A feeling arrived inside Alison as she listened to her mother talking softly and Grandma saying something small now and then. Her grandmother had once been just like Alison. Not just related, but exactly the same, inside and out.

Three years had gone by since the visit. Alison couldn't picture her grandmother's face but she could pull up that feeling. The blue glass box had stayed empty on her dresser all that time. Now the pearl lay on the bottom. Alison lifted the lid partway; the pearl shone like a moon in a lake, but upside down.

After lunch, Alison put on her swimsuit and headed for the river again. She pulled a towel off the line and walked down the road to where the path, slick with mud, angled through the Buchanans' woods. As she picked her way down, voices floated up to her. She reached the top of the giant rock that sloped into the deep pool, and her heart sank. Her brothers and about six of their friends. So much for a relaxing swim. A couple of them spotted her, so there was no way she was leaving. They didn't own the river. She crossed the big rock, staying high, and dropped down to a narrow ledge inches above the water and backed by a tall rock wall. She liked this spot, lapped by the current, with a view upstream where alders and birches bent to shake hands over the water and scattered shifting circles of light and shadow on the surface.

"Hey, Alison!" Lester was standing knee-deep opposite the big rock, smacking his palms against the water again and again with his face turned from the spray. He loved to swim, except he couldn't stand water on his face.

She waved. "Hey."

She dangled her feet in the water and let the minnows worry her toes. The boys cannonballed and hooted. After a while she got bored, found a chunk of soapstone and drew designs on the rock wall. The surface was rough in places, but it worked okay. She drew Sally sitting on her haunches, but it looked more like a turtle, so she washed it off. Her mind skipped to the day before yesterday when Warren had ditched her at Gaynes. She remembered the man who'd offered her a ride and how she couldn't tell if he was a kidnapper or just being nice. Grown-ups were good at hiding the truth and didn't necessarily do the right thing. Warren wasn't a grown-up yet, but he had that down pat.

Someone shouted, "Looky here!" A boy, high school age, coming down the path. He was tall and kind of tubby, at least compared to the rest of the boys, whose skin stretched across their ribs like plastic wrap. Judging by the new boy's light green shirt with the collar turned up and the perfectly white towel slung over his shoulder, he was from out of state. Local kids wore T-shirts, and if any of them brought towels, they were like Alison's: faded, with mysterious stains. He'd probably come from the Greenville Inn, halfway between Adams and Daventry, the nearest ski town. The owners of the Greenville Inn told their guests about the swimming hole, a quaint Vermont attraction, like the cider mill and the covered bridge.

The boy came onto the rock, slipped off his sandals and folded his towel in a neat square on top. Someone sitting nearby sniggered. Warren hoisted himself out of the pool and flung his head to the side to clear his hair from his face. Hands on his hips, he stuck out his chin. "You here to try out our river?"

The boy nodded. "It's hot."

"I'll bet you can do a hell of a cannonball." Everyone laughed. The boy turned red and looked at his feet. Warren puffed himself up more. "Well, come on. Show us what you've got."

The boy sat down, rested his arms on his knees and glanced around at the group, not lingering too long on anyone. When he got to Alison, she smiled at him. She knew what it was like to have Warren on your case.

"Actually," the boy said, pointing to a nearby shallow, "I thought I'd go over there."

Warren's eyebrows shot up and his grin spread wide. The others elbowed each other and shook their heads. Alison winced. Only babies and old people sat in the shallow.

"What do you want to do that for, New Jersey?"

"I'm not from New Jersey. I'm from Poughkeepsie."

The boys hooted. Lester was loudest. "Poo-keepsie. That's funny. And kinda dirty. Isn't it dirty, Warren?" The boys laughed louder and socked each other on the arm.

The Poughkeepsie boy squirmed. Alison said, "The pool's really nice. You should try it."

He shrugged. "I can't. I don't know how to swim."

Warren climbed two steps closer. "Don't yank our chains, Jersey. Everybody knows how to swim."

The boy looked up, jaw working, and locked eyes with Warren. "Everybody? Everybody in the whole world? That's not even physically possible. What a dumb thing to say."

Rooster Cantrell, Warren's best friend since kindergarten, had been sprawled on his back, shades on, hands behind his head. He sat up and swiveled toward the boy from Poughkeepsie. He didn't say anything. He didn't have to. The boy shrank.

A boiling anger rushed through Alison. Being mean made Warren feel big and powerful. The only person he thought about other than himself was Lester. It was a kind of shield. Who could criticize him when he was so protective of Lester? It made him seem to be a better person than he actually was.

Warren was practically standing on the boy's toes. And his face had gone from teasing to looking as if he wanted to pull the legs off something. He knocked his foot against the boy's shin. "You call me 'dumb'?"

Alison stared at the design she'd been scribbling onto the wall. It reminded her of something—maybe in a book? She'd drawn an arc from twelve o'clock to six o'clock and two angled lines meeting on the inside of the arc. Now she drew a line diagonally from the angled line to the arc, then away again and down, at the same angle. She hadn't planned it but, ignoring the arc, it looked like the beginning of a star.

Warren pointed at the boy. "What d'you say we give Jersey here a swimming lesson?"

Rooster peeled off his sunglasses and put them aside. "Radical." He got up and stood next to Warren. A senior named Andy came over and so did a dropout called Juice. The boy from Poughkeepsie fidgeted. He snuck a glance behind him, like he might make a dash for the trail.

He'd never make it. Alison returned to the design, her stomach sour. The lines glowed brighter. She finished drawing the star. It was upside down, with two points facing up and one down. Weird. The soapstone grew hot in her fingers.

"Ready, guys?" Warren grabbed the boy's ankle. Rooster took hold of the other.

"Hey!" the boy said, kicking, but Warren and Rooster held on. "Leave me alone!" He flung his arms around. Andy and Juice laughed and pinned him down. His face went from pink to white. "Leave me alone!"

Some kid started clapping and chanting, "Swim lesson! Throw him in! Swim lesson! Throw him in!" Lester and the rest joined in. Warren and the other three dragged the boy down the rock to where a thick stripe of quartz ran across it. If the water was above the stripe, you shouldn't go in. The river wasn't that high today, but there was a lot of current. Especially if you couldn't swim.

"On the count of three," Rooster yelled.

"Don't, you guys!" Alison said.

The boy's face was a mess of fear. He was wriggling like his shorts were on fire, and trying not to cry at the same time. Grunting, Warren and the others lifted him.

"One!" They rocked him forward. "Two!" They swung him back.

Something nudged Alison from deep inside. She spun to face the drawing. It was burning white, like the middle of a fire. Her hand moved to the bottom of the arc. Without knowing why, she closed her eyes and said: "Warren." She opened them again and the soapstone dropped from her hand. The star was in a circle.

"Three!"

She spun around to see the boy in the air above the pool. As he fell, he threw his arm out, grabbed Warren's forearm, pulling him off balance. Warren's feet went out from under him and he slid into the pool. The boy disappeared under him.

Warren popped up, a look of shock on his face. The boy thrashed to the surface, mouth gaping. He clutched at Warren and climbed on top of him as if he was a life raft. Warren opened his mouth, then closed it as the boy sank him.

The other boys gathered at the edge of the rock, peering into the pool. Lester was standing in the water, laughing his head off, thinking it was all a game. The murky water roiled as the boys grappled under the surface. An arm appeared, then the face of the Poughkeepsie boy, stretched in terror. He gasped for air and sank again. Why didn't Warren push him off and swim away? The boy must be standing on him, or, more likely, Warren was lying at the bottom, waiting for the perfect moment to leap out of the water and laugh at everyone for falling for it. But what if he hit his head going in? Her mouth went dry and she felt strange—dizzy and excited all at once, like the world was spinning on a new axis.

The seconds ticked by. The boys glanced at one another. Rooster said, "That fat kid is weighing him down." He dove in, the bottoms of his feet flashing white in the sun. The Poughkeepsie boy came up again, slapping his arms on top of the water, making huge splashes. He spotted Lester ten feet away. Worry crept onto Lester's face. He stepped toward the boy and held out his arms. "You gotta kick! Kick, kick, kick, kick!"

It was what their mother had told them when she taught them to swim. The boy started kicking, from his knees, which wasn't the way to do it. Nothing he was doing looked anything like swimming, but it was keeping him afloat.

Rooster's head popped up. He shook the water from his face, took a big breath, and dove again. The boy was churning the water like an outboard, making it impossible for anyone to see into the pool.

Warren had been under a long time. Alison stared at the upside-down star on the wall, her heart fluttering. She recognized the design now. Her witchcraft book. The upward points of the star were devil horns. Satan's sign. She'd cursed her brother. A wave of panic flowed through her. She glanced at the swimming hole. The boy had beached himself downstream of Lester and lay on his side, panting. Rooster was diving again and Juice was in the water now, too, searching for Warren.

Alison scooped water and threw it against the star. She tossed water on it twice more and frantically rubbed the markings off. The rock wall was burning hot, but she scraped her palms over it, erasing the star. She tossed more water, her breath sticking in her chest, as if she was drowning, too. She rubbed the stone again and again, ignoring the pain in her palms, not daring to look behind her at the pool. The wall was clean. Exhausted, she leaned her forehead against it. It was cool.

"Hey!" A couple of boys cheered.

Rooster and Juice dragged Warren onto the far bank. Lester hung over him, blocking Alison's view. She jumped in and swam across, her eyes trained on Warren. Rooster rolled him onto his side and water spewed out of his mouth. He coughed, pushed Rooster off him and sat up, flicking his hair out of his face.

"What the fuck is the matter with all of you goddamn pussies?"

Alison let out the breath she'd been holding. She hadn't drowned him.

The boy from Poughkeepsie made his way back to the rock the long way, crossing the river below where they'd dammed it. The water ran fast there and he stumbled on the slippery rocks. He kept checking to see if anyone was coming after him, but they'd had enough fun for one day. He got to the big rock and put on his sandals, shaking, chewing his lip, holding himself together. One of the boys did a cannonball and almost landed on Rooster, making everyone laugh loudly, like they'd all been holding their breath, too.

Lester and Warren stood together, waist deep, swatting at the mosquitoes buzzing around them. Alison hung off to the side, rubbing her arms, wishing she'd stayed home.

"He couldn't swim, could he, Warren?" Lester said.

"No. But he did improve."

"Don't fat people float?"

"Apparently not. Sure sucks when they're standing on you." He glanced at Alison, noticing her for the first time. "What's the matter with you?"

"Nothing."

"Looks like you've seen a ghost."

She shivered. "I'm going home." She almost said she was glad he didn't drown, but since she was the one who had cursed him, she couldn't.

She swam to the wall and stared at the place, still dark and wet. The chunk of soapstone lay in a puddle at her feet. She picked it up and cocked her arm to throw it into the current, but hesitated. Something had happened. Something powerful, not completely under her control, but not outside it, either. She lowered her arm and palmed the soapstone. She pulled her towel down from the tree branch, draped it over her shoulders like a cloak and stole into the woods.

10

Janine

Janine turned right along the corridor to the office. At the far end, Greg Bayliss was leaving the staff room, heading her way. She breathed in deeply, squared her shoulders, ran her tongue over lips and resisted the urge to check her curls. Her hair was flawless this morning. She'd made sure of it. He'd been gone all summer and, finally, here he was. Her man. Her next husband.

Last February, right before Valentine's Day, his girlfriend had dumped him. She was a dreadful creature from Jericho, an earthy type who lived in caftans and clogs. As soon as Janine found out Granola Girl was history, she set to work reeling in Greg Bayliss. Janine wouldn't have hesitated to out-and-out steal him from his girlfriend, but he seemed the loyal type (how quaint!) and she didn't want to ruin her chances, not with a guy that good-looking. There wasn't a better prospect in all of Lamoille County, even if he was only a schoolteacher. To think she'd been counting on becoming the wife of a state senator and, if she'd had her way, the first lady of Vermont. She'd have preferred a bigger state, but now even pathetic little Vermont was off the table. Mitch's death was a pain in the ass.

She befriended Greg first, asking about Granola Girl and commiserating after he admitted they'd split. Janine deliberately dressed modestly during this time, and pretended he didn't interest her much. She was friendly but never flirty, and made sure to ignore him now and then. After six weeks, which she judged the mending period of a man's heart, she baited the hook, cast her line and reeled him in.

Their first date was in early May, an excursion to the fair in Montpelier. He won a stuffed Bullwinkle at a throwing booth (he'd pitched in high school) and presented it to her with a flourish, imitating Bullwinkle's voice.

"Watch me pull a rabbit outta my hat, Janine!"

His dimples showed and she couldn't help being charmed, although she would gladly have exchanged some of his good nature for an extra helping of ambition. They went out again ten days later, to dinner at a restaurant outside Burlington, where he let drop he'd be teaching English as a second language in Mexico all summer. Janine's fantasies of a romantic and productive summer were squashed. It was all she could do not to reach across the table and smack his do-gooding face. Mexico! What was wrong with leaving them to their own language?

She tucked her chin and peered at him through her lashes. "Does it have to be all summer, Greg?"

"The longer I'm there, the more I can do."

"I'm sure you're right." Men lapped up that line. "But don't you need a little vacation? Maybe have a little fun?" She gave him her sweetest smile. He liked nice girls, she could tell. It was a chore but nothing worth having comes easy. Except sex.

"Teaching's fun. That's my vacation."

She studied him from across the table. In this light he resembled Robert Redford more than usual, with his sideburns, worn suede sport coat and faded denim shirt. She wondered whether she should just screw him. They could do it tonight. Hell, give her five minutes and she'd be fucking him on this table with thirty customers watching. Sadly, it was not a viable long-term strategy. Fucking was easy. Husbands were a different business. Maybe she should reconsider

Ray What's-his-name, the banker. His eyes stuck out too far but he had money and didn't give a damn about Mexico. Maybe she should move back to Burlington or to another state. The problem was she had no savings and no marketable skills, other than the ones she was using now. Adams might be a dump, but it was cheap.

He filled her wineglass and she sighed. He had manners, blue eyes and dimples. And she was sure he'd be great in the sack. Who cared about the summer? She'd screw his brains out before he left on his mission. Give him something to think about for a couple of months. Come September, he'd be hers.

She touched her wineglass to his. "You're a very special person, Greg. You know that, don't you?"

They shared a baked Alaska and the waiter brought the check. Greg pulled his wallet from the inside pocket of his sport coat. The label caught Janine's eye: Brooks Brothers. On a teacher's salary? As he stacked bills on the table, she toyed with the possibility his shabby clothes (and that awful Vega he drove) represented not real poverty but wealth pretending not to care about appearances. She'd seen it before, people from the Cape or Long Island with their round-heeled penny loafers and pilled cashmere sweaters, people with so much money they weren't pressed to show it off.

At the school office the next day, Janine had copied information from Greg Bayliss's file and made several phone calls, pretending to represent the school, an alumnae association and a newspaper. Her hunch was right on the money, literally. She didn't need a bank statement, she just toted up the addresses: Beacon Hill, Exeter, Harvard, London, Central Park West. Whatever his reasons for holing up in Adams, Mr. Gregory Bayliss, sixth grade teacher, was loaded.

Summer vacation had been about to start. Janine had snagged Greg in his classroom after the lunch bell and shooed the stragglers out onto the playground. She'd set a pile of summer reading lists on the corner of his desk, taken his hand and pulled him into the coat closet, where she shushed him with one finger and gave him a quickie blow job, one of her specialties. She'd probably left purple fingerprints from the mimeo behind. Good. Every time he caught a whiff of the sweet damp mimeo ink, he'd think of her.

Now fall had finally arrived. Greg was walking down the school corridor, reading from a sheaf of papers. He hadn't noticed her. Janine's scalp tingled in anticipation as she angled toward him, calculating her trajectory as if she were an ICBM and he were the Kremlin. She was a yard away. He raised his head, recognized her and smiled. Those dimples. And he was so tan! It made his eyes even bluer. Maybe he'd decided to go surfing all summer instead of teaching. She imagined him in swim shorts. A swirl of heat flared inside her, moved down between her legs. Lust and ambition had every nerve in her body on full alert. She widened her eyes at him.

"Janine! Great to see you."

"You, too, Greg. How'd the teaching go?"

"Difficult and fantastic. Such an amazing place."

She moved a half step closer, an inch from an improper distance. "Can't wait to hear all about it."

He squirmed (worried someone might see them, no doubt) and peered past her down the hall. "Sure. But I've got a meeting with the other middle school teachers. Can't be late."

"No, you sure can't. I'm off to the mimeo machine myself."

His tanned cheeks flushed red. "Right. See you later, Janine."

She returned to the front office, made a few phone calls and got to the end of her to-do list. Staff day was over. Labor Day weekend was here, and a date with Greg was a near certainty. With the first day of school on Tuesday, he'd always be handy. She'd never looked forward to the start of school this much in her life.

She retrieved her handbag from the bottom drawer.

"One last thing, Janine."

Kawolski would be staring at her from behind his desk, swiveling in his chair, a few degrees in one direction, a few in the other direction, again and again, like a boy would. He knew she was leaving, that it was, in fact, ten minutes past her quitting time, on a Friday, no less. She placed her handbag on her chair and took a deep breath. Her eye caught the letter opener lined up next to the stapler. She imagined plunging it into his neck, right below his oversized earlobe. In three strides, maybe four, she'd be at his desk. She'd be quick. Spring across the desk and jab it in. She was flexible and her skirt had some give. He'd never see it coming.

"Janine? If you have two minutes."

She smiled at him. "I might even have three."

He laughed his girlie laugh. He really was a ridiculous man. But the students loved him, the younger ones anyway, and so did the teachers and the school board. "Such a compassionate man," they said. "A great communicator."

An insufferable idiot.

She entered the office, readying her face for the other person she knew was there: April Honeycutt. The brand new special ed teacher was perched on the edge of a chair as if to make a point about how little space she occupied. She was too adorable for her own good, with her perky bobbed hair that bounced with her slightest movement and her back-to-school wardrobe prim enough to make her look as though she were playing teacher dress-up. Since meeting her earlier in the week, Janine had been trying to think whom April Honeycutt resembled. Now it came to her: Cybill Shepherd in *The Last Picture Show*, although not the scene where she strips on the pool deck. No, April Honeycutt wasn't the stripping type. She had Cybill Shepherd's innocent '50s look, the same doe-eyed face and the same woman-but-really-still-a-girl body. If Little Miss Honeybutt weren't so earnest and, well, vulnerable, Janine would have skipped the preliminaries and gone straight to despising her. But it wouldn't be fair. A small dose of Janine's bad vibes and April Honeycutt would crumble, maybe burst into tears. Janine examined April's face, musing whether she'd be a pretty crier or an ugly one. She couldn't decide.

"Hello, April. How are you settling in?"

"I'm a little overwhelmed, to be honest." She heard herself complain and put on a cheery expression. "But that's how first jobs go, I guess."

Janine tipped her head sympathetically and smiled.

Kawolski ran his fingers down his tie. "Janine, I was hoping you would have time to show Miss Honeycutt how to fill out a requisition. She would like some special supplies for her students."

Special supplies for special ed. A moment's curiosity about what those supplies might be (Training treats? Restraints?) gave way to impatience. Janine fought the impulse to look at her watch.

"As you know," she said to Kawolski, knowing perfectly well he did not, "requisitions won't go anywhere on a Friday afternoon." She addressed April. "We'll see to it your first free period Tuesday, when you're fresh. You've had a big week." A maternal tone had crept into her speech, making her feel old and, worse, maternal.

April smiled sweetly. Janine checked the impulse to kick her in the shin. Instead, she allowed her gaze to drift to the window, signaling that an empty overflow parking lot held greater interest than the biggest week in the young woman's pathetically sincere life.

Kawolski clapped like a circus seal. "If that suits both of you . . ."

His voice paused on an upswing, which meant he'd thought of something else. One Last Thing. Janine wished them a good weekend and left the room. She grabbed her bag and noticed the letter opener again. Not today, she thought without regret or residual anger, and escaped the office before Kawolski could open his mouth.

Janine had decided on the menu within minutes of Greg accepting her dinner invitation for Saturday. Her repertoire was limited; she had, at most, a week of meals suitable for company she could put together without breaking a sweat. Marriage to Mitch had taught her that. He didn't mind eating out—preferred it, in fact—but inviting his business associates and political allies (and their spouses) to his house for a homemade meal was as central to his success as a firm handshake and a well-executed stump speech. Mitch was thirty-two when he proposed to Janine, and political aspirations were forming inside him like the new skin of a snake takes shape before the old skin sloughs off. Janine, barely twenty, had never displayed any interest in the kitchen, other than making coffee and arranging conspicuously small portions of food on her plate.

Carole had taken care of meals, as she had everything else, for most of Janine's life, even when they lived with their hateful Aunt Regina. When Carole was eighteen and Janine was seven, Carole moved them from Aunt Regina's sprawling Victorian into an apartment on Pearl Street. Carole worked at a bakery all day and ran their household. It was the happiest part of Janine's childhood, just her and Carole. Four years later, Carole married Walt. They moved to a single-story clapboard house outside Colchester, and Janine complained about how boring life there was compared to Burlington and about Walt, who'd stolen Carole's attention. When the twins came along, Janine was finishing high school and schemed constantly (and volubly) about how she might flee the pedestrian chaos of Carole and Walt's home. She would, she announced without a hint of irony, take the bus to New York and become an actress. She would marry Drake Connor, the high school basketball star, and follow him to whatever big city team offered the most money. (That Drake Connor was engaged to another girl did nothing to quash this conviction.) She would go to Las Vegas, where wealth spewed like oil from the desert. She would, in sum, do anything other than work.

Mitch was the answer that came to her gradually. He started off as just another old man like Walt. Exactly like Walt, in fact, since they were fraternal twins who might as well have shared an egg, at least as far as looks were concerned. As she emerged from her teens she discerned the differences—Mitch held himself straighter, spoke with authority and had a way of making people around him feel noticed, including Janine. His wife died the year the twins were born, and the pallor of the tragedy made him different again, and intriguing to her, as if misfortune were cologne. Mitch was widowed, childless, wealthy, poised and familiar; a potent mix for Janine. None of the many suitors she had jilted had come close.

The Christmas Janine was nineteen, the whole family, twins included, traveled to Burlington to spend several days at Mitch's house. Lester ran a high fever on the twenty-third and was no better on Christmas Eve. Carole and Walt packed the car to take the children home so Mitch's parties would not be spoiled. Janine sipped wine in front of the drawing room fire and told Carole she would stay.

Her sister held Lester, whose cheeks were on fire, and frowned. "But you belong with us."

"It's only a few days."

"No one else is staying. People will talk."

Janine laughed. "There's nothing to talk about. Yet."

Carole's cheeks turned as red as her son's. "You don't intend . . . Mitchell would never . . ."

Janine put down her glass and recrossed her legs. "What worries you, Carole? That I might get the better one?"

A year later she had her own house to run. She kept the housekeeper Mitch employed after his first wife died, but Janine struggled with cooking. At first Mitch didn't mind. What did he expect when he married a twenty-year-old? But a few years into their marriage, he made it plain that canned vegetables and mashed potatoes made from Potato Buds would no longer pass muster. The wife of one of Mitch's colleagues suggested she watch Julia Child on television. Janine felt an immediate affinity for the triumphantly haphazard woman and accepted her demonstrations as gospel, although she only prepared a handful of the meals, and those under duress. The cooking shows served a more primary purpose: whenever Janine's natural confidence flagged, she thought of the catastrophic collapse of the apple charlotte on national television, and of Julia's equanimity. One could fail decisively and publicly and laugh it off with the help of a swig of wine. Janine studied Julia Child but never mastered her.

Now that Mitch was dead and she lived alone, Janine rarely cooked for herself—she couldn't possibly keep her figure if she did—but she pulled out the stops for Greg: chicken cordon bleu, green beans amandine, scalloped potatoes and apple tarte tatin. So what if it happened to be Mitch's favorite meal? Janine couldn't afford to be sentimental. Love was for schoolgirls. Marriage was business.

Greg appeared at the door in a faded denim shirt, worn chinos and desert boots. His hair was damp from showering. He leaned in to kiss her cheek. God, he smelled great.

"Did you squeeze in some basketball after school?"

He flashed his dimples and stepped inside. "Yeah, the Friday pickup game." He was carrying a bottle of red and a bouquet of orange supermarket mums. She accepted the flowers (Mums? That's what you bring your grandmother) and led the way to the kitchen.

"It smells fantastic in here," Greg said. "You forgot to mention you can cook."

Janine handed him the wine opener. "I didn't forget. I just didn't want to overwhelm you with all my virtues at once."

He laughed. "Keep 'em coming."

They carried the wine and glasses to the porch, where Janine had arranged cheese and olives on a small table covered with a blue-and-yellow Provençal cloth. The yard opened onto a narrow field bordered by oaks and maples, emerald green. The setting sun found a gap in the tree canopy and fell across the porch, igniting the edges of the evening.

"It's so pretty here," Greg said.

Janine stood next to him, taking in the view, but couldn't help seeing the bare trees and piles of snow that would arrive all too soon. "It's Vermont. Pretty is the law." He looked at her sideways, so she added, "It's very pretty. The view's what sold me on the place."

They sat. Greg toasted the start of the school year and Janine took a long sip of her wine. Why not toast the school year? It was, after all, what brought them together. Greg tossed a couple of olives into his mouth and relaxed into his seat. Janine fed him the questions about Mexico she'd been warehousing all week, and he told her stories more interesting than she'd expected and admitted to cultural faux pas that made them both laugh.

Sometime between the main course and dessert, Janine forgot about her marriage campaign. Maybe it was the wine. Maybe it was having Greg in her house, surrounded by objects that carried the memories of her life: photos of her and Carole, and her nephews and niece. Chairs and lamps and linens from the home she had shared with Mitch. Garage-sale plates painted with delicate flowers that lifted something inside her each time she saw them. The shelf of record albums below the stereo, songs of her life. The bedroom, separated from them by a plaster wall, in which she dropped into loneliness each night the same way she lowered herself into a too-hot bath. In this environment, she was hard-pressed to maintain the discipline she'd evinced to get this far with Greg. She was relaxed. A light, warm feeling bubbled along her spine. Happiness?

She crossed from the kitchen to the living room, a dessert plate in each hand. Greg had moved from the table to the couch and was refilling their wineglasses. He looked up at her, his face open, his eyes soft.

"I'm so glad you invited me here, Janine."

She smiled, then, without thinking first what sort of smile it should be. She set the tarte tatins on the coffee table and sat beside him, a flutter in her chest quickly expanding until her heartbeat was loud in her ears, heightening her senses. Something real was surfacing too quickly. She moved to fight it, beat it down, and triggered an internal panic. Where was her control, her focus? She was adrift.

Janine glanced at Greg's knee, three inches from hers. A charge zinged across the space. She'd read about this sort of thing, but hadn't quite believed it and still didn't. He put down his glass and touched her, barely, along the inside of her wrist. She wanted to look at him but her boldness had left her. He reached up and stroked her cheek. There it was again, a true feeling, or what sure as hell seemed like one, fighting its way out through her hard-bitten shell, which was breaking down, splintering. Her fear of being exposed mixed with pure desire and overwhelmed her.

"Hey," he said.

"Hey." She didn't dare move. She'd run out of script. The air between them was like cracked glass a breath away from shattering. If she wasn't mistaken, she was falling in love with Greg.

"Tell you what." He dropped his hand from her cheek and settled back against the couch. "There is no way I'm passing on this dessert, but as soon as I've devoured it, you're next."

She looked at him, her limbs loose with desire, and gave him his plate. "Don't let it get cold."

11

Carole

Carole beat eggs in a bowl and watched Lester, half asleep, hunched over his plate, his hair falling over his cheeks. She ought to have sent him to the barber before school started—both boys, in fact. She'd never before let them show up on the first day this way, even if long hair was "in." Lester bit off the corners of the Pop-Tart, then nibbled around the edges, examining it every few seconds to see if he'd managed not to expose any of the fruit. Satisfied, he gulped down his orange juice and finished off the rest of the pastry. Carole switched the heat on under the frying pan.

"Mom, where's my cross-country stuff?"

She startled, rattling the pan on the grate, and turned to see Warren filling up the doorway, hands on his hips.

"Your what?"

"My clothes. For cross country. Yesterday you said you'd wash them and put them in my room."

"Well, I must've, then."

"Not that I can see."

"Let me make your eggs, then I'll look." Had she done the laundry yesterday? She couldn't remember a blessed thing about yesterday and this worried her. She gathered herself. One thing at a time. She slid the eggs in. Took the toast out of the toaster oven. Buttered it. Put it on a plate. Stirred the eggs. Waited a little. Stirred some more. Put the eggs on the plate and the plate on the table. Short-order cook. That's what Walt always said.

Carole wiped her hands on her apron and went upstairs to the boys' room. Dark green shorts and a white T-shirt were what she was looking for. And white socks with green stripes. Was that it? Or was it more of a uniform? Were they still practicing or was it a race? Did it matter? And shoes. Did she put his shoes with his running clothes?

Clean clothes went in the dresser, or on top, if she was rushed. She crossed to the dresser. All the drawers were open. She scanned for something dark green, something white, pulling all the clothes out of one drawer, then the next, tossing everything on the floor. Nothing. On top of the dresser were two baseball hats and a magazine. Was a hat a part of what he needed? Maybe she'd put the clean clothes on the dresser and they'd fallen off. The floor on either side of the dresser was covered in clothing. She picked it up, piece by piece, and threw it onto the bed next to her. Lester's? Moving around the room, she piled clothing on the bed. Red. Blue. White— but shorts. Stripes. Red. Black. Green—a shirt.

"Mom!" Warren, from below.

Carole stuck her head out the door, glanced back at the bed and hurriedly gathered the clothes in the top sheet. Where? Where else for clothes? She dragged the bundle down the stairs.

"What the hell?" Warren frowned. "It's not there, right?"

She walked past him, down the hall, and went downstairs into the basement. One step, two steps, three steps, four five six seven eight nine ten.

It was cool. Dark. Quiet. The washing machine squatted in front of her, a hulking shadow beside its twin, the dryer. Liar.

"Mom!" The light came on. Warren stomped down the stairs, stepped around the bundle, now burst open, and stood in front of her. She had to look up at him, that's how tall he was. "We gotta go. What are you doing?"

She nodded at the bundle. "Laundry."

"Too late." Warren bent over the basket next to the washer, pulled out a few things. He straightened, stared at her a long minute. "You're acting totally wacked, you know."

She'd failed him. She knew that. But she didn't quite understand how, and that worried her. She couldn't fail him, or any of her children, just like she couldn't fail Janine when her sister was small. She simply couldn't.

Warren nodded toward the stairs, his voice soft. "You coming? Lester likes his good-byes, you know."

"Of course."

They went up to the kitchen, where Lester was waiting. He put his arm around her shoulder, his head against her cheek. "Bye, Mom. See you after school!"

Warren stuffed his clothes into his gym bag and stood back, jingling car keys in his pocket. "Later, Mom."

He resembled Walt so closely in that moment, the ground lurched under her feet. She held on to Lester, gripping his shirt with her damp hands. He thought it was a game and squeezed her more tightly. Warren glanced at his feet, impatient now, sharpening his resemblance to his father, to the man he would become, or already was. High school seniors. Time was a tide, and she was going out to sea with it. See with it. Be with it.

Stop.

A flood of belligerent, cascading emotions swept over her, through her, faster than she could label them. Collapsing. Relapsing.

Stop.

"Drive carefully, Warren. There'll be children about." She kissed Lester's cheek and released him. "Be good. Both of you."

Lester eyes widened in alarm. "Mom, why are you crying? Are you hurt?"

Carole swept a finger across her cheek and was surprised to find it wet. "I'm sad you're growing up." It was true.

Warren shook his head but his eyes were warm. "Mom . . ." He tossed his keys in the air and caught them. "Come on, Lester. Let's boogie."

Carole watched them go. She tidied the kitchen, working by rote. Wipe, dry, sweep. Wipe again. And again.

She checked the clock on the stove. Middle school started a half hour after the high school, so Alison would be coming down before long. Carole was not ready for that. Not steady for that. She left the kitchen, climbed the stairs and entered her room, shutting the door silently behind her. She straightened the bedclothes and lay down, curling her knees to her chest and closing her eyes. Tears stung her nose and she willed them away.

It wasn't just about the boys. It was about her simple life, the ordinary, everyday life she had created with Walt, had cherished, clung to. It might not be much by other people's standards, not even her sister's, but it was everything to her. It was good and right and true.

And it was floating out of her grasp.

"Mom? Mom, where are you?"

Alison's voice from somewhere below. Carole roused herself, unsure if she'd been asleep. She pushed to sitting and waited for the dizziness to subside.

"Mom!"

Alison was on the landing. Carole went to the door, opened it. Alison was bright, excited, flustered.

"The bus'll be here any minute!" She stepped closer. "Are you okay?"

"Of course. Just a little tired."

"You sure?"

"Yes. Did you eat?"

"Uh-huh. I have to go." She rocked from foot to foot like a boxer, her red curls bouncing. She threw her arms around Carole and sprang away before Carole had could do more than touch her back. "See you after school." Alison spun around the stair post and glanced over her shoulder, her brow creased.

"I'll watch you go."

Alison flew down the stairs. Carole followed, catching doors in her daughter's wake, and stood before the office windows. Alison was already across the lot, searching the road for the bus.

"See you," Carole said around the lump in her throat.

Walt came up beside Carole. Alison waved at them and he waved back. The bus arrived, swallowed up their daughter and left.

Carole gasped, fighting tears of confusion and fear. Walt wrapped her in his arms. She buried her face in his neck and sobbed.

"Too big too fast, huh, sweetheart?" he said.

She let it go, too exhausted and terrified to explain. He took her hand, held it to his shoulder and slow-danced her across the office.

12

Alison

The engine of the school bus rumbled as it rounded the bend and lumbered into view. Alison peeked behind her to check on her mother, who'd been super out of it this morning. There she was, next to Alison's father, standing inside the office. Alison waved. Maybe with school starting her mother would have more time to rest.

Alison pulled up her white kneesocks and glanced at her feet one last time to make sure it wasn't obvious her sandals were last year's. White socks, sort-of-white sandals. Like she had a choice. Luckily, it was a sunny day and warm enough that she didn't have to cover up her new yellow-and-orange plaid shirt with an old sweater. Even her hair hadn't frizzed out this morning—another auspicious sign.

Auspicious signs were everywhere, making her think Delaney must've botched the tarot reading. The class-assignment letter came, and she got Mr. Bayliss, the best teacher in the whole school, and the nicest. The other sixth grade teacher was Mrs. Dorfman, and the name said it all. She was crabby and her face looked like it might explode any second. She was humongous, too, her arm as big around as Alison's leg. Some of the boys called her Dorfcow and said she slept standing up. So getting Mr. Bayliss was like winning twice. Delaney got him, too, but she always got the good teachers because her mother made sure of it. Maybe having the same teacher would make it easier for Delaney to be her school friend for the very first time.

The bus braked with a huff and the doors flapped open. Mr. Kiernan, skinny as a skeleton, leaned out of his seat holding the handle. His fingers were so bony that it didn't seem there could be enough muscle to do anything.

"Hi, Mr. Kiernan."

He gave her a friendly nod and grunted as he pulled the door shut behind her. Alison's was the next to the last stop—the kids closer to town had to walk—so the bus was almost full. It was also pretty loud, in a bubbly way. Alison spotted Maggie, Delaney's best friend, and J.J., who was friends with everyone, sharing a seat near the back, and scanned around them for an empty one. A lot of the kids, the boys mostly, were pushing one another and scrambling in and out of their seats like the cushions were electrified, so it was hard to see the free seats.

An eighth grader next to her shouted, "Look, everybody! Twins!" He pointed a few rows back where Dolores Gordon sat by herself.

Alison couldn't believe it. Dolores had on the same shirt as she did. The exact same shirt. One kid after another looked at her, looked at Dolores and burst out laughing. Her cheeks burned. She took a step back. Maybe she'd get off the bus, tell her mom she felt sick. But the bus started moving—it had to be a slugfest before Mr. Kiernan would say anything, much less stop driving—and she grabbed a seat back to brace herself for the sharp turn coming just past the bridge. If she could've crawled under the seats, she would've. Abashed. Such a better word than "embarrassed." "Embarrassed" was soft and silky. "Abashed" hit you in the teeth.

Dolores had been staring out the window. All the shouting got her attention. She noticed the pointing fingers swinging between her and Alison and broke into a wide grin, showing a mouthful of yellow buckteeth and her gums. Everyone hooted louder, and some boys started chanting, "Twins! Twins! Twins!" Dolores laughed, too, snorting and wiping her nose with her palm and slapping her other hand on the seat in front of her, rocking back and forth, back and forth.

Alison stood frozen in the aisle and avoided all the faces, especially Maggie's and J.J.'s. Sweat broke out on her forehead. She glanced at Dolores Gordon, hoping somehow she was magically wearing a different shirt. No such luck.

She'd always felt sorry for Dolores. She got teased a lot about her teeth and her greasy hair and the fact that she was bigger than anyone in the seventh grade, boys included. And there was way more than her looks to feel bad about. The Gordons lived down by the old mill, ten of them in a couple of trailers, and Jim Gordon, her father, was a mean drunk. The Gordon boys—all six of them—carried bruises on them as they ranged down River Road and through town on errands of mischief and worse. Dolores was the middle girl and had problems in school like Lester, although she missed a lot of school. It made no sense because school had to have been way better than those trailers, especially in the winter. Anyway, Dolores might have looked a little scary, with her sticking-up hair and her hands like catcher's mitts, but she was sweet. Anyone could see that.

The boys had shifted around and blocked the other empty seats, forcing Alison to take the only one left, next to Dolores. Alison moved down the aisle and plastered a smile on her face, which she knew for a fact was as red as her hair.

"Hi, Dolores. Can I sit here?"

"Sure!" she yelled. Everyone started laughing again, including her.

Alison sat and arranged her book bag on her lap. Two boys from her class spun around in the seat in front and gawked at them.

"Take a picture, it lasts longer," Alison said. She twisted to face Dolores. "By the way, I like your shirt."

The bus ride took two forevers. Alison got off and headed straight

for the girls' room near the gym, the only one they were allowed to
use before school started. She passed a couple of girls who said, "Hi"
and waved. Alison rushed past, letting out a "hi" in a squeaky voice
she didn't know she had. She whizzed around the corner by the
trophy display and ran smack into someone, an adult.

"Alison! Where's the fire?" Aunt Janine held her by the shoulders.

"I'm going to the bathroom. I'm—" Tears stuck in her throat.
She hid her face by staring at the floor and squeaked her shoe on
the freshly polished linoleum.

Janine lifted Alison's chin. "What's wrong? What happened?"

Her aunt had on a hot pink cardigan over a blouse the color of
vanilla ice cream. Her hair hung over her shoulders in perfect waves.
She was so pretty, all the time. "It's stupid. It doesn't matter."

"Of course it does. Come in here a minute." Janine led her down
the hall to a quiet corner by the girls' locker room. "Okay, so what's
the story?"

Alison told her about the shirt, how she only had two new ones,
how she knew it was stupid to get upset about a shirt. She started
crying and felt even stupider.

Aunt Janine pulled a tissue from her skirt pocket and dabbed
Alison's face. "You know, I've got some things at home I never wear
that I think you might like. Nice things. I don't know why I didn't
think of it sooner."

Alison wasn't sure she wanted grown-up clothes, but anything
was better than the plaid shirt, which she could never wear again.
"Thanks. That'd be great. And do you think you could give me a
ride home after school? If you've got stuff to do, I can wait."

"You bet. Now you better skedaddle. The bell's about to ring."
She gave Alison a quick hug and hurried down the hall to the office,
heels clicking.

Alison watched her go and fought off the sickening guilty feeling that came from a moment's wish that her aunt was actually
her mom.

· · ·

They filed into the gym behind the other sixth grade class for assembly. Alison scooted in beside Delaney and, to her great shock and happiness, Delaney didn't do what she did last year when Alison did the exact same thing: tell her to take a long walk off a short pier. Instead Delaney said to her, "Isn't Mr. Bayliss the bee's knees?"

"Yup. And the cat's pajamas, too."

J.J. was on the other side of Delaney next to Maggie. "What about Mr. Bayliss's pajamas?" They all groaned. "Okay, so don't tell me," J.J. went on. "And just so you know, Mrs. Dorfman is super copacetic."

Maggie rolled her eyes. "Wait till she sits on you."

Mr. Kawolski, the principal, called everyone to attention and made the two new teachers get up and say something. The first one taught third grade. She was short with a tiny face surrounded by tons of frizzed-out hair, like one of those monkeys in *National Geographic*. The other one was Miss Honeycutt, Lester's new teacher. She could've walked right out of the Sears catalog. Her hair was even shinier than Delaney's, plus she was a blonde, which mattered for reasons Alison had never understood. Miss Honeycutt didn't seem stuck-up, though. She stood in front of the microphone and her hands pulled at each other.

Davey Weiner was behind Alison and whistled under his breath. "Get a load of the fox."

Tommy said, "Makes me wish I was a retard."

"Wish granted, spaz."

All Alison could think about for the rest of the assembly was that Delaney was not just her summer friend, something to be tossed away when school started like a worn-out pair of flip-flops. She was her actual friend. For keeps.

Back in the classroom, Mr. Bayliss told everyone to start reading *White Fang*. He went around the room, talking to each kid about the books on their summer-reading list. Finally he made it to Caroline LeClerc, who was sitting behind Alison. Caroline was shy and whispered her answers.

Alison looked up from her book. Mr. Bayliss was standing next to her. She'd never been this close to him before. Unless you got into trouble, you never got close to a teacher until you were in their class. She felt nervous having him right there. But good nervous.

"Nice to meet you, Alison." He picked up her list off her desk and read both sides. "I'm really impressed with this." He smiled at her.

He had a great smile. Mr. Bayliss was so nice, even nicer than everybody said. "Thanks, Mr. Bayliss."

"Your parents must be very proud of you."

Alison could tell he expected her to say that they were, like it was automatic. Alison felt tears gathering behind her eyes. She looked down at *White Fang* and bit her lip. All she could think about was her mother, how she didn't seem to care about her much anymore. Her belly twisted and she bit her lip harder. The words in front of her ran together into rivers of sentences that slid off the page. She would not cry. Not again. Not in front of Mr. Bayliss.

He squatted next to her and touched her arm. "Are you all right, Alison?"

She nodded. What else could she do? She was *not* going to cry.

"It's okay, sweetheart."

Alison made herself look at him and nodded again. It wasn't okay, but while she was here, where Delaney was her friend and Mr. Bayliss was her teacher, she'd pretend it was.

13

Carole

Carole happened to be out by the pumps when Janine drove up. Someone had emptied their ashtray onto the pavement right next to the trash can and it was up to Carole to deal with it. Walt was under a car, of course, and Lester was organizing screws and bolts, talking to himself or to his father or brother—Carole honestly couldn't tell. Warren was in the garage somewhere, too, or on an errand. She'd given up keeping track of everyone. From her desk she'd seen the driver dump the ashtray and drive off and had headed out with her dustpan and a resentful lump in her chest. Not that she minded cleaning. How could she mind it? It would be like minding her life since it seemed she spent it tidying scrubbing sorting filing adding (subtracting) washing polishing. Walt did, too, come to think of it, fixing cars that had met with disaster or simply worn out from use or the passage of time. So much of life, maybe all of it, was making right the disordered decaying broken world.

Creation. Whatever happened to creation much less recreation? She created breakfast or a meat loaf or chocolate pudding from a mix but that was about it. God had his seven days and since then all people could do was try to keep up with it all coming to pieces falling apart falling down we all fall down.

Ashes ashes.

She swept the butts and ashes into the pan and slid them into the garbage wincing at the smell wondering if the insides of the lungs of whoever made the mess smelled as bad as that. Would serve them right if it did and messes in places deep and hard to reach are hard to clean up. A laugh bubbled up and she didn't know what was funny. She turned to go inside where it was quieter or not actually quiet but inside she knew where to expect the crowd sound to come from, how to hum into her ears loudly if she was by herself to drown out the other ones that weren't in the crowd. They had ideas of their own that weren't hers but were in her head yet were hard to shake away break away drown. Drown out. Down and out. So she hummed them out.

Voices pursued her. She couldn't make out the words and was almost inside the side that was in not the side that was out inside out like a sock pulled off in a hurry. Keep your insides in. Keep your outsides out. Sounded simple simple Simon Simon says touch your nose touch your head. Touched head. Dead.

"Hi, Mom!"

This voice came from the outside, she was sure. But it also came from the inside. Maybe it had always done that. She hesitated at the door. Her daughter appeared at her side.

"Oh. Alison." Her face was overflowing with happiness and it rushed into Carole. She smiled at her, reached out to touch her face but fell short and brushed her daughter's arm. She looked past Alison and noticed a red LTD backing up on the lot near the road. Janine's car. Janine scar. Scarred. Barred.

Alison said, "Aunt Janine gave me a ride." She showed Carole a shopping bag. "We stopped at her house and she gave me some of her old clothes, only they aren't really old at all."

"Clothes? Oh." She concentrated on her daughter's face and ignored the rivers of unanswered questions flooding her mind and pulled up an idea that she quickly inspected and called normal. "Ask her if she wants to come in, okay?"

"She's coming. She has paperwork for you."

Paperwork. So much paper. So much work. Carole didn't want it. Too late. Janine was crossing the lot.

Alison stared at her. "Are you okay?"

"Hmm? Yes. Of course."

Her daughter frowned. "Aren't you going to ask about my first day?"

Janine said, "Hi, Carole."

"Hi, Janine."

"I sent the form to you, remember? For Lester?"

"Did you?" Carole noticed Alison staring at her, mad. Bad.

"We talked about it on the phone. It has to be on file. Same thing every year. It isn't like you to forget." She sighed and waved the papers in her hand. "I brought copies."

Janine was mad, too. Everyone was mad bad sad. Carole wanted to run away inside or out. She stepped back.

Janine said, "Aren't we going in?"

Alison yanked open the door. "I am. I'm starving."

"I can't do them now."

Her sister gave her a look and thrust the papers at her. "Have it your way." As she started for her car, she said, "You're welcome."

"I'm sorry," Carole said. Too late.

She followed Alison into the kitchen.

"Thanks, Mom! My favorite."

There on the table was a cake, pineapple upside-down right side up. She'd made it in the morning she remembered now because mornings were best and she didn't want to forget. She'd created something and she smiled at Alison because she'd created her, too, red hair and freckles and boundless energy and secret thoughts and arms and legs that kept getting longer.

Her daughter dropped her bags on the floor and threw her arms around Carole, who took one sharp breath in and Alison was away again and taking down plates and opening drawers and pouring milk.

"You have some, too, okay, Mom?" Alison was fast. The knife was already in, slicing a lifesaver-shape of pineapple into two pieces that couldn't save even one life. One knife.

"Of course. Thank you."

They sat at the table and Carole had milk and couldn't remember the last time she had or why she hadn't but she didn't have long to think because Alison was talking about her teacher and Delaney and a new teacher and another new teacher and Lester and *White Fang*.

She caught it as it whizzed past. "White Fang?"

"Uh-huh. Jack London. Did you read it?"

Carole paused in her concentration on her daughter's words to turn inward, where her memory of *WhiteFang*JackLondon would be kept if it was kept anywhere and the crowd noise was there louder now that she was staring in and not out inside out upside down and a sinister figure colossus loomed guarding the tall library stacks where she first thought to look for *WhiteFang*JackLondon so she backed away in her mind and shut it out but without knowing it, did it on the outside too. She opened her eyes and Alison was staring at her so she spoke over the voices loud now.

"I'm not sure I have. Maybe in school, like you."

Her daughter hesitated as if she'd seen something disappear around a corner and thought about chasing it. She finished her cake in two bites two bits two bites and Carole was glad over the noise everywhere she contained and shrunk from.

Alison pulled clothes out of a bag at her feet. It was like a magic trick with colorful scarves coming out of a hat one after another.

"And these three are golf shirts, but no one would know that, they're just really good shirts and they're a little big but the colors are pretty, don't you think?"

Carole nodded.

"And she gave me these cardigans. The green is my favorite. And next time she goes to Burlington—she goes all the time, I never knew that, did you, Mom?—she's going to pick up some school shoes for me. She knows my size now and I told her you would pay her back."

Pay her back payback. Alison was talking and the pile of clothes on the table became all the clothes her daughter had worn since she was born. A pile of tiny dresses and hand-knit sweaters in white and rose-petal pink with appliqué flowers and one with rabbits on the collar Alison's favorite when she was older and put them on her stuffed animals. Piles of tights and overalls and shorts sets and dresses with bloomers and more piles of coats and sweaters and rain jackets and shoes boots sandals hats mittens a length of yarn between the pair to keep them together never lost.

"All this stuff is so neat, isn't it, Mom? And this dress, I just love the sailor collar, don't you? If you have time, maybe you could take it in and hem it. Aunt Janine said it would be perfect. Do you have time, maybe?"

"Time?"

Alison held up a navy shift dress. "To make it fit."

"Sure. Sure I do. Just leave it in my room."

"Cool! I'll go put it on and you can pin it."

And she was gone.

The next morning, after the children had left for school, Carole pulled the ironing board from the hall closet, set it up in the kitchen and brought down the pile of wrinkled clothing from the flowered chair in the bedroom she couldn't remember ever being used for anything else. On top was the navy dress. She flipped it over and saw the pins and went upstairs again for her sewing kit. To make it fit.

Carole sat at the kitchen table, poked thread through the eye of the needle, and pulled it through with pinched fingers. She secured the folded hem to the skirt with practiced movements, darting in and out of the fabric, stitches spaced evenly and pulled taut until invisible. The motion stirred memories of splitting the seams of her own clothing and remaking them for Janine.

After their mother went to Underhill to rest, her aunts bought her clothes, beautiful clothes, more than once a season, more than she could begin to wear out. Summer dresses and matching hats from boutiques on Cape Cod, woolen coats and cashmere scarves and fine cotton underclothes and flannel nightgowns from Barneys and Macy's, shoes and boots in fine, soft leather, always appropriate for her age and in fashion, but never flashy. It was, after all, Vermont, and the Giffords were staked to tradition.

"Classic" was Aunt Bettina's watchword.

"Proper" was Aunt Regina's.

Carole allowed herself to be dressed and paraded, and did not pretend to herself she had a choice.

Her sister, on the other hand, was a pariah for reasons Carole did not understand for many years, and received next to nothing. Carole, ten years older, clothed Janine, and stored old outfits in a trunk in their room. (She would not permit Janine to sleep elsewhere. She had dreams of Aunt Regina, typically in the guise of a winged demon, whisking her sister off in the middle of the night, and of her mother then going mad, truly mad, more wildly mad than she was now, with the loss.) The underclothes, still perfectly white, she lay in the trunk as well, and one good winter coat a year, plus an assortment of shoes, for feet seemed to grow according to their own schedule, not the laws of nature. In the evenings, when her schoolwork was finished and her aunts did not need her, she reworked the seams and necklines as best she could, and hoped her sister's long hair would hide the worst of her mistakes.

Janine was tightly sprung and careless, so even when she was old enough to appreciate her sister's care she rarely paused to do so. Carole might have harbored resentment for that, but recognized her little sister had her, and only her, on this earth. When she put the girl to bed, tucking the covers snugly so Janine would feel

embraced as she entered sleep, tenderness for Janine warmed Carole's body and calmed her mind. She could not replace what they
had lost nor straighten the road their parents had set before them,
nor could she change who she and Janine were, what they carried
inside them, or what misfortune might overtake them. She could,
however, stay by her sister and remain brave against fate, love her
without fail and shield her from the dark mystery of why she and
her mother were the only ones who did.

Carole was halfway around the hem when Walt called to her from
the garage. She needed to finish the dress or she would forget.
Already her mind was getting crowded, voices corralling her own
thoughts, tossing them around. In the quiet, she might finish. She
might be able to do this one thing for Alison. One hem. Once
around the bottom. For Janine. For Alison.

Walt called again.

Another stitch. Another.

Walt opened the door. "Carole, a customer needs to settle up
and I've got two cars in the air. I'm sorting wildcats in here."

"I'm coming." Carole rose, folded the dress over the back of
the chair and went into the office, placing each foot carefully and
keeping her head still so as not to alert the voices.

A bearded man propped his elbows on the counter, scowling
and slapping his checkbook against his palm. Walt was rummaging
through a box he'd pulled from the shelves between the counter
and the garage entrance. Fan belts. Tuna melts.

Carole picked up the invoice from the desk, two smudged fingerprints on the margin. The name and the amount was all she
needed. Check the name, give the amount. Name and amount.
Name. "Erwin Battle."

"That's right."

"Battle." Battle tattle rattlesnake. Battle tattle rattlesnake.

"That's my name."

Voices pressing hard, pushing behind her eyes. Pushing her eyeballs to the side. They could see. They could see everything. They were coming out. "Battle. Tattle."

"What?"

"Battle tattle rattle—" Her stomach tightened and she felt the corners of her mouth lift. A bubble rose from her chest. She laughed.

The man smacked his checkbook down. "I don't know what you're playing at, lady."

Carole clamped her hand over her mouth to shut off the laugh, to stop the voices escaping. Battle tattle rattle. Battle tattle rattle.

Walt took the invoice from her. "You best go inside, Carole." He steered her by the elbow, pushed the door open, spoke to the man. "She hasn't been sleeping." The door was closing behind her. "I'm awful sorry."

"Awful sorry. Awful lawful story."

The dress on the chair. For Janine Alison. The least she could do. The best she could do. The best and all the rest.

She smoothed the dress in her lap found her place picked up the needle. It shook by hook and by crook.

She pushed the needle through the fabric and into her finger. A bead of blood appeared on her fingertip. She pushed on the finger. The bead grew.

Bad blood. Bad flood.

Bad. Mad. Blood.

Part 2

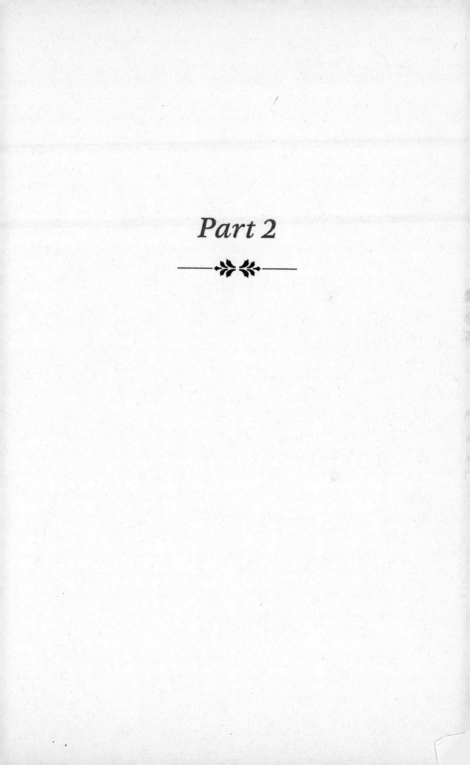

14

Solange

April 1926

Osborn signed the register and turned to face her. The justice recited from a book, but Solange was deaf to him; the only vows that mattered were those she whispered in Osborn's ear at night.

The justice finished speaking. Osborn held Solange's hand lightly, slipped the band onto her finger and smiled the same way he had the day they'd met at the hotel eight months before.

"My wife." He drew her to him, kissing her deeply.

Her heart filled with light. What fate had sent her Osborn? She'd always sensed that as her life unfolded, true happiness would appear, but she hadn't counted on it appearing all at once in the shape of this man: kind, loving, purposeful and so handsome she couldn't stop looking at him. Solange felt blessed.

The justice offered congratulations, as did the witness, a city hall clerk with an alarming overbite. Osborn grasped Solange's hand and they sped from the room, laughing. They tripped down the marble stairs, out the enormous double doors and into the fresh of the day. Osborn's Buick waited at the curb. The pale green tips of the elms lining the street shook in the breeze.

Solange leaned against the car and opened her arms. "Osborn!"

They kissed again, smiling so hard they could barely purse their lips.

Osborn cupped her chin. "Mrs. Solange Gifford, my Scarlet Queen." Their lips met once more.

They set off for three days at Lake Willoughby, the most time Osborn could afford in his final months at Albany Law School. The WilloughVale Inn was rustic and weathered but situated prettily on the lakeshore. A bellman showed them to their suite and placed the suitcases inside. He indicated a large, private veranda where flowers, fruit, cheese and sodas had been arranged.

"Courtesy of the inn. Congratulations."

Osborn tipped him, closed the door and followed Solange to the veranda, where they sat together on the loveseat.

She inhaled the crisp, piney air. "Isn't it perfect?"

"It is." He reached into his jacket and pulled out a flask. "A little hooch to celebrate?"

"Osborn!"

"I'm joking. It's gin."

"Where did you get that? Never mind. Don't tell me." She poured two glasses of lemonade.

Osborn added a finger of gin to each and touched his glass to hers. "To us."

"To us." The gin paved a swath of heat down her throat. Osborn stared at the lake, lost in thought. "What is it, darling?"

"I confess disappointment with city hall. I'd wanted to marry you at the Hotel Vermont, on the rooftop garden, with vases of red roses on the tables. I wanted our families to be there with us, eating lobster and drinking champagne."

"It would have been impossible," Solange said, "and getting the champagne would've been the least of it." She set down her glass and slipped into her husband's arms.

"True. I don't know which of our families approve of us less."

Solange had heard rumors that Osborn's father referred to her as "that pirate girl," using the slang favored by Burlington's elite in describing lake-dwelling families. He hadn't said it in her presence, but Solange knew where she stood. Osborn's stepmother was polite but distant, which sent its own message. Solange's family was no different. Jean-Claude Bouchard had refused to allow Osborn to board the houseboat, addressing him at shouting distance from the rail. Solange had petitioned her father to give her beloved a chance, but he wouldn't budge, despite his typically affable nature. She worried she'd crossed him by following her heart, but she did not doubt her choice. Solange's mother, Rosemarie, would not dream of second-guessing what her daughter believed to be her destiny. But neither would Rosemarie urge her husband to soften his view, knowing pride was in his bones the way intuition was in hers.

Somewhere out on the lake, a loon called, a tremulous wail. A moment passed, then came the answering call from its mate. Osborn kissed the top of Solange's head. "You are so much more than where you came from, darling."

"That goes double for you, Osborn Gifford."

He laughed and pulled her toward him, resting his forehead against hers. "My family will come around once they get to know you."

His optimism touched her, but she wasn't convinced. Osborn's family was part of the cadre of well-to-do Protestants who ran the city. She was kin to French Canadians who lived on barges, not yachts, and wintered, not on the Carolina coast, but in shantytowns near the harbor. But that was their families, not them. She and Osborn were deeply in love, and now they were married.

"I hope they do come around," Solange said, "but honestly, as long as I have you, I don't care."

She was eighteen and Osborn ignited her soul.

. . .

Osborn had been living in a men-only building in Albany, but before the wedding, he'd secured another place off State Street, where the law school was housed.

As they climbed the stairs—four flights in all—Osborn apologized for the simple accommodations.

"Once I land a job, we'll get something better." He opened the door and let her pass inside.

Solange took in the large windows, decorative moldings and solid furniture standing on tastefully worn oriental rugs. She wandered into the kitchen, outfitted with modern appliances, easily four times the size of her family's houseboat galley. Their entire boat could have fit in the living room.

"It's perfect. Really." She picked up a book, tied with a red ribbon, from the kitchen counter: *The Fannie Farmer Cookbook*.

Osborn smiled. "My mother sent that, so we wouldn't starve."

Solange's mother cooked from memory, and Solange had never paid much attention, except when required to shell beans or help make jam. "I may not be able to cook, but I can read."

He took her by the waist and drew her close, his breath hot on her neck. "Let's always have dessert first."

While Osborn was in class or studying in the second bedroom, Solange wandered the outdoor market at Lyon Block, marveling at the vast array of fresh ingredients, many she'd never heard of, much less tasted: artichokes, Jordan almonds, watercress. Osborn gave her cash, more than she needed, and opened accounts at stores selling dry goods, clothes, furnishings—whatever she wanted.

She read the cookbook cover to cover, and was intrigued by the chapter on "Helpful Hints for Young Housekeepers." To clean piano keys, she learned, wipe with rubbing alcohol.

"You don't have to cook tonight," Osborn said frequently. "Let's go out."

If it was just the two of them, Solange was happy; the company of the other law students, invariably unattached young men, made her self-conscious. Her voice sounded too high and her opinions not sufficiently opinionated.

One morning, after weeks of diligent shopping, cooking and wiping, Solange found a collection of novels among Osborn's texts: Thackeray, Hardy, Hawthorne. The books stole her private hours. Soon, she discovered shortcuts to acceptable meals, and the library.

Her life was small, full of comfort and ripe with love.

Osborn scooped Solange into his arms and carried her across the threshold of their new home in Burlington. She gasped at the vaulted entry, the elegant sweep of the staircase, the tall windows in the parlor. A parlor!

"What are we going to do with all this?"

He kissed her. "Fill it with children, of course."

He'd passed the bar exam and slid neatly into the position waiting for him at Reston & Howard, the city's most prestigious legal firm. His father and stepmother helped him buy the house perched on the hillside above downtown, bordering the university. It was three times the size of their apartment in Albany. The excess space left her unmoored, but how could she possibly complain?

Carole was born in November of 1927, a week after a tremendous flood washed out nearly every bridge in the state. Solange's mother claimed it was a good omen, and Solange could not argue. The baby thrived.

"What apples you have in your cheeks!" Osborn exclaimed, lifting his daughter into the air, her butter yellow curls bouncing. "I fancy a bite!" He pretended to gobble her up, sending her into a fit of giggles.

With the help of a maid, Solange took care of the too-large home, especially before visits from Osborn's family, which she tolerated more than enjoyed. There was a layer, like thick muslin, between her and Osborn's relatives, and she had no idea how to remove it. When Osborn was present, his sisters were kinder, his parents less diffident.

She'd tried to explain it to him. "They don't approve of me."

"Of course they do. Don't you see their faces when you walk in with Carole?"

"That's for her, not for me."

As soon as she said it, she heard her own petulant tone, and vowed to be less sensitive and more accepting. She wished both families would embrace the happiness she and Osborn had created, but she couldn't make it so, and resolved to focus on what mattered: her daughter was a joy, and her husband loved her from one day to the next as if love and time were the same thing.

Carole toddled beside her mother down to the shore, holding on to the pram she would climb into for the uphill trek home. On their way to the harbor, they passed the shanties. The jumble of tiny houses, cobbled together from sheets of metal and scrap lumber, were so at odds with the beautiful lake shimmering beyond them.

The sight weighed heavily on Solange. Before the market crash, the shanties would have been boarded up in the summer when the houseboats could sail the lake. Now most seemed occupied; children with sooty faces and tattered clothing chased one another around the junk piled in the narrow alleys; women hung dingy washing on lines strung between the shacks; men sat on oil cans and wooden crates, hunched in shame or defeat. Solange felt a stab of guilt for everything she had, things she didn't even want or need.

The city folks called the place Shappyville, referring to her father's kin. As if anyone would have created it out of desire rather than necessity. Who in their right mind would? Heaved against the rough beach like a pile of driftwood, the shantytown had been forced ashore by the tide of commerce.

Decades ago, after Vermont's trees had been felled and logging ground to a halt, her family and the other lake dwellers had resorted to ferrying goods along the waterways. They had scraped by, but the lake had gradually become a place for moneyed newcomers to travel to, look at, play in and leave. The vacationing millionaires moored their yachts and parked their motorcars in front of stately mansions and took exception to tarpaper shacks and dilapidated barges spoiling their lake views. The lake dwellers had never had much, but they'd sailed their boats up and down the lake in a gritty sort of freedom. Now they'd lost their livelihoods for good.

Leaving the pram at the end of the dock, Solange hoisted Carole onto her hip and made her way to the family boat. Her mother, Rosemarie, was sunning herself on a chair, her feet propped on the railing.

"Hi, Mama."

"Hello, Solange." She smiled and held out her arms. "Bring that beautiful child to me."

Solange obeyed. Carole twined her fingers through the strands of beads around her grandmother's neck.

"What a pretty day it is." Solange swept her hand to indicate their surroundings and noticed, as she did every time she visited, the disrepair and decay of her childhood home—and the Bouchards owned one of the better boats. As uncomfortable as she was in her too-large home, she'd grown accustomed to fine furnishings, modern plumbing and spotless surfaces. Solange had caught herself hurrying home after these visits, eager to reenter the calm, clean comfort of her new life, and felt ashamed.

"Mama, I found some nice blankets and other things in the attic. No one's using them."

Her mother was playing patty-cake with Carole. She finished the song before answering. "You offering us charity?"

"No, Mama. It's not that at all. I just thought—"

Her mother looked at her evenly. "I know what you thought. And we don't need blankets. We don't need anything." She returned her attention to the child. "I do believe there might be some maple candy in the tin."

Carole clapped her hands and squealed. Solange sighed, wondering how she'd forgotten that pride was its own comfort.

After the visit, Solange stopped beside the poor box and filled it with the blankets and clothes she'd offered to her mother. It occurred to her that every house in her neighborhood had to be full of useful goods for the poor. Maybe she'd find a way to get to them.

"Mama!" Carole, spying the empty pram, raised her arms.

Solange placed her inside, kissed her forehead and walked on to the swimming beach, remembering Osborn's comment that morning at breakfast about crime increasing at the waterfront and on Grand Isle. It didn't surprise her. She could see how the risk of losing what little they had would make people angry, and if some used their anger as an excuse to grab hold of what they wanted, well, the blame could be spread around. There were always a few bad apples; that was true. But the other side of the story, the part about having had the best life you wanted and losing it, that was true, too.

They arrived at a grassy area. As she removed the dress covering her bathing suit, Solange stared across the wide water at the Adirondacks, hazy blue like worn chambray, and north, where the big islands coveted their secret shores. She carried her daughter to the water and stood her between her legs. Carole squeezed her mother's hands and made *oohs* of surprise each time a gentle wave lapped against her chest. The water at the edge of the lake felt more like a breeze than anything liquid, and looked like crushed glass glinting in the sun.

"Come on, now." She lifted Carole into her arms and waded

farther in. The child gasped as the water rose to her neck. "I've got you, darling." She kissed her daughter's sun-warmed cheek and tipped her to float prone on the water, holding up her round belly with one hand and laying the other on her back.

"Show me how you blow bubbles."

Carole stuck her face below the surface, blew air from her nose and lifted her head, sputtering and grinning.

"Good girl! Now, kick. You don't want to go under."

The girl kicked from her knees. The splashes delighted her. She knew she was sending water at her mother's face and kicked harder. Solange laughed and held Carole's knee in place. "Kick again, legs straight. That's it. Kick, kick, kick, kick."

A terrifying nor'easter had blown through ten days before. Sidewalks and streets were still blocked by downed branches and trees, and heaps of snow lay everywhere. The slice of lake at the bottom of Main Street was dull as gunmetal in the weak light of late fall. Solange picked her way through the mess, and Carole trotted alongside carrying an armload of sticks she'd collected to build a house. An oak tree, a foot in diameter, stretched across the path, the final obstacle before they reached home.

"You'll have to put down the sticks so I can lift you over."

"No."

"What will we do, then?"

Carole looked to the sky, considering. "Can we build the house here?"

"How long will it take?"

"Thirty hundred minutes."

"We'll miss supper, I think."

The girl frowned with such seriousness, Solange stifled a laugh.

"If you leave them in a pile here, we can get them tomorrow."

Carole stepped off the sidewalk and placed the sticks on the ground, lining them up one at a time. She returned to Solange, who swung her onto her hip and stepped over the log. The girl was so heavy! Less than a year before she'd be in school. Solange hugged her closer, breathing in her daughter's scent of baked pear and sun-drenched linens. "Darling girl. Should we see if Elsie has any cake left?"

Carole burst into the kitchen, Solange hustling after her. A stockpot poured steam into the air, and two loaves of brown bread cooled on a tray. Elsie, tall and square-shouldered, stood over the butcher block slicing carrots, and greeted them with a wide, gap-toothed grin. Osborn had insisted on a housekeeper because his family had always had one. Solange wouldn't have minded the housework but admitted she enjoyed the extra time with Carole. When the depression hit, Osborn had wanted to cut Elsie's days from six to four. Solange convinced him their savings could not measure up to the hardship Elsie and her family would suffer. Osborn capitulated.

Elsie served Carole potato soup and bread, then offered to bathe her.

"Are you sure you don't mind?" Solange said.

"Takes less time the way I do it," Elsie said, not unkindly, and scooped Carole from her chair. The girl yawned and drooped onto Elsie's shoulder.

"Oh, but she loves to play in the water."

"That she does." Elsie pointed at the newspaper splayed open on the kitchen table. "News about that boat wreck. Aren't you kin to them Ploofs?"

"My father is a cousin to the Shappies, so, yes."

Elsie nodded. She wasn't a lake dweller but she wasn't Protestant money, either. Solange kissed Carole's cheek, held open the kitchen door for them and took a seat at the table. She'd never been one for reading news or discussing politics. But she knew the story Elsie meant. Everyone did.

Solange scanned the headlines, mostly about the storm and its aftereffects. She'd been expecting the name "Ploof," but her eyes snagged instead on "Reston & Howard." Her husband's firm.

Reston & Howard to Represent Putnam

Capsized boat case "straightforward," firm contends

Burlington's premier legal group, Reston & Howard, has been tapped to defend Henry W. Putnam against claims filed by Sylvester Ploof seeking restitution in the sum of $2,000 for bodily harm and loss of property during the storm of November 13.

"We're proud to be entrusted with this case," said senior partner John B. Reston, "and intend to see our client vindicated." Asked if an attorney had been assigned, Mr. Reston indicated an announcement was forthcoming. "Telegraph lines were only restored yesterday. We're just getting our feet under us."

According to Chief of Police Timothy Stearns, Ploof and his family sailed on a loaded sloop from Thompson's Point in Charlotte on a northerly heading. Caught in the sudden storm, they moored at a dock on Birch Island, owned by Putnam. The caretaker, Terrance Williams, untied the boat, which later succumbed to the storm and was dashed against the rocky shore.

"We couldn't verify exactly what might've been on board and was claimed as lost," Chief Stearns stated. "It's not like there was a bill of lading." Thievery from vacation homes has risen sharply in recent years, he noted.

Putnam was not available for comment, but his offices confirmed the logging executive has not resided at Birch Island for seven years.

A trial date has not been set.

Solange leaned back in the chair and shook her head. Such a slanted article, implying that Sylvester Ploof moored at the island to launch a raid. The injustice, the prejudice, brought heat to Solange's face. The poor family had lost their boat—their home—and instead of receiving compassion were suffering insinuations of thievery and misrepresentation. It was so common as to be expected, but that didn't take the sting out of it.

The write-up troubled her in a more personal way, too. Osborn's firm had taken the case. As the youngest attorney in the group, he would have had no say in the matter, but the association disturbed her. When the news of the capsized boat first reached them, Osborn had called it "a tragedy," so she doubted he'd be eager to work on the case.

Solange folded the pages, rose from the table and added the newspaper to the pile in a wooden crate next to the kindling.

She went to the living room to read, but her mind was preoccupied by the article. She tidied the nursery then sent Elsie home early and prepared dinner herself. Osborn was eager to play with Carole when he arrived home, so Solange waited until the meal was finished and the child put to bed before broaching the subject of the case with him.

"I was going to bring it up." His tone was casual. "They've appointed me lead counsel."

She froze, her teacup in midair. "It's not a subject for joking, Osborn."

His expression signaled annoyance. "I'm perfectly serious. And frankly, I'm surprised you don't have more confidence in me."

"It has nothing to do with confidence in you. But you're the least experienced attorney. Why would they put you in charge?"

"Well, they suspect the case will spark social tensions in the community. I dare say it already has." He lifted his eyebrows and held her gaze. "If an attorney of Reston's stature takes the case, a liberal-leaning judge might feel more compassion for Ploof."

"And why shouldn't he?"

Osborn shrugged. "I can't speak for the judge. He hasn't even been named. But Putnam has the right to representation."

"Of course. But don't you find it distasteful that a man worth millions is refusing to part with two thousand dollars? His caretaker set a family adrift in a storm!"

"Distasteful? Perhaps, but my job isn't to take offense. And the caretaker was concerned for Putnam's property."

Solange thought of the mansions, and of the shanties. "Property over life isn't a toss-up. And look at it from Ploof's side. He had no choice but to tie up at the first dock he could reach. And if it had belonged to someone of more modest means, they'd never have come to any harm."

Osborn frowned, weighing his words. "As I understand it, the strategy will be to show that Mr. Ploof's reputation caused the caretaker to perceive a threat."

Solange edged forward in her chair, indignation rising in her chest. "If Ploof had earned that reputation, Osborn, you might have a point. But what other reputation could a family labeled 'pirates' have?"

Osborn went to the sideboard, poured a cup of coffee and returned to his seat. "I suspect it will be a long trial, Solange. I don't want it to come between us."

She sipped her tea and stared at the fire, reeling in her emotions. A log hissed and cracked. She lifted her eyes to meet her husband's. His brow softened and she let go a little, too. He'd worked so hard for his position and had done so on his own merits, not by climbing on the shoulders of his father. He was dedicated, talented and serious, and Solange was proud of him.

"It's an honor they selected you. If only it had been a different case."

"It's only the law, darling. There's no need to take it personally."

. . .

Solange arranged to meet her brother, David, in town to buy a gift
for their mother's birthday. Carole had started school, and Solange
devoted her free time to the charity she'd organized in her neighborhood. The work brought her to the harbor, where she sometimes
met her family. But David, several years her elder, plied odd jobs
on the New York side of the lake and was rarely in town, so Solange
was eager to catch up with him.

They'd agreed to meet at two at Abernathy's department store.
Solange was early, so she bought the *Free Press* from the news shop
and found a sidewalk bench from which she could spot David
approaching. Reading the paper had become a habit that at times
she wished she'd never started. The more she read, the better she
could discern the bias in the reporting, not just about the trial—
the two long years of it—but about any topic that ventured near
the divide between rich and poor, landed and lake-dwelling. Burlington was two cities, she saw now.

She skimmed the headlines until movement down the block
caught her attention. In front of city hall, two policemen confronted
a man, crowding him and blocking her view. One of the policemen
reached for his billy club. The man stepped to the side, dodging
them. He wore a flat cap and a worn woolen coat. David.

Solange jumped up and rushed toward them. Her brother waved
a sheaf of papers in the officers' faces. One of the officers grabbed
his arm and bent it sharply against his back. David swore and
lurched in an attempt to free himself. The other policeman, his face
beefy and red, raised his billy club.

"Stop!" Solange cried.

The policeman wielding the club sized her up, his eyes taking
in her tidy dress, her polished shoes. "Don't worry about this fellow,
ma'am. We'll see to him."

David scowled and lifted his chin at her. He'd read the policeman's assessment of her and what it implied, and didn't approve. Did he think she did?

"See to him? He's my brother." Her mind spun in turmoil. "Let him go."

The policeman shook his head, his jaw set. "I'm afraid he was loitering in a public place."

David spat on the ground and held the papers aloft. "I was looking over some paperwork. Since when is that against the law?"

The policemen exchanged glances. The one holding David's arm released him.

"Thank you." Solange exhaled in relief.

David shrugged his shirt into place and wiped the sweat from his upper lip. Solange came to his side.

The red-faced policeman pulled a ticket book from his pocket and extracted a pen from between the pages. "Seeing as this lady is here to vouch for you, we'll let you off with a fine."

He scribbled a moment and tore the ticket from the pad. David snatched it from him and stormed off. Solange hurried after him.

Over lunch, he told Solange this sort of harassment happened all the time to him, to his friends. Even their father had been roughed up a few weeks ago.

"No one told me. Why didn't someone tell me?"

He examined her as if he didn't quite recognize her. "What good would it do?"

"I don't know." Her voice quavered. "At least I would know. I want to know."

"Do you? I wonder." David pushed his empty plate to the side and placed his forearms on the table. "Because you can't be everywhere, swooping in to fix things like you did today."

She nodded, anger and shame swirling inside her. She clasped her brother's hand. He squeezed her fingers once, lightly, and let go. Sympathy, she understood, only went so far.

That evening after Carole had gone to sleep, Solange marched downstairs to the library. Osborn had made a habit of retreating there after supper, avoiding discussion with her, of that she was sure. Most evenings she was relieved. They had laid out their arguments repeatedly, hers becoming bolder over time, his becoming more terse. But tonight was different.

She knocked and stepped inside before Osborn could respond. He looked up from his papers, his face ashen, his eyes rimmed in red. He raked a hand through his hair and propped his elbows on his desk. Solange hesitated—he was exhausted—but found her resolve and took the chair opposite him.

"They fined my brother today."

"Who? For what?"

"For nothing! He went to the courthouse to pick up some paperwork for his boat—new regulations, I'm sure you've heard—and had the gall to stand outside the building looking over the documents. The police charged him with loitering. They raised a billy club to him, Osborn."

He cringed. "Well, there are statutes . . ."

"Against reading a document at midday? It's harassment, Osborn. Surely you can admit that."

"Perhaps it was a mistake. The police are overworked."

"Perhaps they wouldn't be if they didn't insist on writing so many citations for nuisance crimes, and trumping up petty charges. David says it happens all the time, and I know my cousin was cited for truancy and child neglect when his son was home sick."

"I'm sure there's an explanation, Solange. In any case, what do you propose I do about it?"

She rose from her seat, her shoulders squared. "For the last two years, since this case started, the press and the police and all the rest have set out to pillory my family and everyone else who lives on the lake."

"So it's my fault?" He spread his arms in a gesture of appeasement. "Please, darling. Don't get overwrought."

A year ago, even months ago, she would've backed down. She had trusted his perspective on everything, put faith in his authority, and his decency. She had bought into the idea that because the road he walked on was smooth, his understanding was deeper than hers. But she questioned that now. Maybe his road seemed smooth because he viewed it from a great height. Did he view her the same way? She didn't doubt he loved her, but that, she was beginning to see, was not the same as knowing her. "Am I overwrought? Or is it that I have begun to open my eyes?"

He pointed to the papers before him. "I'm an attorney. I'm representing a client. I don't control the press or the police."

"But you lay out the arguments for them. You feed the prejudice. You make the case."

He held her gaze. "I'm after the truth."

She stepped closer, placed one finger on the sleek, polished surface. "There isn't one truth, not when the lies have already been told. Year after year these lies have been laid down like bricks in a wall. And the wealthy folks, including you, Osborn Gifford, are standing on one side of it."

15

Solange

When Osborn's mother heard Solange had consented to attend the mayor's annual fall party, she sent over a demure dress and jacket ensemble, something she might have worn, in brown, no less. But Solange decided that if she was going to be dragged to a highbrow event, she would not be clothed as a mule. She'd ordered the most daring dress she could find on short notice, in emerald green velvet to set off her red hair.

The evening of the party, Solange examined herself in the mirror. The dress was fitted, with ruching along the sides, and cut to the waist at the back. Her hair flowed in waves over her shoulders, as she refused to adopt the cropped, sleek style favored by every other woman. Her only adornment was a headband with a delicate leaf design made of silver filigree and seed pearls. Satisfied with her appearance, Solange gathered her purse and coat and emerged from her dressing room. Osborn was showing Carole, who'd just turned seven, how to fasten his cufflinks.

Her daughter rushed toward her. "Mama, you're so pretty!"

She smiled and took Carole's hands, spinning in a circle to show Osborn the back. He gasped.

"Don't you like it?"

"It's, er, stunning." Osborn collected himself. "You are stunning, darling."

"Thank you, Osborn."

She had no patience for parties, especially ones crowded with politicians, lawyers and bankers. But Osborn's request that she attend was not pro forma. He'd said he wanted her by his side, and she'd softened a little, nostalgic for the time when they could not breathe without each other. Tension had accumulated between them like a rubbish heap, and what joy they did share was mostly in the company of their daughter. In his entreaty, Osborn mentioned that Evelyn Taylor would be there. The mayor's sister was broadminded, kind and fun-loving, but spent most of her time in Boston, so Solange welcomed the rare chance to see her.

When they arrived at the hotel, Osborn dropped the car keys in the palm of the valet and escorted Solange inside. The ballroom chandeliers shimmered and reflected prisms of light off the crystal glassware and ladies' jewels, and playful notes from a jazz ensemble mixed with the buzz of conversation and laughter. Osborn quickly found a group he knew and introduced Solange. She accepted a glass of white wine from the steward and wished Evelyn would hurry up and arrive.

A man whose name she'd already forgotten addressed Henry Perkins, a zoology professor at the University of Vermont. "I read an article about your recent report, 'Rural Vermont.' Fascinating."

Solange had seen the article, too, and knew enough about Perkins's studies and his influence on social policy to be poised to dislike him. In person, he wasn't physically commanding, but his self-assurance was palpable.

Perkins jumped at the chance to describe his report. "Yes, it's difficult to summarize decades of research in a short article, but the paper did an adequate job. The report contains data on fifty-five families, noting defects persisting in the germ plasm across generations."

"A tremendous amount of work," Osborn noted. "And the report's recommendations?"

"Primarily to continue practices already in place: education in heredity and population science in the schools; identification of bloodlines with rampant feeblemindedness, criminality and other defects; and measures to prevent these problems—and all the social and financial consequences—from persisting."

A portly man with a slick moustache turned to Perkins. "I agree we must check the multiplication of the unfit. Rural communities care for the unfortunate and handicapped as best they can, but there is the future to think of."

Solange couldn't believe what she was hearing. How would they stop families from producing children? Could that possibly be legal? She shifted from foot to foot, and searched the faces of each man in the group. Was no one else alarmed by this proposal? Osborn frowned at her agitation and placed a quieting hand on her arm. An acrid taste filled her mouth. She sipped her wine to dispel it.

The conversation turned to the problems endemic to rural Vermont: illegitimacy, delinquency and poverty. Solange watched Osborn carefully as the men discussed whether French Canadian heritage, or Catholicism per se, was the root of the problem. His face was impassive, a natural lawyer. No one, not even she, knew what he believed, where he stood. It aggravated her. On this issue, he'd undoubtedly say it was impossible to tease apart French Canadian heritage from Catholicism, as if that were the point. At least Perkins put his opinions, appalling as they were, on display. She had always taken Osborn's neutrality as a virtue, but neutrality wasn't fairness. If she asked him what he believed in, he'd say "God," "the law," or "you, I believe in you, and Carole." But those weren't really answers. Solange wanted Osborn to take a stance, if only to give her something to push against. Passion was a larger force than love, and in this, he'd disappointed her.

A banker named Reynolds drained his glass and jabbed a finger in the air. "If this city is to become the jewel of New England and continue to attract the right sort of people, the good people of Burlington need to rid the waterfront of those damned shanties once and for all."

She'd heard enough. Righteous anger surged through her. "And what do you propose to do with the people who live in them?"

Reynolds regarded her down the length of his nose, a smile playing his lips. "What possible difference could it make, my dear Mrs. Gifford?" He emphasized her husband's name, to remind her who she was, and in whose company.

"Oh, there you are, Solange." Evelyn slid beside her, radiant in a gold gown that picked up the lights in her auburn hair, and kissed her cheek. "Are these gentlemen boring you?"

Solange said, "Not at all." She fixed her gaze on Reynolds, then shifted it to Perkins. "We were just discussing compassion for our fellow man."

Evelyn picked up her sarcastic tone. "Wonderful. Then all of you will be delighted to drop a check at the table by the buffet. We're taking contributions for a new relief program." She smiled sweetly. "Just to tide folks over until Roosevelt gets his way." She bit off the words, took Solange by the elbow and led her away. When they were out of earshot, she said, "Those men are not worth your time."

Solange paused. "Including my husband?"

"Osborn loves you, my dear. He doesn't care where you came from."

Solange noted Evelyn's assumption that her family was a feature to be overlooked. She frowned in disappointment. "But I do. I care more than I ever believed I would."

Evelyn nodded. "Come meet some decent people. I warn you, though. They drink with purpose."

They threaded their way through the lively crowd, past the musicians and the buffet tables laden with platters of food. Evelyn spotted three of her friends planted near the bar and made her way to them. As she introduced Solange, another joined them. Myra was slender and dressed in pale gray and swayed like a sapling in the wind.

"You should give it a go," she said to Solange, twirling her fingers vaguely at the table behind her, where a woman sat holding a deck of cards. Her black hair was streaked with gray and her shoulders were draped with a richly embroidered shawl. A sign behind her read, in gothic lettering: "Tarot Readings."

"According to her," Myra said, "I'm destined for—oh, what was it?"

"A hangover?" Evelyn said.

"No doubt."

The women jokingly speculated on Myra's fortune. Solange felt the fortune-teller staring at her. It was probably her red hair. Her mother had told her many times how redheads were more susceptible to unseen forces, accounting for why so many witches had red hair. To her knowledge, Solange had never met a witch and wasn't sure she believed in magic stronger than her mother's natural remedies. The fortune-teller continued to watch her. Solange murmured a pardon and slipped from the group to take a seat at the woman's table.

The woman narrowed her dark eyes and bent forward like a hungry crow. This was surely an act, part of the entertainment. The deck of cards was short—just the Major Arcana, for a quick reading. Solange's mother read tarot from time to time, as had her mother before her. Solange had played with the cards as a girl, fascinated by the strange and intricate pictures, and the stories each told.

The woman rearranged her shawl and wordlessly shuffled the cards, eyes locked on Solange. She thrust the deck at her.

"Cut."

She obeyed. A tingle rose along her spine. Her throat was parched and she wished she hadn't relinquished her wineglass. The woman snapped three cards onto the table in a neat row. *Snap. Snap. Snap.* Past. Present. Future. The simplest of readings.

Her index finger heavy with silver rings, the woman pointed to each card in turn, beginning on the left, and gave the reading in a low voice. Solange only half listened. The meanings surfaced of their own accord.

The past, the High Priestess. Intuition and higher powers. Her childhood, her home on the lake, her intuition that Osborn was meant for her.

The present, the Wheel of Fortune. In the center it could only mean one thing: a turning point.

The future, the Fool. Reversed.

The woman's hand darted out and spun the card right side up. Only good fortune was permitted at this party. But Solange had seen, and understood. Foolishness. Recklessness. And a sense of being ensnared.

Solange laughed. She'd never been the slightest bit reckless. The woman raised her eyebrows and scooped up the cards. Solange thanked her, stood and went straight to the bar. Even to her own ears, her laugh had been too high, and thin. She accepted a glass of wine from the bartender with a trembling hand.

Osborn helped Solange spread a tartan blanket on the grass. She knelt to unpack the picnic basket. He set his boater to the side, lay down and sighed contently. "So warm for September. Really, we couldn't have chosen a more perfect day."

Solange paused to admire the colorful hills rising against a vault of blue. The trees bordering the roadside meadow were every shade of gold, orange and scarlet. "It's lovely." She passed him a plate with chicken, bread, a boiled egg and pickled vegetables. As he took it from her, he clasped her hand and squeezed it gently. She smiled at him, a bit unsure. Who could blame her? Osborn worked so much and kept company with men she had nothing in common with. At times she wondered who he was becoming.

"Thank you, darling. Looks delicious."

She smiled again, the tenderness in his face opening a small bloom in her chest. She made a plate for herself, arranged her skirt over her knees and stared across the river valley. "I don't realize how much the city bothers me until I leave it."

Osborn frowned, having taken her comment as a criticism of their life together, but quickly recovered. "Then let's do this more often. I'll have time once the trial is over."

The trial. Always the trial. And it hadn't even started.

He realized his error in mentioning it. "We'll bring Carole."

"She'd love the flowers and the birds."

He called her attention to a pair of blue jays chasing a crow across the treetops, diving and squawking insults at the larger bird. Solange laughed at their antics and lifted her face to the sun. Lingering over lunch, they pointed out cloud shapes and talked about other places they could drive to from Burlington.

They finished eating, sated. Solange placed the dishes into the picnic basket and handed it to Osborn to carry to the Buick while she folded the blanket.

He held open the car door. "Next stop, Underhill."

"I thought we were heading home."

"There's a cider mill."

She climbed in. "Well, if it's not too far." He walked around to the driver's side, got in and pulled on his gloves.

"And it's visiting day at the state hospital."

"Why on earth—"

"I've heard the presentation is educational." His finger rested on the starter button.

Perkins had been bending his ear, no doubt. Solange searched her husband's face for a deeper reason but he betrayed nothing.

Osborn continued. "And you've said we should do more for the unfortunate. You've done so much to help with relief for the poor in the city. I thought we could see what the state was contributing."

She held her breath a moment, disinclined to spoil the fine mood of the day. "All right, then."

He started the car. "We won't stay long."

They drank cups of hot mulled cider at the Wheatly mill and bought a jug to take home. The village of Underhill was fifteen minutes farther, and they had no trouble locating the hospital, set back from the main road, along the river. Osborn parked in the crowded lot and escorted Solange inside.

The receptionist gave them a brochure and pointed to a room across the corridor, where the presentation was underway. Two dozen people sat facing a lectern with a sign identifying the speaker as "Dr. Eugene A. Stanley, Superintendent." Solange and Osborn took seats at the rear.

"The patients you will see first are afflicted with chorea, a progressive, debilitating and, sadly, incurable disease of the muscular nervous system. It is inherited genetically; that is, it is passed on in families. Indeed, the five patients we have here at the hospital are family members. Once you witness the suffering and diseases that genetic defects cause, you will better understand the need to safeguard the future. We care for the chorea patients as best we can and protect subsequent generations of Vermonters from similar harm by halting further transmission of the defect."

Did that mean sterilization? Solange reasoned that the patients must be suffering terribly to have agreed to it.

Dr. Stanley continued. "After the chorea family, we will briefly visit a select group of mental defectives. These patients were brought to our facility due to the unmanageable burden they caused their local communities. While they may appear relatively harmless under our watchful eye, in their towns they were free to express their violent and criminal tendencies, moral degeneracy and, in some cases, sexual depravity."

The visitors mumbled and shifted in their seats. Solange whispered in Osborn's ear, "I'm not sure of this."

He laid a hand in her arm. "Don't worry. They wouldn't endanger anyone. Their mission is public protection and education."

Dr. Stanley motioned to a door to his left where an attendant stood. "This way, ladies and gentlemen."

Osborn and Solange joined the others as they filed into a large room with barred windows. The patients were arrayed in one corner. Two older men sat collapsed in wheelchairs, immobile, staring intently at disparate, distant points. A few feet away, a young woman danced with her back to them. An ethnic dance, perhaps, because her movements were extreme and unschooled, and she emitted a throaty hum. Solange noticed another patient walking with jerking steps and realized the woman's "dance" was a symptom of disease. The patient spun to face them, her features twisted in a grimace of alarm.

Solange's shoulders sagged. "How awful for them."

Osborn said, "Do you suppose only their bodies are affected, or their minds as well?"

"I've no idea. I don't know which would be worse."

Dr. Stanley's voice reverberated off the hard walls and floor. "As you can see, chorea is a debilitating disease. We care for them here at Underhill with compassion and whatever expertise can be brought to bear. What family wouldn't embrace the chance to stop such a scourge from afflicting their loved ones?"

Perhaps, Solange thought, these unfortunate people would be better off without children. How could they care for them?

After a several long minutes, the doctor crossed in front of the visitors and positioned himself by a door on the far side of the room, directing them through. A couple with an adolescent son paused at the door, causing the remainder of the group to amass behind them. The man, tall with a sharp goatee, drew Dr. Stanley's attention.

"It occurred to me, Doctor, that mental disorders and behavioral problems might be less susceptible to the laws of heredity than, say, what we see in this chorea family. What do your studies reveal in that regard?"

Dr. Stanley smiled as if he'd been awaiting this very question. "A great deal, sir. Although we tend to think of dysfunction in character and behavior as more mutable than physical disease, the evidence points to the contrary. One only need examine notorious Vermont families, such as the gypsies and the pirates, in which moral turpitude and depravity are rampant, to conclude that their unfortunate natures are passed down like heirlooms from generation to generation. Blood, as they say, will tell."

Solange stared at the doctor, incredulous. She opened her mouth to utter a retort, but her throat clamped shut. The man who'd asked the question nodded in agreement, as did his wife, her bright red lips pulled into a knowing smile. The crowd seemed to be closing in on Solange, snatching the air from her lungs. Osborn put his arm around her shoulder. He knew, he knew all about her family, her blood. She spun away. The group surged forward, toward the next stage of this gruesome spectacle. Solange pushed through the crowd the way they'd come, ignoring the questioning faces and harsh glares.

She entered the room where the presentation had been held and hurried past the empty chairs toward reception. An attendant blocked the passage and pointed over her shoulder. "That's the way, madam."

Solange's arms flew from her sides. "I know the way. I am leaving."

"Yes, madam. But the group exits through a different door." Perturbed by the breech of protocol, he held his ground, then fixed his attention behind her. She turned. Osborn. "Is this your wife, sir?"

As if she were a forgotten coat or hat. Anger rose within her. "Step aside. I am leaving."

Osborn said, "My wife is unwell. Please excuse us."

The attendant paused, considering his duties and the situation. "Well, if the lady is poorly—"

"I'm perfectly fine!" Solange threw herself past him, burst through the door, crossed the reception area and stormed outside.

Osborn caught up to her on the path. "Darling, I know what you thought the doctor said . . ."

"What I *thought* he said? What he said *in truth*, Osborn. In complete, self-righteous, condescending truth."

"All right, but he was only making a point about heredity. He wasn't talking about you. He doesn't know you."

They'd arrived at the car. Solange circled to the passenger side. Osborn approached and she held up her hand.

"No, he doesn't know me. Or my family. But he wouldn't let that get in the way of his plans, and those of the others, including your friend Perkins, to clean up Vermont's breeding stock by getting rid of all of us." She took a step toward him. "Why did you bring me here? What did you mean for me to see?"

"That the state is serving Vermonters as a whole, and helping the afflicted at the same time. That good is being done, and the interests of the people are being served."

She threw her head back and laughed. "The interests of your people, perhaps, Osborn. What about the interests of the unfortunate? If you looked, if you really looked, you'd see exactly what I see. The unfortunate don't suffer from inherited defects. They suffer from poverty."

He pursed his lips. He struggled to find the right words, the lawyerly ones. How could he not see the plain truth of what she said? When they'd first married, Solange had thought of her husband as a principled man, one with backbone. Now he struck her more often as too eager for the approval of his peers and superiors, and too keen to make excuses for staking claim to morally dubious ground.

Osborn finally spoke. "The doctor made an unfortunate remark. Of course, the people who live on the lake are, by and large, poor, and it's tremendously sad." He opened the car door. "Let's just forget this for now, okay? Enjoy the ride home. Carole will be waiting and we'll have a lovely dinner together."

Solange's pulse slowed at the thought of their daughter. She glanced over her shoulder at the tall brick buildings sitting squarely on the lawn, yielding no clues as to what transpired inside. The sun was strong and reflected heat off the pale granite stones at her feet. She climbed in the car and rubbed her arms, shivering. Osborn should never have brought her here. She would never forget what she'd seen and what she'd heard and wanted nothing more than to leave it behind.

16

Solange

Osborn's case—that's how she thought of it—went to trial the summer of 1936, four years after Ploof's boat had succumbed to the storm. The presiding judge was George Holborn, a man inclined so far to the left, Osborn complained, he appeared likely to fall sideways out of his seat. The trial dragged on for nearly a year, due to ill and misplaced witnesses, blizzards, lost paperwork and the death of Judge Holborn's wife.

One evening after she'd put Carole to bed, Solange intercepted Osborn on his way to his office. He'd taken to sequestering himself there, which struck Solange as cowardly.

"Who was on the stand today, Osborn?"

"I'm tired, and I still have work to do."

"Was it the caretaker? What questions did you ask?" Solange was too impatient to wait for the morning paper and had to know every detail of the trial, including Osborn's version of information she received through other means. She couldn't help herself. It was as if her marriage was being tried and decided upon, her choices, her life.

Osborn grew impatient. "I defend Putnam in court every day, Solange. Why must I come home only to defend him, and myself, again?"

"It's what you chose."

"I do not choose to argue with you."

"I won't be mute when I feel strongly." She could see how worn out he was, but her sympathy grew thin. How could she forgive him for being on the wrong side of things? And he never asked about her activities, her work with the poor, her efforts to document police harassment, which had escalated dramatically that winter. Like boxers in a ring, she and Osborn tended to their wounds in separate corners. Her bright and noble young man had grown cold to her, unmoved by her arguments, immune to her zeal, which his impassivity only inflamed. At night he moved as far from her as possible, leaving a space between them that never warmed. Their love, which Solange had naively accredited with absolute power, had failed to bridge their worlds.

Osborn opened the office door. "I have more on my mind than strong feelings." He slipped inside. "Don't wait up for me."

Solange struggled to quell her frustration. She crossed the foyer on her way to the kitchen for something to drink.

"Mama?" Carole clung to the stair railing. At nine, she'd grown into a watchful child. She no longer slept well and her appetite had dulled.

"You're supposed to be in bed, my love."

"I heard you and Papa talking."

Watchful and diplomatic. The word she meant to use was "arguing."

"I'm sorry." Solange climbed the stairs, led her daughter to her room and tucked her in.

Carole hugged her toy dog to her chest. "Papa's taking me to the pictures tomorrow. If you come, too, I can sit in the middle."

Solange stroked the girl's hair from her forehead. "We'll see." Her daughter's pleas to reunite her family broke Solange's heart. Osborn, too, was distressed. What a place they'd come to, where sadness and pain were what they shared most.

She wished Carole good night and went downstairs, the hollow echoes of her heels resounding through the empty spaces.

Nine months after it had begun, the trial ended. Judge Holborn awarded Sylvester Ploof $450 of the $2000 demanded in the suit. Osborn filed an appeal, and the case continued. Once the dispute became about money and not morality, public opinion shifted in favor of the Ploofs. How could a billionaire be so uncharitable to a poor man who'd lost everything? Solange no longer discussed the case with Osborn. She rarely spoke with him at all.

He went in early and stayed late, and accepted every offer from clients and colleagues for social engagements. Solange's habitual absence at these gatherings was explained away until it became unnecessary to do so, as it was assumed. Burlington was a small city and rumors about the state of their marriage took to the air like seagulls at the fishing piers. Solange strove to stay above it, or far from it, but it was impossible.

Spring arrived as it always did in Vermont, late and in a mad rush. One fine May morning, Osborn entered the sitting room where she was tending houseplants.

"Solange, I've made a decision."

Her hands quieted above a fern. She looked at him, surprised to find a hesitant smile on his lips.

"I've rented a house on Cape Cod for the summer." He stepped closer and tucked a loose curl behind her ear. "For the three of us."

"Leave here? Just go away?"

"Precisely."

"Nothing's that simple, Osborn."

He said he'd arranged for all the holiday time he dared, and would work from the Cape as much as he was able. She could do as she wished. He took her hand. "Please. Let's just go."

The hope on his weary face stirred the same feeling inside her. "All right. We'll go."

They were blessed with a bright day on the car journey south; hillsides cast in the palest green, earth freshly turned in the fields, rivers testing their banks with the last of the snowmelt. Carole slept in the car as she always did. Solange gazed at the scenery, her emotions in abeyance. After a time, she closed her eyes. They skirted Boston and approached the ribbon of land unfurled upon the sea. Carole, now awake, wanted to know about the place names—Sandwich, Mashpee, Truro—and laughed when her father made up outlandish stories to account for them.

Osborn slowed the car as the house, placed with care between the road and the sea, came into view. The drive was lined with a white picket fence nearly obscured by flowers in riotous bloom. The small house and its windmill, clad in salt-worn shingles, looking out upon the ocean but not commanding it, had a fairy-tale aspect, the lines and colors perfectly attuned to the landscape. Sandy paths, idle trails, wound between the dunes and around tidal ponds. From the backseat, Carole let out a gasp of delight.

Osborn parked, opened the barn-red door and stepped aside for Solange. Carole followed her in, dashed across the whitewashed floors and hopped onto a window seat with a broad view of the dunes and beyond to the sea.

"I'm spending my summer right here!"

"And so you shall!" Osborn bent to whisper in Solange's ear. "I want nothing more than for us to be happy here."

She half closed her eyes and breathed deeply. "It's very peaceful."

And it was, for a time. Carole played on the beach and swam with Solange. The sea was nothing like the lake, of course. It was boundless, insistent, with a quality of longing that was new to Solange. The sea claimed the eastern horizon, offering up the sun each morning, reaching after it with grasping waves each evening. Solange found it strange and terrible at first, and resisted enchantment, but as the days at Chatham fell behind her, she yielded to its beauty.

Carole loved everything from the start—the cottage, the dunes, the surf, the seagulls pitching and whirling. She considered the shells, jellyfish and bits of bones the water relinquished upon the strand as personal gifts. Osborn learned to catch bluefish and cook lobster, and on some days he neglected to shave. Their skin browned. The weight on Solange's chest lifted a bit, and she slept late into the mornings.

They'd been at the Cape for a week before Osborn reached for her in bed. She turned to him cautiously, unsure. He'd become a partial stranger, someone she might or might not want to know more deeply. They had not made love in months, but with only each other and their daughter for company, the nights were theirs alone, and desire broke through their cool, raw surfaces. Tenderness followed and spilled into the days. But Solange didn't trust the change and held part of herself back, wary of suddenly abandoning their habitual conflict simply because they shared a different bed. She wanted to return to a place of safety and warmth in their marriage, but achieving that by running away felt cowardly, a clever trick, and unlikely to last.

In mid-June, after they'd been in Chatham five weeks, they prepared to return to Vermont. Solange's niece was to be married and Osborn was needed at the law firm. Solange sent Carole to her room to pack her books and toys and went to the kitchen to box up the perishable food.

Osborn came in and stood before her at the kitchen table, a concerned expression on his face. "Darling, I wanted to speak with you about the wedding."

Solange wrapped the morning's bread in brown paper and placed it in the box. "What about it?"

"A box of papers was delayed and arrived just now. Reston included an article from the *Free Press* about several armed burglaries at the waterfront." Solange looked up at him. "I'm not happy with Carole attending the wedding."

"That's ridiculous." He had not been invited, as he was even less welcome among Solange's family now than before the trial. But of course she would go, as would Carole.

"She can stay with me, or Elsie."

"It's not a matter of her care, Osborn. As you know."

"This summer's recession has made the area more dangerous."

"It's a wedding!"

"And so there will be drinking."

Pressure built in her chest. She clenched her jaw. "I suppose no one drinks at proper weddings in the city?"

"Yes, but—"

"But what, Osborn?"

He exhaled sharply in frustration. "Why can't you just be happy, Solange? I've given you everything. Why do you insist on making things difficult for us?"

"By attending my niece's wedding?"

"By refusing to accept that you no longer live on a boat, scratching out an existence. By dragging our daughter into unacceptable situations."

"They are her family!"

He grabbed the chair back in front of him and leaned toward her. "Have you looked at Carole, Solange? Have you looked at her?"

"What do you mean?"

"I love you, Solange. And I don't care where you came from, you know I don't. But I can't bear to see Carole put in danger, or ruined."

Solange stared at him, her thoughts spinning to make sense of his words. She heard Carole's quick footsteps on the stairs and in an instant the girl appeared, wearing a white sailor dress with a blue collar and a brass anchor buckle at the waist.

"Do you like my new dress, Papa? Aunt Bettina sent it."

"Very much. It suits you."

She flung her arms around him, blonde curls bouncing. Solange looked from her daughter to her husband and to her daughter again. They were so similar. The words of the doctor at Underhill flashed in her mind. *Blood will tell.* Osborn's blood had made a strong showing in Carole. She had no place on a barge, on a lake. She was not a Bouchard. And no one would ever have cause to call her a pirate. Solange knew she ought to be relieved.

"Aren't we going?" Carole asked.

Osborn kissed his daughter's cheek. "Let's pack the car."

Solange placed the lid on the box. Osborn smiled at her kindly, picked up the box and left, Carole at his side.

Solange went to the window, secured the latch and turned her back on the sea.

On the day of the wedding, she sailed on the family boat to South Hero on Grand Isle. Solange's father and her brother, David, talked about the same things they always did: the weather, the fortunes of people they knew, stories about how things used to be different, better. Her mother, Rosemarie, watched Solange closely, searching for change.

"I was only gone a few weeks, Mama."

"I know, but it can be easy to go a long way in a short time."

"Not on this boat." Jean-Claude Bouchard winked at his daughter. With that one gesture, he'd made her feel like a young girl again, unencumbered. She smiled at him and he winked once more.

Rosemarie pulled Solange close. "You know, I've never seen the ocean."

"It's frightening."

They neared Sandbar Causeway, the water glinting like shards of ice. A half dozen boats were moored to the south, the bright colors of the ladies' dresses visible on the lawn that stretched between a modest clapboard house and the dock. Men ferried crates from the boats to long tables arrayed on the lawn. Solange's father tied up and David helped the women out. They made their way ashore, carrying baskets covered in handkerchiefs, pausing to greet everyone they passed.

Solange set down her basket and admired the sprawling bouquets of blue asters, black-eyed Susans, cattails and marsh grasses on the tables. Her mother lowered herself onto a bench.

"Let me get you something to drink, Mama."

"Thank you, dear."

Solange followed two men hauling crates of beer to a wagon parked at the edge of the lawn. An elderly woman—a distant relation, perhaps—ladled lemonade into tin cups from a large crock.

"Two, please."

A voice behind her said, "Solange, isn't it?"

She turned. A dark-bearded man, well over six feet tall, smiled down at her. She might not have known him except for his eyes, a summer sky blue.

"Caleb?" Solange hadn't seen him in more than a dozen years. When they were small, they'd swum and fished together, played hide-and-seek on the boats, counted stars. He'd been two years ahead of her in school—when he was in school, that is—and had been a lanky boy, still adjusting to the length of his limbs and his purpose in the world. Now the set of his jaw and the clarity in his eyes told her he'd found his purpose, or was near to it. "I'd heard, I think, you were welding down in Troy. Are you back now, or visiting?"

"I haven't decided. You know how it is. When you come back, you can't quite remember why it was you ever left."

"I do know." She sensed the heat coming off his body and felt her cheeks redden. She picked up the cups of lemonade from the wagon bed, thanked the woman and looked over Caleb's shoulder. "I promised my mother a drink."

He hunched down a little, his breath in her hair. "Promise me a dance later?"

A dance. When had she last danced? She took half a step back, gathered herself and spoke as if to anyone. "We'll see."

Solange returned to her mother and spent the afternoon catching up with old friends and with relatives she'd forgotten she had. Each time someone recognized her and shared a memory, she remembered pieces of herself she'd buried or cast aside. It was as if part of her, a substantial part, existed in these people, in their memories and in their hearts.

As she wove through the gathering, she caught glimpses of Caleb. Twice he'd been looking at her. During the ceremony, he sat on a bench behind the row of wicker chairs that held her family. She felt his eyes on her. She pinched her wedding band with two fingers as the songs, the hymns and the vows floated over her head like dandelion seeds.

The music began at dusk. The fiddler tapped his foot and spun the first three measures of a reel into the air. An accordion, a guitar and a harmonica joined in. The wedding guests made a circle on the lawn, which couples and giggling children soon filled. Caleb didn't wait long to find her.

"May I?" He took her hand, lifted it high and twirled her in a slow circle.

She answered him with a smile, a twist of guilt in her belly. To erase the feeling, she told herself it was only a dance.

They danced that reel and another, moving easily together, as if they were still children who never thought about their bodies but simply lived in them. Solange could see the boy in Caleb, in his bright, curious eyes, in the way he tossed his head when he laughed, in his mischievous grin. It occurred to her that these childhood memories had been lying undisturbed, awaiting her recognition that she'd always been drawn to him.

A jig played, and they danced, then an air. Caleb pulled her closer. In the pressure of his hand against her back was a knowledge of who she was, of who he was, of who all the people were, dancing together under the stars on an island in a lake, blue as midnight. She hadn't felt so alive, so herself, in years.

17

Solange

Osborn, Solange and Carole had planned to return to Chatham together four days after the wedding, but Osborn was forced to stay to depose new witnesses testifying on behalf of Putnam. That these witnesses likely had been bribed didn't change his obligation.

"Only a few days," he assured Solange. "A week at the most."

"I could go ahead with Carole."

His face registered surprise. He didn't expect her to volunteer to leave town, her charity, her family.

Solange said, "All Carole talks about is the beach."

In truth, she wasn't confident of her feelings and so could not predict her own actions. Nothing had happened with Caleb other than dancing, but Solange didn't trust herself. She felt perilously indifferent; she was a coin tossed in the air.

Osborn said, "Regina is going to Boston tomorrow to shop. I'm sure her driver could take you to Chatham."

"Perfect."

When they parted the next day, Osborn lingered in his embrace. Solange thought of Caleb's broad hand on her back and blushed. Osborn smiled, thinking he was the cause, and she knew she was right to leave.

.   .   .

Rain greeted them at the cottage and continued for days. The heavy sky weighed on Solange. She played endless games of rummy with Carole and helped her identify the birds they spied from the window seat. In the long afternoons they read side by side on the settee, but Solange could not remain fastened to the page. Vertigo overtook her, as if she were balanced on a point and could only steady herself by looking into the distance. The same feeling came over her when she lay down, and she resorted to sleeping with several pillows stacked behind her, nearly upright. She'd never been seasick but guessed this was how it felt.

She did not think of Caleb often, nor did she examine the state of her marriage. Instead, Solange wondered how it was possible that the girl setting tables at the Hotel Vermont, full of expectation and wonder and courage, had become the woman she was now: flailing inside a cage, unable to account for how she had arrived there or why, unable to express what she wanted. Like a dog chasing its own tail round and round and round, she was dizzy with her own impotence.

When the weather brightened, she and Carole returned to the beach. Carole made friends with a younger girl staying nearby, and Solange was pulled into conversation with the family, which she welcomed as a distraction. If she stared out to sea for more than a moment, she felt untethered. There should be mountains. Something solid, not simply water and sky.

Six days passed. In the late afternoon, Solange sat on the veranda fashioning an elaborate braid in Carole's hair. A car clattered down the lane.

"Papa!" Carole sprang up to meet him at the gate, her blonde tendrils slipping through Solange's fingers.

Solange waited, arranging the brush and ribbons in the empty seat beside her.

"There you are, darling!" He came around the house, Carole attached to one arm.

"Hello, Osborn." She took the hand he offered and stood. His face was so bright, as if he'd been the one away at the shore for a week. He pulled her closer, his scent familiar, his touch secure. He kissed her cheek, and she drew away and fingered the crown of her hat as if keeping it in place, but there was no wind. "Did you have a good trip?"

"Yes. And it's wonderful to be here. To see you."

Carole stared up at them expectantly.

Solange smiled at her husband. "You must be thirsty. Carole, is there any iced tea left?"

The few hours left in the day were occupied with their daughter, who had many things to show her father and many stories to tell. They ate an early supper. Carole fell asleep on the settee, her browned legs folded so her shins rested against her father's leg. He reached for a blanket and gently tucked it around her. Solange left the sitting room, wandered into the kitchen and joined Osborn a few moments later, pacing the room.

He motioned to her. "Sit with me, darling."

She chose a chair not quite across from him, perched on the edge and regarded their sleeping daughter.

"Carole was unusually talkative this evening," he said.

"Until she made a friend the other day, she's only had me to speak to."

"Have you been lonely? I've missed you."

"It *is* quiet." It wasn't the response he'd wanted, but what could she do?

Osborn blinked at her, then continued. "I wanted to discuss something with you, something I thought about on the drive down. Chatham seems to suit both you and Carole so well. Why don't we look at property here?"

"For holidays?"

"No, to live. I'm certain I could find a position nearby, or in Boston. We'd be far from all that . . . business."

Her fingers stilled on the silver bangle she'd been toying with. He couldn't mean what he'd said. "Move here? Permanently?"

"Yes. That was my thought."

"But what about our families?"

"I'd sacrifice that." His Adam's apple bobbed up and down. He pulled away from Solange's gaze and stared at Carole. "For us. For you."

A silence as dense and static as the bottom of the ocean filled the room. Carole turned onto her shoulder, sighing in her sleep.

Solange uncrossed her legs and placed her feet on the floor. "I should put her to bed."

"But what about my proposal?"

"I won't leave my family."

He swept his arm to encircle her and their daughter. "But we are your family. You can visit Burlington as often as you please. You and Carole and I can be happy here. Nothing else matters, don't you see?"

"And what would I do here all day?"

"What you have been doing. Be Carole's mother. Be my wife."

He meant to sequester her here, make her forget her parents, her work, the desperate needs of others, and return her to her throne as his Scarlet Queen. The artlessness of his proposal moved her, but only a little. She had no clear vision of how their relationship would play out in the future, but it was far too late to go back to the naive place where they had begun. They were different people now; at least she was.

"I don't want to live here, Osborn. I won't leave my family. Nor the lake."

He jerked as if she'd struck him. "The lake? I've never understood your obsession with it. Why do you need a lake when you can have the ocean?"

"My obsession? It's my home."

His face darkened. "We're married, Solange. Your home is with me." He waited for her to agree, but she could not. "Perhaps Carole and I will look at houses tomorrow. She'd enjoy it."

She stared at him in disbelief. "Osborn, you wouldn't."

"If you force my hand."

"I'm her mother. You wouldn't." Her throat closed. "You can't."

"A mother thinks of herself last, not first." He stood and gathered Carole into his arms. "To bed, little one."

Solange rose to stand in front of him, her pulse quickening. She'd never seen him so closed off. "Osborn . . ."

He edged around her.

She followed them to foot of the stairs. "Please don't. Please." She felt her knees give way and clasped the doorframe.

He started up, ducking under the low ceiling. "I'm only taking her to bed. You needn't fuss."

She waited for Osborn in the living room, expecting him to apologize for the threat, but when he returned he picked up the newspaper and retired to the patio to read in the failing light. Solange imagined he was already reshaping her staunch refusal into a change of heart that would require time. She didn't want to argue with him yet again, and she certainly didn't want to hear him say he would take Carole from her, not even if it meant allowing him to believe something other than the truth, so she let it go.

It was simple to release her grasp here. The salty worn air seeping in through the open windows and the angled, diluted light conspired to soften her. Time washed in and out with the tide, traveling backward as well as forward, engulfing the beach and giving it up again. She listened to the waves beyond the dunes slap the sand and shrink away, again and again, and pictured her desires moving into and out of her outstretched arms, hers for a moment and then stolen by another power. She pretended to be water, yielding to the pull.

That night and in the days and nights that followed, Solange and Osborn inhabited a twilight space, lit by the laughter of their daughter and shaped by the waxing moon. It was a fantasy of a life, not unlike the one they'd had when she believed their souls were twinned. This fantasy, weak and easy, also would not last. Nothing, she would realize, lasts longer than the truth of who we really are.

One day in mid-July, they wandered the streets of Chatham, arriving at a block of half-timbered buildings with steep, dormered roofs. Osborn ducked into the post office to collect the mail.

"We'll be in the general store," Solange called after him.

She and Carole tried on hats, laughing and admiring each other. Osborn rejoined them, holding an envelope, his face solemn. Solange's mouth went dry and she carefully placed the sunhat she'd been considering onto its stand. Osborn led her outside to a nearby bench, Carole at their heels.

Carole said, "What is it, Papa?"

"A telegram for your mother."

He sat beside Solange. She opened the envelope with trembling hands and unfolded the paper. She scanned the letter and turned to Osborn, his face blurred through her tears.

"My father has died."

Osborn pulled her into his arms.

Solange was unaware of the passage of time. Stunned into helplessness, she looked on as Osborn composed a reply to her mother, saying they would leave in the morning. There wasn't time to drive today, he explained. Solange was dimly aware of Carole clinging to her arm, whispering questions that her father may have answered. Solange said nothing.

They returned to the cottage. It seemed so unfamiliar; she was bewildered to find her belongings there. Osborn settled her in the living room, asked her what she needed. She shook her head. He left, spinning in and out of her view—into the kitchen, up and down the stairs, back and forth to the car—Carole trailing along. They brought her water, tea, supper, a blanket. She waited for night, for the crushing stillness.

Osborn knelt before her. "Please come to bed. You need to rest."

"I'll just stay here."

He lingered a moment, then was gone.

Solange rose and shut the windows to mute the sea. It was invisible, hidden behind the reflection of the lamp in the glass. Good.

She stood at the window, clutching the blanket around her shoulders. No one could have foreseen the sudden death of Jean-Claude Bouchard, but she was nevertheless nauseous with guilt for having been here when he collapsed on his boat and slipped into the lake like an anchor. She could have spent the last several weeks with him. She could have been with her mother, at her side as she bore the news. Instead, she had agreed to escape here with Osborn, an act she regarded now as spurred by cowardice, not hope.

But those lost weeks were nothing when added to the eleven years she'd lived on the hill, high above the lake, stumbling around in an oversized house, in a life that didn't fit her, bound by marriage to a man who did not understand or accept her nature, and whose conscience was muffled by his ambition, whose faults were disguised by breeding and success. Solange stared at her ghostly reflection and opened her mouth, afraid she would suffocate under the weight of her regret. She'd been blown off course and was lost. This was her true grief, and it had first entered her like a sickness after her niece's wedding. Her grief for the self she had betrayed, crystallized by her father's death, was so large she could not contain it. It lived beside her, another being, and her guilt gave it a beating heart.

They left Chatham early the next morning under a vermilion sky. Solange dozed, half dreaming about what she might have been doing when her father had fallen from his boat. Rubbing sand from Carole's feet, perhaps, or listening to Osborn comment on the beauty of the ocean. Her thoughts drifted to the telegram, the staccato message like final heartbeats. *Come home STOP.* She was unbearably tired. Her skin felt abraded, her nerves too close to the surface. Deep inside, she was numb.

When they arrived home, Solange left Carole with Osborn and, against his protestations, descended on foot to the waterfront. She found her way to the family houseboat and boarded it. Her brother was slumped against the wheel as if asleep, but his eyes were open, his face hard with pain and anger.

"They're saying it was probably his heart. It was, you know, but not in the way they mean. Too much trouble and too little money for too long."

She reached for him. "David—"

He looked away, pulled a tin from his pocket and began to roll a smoke. "Go see Mama. She's below."

She descended, gripping the rail, and felt her way in the dim light to where her mother lay.

"Mama."

Her mother stretched out her arms and Solange collapsed into them, sobbing. Her mother's embrace was warmer and stronger than ever, so many years of love now strengthened by loss. Solange felt small and brittle.

At the funeral the next day, Jean-Claude Bouchard's favorite objects (his pipe, his compass and his slicker) were burned and cast into the lake. Solange slept in her childhood berth that night and the next. On the third night, she leaned against the deck railing, stars bright overhead, bats skimming the water, wheeling into the moist midsummer air, black against black.

Solange descended the companionway and found her mother at the sturdy oak table holding a tin cup of steaming coffee. Dressed in black, her face was pale but resolute.

"There's more, if you'd like."

"No, thank you, Mama." Solange lowered herself onto a chair. "I've made a mistake."

Her mother nodded, but said nothing.

"I've loved him. I truly have."

"I know you did. It's all right."

"How can it be all right? Osborn wants to move us to the Cape, to Chatham. When I objected, he threatened to take Carole from me."

Rosemarie raised her eyebrows. "He said that?"

"In so many words. What am I to do? He'll never divorce me. I'll be stuck with him, playing the part of his wife, his supporter. Osborn is headed for public office, I'm certain of it. What will I do then?" She paused, allowing the truth to surface. "He's not the man I thought he was."

Her mother rose from the table and disappeared into the sleeping quarters at the bow. A few moments later, she placed a square box in front of Solange, made of blue glass and as long as her thumb.

"What's this?"

"My mother gave it to me when I was eighteen. I'd fallen for a young man who'd come to our island looking for healing for his younger sister."

"Not Papa?" Solange had never considered that her mother could have been in love with anyone else.

"No, not your father. This fellow, a logger, was from Essex."

"Not from the lake."

"Definitely not, and Protestant besides. When my mother found out about us and our plans to be together, to leave the lake, she sat me down and gave me this box. I asked her why. 'Blue for the water,' she said. 'To bring you back to us.'"

"And that's what happened?"

Rosemarie cast her eyes down. "In time. That October, he had an accident. A tree fell the wrong way. He died the next day."

The air in the hold grew oppressive. Solange swept damp hair from her forehead. Her throat was dry and cinched. "And then you met Papa."

Her mother smiled. "That's right. Less than a year later."

Solange placed a finger on the box and traced the bead of lead along the rim. "I don't love Osborn anymore, Mama, but I don't want anything to happen to him."

"Logging's a dangerous job. It could've happened anyway. And I'm not saying I wasn't torn apart. When he died, seemed like I died, too." She paused, remembering. "But the box reminded me of where I belonged, that I could go back and my life would still be mine. And it was." She fixed her gaze on Solange and laid her words out straight. "You can't know how things will turn out. That's not in our power—or anyone's. But you can know where you belong."

Solange nodded, her throat too clogged to speak. She ached for the years she'd squandered, and for losing Osborn, the man she'd loved. She wasn't sure what to hope for. So much depended on luck, good and bad. A tarot card is reversed or it isn't. A child is born on a boat or in a mansion. A daughter is like her mother or her father.

She picked up the blue box and cradled it in her hands. It was heavier than it appeared.

That night, Solange stashed the blue box in her bag and waited for her mother to fall asleep. She thought about the fortune-teller at the party, about the Wheel of Fortune card and the turning point it had signaled, on which she was now poised, and the Fool, whose significance had, until this moment, escaped her. She would not be ensnared.

She climbed off the boat, her bag slung over her shoulder. The moon had risen above the island hills. She nodded to several shadowed figures huddled drinking and smoking, then made her way down the dock, water lapping against the piers, the air rich with the smell of diesel, wet wood and barnacles. She knew where to find him, which boat, assuming he'd stuck around. He'd mentioned his place in passing and she'd fixed it in her mind without knowing she had.

A pulse quickened through her, up from the water below the rough boards. Her fingertips tingled and a longing like hunger moaned deep in her belly. Her anxiety about who she was and in what she believed was torn from her mind in shreds, leaving clear, cold space.

She arrived at her future and abandoned herself. She was foolish, and reckless—and free.

18

Carole

Carole couldn't think of anything she wanted more than a baby brother or sister. She'd prefer a sister—they would have so much in common—but either would be wonderful. She was tired of dolls and, at ten, too old for them, really. Her parents wouldn't allow her to have a dog or a cat, so a baby to hold and dress and sing to and, later, to play with, would be the best.

When her parents announced a baby was coming, Carole was too happy to speak. The baby would arrive in the spring, so she thought right away that next summer they could all go to the beach house in Chatham. It was a better there than in Vermont, because her parents argued less, maybe because her father wasn't working all the time. Her mother told her she missed her family and the lake when they were at the Cape, but she was calmer there, especially when it was just the two of them, with no plans, one day drifting slowly into the next. Sometimes when Carole was reading or drawing, she'd look over at her mother and find her staring out at the sea. Carole asked her once if she was looking for whales, which made her mother laugh. A baby would distract her mother from whatever she was searching for across the water, and Carole would never be lonely again.

Her mother didn't feel well, especially in the mornings, and slept a lot.

Papa told Carole not to worry. "Your mother was a little sick in the beginning with you, too, and look how wonderful you turned out." He was as excited about the baby as she was.

One day in December, Grandma Rosemarie showed up at the door. From her room upstairs, Carole heard Elsie let her in, probably because Carole's father was at work. Grandma Rosemarie hardly ever came to the house, and her mother's other relatives never did. It was one of those rules that didn't need to be written down. Carole guessed it had something to do with her parents' fights but wasn't sure.

Before her mother got pregnant, Carole would often hear raised voices at night. She'd creep down the stairs, wanting to hear what it was about.

"You don't care what happens to families like mine," her mother said.

Her father answered by talking about the trial. Not much of what they said made sense, and Carole gave up trying to get close enough to make out all the words. She'd sit on the stairs, her nightgown wrapped tight over her knees, her stomach sick with worry. The sharp words sliced through the air like bats.

From what she could tell, her mother thought her father didn't like poor people enough. Grandma Rosemarie was poor, so that fit. Carole never said so, but she didn't like Grandma Rosemarie that much, either. She smelled like a wet dog and had a funny look in her eye, like she was trying to see straight into Carole. It made her nervous.

Now Grandma Rosemarie was talking to Elsie in the parlor. Carole went down to see what was going on. Her grandmother pulled her close for a hug, then held her by the shoulders and smiled. "Carole, dear, look at you."

Carole felt her cheeks redden. She said the first thing that popped into her head. "Did you know Mama's having a baby?"

Grandma's smile disappeared. One second later, it was back, on her lips anyway.

Elsie looked confused. "I guess she hasn't had a chance to tell you. She's been unwell, hardly leaving the house."

"That's why I came. I was worried something had happened."

"Just a baby," Elsie said, leading Grandma Rosemarie up the stairs.

Her mother's belly was getting rounder and the rest of her was shrinking. Carole brought food to her room, but Mama said she wasn't hungry. Christmas and New Year's came and went, and pretty soon her mother hardly came out of her room at all. Papa and Elsie checked in on her all the time, so they were worrying, too, and Carole never asked the hundreds of questions she had about the baby so as not to be a bother.

One day after school, Carole went into her mother's room. It was so stuffy, Carole went straight to the window, threw open the drapes and pushed up the window.

Her mother shielded her eyes from the sudden light. "Close that, Carole. It's too cold."

"You told me fresh air is healthy."

"Please close it."

Carole hesitated, then waved some cool air inside before lowering the window. "Let's go for a walk. I can show you where they're building a new hotel."

"That's too far."

"Please?"

Her mother shook her head and pulled the covers up over her huge belly.

Carole tried to think of something, anything, they could do together. "What about a walk in the garden? That's not too far."

"Not today."

Carole sighed and chewed her fingernail. She came around to the front of the bed so her mother could see her doing it, but her mother didn't scold her. She didn't say a word.

"Can we play cards?"

Her mother didn't answer, which was poor manners, except when someone was ill.

Carole told herself to be patient. Soon she'd have her mother back, plus a new brother or sister. Her father would be happier, too, because he wouldn't have to worry about her mother and the baby anymore. Everyone would be fine. Better than fine.

Aunt Bettina and Uncle Tyler lived a few houses down the street and, as the baby's time got closer, her aunt came over nearly every day. She always had a smile ready, but Carole could tell she didn't approve of "the state of things," as she'd overheard Aunt Bettina say to Papa. Mama was stubborn, though, and with her belly so enormous, it was hard to make her do anything. Carole went to her parents' room with her schoolbooks and read and did her math exercises on the rug at the foot of the bed. When her mother fell asleep, she'd open the windows and let fresh, cool air in to help Mama be healthy for the baby.

On the Wednesday before Easter, Carole was playing jacks in her room, next to her parents' bedroom.

Her mother moaned loudly.

Carole dropped the jacks, let the ball bounce away and ran next door. Mama lay curled on her side, her eyes squeezed shut. Her forehead was sweaty and the cords in her neck were like the strings inside the piano.

"Mama! Is it the baby?" Carole was caught between fear for her mother and excitement that the baby would soon arrive. "Should I call Papa?"

Mama opened her eyes, rimmed in red. "The doctor. Call the doctor."

Carole ran down to the telephone, taking the stairs two at a time.

She didn't know whether her mother wanted her to call the doctor instead of her father. She called both. And Aunt Bettina. She called everyone.

Aunt Bettina arrived first. Elsie ran around the house with linens and towels and set water to boil on the stove.

Carole felt her mouth drop open. "What is *that* for?"

She slammed the lid on. "Don't get underfoot."

Carole jumped to the side, swallowing the millions of questions she had.

Papa strode into the kitchen like he was late for an important meeting. "Where's the doctor?"

Elsie shrugged. "Not in here."

He turned to Carole, noticing her for the first time. He gave her a quick smile, but he seemed worried, not happy. "Your aunt Regina is here to take you to her house."

Aunt Regina was her father's other sister, the older, crabbier one. Carole did not want to go anywhere, and certainly not with Aunt Regina.

"But I want to see the baby, Papa."

"You will, but not today."

"But—"

He kissed her cheek and left without a word. She ran after him into the hallway, around the corner and straight into the monstrous bosom of Aunt Regina, carrying a small suitcase belonging to Carole.

"I've packed a few things for you. Your uncle Harold is waiting in the car."

She opened her mouth to protest, saw the terrible look in her aunt's eyes and changed her mind.

"Come now, Carole. A birthing is no place for a young girl."

Carole followed her out, her mother's muffled screams in her ears.

19

Solange

Osborn appeared at her bedside and reached for her hand. A contraction seized her, a giant fist squeezed in rage, and she lurched away.

"It's not too late to go to the hospital, Solange."

It was too late. The contractions were only minutes apart. The pain rolled through her lower back and into her groin, a fierce hot pressure. She panted, waiting, counting. The contraction eased. She fell against the pillow. "No."

He let out an exasperated gasp. "But the doctor—"

"The doctor can have his babies wherever he wants. Is the midwife here?"

"She's in the kitchen instructing Elsie."

She nodded, saving her strength. Carole had been born in this house, but Osborn wanted a hospital birth because that's what all the wealthy women had now. Osborn's sister Regina had told her how they had drugs "so modern you didn't have to be awake for any of it." Solange needed her wits about her. She needed to see this child, to hold her in her first moments and know whose she was. "Her," because it was definitely a girl.

For her entire pregnancy, Solange had suffered in turmoil,

knowing the child's parentage would determine her fate but not knowing which outcome she dreaded more. If the child was Caleb's, Osborn might throw her out. That she could handle, even welcome, were it not for Carole, whom Solange was certain Osborn would withhold from her as punishment. Hadn't he shown himself capable of that? Solange had hardly been able to bear the sight of her daughter these long months, knowing what she had jeopardized. Self-recrimination had made Solange physically ill.

If the baby was Osborn's, Solange would be bound tighter to a man she neither loved nor respected. She would lose her integrity, what little she might yet salvage. Carole would hardly be better off living in such a household. Either way, the baby would be born into regret, and perhaps shame, and that, too, had sickened Solange. In her bleakest moments, her despair was so great she considered taking her own life, but her love for Carole and the blameless child inside her caused her to turn from that idea.

Another contraction gripped her. She gasped, clutching the bedspread. Osborn stared at her helplessly. He saw nothing but his wife in the throes of labor.

The contraction grew stronger, steel bands cinched tighter and tighter. The pain dissolved the sympathy she had for Osborn. She could not bear his obliviousness, especially of his own culpability. Not now.

She spoke through clenched teeth. "Leave. Please."

"I'll see if the doctor can come." He left, casting an uneasy glance over this shoulder.

The baby howled as the midwife wiped her down, swabbed alcohol on the cord and swaddled her. Solange was disoriented and couldn't guess how long the labor had lasted. Late in the birthing, when the contractions came so hard and fast she had no desire in her soul except that it would end, she'd been vaguely aware of a male voice barking orders. A pinch in her arm had followed, and she'd been floating since.

Yet her baby's cries pulled a warm throb from deep inside. The midwife handed the child to her, as one would pass a loaf of bread across a counter, and moved about the room collecting her belongings.

Elsie bundled up soiled linens and towels, paused at the foot of the bed and offered a tired smile. "I'll bring you a fresh washcloth in a minute. And some tea."

"Thank you." Her voice sounded as if it came from across the room.

She arranged the swaddled baby in the crook of her arm and pushed a bed pillow under her elbow for support. Her daughter whimpered, her face red and puckered from the trauma of coming into the world. As the baby quieted, the fullness of her lips became plain. Despite everything, Solange smiled at her daughter's innocent perfection.

One night with him, and this.

She unbuttoned her nightgown and gave her daughter her breast. She stroked the child's cheek with her fingertip and brushed the coal black strands from her tiny brow.

A damp layer of dread settled over Solange. "It's all right, little one."

Her first lie to her child.

She woke slowly, as if swimming up from a great depth. The room was dim. A dull ache pulsed in her groin. She placed her hand on her belly. The baby. Panic roused her. She rolled over to find Osborn in a chair beside the bed. In the bassinet next to him, the baby mewled.

"Are you all right, darling?" he asked.

She nodded, fear awakening in her chest, sending spikes down her arms. "Could you please give me the baby?"

He rose and lifted her with all of the tenderness he'd shown Carole as a newborn. Solange, groggy, pushed herself to sitting.

He placed the child in her arms. "She's beautiful."

"Yes." She slipped her nightdress from her shoulder, her fingers trembling.

"Elsie says black hair often falls out. A different color follows."

"I've heard that." She watched the child close her eyes in contentment, her tiny fist unfurling. Solange felt her husband's eyes on her. He sensed something was wrong, no doubt, but for months she'd hidden behind the pregnancy, the illness. Now the baby was here and did not belong to him. In anticipating this moment, she had vowed not to lie or pussyfoot around the truth. She might have gotten away with passing off the child as his—and had, in fact, considered it several times—but could not. This shred of honesty held all her remaining dignity.

Solange looked up from the baby and faced her husband. He smiled at her in the tired, cautious way he'd adopted. She pitied him for having fallen in love with her; he could not be responsible for that. Her pity exposed the revelation that if the child had been his, she would have stayed with him. She would have done her best for their daughters and, therefore, for him if the coin had landed the other way up.

Osborn saw the shift in her and edged forward in his chair. "Solange," he whispered.

The truth. He'd have to live with the truth. They all would.

"Osborn, you are not the father of this child."

He frowned. "What did you say?"

"This child is not yours."

"Not mine?" He sprang to his feet. "Not mine? What are you talking about, Solange?"

She tried to swallow but her mouth was dry.

Osborn's eyes narrowed. He was thinking of the last months, the last year, perhaps further back, perhaps unraveling their life to the beginning, slotting in this new information, recalibrating. "What are you saying? Are you saying you had an affair?"

"I'm sorry." And she was. For him. For herself. She was very sorry for the baby. And for Carole most of all.

"Sorry?" His voice was a keening. He paced the room, then halted suddenly. "Whose is it?"

"It doesn't matter."

He laughed, the first syllables bursting out, then sliding into a harrowing sound, like a dog that had been kicked. He stood rigid, his face knotted, his eyes searching.

"It matters to me! You are my wife! Who is it?"

"It doesn't matter."

"Do you love him?"

"No."

He balled his hands into fists, punched the air above his head, again and again. "You betray me. You destroy our family, and for what?"

Solange drew her knees up, held the baby closer. Her heart beat in her ears.

Osborn strode to the closed door as if he meant to go straight through it, then took two steps toward the bed and thrust his finger at her. "You won't have Carole! Whatever you do, whatever it is you think you want in this world, you will not have Carole!"

He yanked the door open and slammed it as he left. The baby startled as if electrocuted and released a cry Solange felt in her marrow.

20

Carole

Early the next morning, Carole awoke, confused at first by the too-heavy bedclothes and the strange angle of the light. Remembering where she was, she found her robe on a chair by the bed and ran downstairs to the breakfast room where Aunt Regina sipped her tea and Uncle Harold hid behind the *Free Press*.

Carole flew to her aunt's side, her heart fluttering. "Is the baby here?"

"'Good morning' would be a better start."

"I'm sorry! Good morning! But what about the baby?"

She set her teacup onto the saucer. "Late last night, your mother gave birth to a girl."

Carole's breath caught in her throat. "When can I see her? Can we go now?"

"No, we certainly cannot. Your mother needs to rest. Now get dressed and brush your hair. You look like a ragamuffin."

Carole was trapped at Aunt Regina's for three more nights before she decided to take charge of things. Even if her mother was tired, Carole knew she could help her, not add to her burden. It was Easter Sunday. She would have left first thing that morning, but missing church on Easter seemed a poor idea, adding to the deceit of leaving the house without permission. After church, she told her aunt she had a stomachache and went to her room. She put on her most comfortable shoes and a sweater and crept downstairs. The voices of her aunt and uncle came from the parlor, and someone clattered in the kitchen. She slinked down the hall and out the back door.

She knew the way home. It was far, maybe three miles, but she was determined to meet her new sister. She hurried along the sidewalk, leaping over mud puddles and making sure to watch for vehicles at the corners. The sun heated her back and the air smelled of garden soil and earthworms. Here and there, tender green shoots had appeared. Daffodils, maybe. Her stomach growled and she realized she hadn't eaten since before services. Maybe, she thought, after she held the baby for a while and helped her mother, she could go to Aunt Bettina's for Easter dinner with her father. Or they could save her a plate.

She entertained herself by picturing what the baby would look like. Her feet became sore—she wasn't used to so much walking—and once she almost got lost, but soon the neighborhood became familiar and she knew she was home. Home free!

Carole ran up the steps but hesitated at the door. She would have to be careful not to be caught and sent back to Aunt Regina's before she saw her mother and her sister. She opened the door slowly—it was always unlocked during the day—and was relieved to see the parlor empty. She headed for the stairs, listening for sounds from the kitchen or from the hall that led to her father's office.

A grating noise—a pot sliding across the stove—came from the kitchen. Elsie, probably.

She must be quick! Her heart beat in her ears as she tiptoed up the stairs, scurried down the corridor to her parents' room and listened at the door.

Silence.

She twisted the knob and went in.

Sunlight spilled in through the tall windows. Her mother was in bed, the covers pulled to her chin, and seemed to be asleep. Carole approached the bassinet beside the bed and peered in. The baby was awake, her dark eyes wide, her pink bow of a mouth shaped in a little circle of surprise. How small she was! A warm, syrupy feeling flowed into Carole's arms and legs. She smiled at her sister and reached for her. She didn't dare pick her up—she'd never held a baby and dolls didn't count—so she stroked the baby's cheek with a finger, marveling at how impossibly soft her skin was. Carole felt her sister's hair, fine and black.

"You're beautiful."

The baby's face pulled tight like a string purse, then her mouth opened in a yawn. It was the sweetest thing Carole had ever seen.

"Carole." Her mother's voice was hoarse.

"Mama." Carole moved to the bed and kissed her cheek. Her mother's eyelids seemed too heavy for her. Her hair was unwashed and lay in strands on the pillow. "Are you all right?"

She nodded. "The doctor gave me something. I just sleep and sleep."

"The baby's so small, and so cute."

"Yes. She's perfect." Mama closed her eyes like she was hurting. "You'll be a good sister to her, won't you? Watch over her?"

"Sure, Mama." Something in the way her mother said it made Carole's insides twist. "I can help you with her. I really want to. Can't I come home now?"

Her mother turned away. "That's for your father to decide."

Carole waited for her to speak again, but she appeared to have dozed off. Carole thought of her words. Maybe all mothers asked the big sister to watch over the little sister. What about Papa? Wouldn't he look after the baby, too?

The infant gurgled. Carole got up from the bed, knelt by the bassinette and stroked her sister's tummy until she quieted.

Downstairs, the door chimes sounded. Carole went to the bedroom

door and opened it a crack. She didn't know how much trouble she'd
be in if her father caught her—she was only visiting her own mother
and sister—but Mama's words had made her wary.

A man and a woman spoke near the door, but she couldn't make
out the words. As they moved farther into the parlor, closer to the
stairs, Carole recognized her father's voice and, she thought, Aunt
Bettina's. Papa's tone was harsh, worse than when he argued with
her mother. Carole slipped into the hallway and left the door ajar
behind her.

Papa bit off his words. "She won't say who it is." The woman
replied too softly for Carole to hear. Her father spoke again. "How
do you expect me to remain calm?"

The woman said, "Such a dreadful accusation. Are you certain?" It was definitely her aunt.

"She admitted it. Why do you think I'm like this?"

Aunt Bettina's voice was steady. "And what will you tell Carole?"

Their voices faded as they moved off, deeper into the house,
where Carole could not imagine what was said next.

She returned to the bedroom, thinking she would say good-bye
and go back to Regina's before she got into trouble. The baby
mewled and a moment later began crying in earnest. Her mother
was sleeping, so Carole went to the bassinet. She slipped her hands
under the swaddled infant and picked her up. The baby's head
drooped and she cried more loudly, her face red and pinched. Carole cupped her sister's head, held her to her chest and brought her
to the window.

"Look outside. It's a pretty day."

The baby did not look out the window. She cried and cried, no
matter what Carole did. She rocked her in the bassinet, sang her
songs and talked to her about the cottage at the beach. "It's a
wonderful place. We'll make sand castles and eat ice cream every
day. I'll show you the tide pools where the starfish live."

Finally, the baby drifted off to sleep and Carole crept downstairs. Voices came from the kitchen, and she slid down the hallway to the door where she could hear easily.

Papa was angry. "Regina agrees, by the way. I spoke with her earlier. 'Toss them to the dogs' was her suggestion."

Before Carole could wonder who "them" might be, Aunt Bettina spoke. "Osborn, remember you are a Christian man."

"What would you have me do, then? I have a place in this community. I have earned respect. Solange had a place as well, as a reflection of me. As a courtesy. Now look!"

"Calm yourself. Your anger isn't doing anyone any good."

Carole heard her father pacing. "You know what I think? It's her bad blood. Perkins had it right. You can't change what's in the blood. Blood will tell."

Who was Perkins? And how could blood tell anything?

Papa kept talking, his voice sharp. "And wantonness is in the germ plasm. Perkins proved that."

What was "wantingness"? Or "germ plasm"? Carole's palms were slick with sweat. Her father's words didn't make sense, but she could tell something was very wrong.

A cup rattled against a saucer and a chair scraped the floor. Aunt Bettina said, "Osborn, that's enough of that talk."

"I need some air." Hinges creaked. Her father was going into the yard.

"Fine. I'll check on Solange."

Carole jumped in alarm and raced toward the front door as quietly as she could. She twisted the doorknob and glanced over her shoulder.

"Carole." Her aunt kept her voice low. "What are you doing here?"

Aunt Bettina looked sad and tired, but not angry. Carole explained about wanting to see her sister and her mother. She didn't let on about what she'd overheard, not that it made much sense anyway.

"You poor dear. Why don't you go on to my house while I see to your mother."

"Why can't I stay here? I can help you with the baby."

Her aunt's brow furrowed and she blinked several times. Why was everyone so upset and nervous?

Aunt Bettina opened the front door and shooed her out. "Your mother must rest. You can stay with me. I'll have a word with your father."

Carole expected to be able to see her mother whenever she wanted, now that she was only a few doors away, but she was wrong. Aunt Bettina made gentle excuses and insisted Carole go to school as usual. How could she possibly pay attention? She almost asked her aunt about what she'd overheard in the kitchen—especially about wantingness and bad blood—but decided she'd have to get her own answers. Her father joined them for dinner most evenings, so tense and frayed that he seemed about to shatter. He was nothing like the father she knew; she almost wished he wouldn't come. Carole stopped asking to see her mother and pretended not to be curious about the harsh whisperings she heard behind closed doors. Instead, she was patient.

Exactly a week after she'd arrived at her aunt and uncle's, she woke before dawn, dressed in the clothes she'd laid out the night before and slipped out the back door by the kitchen. A light rain fell and she hurried along the sidewalk, her feet confident on the familiar path, her head down so she wouldn't see the reach of the dark.

In a few minutes Carole arrived at her house and climbed the rain-slick steps with care. She turned the doorknob but it wouldn't budge. How could she have forgotten it would be locked? She'd waited a week and now this. Her nose stung with tears and she rubbed it with a damp hand. She remembered, then, the key for the back door. Elsie was always misplacing hers, so they'd hidden one in a planter.

Carole crept into the kitchen, closing the door gently behind her. Her wet shoes squeaked on the floor, so she took them off and carried them through the hall and up the stairs. A light shone under her parents' bedroom door—really, her mother's now. Carole hesitated, debating whether to knock, wondering if Papa was also inside. Holding her breath, she let herself in.

Mama clutched the baby to her chest like someone was about to snatch the baby away. As soon as she saw Carole, she smiled broadly and signaled her to close the door. Tears flooded her mother's eyes as she held out her arm to Carole.

"You've come."

21

Solange

Carole slipped into the room like an angel answering a prayer and folded herself into Solange's embrace.

"You've come."

"They don't know I'm here." Her daughter's gaze fell to the small suitcase beside the bed.

Hours ago, Solange had tossed clothes for her and the baby into the suitcase without considering what she might need. She'd refused the pills for two days now and was no longer groggy, but the path forward had not become any clearer. Her thoughts were swamped by guilt, dread and despair. She should do something to aid herself and her baby, but what? What? Carole was under Osborn's control; what could Solange do to alter that?

She smiled at her daughter and guided Carole's chin with two fingers so their foreheads nearly touched. "Will you help me? Will you come with me?"

"Where?"

"To the lake." She glanced at the baby. "To her home. Our home."

"Why, Mama? Why can't we all stay here? Why can't we stay with Papa?"

"We have to go now. Hold her."

She pressed the bundle into Carole's arms and scurried to her dressing room. Clothes were scattered on the floor, hanging out of half-open drawers. Scarves and shoes and baby things covered every surface.

Solange had awoken earlier, in the dark, from shallow sleep. The baby had been crying in earnest. She reached for the bedside lamp and switched it on. She startled, knocking over a water glass.

Osborn stood by the bassinet, in silhouette. He dangled the child in front of him, his hands around her chest, her gown crumpled between his fingers. His jaw was set in a hard line.

Solange kicked off the covers and pushed herself upright. "Osborn! What are you doing?"

He ignored her and squeezed harder. The baby wailed, her face bright red.

Solange leapt from the bed.

"Stop!" She pulled at his wrists, clawed at his fingers. The baby shrieked. Without warning, Osborn released his grip and the baby dropped into Solange's hands. Solange drew her close, ran into the dressing room and shut the door. There was no lock. She leaned her back against the door, her heart hammering, and listened as Osborn's footsteps retreated. The door from the bedroom to the hallway opened, then closed. She'd soothed the baby, rocking and murmuring to her. How much time passed, she didn't know. She'd packed a suitcase without her own awareness.

Now Carole had appeared. Solange took it as a sign.

She roughly knotted her hair at her nape and swung a black hooded cloak over her shoulders. Returning to the bedroom, she grabbed a blanket from a chair, took the baby from Carole's arms and wrapped her securely.

"The suitcase, Carole. Now."

"But, Mama—"

"Shhh."

Solange slid into the hall, her pulse quickening. She concentrated on keeping her steps light, being careful not to miss a stair in the near darkness, willing the baby not to cry. At the door, she unlocked the deadbolt, and she and Carole stole into the dawn, obscured by drizzle.

Light-headed and weak, Solange weaved along the sidewalk. The act of leaving had taken all her strength. Carole tried to steady her, and asked her again and again what they were doing. Solange didn't respond. It was all she could do to hold on to the baby and continue walking. The shadowy hedges and looming trees menaced her, and every few steps she glanced over her shoulder to see if someone was following them. No one was there, but she walked faster, nearly running. Her legs felt like stilts and her breathing was ragged.

Carole pulled at her arm to slow her. "Mama!"

"We have to hurry!"

"Why?"

Solange heard the desperate tears in her daughter's voice but could do nothing about them. Escape. That was all that mattered.

They neared the waterfront. A handful of people moved along the docks or toward the town. Panic rose inside Solange. No one could have known she was coming. The baby fussed. Solange jiggled her as she hurried past a group of men smoking and staring at the lake. She passed one dock after another, searching for a familiar boat, praying her family, or someone she knew, would appear.

Solange stumbled on the steps leading to the last pair of docks and pitched forward. Carole grabbed her shoulder, breaking her fall. The suitcase clattered to the ground. Solange landed on her back, the baby clutched against her chest.

Carole squatted beside her. "Mama, are you hurt?"

She sat up slowly, her insides churning, her mind flooded with fear.

Planks along the dock rattled. A figure loomed over her. A man. David. He knelt beside her. "What's wrong?"

"Help me."

A whistle sliced the air. Two policemen ran toward them brandishing billy clubs. Behind them, Osborn, his coat flying open.

Carole jumped up. "Papa!"

Solange screamed.

David stepped forward to block the policemen.

The one in front, built like a dray horse, raised his club and bared his teeth. "Stand back! Get away from her!"

The other moved to the side to corner David.

"Grab her!" Osborn ordered. "For God's sake, grab her!"

Solange staggered to her feet, sidled toward Carole and thrust the baby into her arms. "Protect her."

A policeman yanked Solange by the arm. Her hood fell back, her hair flew in her face. She kicked at his shins. "You can't do this! You can't!" The policeman twisted her arm into her back. She cried out in pain.

As he dragged her toward a van parked in the lot, the other policeman swung his club at David's head. David ducked and drove his fist into the policeman's stomach. Osborn reached for the baby in Carole's arms.

"No!" Solange tried to wrest herself free.

"Cut it out, lady!" The policeman jammed her arm farther up her back.

Solange collapsed.

The sharp bite of metal on her wrists. The cries of her child, her baby. Both her babies.

Inside the van, black silence.

22

Carole

The policeman pushed her mother into the van.

"Papa! Stop them!" Carole started toward them, but her father caught her arm.

"Carole, give me the baby."

He was angry, about to burst, and Carole was afraid. "I want to hold her." The baby was crying, so Carole rubbed her back. She looked around for Uncle David, but he'd disappeared. Both policemen were climbing into the van.

"Papa, what's going on?"

He was watching the policemen, too. "Your mother isn't well." He turned to her, stern. "You could see that, couldn't you?"

She nodded. Her mother was definitely not well. Running out of the house with the baby didn't seem right. Then again, nothing about any of this seemed right to her. It was a big mess and she didn't understand any of it, only that she was scared. "Where are they taking Mama?"

"To the doctor." He stared at his feet.

Tears flooded her nose, her eyes. "Papa—"

A car pulled up to the roped barrier as the police van drove away.

"Here's Bettina and Tyler." Her father guided her toward the car. "Your aunt called me when she realized you were gone. You worried us."

Without a word, her aunt took the baby from her. Carole slid into the backseat, numb and hollow inside, her arms tingling from holding her sister for so long.

As they drove up the hill, Carole asked her aunt and uncle where the police had taken her mother and why. She didn't completely believe her father. Her uncle said nothing, as usual. Aunt Bettina told her she didn't know, and it seemed to be the truth.

That night, Carole couldn't sleep, and thought about sneaking off to her house again, in case her mother was there, but was afraid to leave the baby. She had promised to watch over her.

The sun rose weakly in a gray sky. All day, Carole went from window to window, as if her mother might appear. A woman, a stranger, nursed the baby. Carole held her sister the rest of the time and napped fitfully in the sitting room, waiting for someone to tell her what had happened to her mother. She made a bet with herself that if she took good care of her sister, her mother would come back.

Late in the afternoon, her father came to the house, greeted her with a solemn nod and went to the parlor to whisper with her aunt. Carole put her ear to the door but her aunt's maid shooed her away. After what seemed like hours, her father and her aunt came into the sitting room where Carole held the baby in her lap. Her aunt took a seat beside her.

Her father stood with his arms folded. "Your mother's in a special hospital called Underhill."

"Why? What's wrong with her?"

"She's resting. There are doctors and nurses to look after her."

"Why can't she rest at home? Or here?"

Aunt Bettina spoke carefully. "You know how ill she was the whole time she was carrying your sister." Carole nodded. "It's taken a toll. She's not herself. She became very agitated at the police station."

"Out of control," her father said.

Carole turned to him. His grim face worried her even more. "How long until she's better? How long until she's home?"

"The doctor couldn't guess."

"Can I see her?"

He shook his head. "No." He swallowed hard. "I'm sorry."

Carole felt the floor dropping away beneath her. She remembered what she'd overheard in the kitchen. "Is it because of her wantingness?"

Aunt Bettina exchanged a questioning look with Carole's father. Of course they didn't know Carole had been snooping.

Her aunt put her fingers to her lips. "Her wantingness. Well, maybe."

"What is it?"

"It's when you want something you can't have. Or shouldn't have."

Her father threw up his hands. "For the love of God!"

A thousand questions zinged through Carole's mind, but before she could settle on the right one, her aunt spoke again. "That's enough for now. These are the cards we've been dealt, and there's a baby that needs us."

There was nothing Carole could do except nod.

Her mother had told her a while ago that Aunt Bettina had wanted children, but they'd never appeared. Now it seemed like she'd forgotten she ever wanted any. She wasn't mean to Carole or the baby, but she didn't dote on them, either. The nurse tended to the baby. When Carole was not in school, she rocked and sang to her fussy sister, modeling herself after the nurse, and was occasionally rewarded with a toothless smile.

Carole's longing for her mother seemed larger than she was, an illness she felt everywhere inside her, and it played with her mind. She'd believed she spotted her mother walking down the sidewalk, or across a field near the school, and a fresh sadness filled her when she realized she was mistaken. She'd had her mother every day of her life, had relied without knowing it on the unspoken and unquestionable bond between them, and now she was gone.

Carole poured her longing into her sister as if it were milk. It was the only thing to do. Carole saw her father at her aunt's house, mostly, because being at their house without her mother was strange; sadness hung in the rooms like a mist. Carole loved her father, but he had edges now, and moods. The first few times she saw him, he asked her to come home to stay. She had refused—she wouldn't leave the baby—and that left a giant gap between them. Carole felt torn in two, wanting to be with her father and make him happy like she'd always been able to do, and wanting to keep her promise to her mother to be a good big sister. She couldn't do both, and the baby was little and needed her, so Carole stayed at Aunt Bettina's, wishing her mother would come home, wishing her father would start loving the baby, and knowing deep in her heart things would never be the same again. At night, she sometimes dreamt of being with her parents at the beach house, with the baby, too. She awoke, tasted salt on her lips, and felt more alone than ever when she discovered it was only tears.

Two weeks after her mother had been taken to Underhill, her father came to Aunt Bettina and Uncle Tyler's for dinner. While they ate, the adults talked about boring things, mostly a man named Hitler. The maid brought dessert, then cleared the dishes, and her aunt and uncle left to have coffee in the sitting room. Her father stayed where he was like he was frozen.

Carole crossed her arms and pulled at the skin on her elbows, pinching and twisting it until it hurt. One elbow was scabbed from doing this before. She picked at the scab until she felt blood ooze. That gave her the nerve to ask the question she'd been holding on to.

"Papa?"

He folded his napkin, as if he hadn't heard.

"Papa?"

He looked at her, surprised to see her there. "Yes. What is it?"

"Why don't you like the baby?"

He blinked hard. The granddaughter clock in the corner ticked and ticked. Her father's eyes glassed over and tears slid down his cheeks.

"Papa?" Carole had never seen him cry.

He stared at the table and shook his head over and over.

Carole didn't ask again, but she thought it over long and hard. The best she could figure was that her father, and her aunts, blamed the baby for making her mother tired and sick and full of wantingness. It seemed wrong to blame a baby, but Carole knew it was impossible to change adults' minds. The baby would have to do without her father, just as she was doing without her mother. Both Carole and her sister would have to do without their parents, who were tangled up in a terrible web made of invisible silk.

Carole did her very best. She told her sister again and again how much their mother loved her. Saying it reminded her that her mother loved her, too. But with each day that passed, it felt more like a reminder and less like a fact.

One afternoon in May, a month after Carole's mother had gone, Rosemarie Bouchard, Carole's grandmother, appeared at Aunt Bettina's house. School had let out for the summer, and Carole was settling the baby into the pram in a patch of sun near the front porch. The baby was crying as usual, but Carole was used to it and hummed over the top of the noise as if crying were another kind of singing.

Grandma Rosemarie swung open the low iron gate at the end of the walk and came up to them. Her dress, once red but now a dusky pink, was tied at the waist with a man's leather belt. She carried a large quilted satchel and her graying hair was gathered in a long, loose braid. The braid, and of course Grandma's face, too, brought to mind her mother so vividly that Carole had to blink away the rush of tears. The last time she'd seen her grandmother was in the winter when she'd come asking after Carole's mother. So much had happened since then.

"Hi, Grandma."

"Hello, my dear girl." She gave Carole a hug, then held her by the shoulders. "You're skinny as a switch." Her eyes were somewhere between gray and green, like her mother's, but didn't hold the same light. "I hope your aunt won't mind I stopped by."

"She won't." As soon as she said it, she realized it might not be true. She wasn't exactly sure how her aunt felt about her mother's family, but if she had to guess, Aunt Bettina didn't approve of them any more than the rest of her father's family did. She was just more careful about what she said. Uncertain what to say, Carole bent over the pram and fussed with the baby.

Grandma said, "I'll only stay a moment." She came beside Carole and peered into the pram. She reached in and laid her hand on the baby's chest, exactly as Carole had done the first time she'd seen her. "Doing battle with the world already, are you, wee one?" The baby stopped crying, opened her eyes wide, then set off howling again. Grandma's mouth was a thin line.

"Mama's at Underhill," Carole said before she knew she would.

"I know. I'm sorry for you." She placed her palm on Carole's cheek.

An ache filled Carole's chest. "Have you seen her?"

"We tried. Went to see her doctor in town, but he said he couldn't tell us anything."

"Why not?"

"Rules, he said."

"But I want to go to see her. Can you take me?"

She frowned. "Tried that, too. Your uncle David borrowed a car and we drove all the way out there. 'No unapproved visitors,' they told us."

"How long will she be there? No one will tell me."

Grandma shook her head slowly. "I haven't any idea." She touched Carole's cheek again. "I'd best be going." She leaned over the pram and kissed the baby's forehead.

Carole had so many more questions—about her mother, about her father, about Underhill—but her grandmother didn't seem to have any answers.

Grandma Rosemarie said, "Your father's family will take care of you. I know they will. But if you need us, you know where we are."

Carole pictured the shabby houseboat, the narrow berths, the rats scurrying along the docks, but she didn't want to be impolite. "Thank you, Grandma."

Her grandmother started to leave, then paused and pointed at the pram. "You ought to give her a name."

"Me?"

"Who else, my dear?"

Carole watched Grandma Rosemarie amble down the sidewalk, round the corner and disappear onto Orchard Terrace. A wide swath of longing for her mother opened inside her, a longing so familiar and yet powerful enough to make her unsteady on her feet. The baby wailed—Carole had ignored her too long.

She picked her up, dabbed her face with a corner of the blanket and held her to her shoulder. Her sister's wriggling warmth calmed her. "What should we call you, then? Nothing too plain. You're too precious to be a plain Jane."

Four years later, when Carole was fourteen, her father announced he was joining the navy. She knew he'd registered for the draft two years before—all the men had—but she never imagined he would actually go to war.

She and her father were walking home from a Fourth of July celebration at Aunt Regina's house. It was a small, quiet party, because of the war. Aunt Bettina had left early to put Janine to bed. The air was moist and still as they ducked under the leaf-heavy branches along the street.

Carole's step slowed. "Do you have to go, Papa?"

"Yes. It's my patriotic duty."

Carole reached for her elbows, running her fingers along the raised scars. She pinched each spot hard, digging into the soft, fresh skin around the scars, then let her arms fall to her sides. The sweet release from the pain flowed into her belly.

No one as old as her father had to fight in the war, not unless being a soldier was their job. She knew that from school and from conversations behind closed doors. She'd overheard Aunt Bettina pleading with her father to reconsider, reminding him of "his responsibilities."

He'd laughed bitterly. "I might as well go where I can do some good."

He was leaving in a matter of days, and she wanted him to change his mind or at least to say he was coming back, to promise. But she wasn't a silly girl. She understood you didn't leave for war and make promises, not ones you intended to keep. She wanted him to say it anyway, to try to make up in some way for leaving her and her sister.

The day her father left for basic training, her aunt called her from her room to say good-bye. Carole hesitated on the stair landing.

He stood at the door holding his hat, a brown leather bag at his side. His expression was stony, and she saw behind it that he wasn't leaving because he needed to go, but because he couldn't stay.

She ran down the stairs and into his embrace, as she had done countless times in her childhood.

"Be good, my darling Carole."

She watched him go without a word.

Less than a year after Carole's father was sent to fight the Japanese, Aunt Bettina and Uncle Tyler decided to move to Buffalo to bring his metal engineering business closer to the manufacturing centers. Carole and her sister had no choice but to live with Aunt Regina, a situation that pleased no one. The woman would hardly look at five-year-old Janine, and repeatedly threatened to throw her out on the streets or into the harbor. The girl's willfulness did nothing to help. Regina's husband, Harold, a taciturn property broker, never countermanded his wife, especially where children were concerned, as she had raised four fine boys without his interference.

After the girls moved in, Carole got up the nerve to confront her aunt about her attitude toward Janine.

"Why are you so harsh with her?"

Her aunt's eyebrows shot up. "Why am I so harsh? A better question is why we consented to take her in at all. And if you wish to stay here, you'd better not bring it up again!"

With no levers at her disposal, Carole protected her sister's feelings as best she could.

The week before Christmas, Carole lied about visiting a friend and hired a driver to take her to Underhill. The absence of both her father and Aunt Bettina had ignited Carole's desire to reconnect with her mother, whom she hadn't seen in five years, but whom she still hoped would recover and be restored to her. Aunt Regina refused to take her to the hospital, so she decided to act on her own.

The snow-covered grounds and brick buildings were imposing and much larger than she'd expected. As she entered the main

building, her excitement and anxiety turned to shock. In her imagination, Underhill was a restful haven, filled with soft furnishings,
colorful paintings and vases of fresh flowers, more of a hotel than
this harsh, gray prison. Carole's mouth felt lined with tissue as she
approached the main desk. A matronly nurse in a white uniform
greeted her.

"I'd like to see Solange Gifford, please? I'm Carole. Gifford."

"One moment."

The nurse consulted a piece of paper attached to the desk, op-
erated the switchboard and spoke briefly. A few minutes later, a
slight man in a short white coat came through a side door.

"I'm Dr. Bishop." He shook her hand and ushered her into a
small consulting room.

Carole took a chair and introduced herself. "I'm here to see my
mother."

"I'm afraid Mrs. Gifford cannot see anyone at this time. She is
asleep."

Asleep. It sounded hopeful, and normal. "I can wait."

He smiled. "We are in the midst of administering a deep-sleep
treatment in combination with twice weekly electroconvulsive
shock therapy. She will be asleep—that is, under deep sedation—for
a month, possibly longer."

The blood rushed from Carole's head and she gripped the arms
of the chair. "For a month?"

"Or longer."

"That can't possibly be good for her. It's not normal."

The doctor raised his eyebrows, indignant. "I assure you the
treatment is perfectly safe. All the best hospitals are using it." He
leaned back in his chair, interlacing his fingers behind his head. "I
recently took over for Dr. Schulkyl, her former physician. He'd given
your mother day-long colonics for quite some time. That was his
pet treatment. A bit—how shall I say?—European for my tastes."

"Colonics? To treat what?"

"Dr. Schulkyl prescribed it for most illnesses. Your mother's current diagnosis is depression."

"What was it before?"

He shrugged. "She hasn't been in my care long. Hysteria, most likely."

Hysteria. It brought to mind her father saying her mother had been out of control. Carole pressed on. "And you can treat depression with sleep? And shock?"

"I wouldn't prescribe it otherwise."

"Of course. I only meant—" The doctor peered at her with interest, and Carole shifted in her chair. The room was close and too warm. She thought of her mother here, in this bleak place, and guilt overwhelmed her. She should have come a long time ago. She should have tried harder. Her chest tightened. Tears welled and she hid her face.

Dr. Bishop said, "Are you all right?"

She nodded. "It's only that I haven't seen her for so long."

"I understand. It's a very difficult situation."

Carole searched through her jumbled thoughts. "How long will it take, the cure?"

"'Cure' is a hopeful word, Miss Gifford. Your mother has been ill for five years. It's wise to be realistic."

Carole had never been a dreamer, but realistic is exactly what she became, not only about her mother's prognosis, but generally. She accepted that her sister would always be headstrong and self-centered. She was realistic about her father as well, admitting to herself that his decision to go to war at age thirty-nine had less to do with patriotism than it did with despair, and that she would probably never understand the cause of it. Carole was also realistic about hope, which she could hold in abundance and yet never have enough.

But realism, as helpful as it was, was insufficient. Like ration cards, realism never went far enough. In the places where her logical mind, stretched to breaking, failed to reach, Carole was exposed and utterly abandoned. At times she could not stop herself from fixating on the monstrous unfairness of it, and the exposed places went from raw to red-hot. Rage flamed inside her.

23

Carole

Carole arranged the spaghetti straps across her collarbones and pivoted to view the back of the dress in the mirror. Tangerine lace over peach taffeta wasn't her first choice, but Aunt Regina was in charge—as usual. The color was cheery for November, though, and the enormous bow at the back made her smile.

Her aunt had proposed the party a month ago. "We didn't celebrate your sixteenth properly because of the *war*"—stressing the word to reinforce her disapproval of the personal inconvenience it had caused—"but now that it's over, your eighteenth can make up for it, within the bounds of decorum." Carole understood her aunt's elliptical reference. The war wasn't quite over for them because her father had been missing in action since February. She hadn't realized how much his sporadic letters had meant until they stopped arriving. There was very little news of him in those pages, but his questions and speculations about life at home helped maintain the rickety idea that she had a father who cared about her.

Carole was wondering which of her shoes would suit the dress when Janine burst into the room. "Wow. You look like an exploded orange." She began to giggle.

Carole smiled at her. "I'll have you know exploded fruit is all the rage this season."

Janine stood with her feet apart, arms akimbo. "Where's *my* dress?"

"I have it right here." Carole dipped into the closet and retrieved the dress she'd pieced together from others she'd outgrown. It was white taffeta with a pink lace overlay, similar in style to her birthday dress. She displayed it for Janine.

Her sister's mouth dropped open. She didn't like being caught off guard and quickly pursed her lips. "I guess it'll have to do."

Carole wasn't fooled. Janine loved it. "Want to try it on?"

She helped her into the dress and spun her to face the mirror. "Look how beautiful you are!"

Janine raised her arms in a ballerina pose and tiptoed in a circle.

Aunt Regina strode into the room without knocking. "Carole, we'll be late for the hairdressers—" She stopped short and raised her eyebrows at Janine. "Where did that dress come from?"

The girl lifted her chin and jammed her hand onto a cocked hip. "None of your business."

Aunt Regina's nostrils flared. Carole stepped between them. "I made it for her. For the party."

"Your birthday party? With all of our friends? I don't think so."

"She can sit with Ruth and Emma." Her best friends—her only friends—wouldn't mind.

Her aunt shook her head.

Janine said, "I'm going. Carole invited me and it's her party."

Regina ignored her. "I won't have her there, Carole. It's impossible."

Janine slid her hand into her sister's. Carole squeezed it, hoping Janine would feel her love and not the frustration building inside her. Her aunt's treatment of Janine was harsh, even accounting for the woman's gruff nature. Carole had always supported Janine without directly confronting Regina—the two of them, after all, had nowhere else to go—but lately she'd found it increasingly difficult not to speak her mind.

Breathing deeply to quash her frustration, Carole knelt in front of the girl. "I have a few more stitches to finish on the dress, so let's take it off for now." Janine complied. Carole slipped her sister's wool dress over her head and fastened the buttons. "Why don't you go downstairs for a bit?"

Janine frowned and stomped across the room. She paused at the door and glowered at her aunt. "You're a witch!" She fled the room.

Aunt Regina's face was red and her bosom heaved. "That's precisely what I mean. She's not fit for polite society."

Carole squared her shoulders. "What do you expect?"

"I beg your pardon?"

"What do you expect, considering how you treat her?" Carole swallowed hard. Her habitual impulse was to apologize before her aunt could respond, but her anger was too large. It would tear her apart from the inside if she denied it.

Her aunt narrowed her eyes. "It's not your place to comment."

"Yes, it is. She's my sister! And you've never been fair to her."

"Fair? Your uncle and I took you both in. We should've realized what trouble that girl would be."

"Stop calling her 'that girl'! And how do you expect her to behave when you show absolutely no love for her? If you kick a dog every day, you can bet it will learn to bite!"

Her aunt froze. Carole had never raised her voice to her, not once. She'd always been calm and reasonable. Compensating for Janine's unruly behavior was part of fulfilling her promise to her mother.

Aunt Regina sniffed as if Carole had wounded her. "Because it's your birthday, I will overlook that outburst. But don't think I won't remember if you dare speak to me that way again." She headed out of the room.

Carole followed, her muscles strung tight, her face burning. "If Janine can't come then I'm not going!"

Her aunt glared at her. "Don't make threats, Carole. It's unbecoming."

"I mean it. You can't make me go." She heard the childishness in her words, but it was too late to back down.

"You'll go. Everyone is expecting you."

"Then let Janine come."

"I've made up my mind, Carole. Don't be impertinent."

"Janine's right. You are a witch!"

Aunt Regina's voice was dead calm. Only the quivering of her jowls betrayed her. "I've been so pleased, relieved even, to see so much of your father in you. But now I see your mother as well. What a shame."

Carole's fury, blinding hot only seconds ago, dissolved into a bitter pool of sadness and pain at the mention of her mother. What she would give to have her here, to hold her. Through her tears, Carole watched her aunt turn down the hall and descend the stairs. She thought to run after her, make her account for her words, but instead Carole returned to her room.

Her hands shook as she untied the bow of her dress. How was she more like her mother now? Because she'd spoken out on behalf of her sister? She recalled, as she had so many times, her father's explanation for why her mother had been sent to Underhill: she had been "out of control." "Hysteria," the doctor had said. Carole's rage had erupted to the surface from some unknown and unexplored depth, but that wasn't the same as being hysterical. Or was it? Maybe this was the beginning.

She wiped her tears. A chill came over her. She unfastened the opening along her side, stepped out of the dress and put on woolen stockings, a knit dress and a sweater. She hoped her aunt was on the telephone canceling the party, because Carole was not going to change her mind. Her heart ached at the realization that she would always remember her eighteenth birthday this way. Maybe she could salvage something. She went to the window to check on the weather. The air was brittle with cold, but at least it was clear. Maybe she would take Janine to the Woolworth counter—her favorite.

A bicyclist wheeled down the street toward the house. At first Carole thought it was the boy who delivered telegrams—not many people rode bicycles in November—and immediately thought someone had sent her a birthday telegram. Who would do that except her father? A thrill awakened in her at the possibility he was safe.

But as the bicyclist neared, Carole realized it was not a boy at all, but a man. He dismounted and leaned the bicycle against the fence bordering the street. As he faced the house and straightened his coat, she saw it was Mr. Balducci, the manager of the Western Union office on Pearl Street, a kindly man, aged visibly over the four years he'd been charged with these grim errands. The blood drained from her head. She closed her eyes, hoping she had imagined him, and that it really was the boy, or no one at all.

She opened her eyes. Mr. Balducci strode toward the door with a heavy step. Before he disappeared under the porch eave, he removed his hat.

24

Carole

She made her way downstairs on wooden legs, her head floating somewhere above where it ought to have been. Her aunt's sobbing filled the air, a sound out of proportion with the slim needle that pierced straight through Carole's heart, preventing her from taking full breaths or moving too quickly. She wished her aunt would be quiet. Her noise was monstrous.

Uncle Harold was at the front door, supporting his wife under the arms, moving her toward the parlor in a slow shuffling dance, his back to Carole. Mr. Balducci had gone. Carole followed her aunt and uncle with mincing steps so as not to dislodge the needle and puncture a lung, or something else. The pain made her dizzy.

Her uncle deposited her aunt on the settee and arranged a cushion behind her head. Despite her wailing, her aunt's face was dry. Uncle Harold knelt and clutched his wife's hand.

Janine appeared at Carole's side. "What happened?"

Carole picked up her sister. She was heavy, too big to carry, but Carole held on.

"What happened?" Janine said again, squirming.

Uncle Harold turned to them. He looked from one to the other, to Aunt Regina, hunched and sobbing, and to the children again. At last he came over to Carole and gripped her shoulder.

"A telegram came from the war office. Your father's body has been found. I'm very sorry, Carole."

Janine yanked on her sleeve. "What does that mean?"

Carole stared into her sister's dark brown eyes. The girl had only been five years old when their father enlisted, and he'd hardly spent any time with her before that. Janine never knew the father Carole had once known, and Carole had spoken of him as little as possible, thinking it was best for her to forget. Still, a father meant something.

Carole cupped her sister's chin. "It means Papa's dead."

Janine frowned. "He was missing and now they found him, but he's dead?"

"That's right."

"They found his bones?"

Aunt Regina pulled herself upright, moaning. "For pity's sake, take her away!"

Janine scowled at her aunt. "Where, Carole? Where are his bones?"

Carole pulled her into an embrace, covering her sister's ears with her arms, knowing her aunt was not finished, that somehow her father's death was her sister's fault, and her mother's, and hers. They would all be punished.

Aunt Regina cried, "Take her away! Take that pirate child out of my sight!"

Carole pulled Janine out of the room and up to their bedroom. She fought back tears as she consoled her sister on the rug between their beds, telling her their mother's family were called pirates by mean and stupid people, and she shouldn't pay any attention.

"Like when they tease me about Mama being at Underhill?"

"Yes. Exactly like that."

"So you're a pirate, too?"

"I must be." And yet their aunt had singled out Janine. Always. Her sister noticed her hesitation. "But, I guess I've lost my eye patch."

Janine smiled, her eyes bright.

Carole burst into tears, unable to hold back a moment longer.

Her sister patted her arm. "There, there. It's all right," she said in the same tone she used with her dolls. After a few moments, she jumped to her feet. "I'm going to see if Marie is in the kitchen. I'm hungry." She paused at the door. Carole could barely catch her breath between sobs. "I don't really care about Papa, I guess. Not like you." And she left.

Carole envied Janine. How much easier it would be not to feel the pain of loss sharpened by the bitterness of disappointment. Their father hadn't had to go to war. He didn't have to die. He didn't have to destroy the shred of hope she'd clung to that he might return to them as a father, not a ghost. He hadn't cared enough. He hadn't loved her.

She could not bear another minute in this house. She grabbed her coat and her handbag, leaving without a word to anyone.

The frigid air stung her cheeks as she found her way to the waterfront. She'd seen her grandmother only once or twice a year since her mother left; Carole had never felt strongly about her, and Aunt Regina had told Carole she was forbidden from "consorting with" her mother's family if she wished to have a roof over her head. But Carole had had enough of Aunt Regina's cruel restrictions, and Grandma Rosemarie was her sole link to her mother. Carole hurried along the darkened streets, moving faster the farther she traveled from her aunt's house until she was running, the cold air searing her lungs.

She raced down the hill and past the shantytown, the pungent sting of kerosene fires in her nose, and came to a halt at the last dock. She doubled over, her chest burning, eyes streaming. A single light shone ahead; her grandmother would not leave her boat until the first snow.

The dock boards rattled under Carole's feet. "Grandma! It's Carole!"

An arm emerged through a crack in the door and beckoned her in. Carole slipped inside. Her grandmother was bundled up in several layers of clothing and wore a fur hat with earflaps.

"What on earth are you doing here, dear?"

Carole's mind whirled in circles. She had so many questions but she didn't know where to begin. She opened her mouth to speak and let out a low moan.

Her grandmother folded her into her arms, led her to a bench and brought her a steaming mug of tea. "I was thinking of you today."

It took Carole a moment to remember it was her birthday. She wiped her nose on her sleeve. "There was supposed to be a party. But I had a fight with my aunt. Then a telegram came." Her throat closed. "My father is dead."

"You poor thing." Her grandmother clasped Carole's hand. "He'd been missing a long while, but it's human nature to hope. Is that why you came, because of your father?"

"I'm not sure." Her grandmother sat patiently, her eyes haunting and familiar. "I miss my mother so much."

"I know you must."

"I can't stay with my aunt anymore. I just can't."

Grandma frowned. "Can you tell me what you fought about?"

"Janine. Aunt Regina hates her. She called her a pirate!"

Her grandmother was very still. She pursed her lips and looked to the ceiling, as if for guidance.

"What is it, Grandma?"

"There's something you should know. I've kept it from you because you were too young, and to spare your feelings. But now I think it's better that you know."

Dread curled around her spine. "Know what?"

Her grandmother sighed. "Janine is your half-sister. You have different fathers."

"What do you mean?"

"Exactly that. I know it's hard to hear."

Light-headed, Carole steadied herself against the seat. Her mind was a torrent of thoughts rushing by too fast for her to grasp. Different fathers? She recalled her father's rejection of the baby, her mother's anguish.

Grandma Rosemarie spoke. "Your mother had an affair."

An affair. Her mother betrayed her father. "My mother wouldn't do that."

Her grandmother nodded, expecting Carole's denial. "His name was Caleb Ploof."

Ploof. Like her father's trial. A pirate.

Carole searched her grandmother's eyes for signs of doubt, and found none. But something else was hiding there. Her grandmother knew more than she'd let on, was somehow part of what had happened.

Carole shuddered. "I have to go." She stood, swaying.

"Stay awhile, dear. You've had a shock."

She moved to the door. Too small in here. Too cold. She would fly out of her skin if she stayed. She would spin out of control, smash things, hurt things. Carole yanked open the flimsy door. A blast of wind hit her face, creating a small clearing in her mind. "You said his name was Caleb Ploof."

"Yes."

"You said 'was.'"

"Yes. He died a couple years ago, somewhere in France." She rubbed her arms. "Shut the door, Carole."

Janine's father. Carole had to remind herself; the facts weren't sticking yet. Her sister's father was dead. Like hers. Caleb Ploof had materialized moments ago and already he'd been erased. Panic rose in her chest, a burning acid rushing into every void.

"I'm going, Grandma." The words belonged to someone else. She pushed off the doorway, crossed the deck, leapt from the gangway to the dock and ran off.

Her grandmother shouted after her. "Carole!"

She ran, not caring where she was going, until the burn in her lungs overwhelmed her. She sweated under her coat and the cold moved inside her. She cinched the belt of her coat tighter and thrust her hands deep into the pockets. Only a few of the houses around her had lights on; it was late. A couple—arms linked, laughing, huddling close—approached her. She crossed the street to avoid them.

She wandered through the neighborhoods, her feet numb with cold, her mind too distracted to register where she was. Her parents hadn't loved her. Her father had chosen to risk his life at war instead of staying with her. His wounded pride at having been betrayed was more important to him than she was. Her memories of him loving her were nothing but childish fantasies.

And her mother, the mother she'd longed for every day for eight years, hadn't loved her, either. Her mother had chosen Caleb Ploof over her husband, over her daughter. Carole had poured her love into Janine for her mother's sake, at first simply because she'd loved her mother, and later also because she pitied her for her being crazy. But her mother's madness had come after her affair, not before. One day her mother had been braiding her hair and tucking her into bed, and the next she'd jeopardized the very possibility of her daughter's happiness.

This was her legacy. She was the child of cowardice, betrayal and madness.

Carole pulled her hands from her pockets and into her sleeves, driving her fingers under the cuff of her sweater. Her nails scraped hard against the underside of her forearms. She pinched and twisted the skin on her elbows, digging her nails into the flesh. The slicing pain made her gasp.

Her toe caught the pavement where a tree root had heaved it. She stumbled. Her shoulder smashed into a fence post. She fell onto her knees and cried out.

"Hey, miss! You all right?"

A man stood beside a car a few yards away. The streetlamp

behind him cast his face in shadow. Carole disentangled her hands from her sleeves and scrambled to her feet.

He came around the front of the car. "Are you hurt?"

"No." Her voice seemed to come from somewhere else.

The man stepped closer. He was about forty, with sharp features. He could grab her if he wanted.

"It's a cold night for a girl to be out walking. You need a ride someplace?"

Someplace. Any place. What did it matter? He could drive her to the edge of the earth and toss her off and it wouldn't matter a damn.

"Sure." She headed to the car. She couldn't feel her legs.

He caught up, opened the door for her. "Where're we going?"

She got in. "Anywhere."

He jogged to the driver's side, slid behind the wheel and started the engine. "I'm Ray."

She didn't answer. Nothing she said would tell him the important thing, the only thing that mattered. Whatever he wanted from her, maybe nothing, he didn't want to know it. No one would ever want to know that sort of truth, the truth that not even her parents could love her. She was invisible to Ray, to everyone. Until today, not even she had known how ugly she was inside.

He drove slowly. Carole sank into the seat, leaned against the door, her mind blank, her mouth dry, sour. They wound past Battery Park, through town again, then south. Ray talked a little, asking questions she didn't answer.

He lit a cigarette, cracked his window. In between drags, he hummed an aimless tune. He put out the cigarette and laid a hand on her knee.

"You can tell me what's wrong. I don't bite."

His touch was a jolt of electricity. She grabbed the door handle, fumbling.

"Hey, hey, hey." He swung to the curb, brought the car to a stop. She yanked the door open, jumped out.

"Hey, where's the fire?"

Carole ran down the long block to the corner, her blood pumping hard. She recognized the intersection and turned right toward the center of town, listening for the sound of Ray's car behind her. She ran until her legs felt wobbly. She slowed a little and glanced behind her. No one. Pulling her coat tighter, Carole arranged her bag on her shoulder and hastened down Main Street. The show at the Flynn was letting out. She was comforted to see the crowd, but skirted around them, avoiding eye contact. She couldn't face anyone she knew.

Overcome with exhaustion, unable to think where else to go, she headed up the hill to her aunt and uncle's house. She was too wretched to care what they might say about her being out so long without notice, or about anything else, and focused her flagging attention on making it there. But as Carole turned up the familiar walk, her resignation was mixed with relief.

She let herself in. The house was quiet. She climbed to her room, opening the door slowly so the hinges would not creak. Already overly warm, she peeled off her hat and coat and crossed to Janine's bed. The girl lay on her side, the bedclothes pulled to her chest, her braid curled on her shoulder. Her lips were opened slightly, as if she'd been about to say something, and her cheeks were touched with pink.

"Our fathers are dead," Carole whispered, "and our mother has wronged us. But here you are, my little sister, safe and loved, if only by me. I've kept my word. If there is anything good in me, it's yours."

25

Carole

Carole reached the paper-wrapped loaf across the counter to Mrs. Caldwell, who tucked it into her shopping bag, her arthritic fingers struggling with the simple task.

"Thank you, dear." She opened the bakery door and the bell at the top tinkled.

"You're welcome, Mrs. Caldwell. Have a good evening."

The shop was empty for the first time since lunch. Carole lowered herself onto the stool beside the register to rest her feet for a moment. She'd begun working part-time at Pedersen's a year before the war ended, immediately after graduating from high school. Mrs. Pedersen was shorthanded because her husband had been called up for active duty in Europe. Aunt Regina had been opposed to Carole taking the job, saying she'd expected her to have aspirations beyond being "a lowly shopgirl." Carole insisted it was her patriotic duty, which was true, but it was equally true she was dying to get out of the house.

After the war ended and Ludo Pedersen came home, Carole had expected to be let go. But Mr. Pedersen did not return whole. He jumped at the slightest sound and could not remember the recipes he'd been using since he was fourteen, baking alongside his father.

He set the oven too high, mistook baking soda for flour and could not be left unsupervised. So Carole remained behind the shop counter and the Pedersens baked together.

Mr. Pedersen's condition aside, her job was more pleasant now than in wartime. Sugar and flour were plentiful again, and customers no longer had to present ration cards. Carole had never gotten used to having to deny anyone something as basic as bread and had always been aware of how she had never really suffered during the war because of her family's money.

The bell tinkled again and Carole rose from her seat. Janine strode in, tossed her book bag to the side and came behind the counter.

"Did you save me some gingersnaps?"

Carole bent to kiss her cheek. Her sister made a face but accepted the kiss. "Hello to you, too."

"Well, did you?"

Carole prepared her sister's snack, which she ate on the stool while Carole served the day's last customers. She said good-bye to the Pedersens, flipped over the Open sign and walked with Janine to their apartment on Pearl Street. They'd lived there since shortly after her eighteenth birthday, when she'd learned the hard facts about her parents. Carole realized she didn't need to fight with her aunt about Janine, or anything else; she could simply leave. Aunt Regina had surprised her by not arguing, and had in fact helped subsidize the apartment so the girls wouldn't bring shame on the family by "living incorrectly." Her aunt was happy to be rid of Janine, that much was clear. Both aunts had known about Janine's real father but had kept the secret to avoid scandal. Carole would keep the secret as well, for her sister's sake.

Janine was delighted with the new arrangement. Carole wasn't much of a disciplinarian, not that discipline or reason or cajoling had much of an effect on the girl. If Carole really needed Janine to do something, she resorted to bribery, but since Janine had Carole's full attention, she behaved reasonably well.

On a sweltering Saturday in July, Carole was arranging cookies inside the bakery's display case. One leg dangled in the air behind her as she maneuvered toward the front row, concentrating on not ruining the intricate icing. She positioned the last cookie and glanced up. A man grinned at her from the other side of the glass. She startled, knocking her head against the case.

"Ow!" She extracted herself, brushed the sugar from her hands and touched the sore spot on her head. The man was her age, about twenty, and broad-shouldered, wearing blue gabardine trousers and a matching shirt, neatly pressed.

He winced. "Sorry! Didn't mean to surprise you. I was just trying to get your attention."

His eyes were the brightest blue she'd ever seen. "Well, you've got it now. How can I help you?"

"Are you sure you're okay?" He leaned toward her. His gaze was direct but not cocky.

She nodded.

A smile spread across his face. "I'm a sucker for cinnamon rolls."

Carole returned his smile and felt herself redden. She picked up a set of tongs and reached inside the case.

"I'd like the one all the way in the front," he said.

She stretched toward it, her foot leaving the floor, and began to laugh. He broke out laughing, too, a sound like a spring river. She grabbed the roll with the tongs, then dropped it, which made them both laugh harder. Finally Carole backed out of the case, still chuckling, and dropped the roll into a paper bag.

"Will that be all, sir?"

"I hope not."

She shifted from one foot to the other but didn't drop her gaze. He was steady; she could see that in the solid way he stood without fidgeting or gesturing. She didn't want him to leave, but she couldn't think of what to say that didn't sound silly or forward. Plenty of

boys and young men had shown interest in her, but she'd been quick
to turn them down. She didn't talk much, but that line she had
down pat.

"I'd like to see you," he said.

"Okay."

He grinned. "Okay."

"I'm Carole." She offered her hand.

He lifted his open palm to hold it, as if it was a bird that had
alighted there. "And I'm Walt."

Carole had no idea how Walt had convinced her to visit her mother
at Underhill. They'd only been dating six months, and here they
were, bouncing along the snow-packed roads in his Packard, heading to see Solange Gifford. It had been eleven years since Carole
had watched her mother handcuffed and shoved into the police
van. During the last two, Carole's hatred for her mother and disgust
with her actions had not dulled. She didn't dwell on it—that wasn't
her way—but neither had she altered her view that her mother had
wrecked their family.

Rain began to fall. They were in the middle of a January thaw.
Walt switched on the wipers. "When did you say you came out
here on your own?"

"About five years ago. But I couldn't see her because they'd put
her in a coma."

He shook his head in sympathy. "Do you think maybe that'll
happen again?"

"I have no idea." Secretly, Carole hoped it would. She remembered how devastated she'd been to learn she couldn't see her
mother. She'd been so naive.

Walt nodded, accepting the possibility the trip might be pointless. That was so like him, never worried that spending time might
be wasting it. Regret was useless to him. He made his choices, did

his best and searched for things to delight in wherever he could. Maybe it was how he was wired, but Carole suspected it had as much to do with his background. His family owned a hardware store. They were neither poor nor wealthy, so Walt didn't expect the world to be harsh and unfair, nor did he expect to have whatever he pleased. He had invited her into a world where contentment was neither a sign of privilege nor a second-place prize.

After they'd been dating for a while, Carole had no choice but to tell Walt her mother had been committed, but her mother's affair, and Janine's parentage, remained a secret. As for her father, well, so many men had died in the war, Osborn Gifford was just one more casualty. She'd admitted she didn't get along with her aunt, and that was all she'd needed to explain her situation. Why embarrass herself? Why risk scaring him away?

Walt gestured at the town of Underhill as they drove through. "What do you think of a place like this?"

She considered the general store, the coffee shop, the second-hand clothing store. "It's quiet, all right."

"Quiet's good, don't you think? I could set up in a place like this."

He smiled at her, those blue eyes lively and warm, telling her "I" really meant "we." She touched his cheek. "Yes, quiet's good."

A few minutes later they entered the reception area of the hospital, as dingy and depressing as Carole had remembered. She spoke to the woman behind the desk and crossed the waiting area to sit beside Walt.

He held her hands. She knew how cold hers were from the warmth of his.

Walt said, "Are you worried about seeing her?"

"Yes."

"I can go outside while you visit with her."

"No. Please stay."

Carole couldn't sort out her feelings. Her anger with her mother was still acute, but it was attached to a recollection of her mother that had become vague. It was like hating a shadow.

They waited for so long that Carole got up to ask the reception-ist when her mother might be coming.

The woman didn't look up. "They're getting her ready."

As she wondered what that might entail, a nurse came through a set of doors to her left. A woman in a pale gray shift and a baggy cardigan followed behind. If it weren't for her mother's red hair, Carole might not have recognized her. She was forty years old but looked sixty. Her skin was nearly translucent and her gait was unsteady. Carole could not breathe. Walt appeared at her shoulder and she steadied herself.

Her mother cast her gaze around the room as she entered, hug-ging her arms to her chest. She smiled uncertainly at the reception-ist, looked at her daughter, then at Walt. Her mother came closer, her confusion deepening.

Carole pushed out a whisper. "Mama."

Solange glanced at the nurse behind her and twisted a button on her sweater between her fingers. The button was on the verge of falling off.

"Mama. It's me, Carole."

Her mother looked at her intently this time. Her eyes widened and filled with tears. She grabbed Carole's forearm clumsily, as if testing to see if she was real. "Carole. My darling girl."

Although Carole had imagined this moment—as a child full of longing and as a young woman full of resentment—she wasn't prepared for it. She froze, at an emotional impasse.

The nurse ushered Solange into the waiting area, led her to a chair and left to chat with the woman behind the desk.

Walt said softly, "Let's sit down with her, all right?"

As Carole took a seat beside her mother, she noticed Solange's hair was damp and she gave off a peculiar odor, like ether or a solvent. The skin on her neck and wrists was dotted with red marks, from punctures or bites, and her fingernails were bitten down to the quick. What sort of hospital was this? The brittle anger inside Carole began to crack.

Walt introduced himself to Solange, who nodded in reply, her gaze wandering. Carole fidgeted with the strap of her handbag, wishing she'd thought about what to say. Should she mention her father's death?

Without warning, her mother twitched violently and clutched Carole's hand. A terrified expression came over her. "Is the baby all right?"

"The baby?"

"Yes! The baby! The baby!"

The nurse approached, annoyed for the interruption.

Carole said, "Oh, you mean Janine. She's ten now."

Her mother scowled. "No, the baby."

"Her name's Janine."

"Who's Janine?"

Carole glanced at Walt, flustered. It hadn't occurred to her that her mother wouldn't know her daughter's name. "My sister. Your daughter. She's ten years old."

Solange shook her head and swayed. "No, no, no, no, no."

The nurse addressed Carole, her tone matter-of-fact. "She worries all the time about a baby. Screams all night about it."

Carole moved her face closer to her mother's. "Mama, listen to me."

"No, no, no, no, no."

"Mama, listen to me. It's Carole."

Her mother fell silent. She stared at her daughter, anxious and imploring.

Carole squeezed her mother's hand. "The baby is fine. She's perfectly fine."

Solange exhaled in relief and smiled. "I'm so glad. She's such a good baby."

Part 3

26

Carole

October 1972

Carole had made her appointment with Dr. Carvalho for early morning, hoping to be on the right side of normal, and took care with her appearance. The appointment was Walt's idea, of course. He'd insisted after the incident in the office with Erwin Battle. How could she refuse? Walt was concerned, and she wanted to tell him the truth, but it would only make things worse for him and no better for herself. In the days since she'd lost control, the voices had receded and a small light in a corner of her heart grew brighter. Maybe something to help her sleep was all she needed.

Perched on the exam table, wrapped in paper, she told Dr. Carvalho about her insomnia and no more. She relaxed the muscles in her face and ignored her palms sticking to the paper.

"Headaches?" the doctor asked.

"A few mild ones."

"Appetite?"

"Fine."

"Sexual interest?"

She looked past him, at the eye chart on the wall. "Well, normal, I suppose."

"Any hot flashes?"

"Maybe. I do get hot."

"Any unusual stress?"

"Just the sleep problem."

He took notes, performed a routine physical and handed her a prescription for Valium. "For the insomnia. You might be in early menopause, too. Give it a couple of months and come see me again if you're not better."

Early menopause. That's what she'd tell Walt.

The pills did seem to help. She got a little more sleep and felt better. Not normal, because she didn't trust her recollection of that, but more stitched together. It wasn't something she could relax into, though. She scrutinized herself and how other people reacted to her, so it was like living in a movie in which she was both actor and viewer and not comfortable in either role. Carole didn't think of herself as someone who took much for granted, but now she did. She had taken her sanity for granted, had treated it with the same certainty as gravity or nightfall. When you have nothing to stick you to the earth, and nothing to mark your days, you are changed forever.

Wiped smooth by Valium, Carole existed in a state of tentative normalcy. She tended to her family and the garage and the house, keeping her excursions into the greater world as infrequent and brief as possible. She saw no point in testing limits. And her family, especially Walt, treated her with an extra dose of politeness and an extra breath of patience. They probably didn't even realize it. Carole couldn't blame them, not when she was so conscious of her own actions, but her family's behavior increased her sense that something irrevocable had happened. She would never get her old life back. She could accept that, she thought, as long as the life replacing it was not her mother's, as long as she didn't end up locked away from her family.

Two weeks after the doctor's visit, Walt offered to take Carole to visit Solange, an example of his new solicitousness. He'd never been unkind or impolite, but if she needed to go somewhere, she went, and if her husband wanted to join her, he did. Now she was handled. She needed handling. It was prudent.

Her mother was waiting, as usual, by the patio doors, and smiled broadly when Carole entered. "Carole, my dear." Solange hesitated, then smiled again. "And Walt. What a nice surprise."

They sat at a table in the lounge. Her mother did not ask why Carole had not visited recently, as Carole feared she might. Solange seemed more satisfied and calm than she had ever been, and Carole wondered if that was a symptom of her own changed state of mind; her mother appeared more normal because Carole was not. A vein of resentment opened up inside her. Did her mother deserve to be satisfied and calm, after what she had done to Carole, to Janine, to their father? Did she deserve to feel better than Carole did?

Solange peered out the window. "Last week it was so warm we had lunch outside."

Carole felt her face flush with shame.

As they drank coffee from heavy mugs and spoke of small things, Carole became confused as to why they—any of them— were there. It was fleeting, but Walt noticed. He had been watching her, she realized, and perhaps comparing her to Solange. Of course he would. She did, too. Every day, Carole searched for her mother in her reflection in the mirror until she became nauseous and dizzy, as if behind her eyes she'd find a telltale sign, a link to her mother's broken mind.

Forty minutes passed in the hospital lounge until Solange tired and became unfocused. Carole and Walt kissed her cheek and promised to return soon. As they left the building, Walt remarked on how lucid her mother had been. A flood of truths welled up inside Carole, and she coughed to stop them from slipping out. Walt patted her on the back, and they drove from Underhill in mutual silence toward the duties and distractions that would welcome them at home.

On a Tuesday afternoon in late October, Carole folded laundry in the living room. A soap opera was on the television, but she wasn't paying attention to it. She'd turned it on to drown out the murmuring. It had started mid-morning and was getting louder, closer, filling her with dread. Every few minutes, a distinct voice would shout above the others, nonsense phrases, strings of words with the cadence of a foreign tongue. It was a splinter in her brain pushing deeper.

Carole busied herself, paired athletic socks—green stripes, blue stripes, plain—folding one cuff over the pair, uniting them.

Upside down.

It came from behind her left ear.

Upside down.

On the television, a woman cried, clutching the arm of a man. The woman's mouth moved, but a man's voice said, "Upside down. Inside out. Worthless. Like your mother."

She placed the socks on the pile and rubbed her fingers into her temples. The murmurs merged, tones knitted together into clearer sounds, a mass of blurred words coalesced, sorted into louder stronger phrases, coming from inside her head out from the television surrounding her from everywhere all at once.

Inside out. Like your mother.

Bad blood will tell. Bad blood will tell. Bad blood will tell.

She clasped her arms around her head and dropped to her knees, shielding herself from the voices outside, collapsing over the voices inside. A sickening wash of fear sloshed through her. Her temples pounded, the pulses in time with the voices, chanting now.

Inside out. Like your mother.

Bad blood will tell. Bad blood will tell.

She rocked and hummed against the tribe in her head and all around. Rocked and hummed, rocked and hummed. Grasping her elbows, she squeezed the nubs of old scars, pinched the skin between her fingers and twisted as hard as she could, dug her nails into the skin, twisting and digging.

Something soft rubbed against her. She looked up. The cat circled, rubbing its flank along Carole's upper arm and came to face her, inches away. The cat's pupils sprang wide open, black, malicious. Carole was paralyzed.

The cat spoke with a voice like tires on gravel. "Inside out. Upside down. Like your mother. Bad blood will tell."

Carole shrank from it. The cat put its paws on her knees, advancing, chanting. Carole struck out with her arm. The cat fell back swiped with a paw catching a claw on Carole's skin. Ripping slipping.

The cat ran away with the spoon and the voices stayed and played all the livelong day. The world was inside outside pineapple upside-down cake take the cake bake the cake.

Carole crawled across the carpet staying low going slow to the television. They might not see her down here crystal clear. She reached up switched it off. She stood mind over matter mad as a hatter and climbed the stairs to her room to the moon Alice to the moon.

When the voices receded, she stumbled to the bathroom and took two Valium. Sometime later—she had no idea when—Walt came in to see if she wanted dinner, but she was too groggy. Later she came downstairs and sat with Walt and the kids while they watched television. She couldn't follow the programs. Before going to bed, Carole took another Valium and fell asleep before Walt.

In her dreams, she was lying in an unfamiliar bed, her head resting on the chest of a man whose face she could not see. His arm was around her, his naked body warm and strong down the length of her. Shadows stretched across the walls; it was dusk.

The door opened. A man entered, his outline and movement so familiar she gasped even before he turned to face them. Walt.

She hid her face, sickened with shame. Panic surged through her, every muscle in her body primed, urgent, but she could not move. Bile rose in her throat.

The scene shifted. Relief and apprehension swirled inside her.

She stood in a doorway, a bag at her side, facing an opulent, cavernous foyer.

In the center stood Alison, her face a mask of reproach. Alison held a bundled infant to her chest.

"Be good," Carole said.

The dreams haunted her every night, and she came to fear them more than the voices.

27

Alison

Her classmates piled out the door for recess, but Alison stayed behind because it was her turn to help Mr. Bayliss clean out Yertle the Turtle's cage. They talked about *White Fang*. Mr. Bayliss wanted to know if the ending made sense to her.

"You mean that White Fang was happy, even after everything that happened to him?"

"Yes."

Alison handed Mr. Bayliss one of Yertle's rocks, which she had washed and dried. "I think so. He didn't have to fight anymore. He was safe in California, and could lie in the sun instead of freezing up north."

"And he had all those puppies."

She laughed. "Yeah, a lot of puppies." She thought for a moment. "But I don't think he forgot how hard everything had been, do you? It seems like too much to forget."

"Even for a wolf."

"Oh, I think animals have good memories, maybe even better than people."

"Do you? Why?"

Alison shrugged. "People talk themselves out of things, cover things up with words, make up stories. A wolf can't do that. A wolf has to feel and remember."

Mr. Bayliss was lowering Yertle into his cage and stopped halfway. The turtle's legs kept moving like he was swimming. "I hadn't thought of it that way, but you're right." He put Yertle down, pulled the cover over the terrarium and looked her straight in the eye. "You're amazing, Alison. Did you know that?"

Her cheeks turned hot. She smiled at him, her insides sliding around. The bell rang. Kids would burst through the door any minute. Without thinking, Alison threw her arms around Mr. Bayliss's waist. He hugged her back—it felt so good!—and she said, into his shirt, "So are you." She let go and went to her desk. The classroom door opened and kids streamed in, playground noise following them.

"Okay, class," Mr. Bayliss said, putting the lid on the terrarium. "Inside voices."

Alison slid into her seat, happiness shooting down her arms and legs until she thought she might melt. She worried that everyone would see how much Mr. Bayliss liked her and be jealous, so she tried to pretend she was the same as every other kid in the class and not, in fact, amazing.

After lunch, the usual gang, Alison, Delaney, Maggie, J.J. and Caroline, chilled out on the monkey-bar dome. Maggie and Delaney started talking about horses and five seconds later were in the middle of a fight about which one's colors were prettier: palominos (Maggie's horse) or dark bays (Delaney's).

"Blondes have more fun, or haven't you heard?" Maggie said.

"That's an ad, not a fact," Delaney said. "And plus that's people. Horses don't even know what color they are."

"My horse does. She knows she's a gorgeous blonde." She flicked her dark blonde hair off her shoulder, lifted her chin and did the sexy-eyes thing.

"That just proves she's as stuck on herself as you are."

Maggie looked like she would spit. "You're the one who can't stop playing with your hair, Delaney. Oops, I mean 'your mane.'"

Alison winced. Nobody criticized Delaney's hair and lived to tell about it.

Delaney pretended she hadn't heard. She pointed her finger at J.J., who was all the way at the top. "You're on my side, right? You're a brunette."

J.J. pulled a lock from behind her ear to check. "Looks that way. But I think I was born with blonde hair. Or maybe red."

"Well, you're a bay now."

"No, I forgot. I was born bald."

"It doesn't matter, J.J. You're on my side."

"Actually, I've been thinking about dying it blonde."

"No, you haven't."

"I have, too. Just yesterday. I even went to the drugstore and looked at the boxes."

"No, you didn't."

"Did, too."

Delaney let out a huge breath. She was going to lose her rag in two seconds. "J.J., you've got brown hair. You're automatically on my side."

J.J. studied her hair again. "If you say so."

Maggie gave J.J. the evil eye. "You're with her? Thanks a bunch." She nudged Caroline, who was sitting next to her, swinging her legs and hoping to become invisible. "Then you're with me." She wasn't asking. "All the blondes are. Automatically." She got up and pulled Caroline's sleeve. "Come on! Let's get all the prettiest girls, the blonde ones, together." Caroline stopped swinging her legs. She looked at Alison, who shrugged. Caroline jumped down and scampered after Maggie. Alison couldn't blame her. Maggie had a terrific temper.

Gretchen Wilner walked by. Delaney climbed out of the bars

and called to her. "Gretchen! You're with J.J. and me. We're the Brunette Bay Bombshells!"

"We are?" Gretchen looked worried. Delaney had never said a word to her before.

"Yup. Go get all your brunette friends, okay? Bring them over here." The girl stared with her mouth open. "Get the lead out!"

Alison said, "Delaney, this doesn't seem like such a hot idea."

"Why not?"

"It's just the color of someone's hair."

"So?"

"You and Maggie are friends."

"We *used* to be friends."

Alison's heart sank. She wanted to run inside to the classroom, where things were simpler, but no one was allowed during lunch. She thought about walking off, but where would she go? Most of the boys were in a circle playing dodgeball, laughing and shouting. If only she could play with them. Try not to get hit by something she could actually see coming.

Since school started, Delaney had been a real friend some days and a real turd others. Alison never could predict. Yesterday, Delaney had been teasing Alison about having a huge crush on Mr. Bayliss, and Alison had gotten really embarrassed, even though it wasn't true. No way she could make Delaney understand what it meant to be special to Mr. Bayliss. Delaney thought she was special every minute of every day to every single person in the universe. What would she know?

Delaney was whispering in J.J.'s ear. She saw Alison staring at her and cocked her head to the side. "What?"

"Which side do I get to be on?"

Delaney gave her the don't-be-a-moron face. "Duh. Neither."

Alison slid off the bar and went to the water fountain, not knowing what else to do. She had a drink, pulled up her kneesocks and leaned against the wall watching the blonde and brown heads move around the blacktop, blondes moving with blondes and away from browns, and browns doing the opposite. It was so stupid. Mr. Bayliss sure didn't think her red hair was a problem. In fact, she was pretty sure he liked her exactly the way she was.

Rain was coming down in sheets when she got off the bus. She made a mad dash for the office, hugging her book bag to her chest. She pushed open the door. The chimes went off and she nearly slipped when her shoes hit the linoleum. She was about to go into the kitchen when her dad came in from the garage wiping his hands with a rag.

"Hey, sunshine. Great day for ducks, huh?"

"Yeah. I'm soaked."

"How was school?"

"Fine."

"That's good." He paused and rubbed his cheek the way he did when he had something to say. Alison pushed a damp curl out of her face and waited. Her dad shifted his feet around. "Your mother's upstairs lying down, so no watching television, okay?"

"Is she sick?"

"No. Just didn't have a good sleep. And she has a headache."

"I thought she was better. She has pills."

"It's not that simple." He fiddled with his fingernails. "Be best if I leave it to your mother to explain."

"Explain what?"

He sighed. "Seems she's got what you call 'the change of life.'"

Alison didn't like the sound of it. "What's that?"

"Oh, it's when a woman, like your mother, when she gets . . ." He shook his head, then looked at her. "Like I said, when your mother's feeling better, she'll explain it to you, all right? That'd be best."

Her mother had been feeling better, and she hadn't explained anything yet. Nobody ever told Alison anything.

Her father went on. "One other thing, and then I've got to get back to work. About Sally."

Alison's throat squeezed shut and she almost let go of her book bag. "Is she okay?"

"Oh, sure, she's fine. But she's been acting peculiar, so I want you to keep her outside while you're at school."

"There's nothing wrong with Sally."

He held up both hands. "Your mother said she was acting peculiar and I'm not getting in the middle of it. The easiest thing to do is put her outside in the morning."

"But what if it's raining? Or if it snows?"

"Put her in your room, then. Your mother's not feeling a hundred percent and has lots to do besides worry about a cat."

Anger boiled up inside Alison. It was so unfair. How would her dad or her mom like it if they had to stay outside in the rain or the snow? Sally was her cat, and it seemed that what mattered to Alison was always the last thing on everyone's list.

Her dad must've seen her face. "Now, Alison, you know I like Sally just fine. If the weather turns bad when you're out, I'll put her in your room for you."

"She doesn't like being locked up."

"She'll be just fine. Right as rain."

"That's what you said about Mom, but it isn't true!"

She stormed into the house, dropped her bag on the kitchen table and went straight to the back door and called for her cat. It was raining so hard she couldn't see past the toolshed. Sally streaked across the lawn, flew up the steps and ran inside. The cat was soaked, making her look tiny and pathetic. Alison stroked her. "Poor Sallypants."

She got a towel from the oven door. The cat let Alison dry her for a minute, then scooted out from under the towel, rubbed against Alison's shin and meowed.

"You hungry? Me, too."

Alison opened a can of cat food and mixed it with some kibble, adding more of the wet food than she was supposed to. "Just the way you like it." The cat purred as she ate.

Alison got some milk and made a peanut butter and honey sandwich. She took a bite and tried to purr, but it made her choke. She listened for her mom, wanting to see her, but all she could hear was the drumming of rain on the roof. Outside the window, the rain beat down as if it was mad at the ground, forcing it to soak it up, to drink. The river would be high, eating away at the banks, greedy. Leaves fell down, not drifting slowly like notes in a lullaby, but dropping wet and heavy, starting to rot before they hit the earth.

Why couldn't her mother be herself again? It was so unfair. And getting the Change of Life didn't make sense. Maybe it was something everyone got, at least all the moms. Why hadn't she ever heard of it, then? Why did some people get headaches and ignore their kids and forget stuff, and other people didn't? Sounded more like a disease. Alison wanted to ask someone about it, but there wasn't anyone. Loneliness made her stomach sour, and she tossed the last corner of her sandwich in the trash.

She grabbed her bag and her soggy sweater, one of three Aunt Janine had given her. Aunt Janine. Why hadn't she thought of talking to her before? Alison left her stuff behind and went to the hall and dialed her aunt. On the third ring, Aunt Janine picked up and said hello.

"It's Alison. Hold on a sec." She unkinked the cord and angled into the kitchen, wedging the door shut behind her for privacy, and slid down the wall to sit on the floor.

"Alison, is everything all right?" She never called her aunt, so of course Janine thought it was an emergency.

"Yeah. I mean, nobody's hurt." She should've thought of what to say before she'd called. What *would* she say?

"Oh. So what's going on?"

Alison heard her aunt moving around. She'd just gotten home

from work and was busy. This was a dumb idea. "I wanted to ask you about something. About my mom."

"Okay." The crackle of ice cubes falling from a tray.

"Well, she's been acting weird."

"Weird? Weird how?"

"Forgetting stuff, like that paperwork you brought over, remember?"

"Everyone forgets things."

"Okay, maybe." Alison searched for a better example, something solid. "She doesn't pay attention, even when she's not doing anything important. It's like she's not there. Or she's there but too busy in her own head."

The pop and fizz of a soda can being opened. "People get distracted. It doesn't mean anything other than they have things on their mind. Adults have a lot to think and worry about."

The way she said it put a big space between adults and Alison. As if Alison didn't have anything to worry about. She picked at a loose thread on the top of her shoes. There really was something wrong with her mom. She was sure of it. "My mom has headaches. And she seems scared."

"Scared?"

"Yeah." Alison realized that was really the biggest change. Not forgetting, not ignoring, not all the rest.

"If you're worried about your mom, you should talk to your father."

"I did."

"What'd he say?"

Alison hesitated, pinching the coils of the cord closed and letting them open again and again. Oh well. Hadn't she called her aunt so she could help? "He didn't explain what he meant, so I'm confused."

"So what did he say?"

Alison let out a big breath. "He said she was going through the Change of Life."

"The what—oh, that!" Aunt Janine sputtered, then laughed, on and on and on. "Oh God, that is hysterical! The change of life. Oh, Walt." She laughed some more, but in the background, like she'd put the receiver on the counter.

An empty space opened up inside Alison. The hand holding the receiver felt bigger than normal and numb. She rubbed tears from the end of her nose.

"Alison?" Her aunt fought back laughs so big she was choking on them. "Alison, are you there?"

Alison pressed the phone against her chest, hard enough for it to hurt. She pushed with all her might but the stab of pain was nothing against the poisonous, sinking ache that spread all through her. She sat there until she could breathe around the ache, and then got up and put the receiver back on the base.

28

Janine

They were supposed to be away the whole weekend, at least that's what Janine had planned. She'd chosen the place: Lake George. In fact, the trip itself had been her idea. Greg agreed to it immediately, but he would have agreed to anywhere she suggested. He wasn't a control freak, which was a relief, although she hoped he didn't defer to her because he was weak. Laid-back was one thing and weak was another. She wanted someone she could respect, like Mitch, and there was no bigger turn-off than someone who'd stand there and let her eat him alive. She needed a man who would stand up to her. He had to know when, of course, and how.

Lake George was a two-hour drive, far enough to feel like a destination, to have a car trip that would be the first and last chapter of the story of their first weekend together, but not so far as to require extra logistics. She wanted an exciting, romantic place to hang out in the sack with him for two and a half days, away from Adams, where it seemed a daily bulletin was issued with details of what in a reasonable world would be considered private business. She doubted whether anyone cared what she did and who she did it with, other than that it was something to talk about while filling up a car or choosing oranges at the Grand Union. Anonymity made her feel less like she was dragging her past behind her like toilet paper stuck to the bottom of her shoe.

Greg offered to drive. Friday afternoon, he pulled into her driveway. She came out of the house with her small suitcase, locked the door and stood watching him throwing junk from the front seat into the rear.

"Hey there, handsome." His Ford Pinto was a rolling locker room, filled with basketballs and sneakers and clothing that looked like the Before shot in a Tide commercial.

He peered at her over the roof and flashed his dimples. "Hi." He finished clearing off the seat and stood beside the car. "Sorry about that. Didn't have time to spiff it up."

She forced herself not to wrinkle her nose and gave him an understanding look. "Why don't we take mine? You can still drive, if you want."

He eyed the LTD, chrome gleaming. "Cool."

They listened to the radio and swapped stories about the school staff. Janine told Greg about how Lane Snelling, the guidance counselor, called into WDEV radio every morning and requested Cat Stevens's "Morning Has Broken."

"No way."

She nodded. "And if you walk by his office when they play it—and for some reason, they always do—he'll be sitting there with his eyes closed, swaying in his chair and mouthing the words."

Greg shook his head in disbelief.

"Do the kids know this?"

"We've kept it quiet for now, but it can't last."

"You could leak it to your niece."

Janine remembered Alison's call earlier that afternoon and almost burst out laughing. "Oh, I doubt she'd tell anyone even if I did."

"You're right. What a sweet kid."

She reached over and ran her hand up his leg, stopping short of his crotch. "Runs in the family."

The prospect of checking into a hotel with Greg intoxicated her. They'd be announcing publicly—well, to the clerk and whoever else was around—that they were going to have sex in the room. She hadn't felt this way before: thrilled with the actual fact of the relationship as much as with the idea of it. When she had packed her bag for the weekend, her emotions were whipped into a froth of horniness and vindication. Now, together with Greg in the car, she could barely contain herself.

It hadn't been the same with Mitch. How could it? He had been too old. It was a sport for her, and not a challenging one. And before Mitch there had been boys, or boys masquerading as men. She'd fallen for a couple of them—raw attraction was not to be underestimated—but had quickly regained her senses, and put herself firmly behind the controls.

Finally, with Greg Bayliss, she sensed a chance for it all: a great-looking guy with deep pockets who was stuck on her. It'd been six weeks since the first time they had sex—the night she'd made him chicken cordon bleu—and every time they got together, he couldn't get enough. Because of his schedule (school, basketball and volunteering, of all things) it hadn't been as often as she wanted, but there was nothing wrong with keeping a man hungry.

So she was frustrated when they neared Lake George and Greg announced he had to be back in Adams by noon on Sunday. His parents, he said, had called the night before to say they'd be stopping by on their way home from a week in Montreal and wanted to take him to lunch. Janine had hoped her weekend with Greg would last longer—through Sunday night, in fact—but made sure her tone was light when she spoke.

"Oh, that's fine. I have a lot to do at home before Monday." For an instant she wondered why he didn't invite her along to lunch, but decided meeting his parents at this stage might not help her cause. What if their idea of a daughter-in-law didn't include widowed secretaries? No, she would put that off as long as she could. "Where are you going with your folks?"

"The Greenville Inn."

Of course. Nothing in Adams would do for the big city elite. "I adore their popovers. We should go sometime."

He nodded, or she thought he did, and turned up the radio. That Neil Young song, "Heart of Gold," was on. Greg sang along in a clear tenor, playing it straight at first, then hamming it up, strumming an air guitar and howling mournfully during the chorus. She laughed and forgave him his devotion to his parents.

On Sunday, they were delayed by an accident on the bridge over Champlain and didn't get to her house until eleven forty-five.

Greg dropped the keys into her palm and grabbed his bag from the backseat. She scrambled out of the car and he came around to give her a quick hug. "Sorry to rush off. I had a blast."

"Me, too." A blast? Oh well. She supposed it was apt enough for an eight-orgasm weekend, not that she was counting. "See you tomorrow at the monkey house."

He was already in the Pinto, pulling the keys from above the visor. "You bet." He backed out, waved as he passed her, and headed up the drive.

She watched him join the main road and waved to him again. He faced straight ahead, eyes on the road. He hadn't thought to look at her one more time.

The air was chilly where she stood under the oak. Clouds had knitted together in the last hour or so, shutting off the sun. Janine rubbed her arms and retrieved her bag from the car. It would have been a perfect afternoon to curl up with Greg on the couch, maybe watch a movie or even a football game. She didn't get football, but if Greg wanted to watch it, she would. Maybe she'd invite him over next weekend for a game, some beers and onion dip. God, listen to me, she thought. She'd have to watch herself. She was beginning to sound like a schoolgirl with a crush.

She unpacked, made coffee and sat at the kitchen table, leafing through the newspaper. She glanced at the horoscopes but rejected the idea of an easy glimpse into her future and moved on to the entertainment listings. It'd been ages since she'd seen a movie. *Lady Sings the Blues* was playing in Montpelier and the matinee at two was the last showing. What better way to blow a couple of hours than listening to Diana Ross?

Parking was tight, so the previews were nearly over by the time she entered the darkened room. She preferred to sit close to the front but saw from the array of heads she'd have to climb over people, and chose instead a spot a few seats in near the middle. An elderly couple took the first two seats in her row. The woman had difficulty arranging her coat, purse and popcorn—how difficult could it be?—and got up several times, clucking all the while, until she was satisfied.

The Paramount logo of the mountain with the circle of stars appeared on the screen. Light from the lobby spilled into the far side of the room, then it became dark again as the door closed. Janine glanced at the latecomers, two of them, their faces shadowed. She watched as they stood shoulder to shoulder looking for seats. There was something familiar about them, their outlines.

Two rows behind Janine's, the couple slid in, crouching, moving past angled legs, and sat down about a dozen seats to her right. The woman, or the one who seemed to be a woman, bent and disappeared behind the seat back. The light from the screen shone on the man's face. Janine stared, unbelieving. Greg. What the hell was he doing here?

Before she could begin to calculate whether he had time to drive to Montpelier after having lunch with his parents, the person next to him straightened. A woman. Young. Light flashed and her features were illuminated. April Honeycutt. That little blonde kitten. April flicked her hair and smiled at Greg. Janine's stomach lurched. She sank into the seat.

Her mind raced, running through the possibilities, doing the calculations. He'd met his parents, then come to movies. He'd run into April, either here or at the inn. She was new in town; it was friendly of him. Greg would have made it to the inn at noon at the earliest. Lunch would take—what?—an hour, an hour and a half? His parents would have wanted to be on their way. They had a lot of driving in front of them. It would have taken him thirty minutes tops to get to Montpelier. He'd seen April buying her ticket, or maybe she approached him—why wouldn't she?—and he couldn't do anything other than invite her to sit with him.

On the screen, Diana Ross, barely recognizable, was being tossed into a cell like a slab of meat. Janine stole a glance at Greg and April. The scene was so dark, little light reflected on them. The scene shifted, black-and-white photographs. A band of light washed over the audience. Janine stared as April covered her eyes with one hand and clenched Greg's shirtsleeve with the other. The little bitch! Janine grabbed the arms of her seat to stop herself from vaulting over the rows and smashing that face with its pert little nose. How dare she touch him! Or grab his shirt! Janine watched him put it on this morning in their romantic, lakeside room, after his shower. After he'd washed off *her*.

Blood rushed to her head. She had to get out of there, but if Greg or that blonde bitch saw her, she'd lose it. She slouched in the seat and forced herself to stare at the screen. Diana Ross was flipping out, crazy or in withdrawal. Men stuck her in a straitjacket. Janine didn't give a damn. She just needed it to be dark for ten seconds so she could split. The camera zoomed in and the music got louder. Janine clutched her bag to her chest, whispered, "Excuse me," to the woman next to her. The woman startled. Janine got up and pushed past, hitting the woman's knees and her husband's, too. She stooped and darted for the exit. She pulled open the door and fled into the light.

She didn't remember much about the drive home. Her mind was filled with the image of April pawing Greg. As soon as she opened the front door, she threw her purse on the table and went straight to the bottle of good red wine she'd bought to share with Greg that evening when she thought they might end up here, before he told her about his parents visiting. Had that all been a crock of shit? Had he actually blown her off because he wanted a few hours, or a whole night, with Little Miss Honeybutt?

She opened the bottle, filled her glass and drained it in two gulps. She refilled her glass, carried it to the living room and sat heavily onto the couch. *Get a goddamn grip, Janine.* What if Greg actually had lunch with his folks and met April by accident at the theater? Maybe she was the touchy-feely type. Maybe pawing Greg didn't mean a thing, but Janine had to find out. She'd invested so much energy into Greg, launched a campaign to get him to the point where he'd propose to her as if it was meant to be. He wasn't on the verge of asking yet—making someone fall in love with you couldn't be rushed—but she'd made real progress. And somehow, her heart had gotten tangled up in the strings of the web she was weaving. Ideally, her emotions would have been sidelined. She hadn't needed to fall in love with Mitch to have been married to him for ten years. It hadn't been a fairy tale, but she hadn't minded. Then he had to go and die. Bastard!

Janine poured the last of the wine with an unsteady hand, cursing the fact that Greg had gotten under her skin. The way he'd looked at her across the table last night at the lakeside restaurant, drinking her in with tender fascination. She hadn't imagined it. And she hadn't imagined how she'd felt in response: liquid, naked, open. Recalling the moment and her vulnerability brought a surge of sadness and fear, as it struck her what losing him might truly mean. She wanted him to know her, to love her, to care for her, and she wanted to make him happier than he'd ever been because she loved him. Janine wiped tears from her eyes. She willed herself to stop crying but the tears fell and fell. She didn't want to spend the rest of her life alone. She wanted to spend it with Greg.

Janine sank into the couch and cried until her tears were spent. She pulled a tissue from the box on the side table, blew her nose and finished the last of the wine. Her feelings for Greg were real, as much as she could tell. All the more reason to find out whether April Honeycutt had her claws in him. Greg was an idealistic man-child and easily led around by the nose, and Janine vowed to stop whatever plan April had in her vacuous blonde head. Greg was hers.

29

Alison

Alison woke to the sounds of her parents talking loudly downstairs in their bedroom. She couldn't hear everything they were saying, but her mother repeated the same thing over and over: "You were talking about me." No way Alison could go back to sleep, so she threw on some clothes and tiptoed down from the attic. As she passed her parents' room, her father sounded really hacked off.

"I wasn't. I was talking to Randall about his truck. Now, that's the third time I've said it and I'm done."

"But you were."

"Oh, for Pete's sake. I've got three oil changes to get to this morning, plus God knows how many state inspections. I can't stand here and argue in circles with you."

Alison paused at the top of the stairs, holding her breath.

Her mom's voice was lower than before. "I'm sorry, Walt. I guess I had a bad dream. A nightmare."

Alison went down to the kitchen and opened the fridge. No milk. Yesterday she'd used the last two pieces of bread to make a sandwich, but she checked the bread box anyway and found an open package of English muffins. Through the plastic she could see that the last two muffins were covered in green mold.

Her father walked in. "Morning, Alison."

"Hi. There's nothing to eat."

"Nothing?" He opened the cabinet next to her. "There's oatmeal. And your cereal."

"No milk."

"There's Pop-Tarts."

"Lester would have a cow. He counts them."

Her father sighed and hung his head like it'd gotten heavy. "When Warren gets up, I'll send him to the store. You make a list for him, all right?"

"Sure." She opened the freezer. "Did you eat already?"

"Just coffee."

"I'm having ice cream. You want some?"

He smiled a little. "No, but you go ahead. I'm off to the mine." He patted her shoulder as he passed behind her and went into the garage.

Alison watched cartoons and ate strawberry ice cream straight from the container. She almost got up to check for some chocolate syrup, but then Elmer Fudd came on and she didn't want to miss any of it. When she'd had enough ice cream, she put it on the coffee table. Sally waltzed in, jumped up and sniffed the container.

"Help yourself."

Sally licked the rim suspiciously. Elmer Fudd stomped off into the sunset, muttering about Bugs Bunny. Alison flicked off the television, got the notepad from under the phone and started on the shopping list: milk, bread, Oreos, bananas, bologna.

"Anything special you'd like, Sally?"

Sally looked up for a moment, then went back to her licking. Alison thought maybe she should put down something for dinner, just in case, so she added carrots (her favorite), potatoes, butter (potatoes were gross without it) and hamburger. She chewed the pen cap. The menu was too boring. She added Hamburger Helper and put a smiley face next to it.

Somebody clomped down the stairs. Warren appeared in the doorway. He must have skipped looking in the mirror because his hair was sticking straight up on one side.

"Don't let the cat eat ice cream."

"It's pretty much gone."

"It's gross."

"Not according to Sally." Alison got up and gave him the shopping list. "Dad wants you to go to the store."

He stared at the list like it was written in Chinese. "How come? That's Mom's job."

Alison wanted to tell him about the Change of Life, just to see if he knew about it, but if it made her father anxious to talk about and made Janine laugh, it probably wasn't a safe topic with Warren.

"She's not feeling well. She had a nightmare."

"A nightmare? What is she, four?"

A hot bolt of anger shot through her. He would never notice anything was wrong with their mother until he wanted something from her. "Don't be such a jerk."

He jabbed a finger into her shoulder. "What'd you call me?"

She ducked past him, ran upstairs and stopped halfway. "A jerk!"

Warren twitched like he was coming after her, so she bolted. She got to the top, turned the corner and peered over the railing. He'd disappeared. Good riddance.

The next day in school her class presented the poems they'd written. Alison got the idea for hers from the newspaper and had worked on it in her room all yesterday afternoon, hiding from her family.

Caroline went first. Hers was about her dog and how he'd almost died. She was worried about rhyming "Waffles" with "awful," but Mr. Bayliss said it was fine because it was close.

He called on Alison next and she got up. She hadn't been nervous until now. She glanced up from her paper and Mr. Bayliss smiled at her. He couldn't wait to hear her poem.

"It's called: 'Obituary for a Star.' It doesn't rhyme. Did it have to rhyme?"

"No," Mr. Bayliss said.

"Okay. 'Obituary for a Star.'"

> *Unknown Star went out ages ago*
> *after a long illness.*
> *Before its light went out,*
> *it was surrounded, at a distance,*
> *by other Stars,*
> *all belonging to a constellation*
> *no one could find.*
> *Unknown Star was well-known*
> *in its galaxy*
> *for shining on its planets,*
> *and a few orbiting moons,*
> *during their days.*
> *One might have life on it.*
> *Unknown Star is survived*
> *by its own light.*

No one said a word. Alison shuffled her feet, not daring to look at anyone's face. The ticking of the clock on the wall sounded like a bomb about to go off.

"Alison," Mr. Bayliss said.

She raised her head.

"It's beautiful. Sad, but beautiful." He looked at her a couple of seconds more, then called on Susie Waterman. Alison sat down, holding the piece of paper lightly between her fingertips as if the beauty he had seen in her words might grow wings and fly off.

After all the kids had read their poems, they lined up for PE.

Delaney was next to her. "Yours was really good. I'm serious. You should enter it in a contest or something."

"Really?"

"Yeah, you should."

"Thanks."

"Just think." Delaney cocked her head to the side, her eyes twinkling. A caterpillar of dread crept along Alison's neck. "If you win, you could dedicate your prize to Mr. Bayliss."

Alison wanted to look around to see if anyone was listening but didn't dare. Her face felt as if she'd stuck it in a bonfire.

Delaney's eyebrows shot up. "You have such a crush on him, Alison LaPorte."

The kids around them were covering their mouths, trying to swallow their laughs.

Alison whispered, "Do not."

Delaney said, "It's not a crush?" A girl behind them giggled. "What is it, then? True loooove?"

A bunch of kids snickered. Davey Weiner imitated Delaney saying "true loooove."

Principal Kawolski was standing near the trophy case. "No chatting in the halls, now. This is a place of learning."

Alison kept her eyes straight ahead. Someone poked her, but she ignored it. Delaney marched along, proud of herself, like she'd made some great discovery. What did Delaney know about her, or Mr. Bayliss? What, as a matter of fact, did Delaney Dalrymple know about anything, other than her stupid horse?

On the bus ride home, Alison stared out the window and thought about Mr. Bayliss. She didn't have a crush on him, but she often thought about being with him outside of school. They would have lunch together, maybe by the river if the weather was nice, or they'd go fishing. They would read, sometimes the same books, sometimes different ones. There'd be so much to talk about then. They might go on a trip together, to a city, Boston or New York, and visit an art museum. She didn't know anything about art, but it was a grown-up thing she was interested in learning about, and Mr. Bayliss probably had been to all sorts of museums. While they were in the city they could go out to dinner. Nothing fancy, but they'd be hungry after seeing all the parks and museums. Sometimes the next thing Alison thought about was where they would stay overnight, because it was too far to Boston or New York to come back the same day. Her ideas petered out there, like a straight road her eyes could follow into the distance, perfectly clearly, before it disappeared over a hill or the edge of the earth. When she got to that point, she'd start nearer the beginning again, at the part where Mr. Bayliss tells her during lunch at the river that he wanted to take her to see the Metropolitan Museum in New York. Alison felt deliciously warm and sweet inside as the conversation ran in her head.

Alison got off the bus and ran into the house, dropped her book bag at the bottom of the stairs and opened the back door to let Sally in. Her cat had been waiting and dove inside like she'd been shot from a cannon. Alison made a bologna and pickle sandwich and accidentally on purpose dropped a slice of bologna. Sally gobbled it up and together they went to the living room to watch *Dark Shadows*. Alison had already seen this episode but didn't want to get up to change the channel because Sally had just gotten comfortable on her lap. The poor thing had been stuck outside in the cold all day.

Halfway through the show, her mother appeared in the doorway. She pointed to the far side of the television stand. "Alison, would you mind handing me my glasses?"

Alison stared at her, confused. The glasses were next to the television, about five feet from where her mom was standing.

"Alison, did you hear me?"

"Yeah, but you're right there."

Her mom was twisting her fingers like she wanted to unscrew them. She'd been doing that a lot. "The television is on."

"So?"

"It was bad enough when they could only hear."

"Who?"

Her mom scrunched her shoulders in. "Please." She drew it out like a kid begging for ice cream.

Before Alison could ask another question, she heard the door from the office to the kitchen open. Her dad's voice boomed. "Carole! Where on God's green earth are you? The Stouts are waiting!"

Her mother's eyes shot wide open. Alison wasn't used to hearing her father raise his voice. She scooped Sally off her lap, got up and gave the glasses to her mom. Without a word, her mother hurried out to the office, muttering under her breath.

Alison went back to the couch, picked up Sally and hugged her tightly. She thought about what had happened, trying to make sense of her mom, wondering how the Change of Life could make a person into something totally different, the way Barnabas Collins changed into a bat. She had to talk to her dad again, even if it made him nervous. Her mother was getting worse, and Alison needed to know what the Change of Life really was and whether it included being afraid the people on television could actually see you. She wondered if the Change of Life was what her grandmother had, if it made her think crazy things, if that was why she was locked up in Underhill. Maybe her mom would end up there, too.

She flicked off the television and went to her room. Feeling sick to her stomach and dizzy, she lay down on her bed and curled onto her side.

If only she could march downstairs and tell her father about her mother and the television, and about all the other things her mother had said and done that up until now she'd pushed into a corner of her mind where they couldn't amount to anything, where they couldn't add up. She wanted to tell him, and she wanted her mother to hear her tell him, so nobody could make excuses or pretend there was nothing wrong. But Alison knew how it would go. Her mother would deny it, say Alison had heard wrong. Her father would side with her mother, because he didn't want to believe anything was wrong with her: she's always right as rain. If Alison was going to help her mother—and she was desperate to—she'd have to do it herself.

She stared at the pile of books next to the bed. The spine of the witchcraft book, near the bottom, caught her eye. She glanced at the blue box on the dresser, where she'd stashed the pearl. The soapstone was at the back of the top drawer, inside a bobby sock.

She sat up, pulled out the book and flipped to the section on healing spells. She knew she had power, and the universe had been sending her signs. Maybe this was why. She'd pulled a giant fish from the murky river and plucked a pearl from its belly. Obviously she was supposed to use it to help her mom. And she'd drawn a Satan's circle with the soapstone (and almost drowned her brother) so she'd understand its power and use it now. Maybe the blue box was part of it, too. The book would help her figure it out, and she'd listen to her inner voice, like the High Priestess card said she should.

She pored over the book for more than an hour. Some of the spells used stuff she could find or substitute, but the words that went with them didn't seem right for her mother's problems. To her relief, at the end of the section, it said: "You will find it advantageous to devise your own incantations, as the majority of witches do." Timing the spell was important, too, according to an old witch verse:

> *Pray to the moon when she is round*
> *Luck with you will then abound*
> *What you seek for shall be found*
> *In sea or sky or solid ground.*

A full moon was best. Alison looked out the window at the night sky but couldn't see the moon. Remembering she'd used the Sunday paper to get ideas for her poem, she dug it out from a pile of clothes at the foot of her bed and found the weather page.

Her heart fluttered. Another sign. The moon had been half-full on Sunday and was waxing, getting bigger. So this coming weekend it would be full.

Alison went to the dresser and opened the blue box. The pearl shone its pure light, just like the moon.

30

Janine

Three days had passed since she'd seen April Honeycutt hanging all over Greg at the movies, and Janine still wanted to gouge the little hussy's eyes out. She'd picked up the phone two dozen times, dialed Greg's number, itching to let him know exactly what was on her mind—how she would not put up with him two-timing her, even if it was the era of free love—then hung up before it could ring. She didn't believe in that crap. There was nothing free about love and never would be. Venereal disease, now that was free.

Two things stopped her from confronting Greg about April. First, she had her pride. What was she going to do? Make a scene and beg him to stop playing the field and commit to her? She wanted that commitment, she would get that ring, but not by begging. She might get on her knees in front of Greg, but not to plead. She was in control. Second, Greg might not have gotten April into the sack yet. Janine had driven by his house too many times to count—and by April's, too—and hadn't once seen the other's car at either place at a suspicious hour. April was naive, no doubt about it, but she didn't scream "easy." In fact, Janine had her pegged as a prude. April would expect a gradual progression of dates from Greg, to be led around the bases. Janine would do her damnedest to make sure Greg and April didn't score, or at least that they would chalk up as few runs as possible.

She kept things with Greg light and professional at school and was as sweet as maple candy to April. Thursday night she called Greg "just to catch up" and he proposed they get together the next night. Luckily she was prepared. She'd gone to a lingerie shop in Burlington and splurged on a naughty red teddy. Paired with her red spiked heels, she'd leave that poor little rich boy so speechless it would be all he could do to remember to thank her afterward.

Over the phone, Greg suggested they grab a bite at a beer-and-burger place in Greenville, but when Janine said she was dying to cook for him again, he didn't argue. "I'll bring wine and an appetite."

Friday night they chatted and drank, and the conversation flowed the way it always had between them. Midway through the pineapple chicken, Greg put down his fork. His expression became serious.

"Can I ask you something personal, Janine?"

"Sure." She wasn't sure at all. "I'm an open book."

"You were married for quite a while, right?"

"Nearly ten years."

"But you never had kids."

"No." She hesitated at the entrance to this minefield, not sure of the answer he was looking for. Plenty of teachers had had enough with riding herd on a classroom of kids all day without wanting any of their own. Greg had made it nearly to thirty without starting a family, so he couldn't have been that gung-ho on the idea. Certainly she wasn't going to admit she didn't want to be responsible for more than, say, a reasonably independent house cat. Once she and Greg were married, there were lots of ways around the issue of children. A partial truth would do for now. She cast her eyes downward. "We couldn't. I mean, *he* couldn't. And it was fine." She met Greg's attentive, caring gaze. "I'd promised to love him and that's what mattered most." She pushed on before he could tease her words apart. "As for me and having kids, well, right person, right time, don't you think, Greg?"

"Absolutely. That's exactly how I feel. Some days I think twenty-five is plenty."

She laughed. "I can imagine." She slipped off her shoe and ran her foot up his leg. "I haven't mentioned it—I mean, I assumed you knew I'd take care of it—but I'm on the pill."

"I should've asked, but, yeah, I figured."

"I'd never trap a guy that way."

He smiled, a bit warily though, as if the possibility hadn't occurred to him. "That's a little dated as a strategy, isn't it?"

"Oh, you'd be surprised. It might be 1972, but lots of women are still searching for a shining knight and a house full of babies." Janine slid her foot into his crotch and widened her eyes at him.

His Adam's apple bobbed in his throat. He reached across the table and played with the bangle on her wrist. A smile teased at the corners of his mouth. "What about you, Janine? What do you want?"

She took a long sip of wine, got up from the table and slowly unzipped the front of her dress, selected for precisely this moment. Her eyes never left his, not even as the dress fell to the floor. Greg broke her gaze, swept his eyes over her body and the red teddy that did not cover it, and exhaled in joyful resignation.

Janine stretched her hand out to him. "You."

By candlelight, she studied him in his sleep, admiring the way his sandy hair fell across his forehead, skimming his cheekbone. One of his arms was draped across her hip, the other angled beneath hers, their fingers entwined. His lips, slightly parted, invited her kiss, but she would not disturb him. He was absolutely perfect just like this. A man with some boy showing through, full of ideals and laughter and lust. The ideals she couldn't relate to, but they looked good on him, lending him a special shine. He was handsome and privileged, but the pampered life he'd enjoyed hadn't ruined him. Early on, she'd searched for and hoped to find some ugliness within him, just a smear of something dark. Now she accepted his goodness, not as a fault, but as a trait she hoped to be able to live with. Learn from? Never. Live with. Admire a little, as one might a child kneeling by their bed, head bent in prayer. You didn't have to believe in God, or anything really, to find it sweet.

She pulled the quilt over his bare shoulder. He sighed and settled once more. A surge of protectiveness moved through her, with jealous righteousness right behind it. There was simply no way she would share this man with anyone, certainly not a bland mouse like April Honeycutt. That girl-child would drag him into normalcy. He'd be pinning diapers and driving a minivan before you could say "picket fence." No, Greg Bayliss needed someone stronger, someone with teeth. He needed a woman who wasn't afraid to give his butt a hard slap when he was about to come, and generally show him a better time than he knew to ask for. Janine was also prepared to give Greg a quick tutorial on how to spend his money.

But first she needed to get rid of April. Greg could not be relied upon to simply choose Janine over an adorable special ed teacher with a heart of gold. He didn't even realize he had to choose. It wasn't his fault and she certainly didn't blame him. If Janine were a man, she'd do precisely what Greg was doing. Actually, she'd be a complete prick. Women didn't have that luxury, so instead she'd have to simplify things for Greg. The real work would start next week at school. For now, she snuggled close to him and allowed herself to doze. If he stirred, she'd be there, ready to satisfy him (and herself, of course) in every way he could imagine, and a few more besides.

Gossip was a sport for those with no imagination, and Janine hadn't cared enough about what the teachers and staff did to bother. But in her quest for Greg she made an exception. A few exceptions, though she was careful not to appear to be the origin of any of the rumors that spread like the flu. Ruth Singletary couldn't keep her mouth shut about anything, and if Janine let slip that she'd over-heard a teacher say April Honeycutt had given up a child for adoption because the father was a black man, Janine only did so to emphasize how wrong others had been to repeat such obvious non-sense. She also made sure the elderly Mrs. Penney witnessed her tearing a note into small pieces. When the woman raised her eye-brows, Janine blushed and said Miss Honeycutt had accidentally left an intimate note on the office counter. Janine was destroying it to avoid an embarrassing situation. Of course, Mrs. Penney was nearly deaf, so Janine had to practically shout, and whoever was in the teacher's lounge just might have heard.

Janine was careful not to launch too many missiles at once and relied on the nature of people with empty lives to exaggerate any worthy speck of dirt. Sure enough, less than a week into Janine's campaign, Ruth Singletary buttonholed her in the office after school had let out for the day.

"I suppose you've heard that April Honeycutt left her students unsupervised for a full fifteen minutes today."

"No, I hadn't."

"Chatting in the hall, while her poor students did lord knows what." She tilted her head toward the principal's office. "I'm con-sidering mentioning it to Ike."

Janine feigned disinterest. "Who was she talking to?"

"Greg Bayliss, of course." Ruth's eyebrows darted up.

Anger exploded inside Janine. She spun her chair around so Ruth couldn't see her face. Her mind pushed an idea past the bloodred curtain of her rage. Janine glanced at the clock. "Oh! I'm late for an appointment. See you later, Ruth." She grabbed her handbag and sweater and slipped away.

As she rushed down the corridor, the clicking of her heels

reverberating off the walls, she quelled her anger and frustration by telling herself it was just another rumor. April was too dedicated to those messed-up kids to leave them alone even for a minute. That was April's problem. She was too selfless. Too young. Too adorable. Too perfect. Too *blonde*. She'd never had to cope with anything. Janine didn't have to know her history; she could smell April's happy childhood on her, that baby-shampoo scent that told her everything. April's father adored her and called her "princess," not just at home, but in front of everyone, without a hint of irony or shame. Her mother's arms were always open, and April depended on and confided in her still. Her older brother stood up for her, and her little sister, her exact duplicate, admired her. She'd gone to Brownies and Girl Scouts and to summer camp, where she'd made friends for life on the very first day. April played tennis, well enough to win a mixed-doubles trophy with her father at the club. He kept the trophy on his office desk. She'd gotten drunk once in high school, and her boyfriend had stayed with her, sobered her up, brought her home. April had gone to a respectable college, but near to home because she would be missed, and, because she loved children and had a big heart, she'd studied childhood education. But not even that had been enough. She'd wanted to help the damaged children, the unfortunates, the ones whom God loved as much as He loved her, perhaps more.

Janine strode down the hall and pushed open the front door. The air was bright and cold. Her mind was as sharp and clear as a shard of glass. How easy it was to be good. How simple it was to walk through life with sunshine on your shoulders and a breeze at your back. How perfect each day was, the mornings full of hope, the afternoons filled with purpose and the evenings a song of peace. How fucking wonderful it was to be April Honeycutt.

Several girls crossed the path in front of her on their way to the sports field, arms linked, giggling. Had she ever been that carefree?

She doubted it. Her childhood was a haze. She didn't remember her father, her mother was locked in an asylum, and her husband was dead. What did she have? Carole. Walt, too, she supposed, and their kids, as part of the package. That was it. She deserved so much more. She had a right to what everyone else had. More, actually, because she had so much more to offer. She wasn't whining or jealous. It was the simple truth.

Janine rounded the corner of the building and crossed the lot toward her car, in its usual spot, as far as possible from the playground and errant balls. The lot contained more cars than usual— she had left a bit early because of Ruth—and she wove among the vehicles on her way to the LTD. Movement to her left snagged her attention. Two people at the end of the classroom building, the windowless wall facing the empty playground. April Honeycutt, up against the wall, and Greg Bayliss with his hands on her hips, his body pushed onto hers, nearly covering her. If it weren't for April's blonde hair, Janine might not have known who it was. But she did know.

Rumors weren't going to change a thing.

A calm certainty spread through Janine as Greg lowered his head and kissed April Honeycutt long and hard. She didn't know exactly what she would do, which hand she would play, but there was no doubt in her mind what the outcome would be. Her life was going to be absolutely fantastic. And Little Miss Honeybutt? Well, she'd had it too good for too long.

Janine drove home and poured herself a glass of Chablis, not bothering to cork the bottle, knowing she'd finish it by dinnertime, if not sooner. She paced through the living room, drinking as she went, thinking how much work it was to have to shape your own destiny. She'd had so little help, other than Carole. As much as her sister had done for her in the past, she was useless to her now.

Janine stopped in front a framed photograph of her parents

propped on a bookshelf. Carole had taken it at the beach house in Chatham. The shadow cast by her mother's hat hid everything except her thin-lipped smile, but her father's boater was tipped back and he was laughing, presumably at Carole. Janine didn't remember him at all and it dismayed her. If only he'd not gone off to war and left her with his bitch of a sister. He'd have made sure she was taken care of and ended up with the right man, a man of his own caliber.

She drained her glass and returned to the kitchen for more. How unfair life was. How damn unfair.

31

Carole

The wall calendar said today was October 27, a Thursday. She'd started making an X in the corner of each day to be certain. Remembering the date wasn't crucial, but she pinned down everything she could think of right when she thought of it in case her mind went sideways and things stopped making sense, or voices in her head said things she didn't want to hear but had no choice about. She kept a small notepad and a pen in the pocket of her dress and wrote down everything she needed to know and remember. At least she thought she did. Yesterday she had looked at what she'd written the day before and found page after page of senseless scribbling, random numbers and symbols repeated and crossed out and repeated again. She'd torn out the sheets and stuffed them in the bottom of the trash.

Dr. Carvalho had given her pills for insomnia. She'd slept better at first but not anymore. Not any more out the door like before. Valium was for anxiety. Everyone knew that. She was anxious all right, but she hadn't told him about the voices or the things people murmured whispered shouted or the accusations she made of her husband or the way the television had gone inside out and backward so you didn't see it instead it saw you. She didn't talk about any of that. She didn't trust the doctor. He would send her away would take her from her family he had eyes that looked the wrong way like the television and he might have been the devil. She didn't want his pills and she wouldn't go back there not even for Walt.

She marked the X in the corner of the square and kept track with her notes to pin things down nail them down to the ground. Sound. Nail them down to the ground without a sound.

On Saturday, in two days, it was her mother's birthday. Carole couldn't go shouldn't go. She saw herself walk up to the reception desk asking for her mother waiting to be taken inside going through those doors the double doors made of steel hearing things bad things frightening things and her mother as witness. Witness to the business. And never coming out again.

She couldn't go but Janine could. It was just after nine. Carole held the plan firm in her mind and went into the hallway, picked up the phone, called the school. The number came straight from her brain into her dialing finger. One ring another ring another.

"Good morning, Adams Schools. Janine LaPorte speaking."

"Janine. It's Carole."

"Oh, Carole. Is everything all right?"

Carole never called the school except to excuse one of the children. "Is everything all right?" That was the wrong question an impossible question.

"It's Mama's birthday on Saturday."

"Already? I suppose that's right."

"I'm hoping you would visit her."

"Well, I don't know. I have a lot on my mind at the moment."

"You did say you would—"

"I said I might."

"You said you would. And I can't."

"Why can't you?"

"I just can't. I'm not feeling well."

"But by Saturday you'll be fine."

"Please, Janine. Please."

There was a long pause. Perhaps they'd gotten cut off. Sliced through. Severed. Amputated. Bleeding out. Blood. Bad bad blood. Bad mad blood. Carole grabbed the doorframe time frame no pain no gain. Moored herself.

Janine said, "I've got to make the morning announcement now."

Carole hung on to the receiver as if she were underwater and it was a regulator. "Please. This once."

Janine sighed hugely. "If she's acting crazy, I'm not staying."

Carole saw light shimmering on the surface. In a moment she'd be through she could breathe she could lie down she could give in. "Come by early. I've got something for her."

"I don't know why you bother, but all right. I have to go, Carole."

"Thank you, Janine."

"Go see a doctor maybe."

"Of course. Good-bye."

"Bye."

Carole hung up the phone and drowned.

The next day, Walt made them each a salami sandwich for lunch. He remembered not to put mustard on hers and he cut them on the diagonal—"restaurant style," he said with a grin. She wasn't hungry but ate to please him. She could trust him. None of the nasty voices sounded anything like him. He was a good person the best person. She looked at his strong hands, black in the creases, the gold band. A tide of bittersweet love washed over her. She would be swept away, swept into him. It wouldn't be a bad thing. If she could melt into her husband and stay safe there. Away there. Away inside him where her mind did not matter.

"Carole?"

She could not tell him. What she felt made no sense, not even to her. She pretended to find something interesting outside and went to the window carrying her sandwich. "Yes?"

"I said I had to go back to work."

"All right." She went to the table, put the plates in the sink.

Walt came up beside her. "You seem a little . . . Did you take your pill?"

"Of course."

"Well, you know where to find me." He smiled, his voice light, but his eyes were looking behind hers, probing.

She ran the water and he slipped away.

Carole washed the dishes, wiped the counter and retrieved the mop and bucket from the hall closet. She filled the bucket with hot soapy water, placed it on the floor, wet the mop, wrung it out and pushed it back and forth across the kitchen floor. Again and again, wet wring mop, wet wring mop, wet wring mop, for too long, she suspected, but the rhythm was like humming and rocking; the voices became part of her movement. Vacuuming was the same except not in the living room because of the television. The house was very clean.

The doorbell chimed. She paused, questioning if that's what the sound was. She wasn't certain—how could she be?—but she would check. She leaned the mop against the wall by the refrigerator, went down the hall to the front door and stood before it. She didn't want to see anyone. Already the voices were louder, more insistent.

Carole closed her eyes, put her hands to her ears. "Stop."

She turned down the hallway, into the kitchen, and began mopping. Back and forth and back and forth and back and—

The doorbell chimed.

She dropped the mop, stepped over the handle and strode to the front door and pulled it open.

A man carrying a toolbox. Walt's friend.

"Hello, Carole. Sorry I'm a bit late."

Pete. That was it. "Hello, Pete." But why was he here?

"How you been keeping?"

"Just fine, thanks." She stepped aside, inviting him in, before she knew she had.

He started down the hallway. "Wish I could've come before now, but I've been working every hour God sends." He rounded the corner and went into the living room. Carole followed but no farther than the doorway.

Pete stopped in front of the television and set down his toolbox. "On the phone I think you said there's a problem with the signal. That right?"

She'd called him. To fix it. When had that been? "The signal. That's right."

"Okay, then, let's have a look." He switched on the set and stepped back.

It hummed to life. A conversation. A man and a woman.

Pete studied the picture a long moment, frowning a little. He changed the channel. Once, twice. He gestured to her. "Looks fine to me."

She shook her head.

"Have a look," Pete said.

He could fix it. She knew he could. He was a good man. He'd always been kind and helpful. He wasn't like the others, not Pete. He was like Walt, that's why she'd called him. He knew televisions. He could make it stop. He could stop them. From seeing. She needed to vacuum the room. Even from here she could see the dirt. Pete could fix it. She would clean it. Fix it. Mix it.

"Carole? You don't look so good. You want me to get Walt?"

If she told him he could fix it. He knew the problem it had to be common. He'd seen it before coming in the door. It was his job. And he was a good man. Not like the ones who could see. He was here to help, she could see clearly now.

"I didn't explain it right," Carole said. "It's when it's off."

"When it's off?"

"Except it isn't off. There's no picture but if you're in front of it, they can see."

Pete tilted his head. He was listening. He was a good man.

She said, "You really shouldn't stand in front of it."

He frowned at the television, rubbing his chin, then looked at her. "Have you mentioned this to Walt, by any chance?"

"Oh no. Walt doesn't understand televisions. That's why I called you."

Carole heard the door to the garage open. Walt. Her mind had been so clear and calm while she explained things to Pete. He understood her perfectly. Now her mind roiled with mud-spattered thoughts she could not tell apart, much less grab hold of. She gripped the doorjamb.

Walt appeared and shook hands with Pete. "Saw your truck. How're you doing?"

"Busy. You?"

"Can't complain. Carole, is there a problem with the set?"

"Well. I don't know." She didn't know. There was a problem and Pete would fix it but now Walt was there and she wasn't sure of anything. She'd been so calm and the voices only a crowd whispering low and Walt came and everything was a jumble. Bumble. Humble pie fish to fry.

Pete cleared his throat. "Carole was explaining it to me. A special problem with the signal."

Walt said, "What sort of a special problem?"

"I've seen it once before. You remember Annabelle Carr, Rusty Carr's mother?"

"Sure I do."

"Before she went to the nursing home in Winchester, her set was the same."

Walt went still, his eyes on the television.

Carole said, "You see it now, don't you, Walt?"

Pete reached for the on-off knob. "Here's the fix when you're getting transmission in the wrong direction." He glanced at Carole, then at Walt, to make sure they were watching. "Dead simple. You just switch it on and off three times real quick." He demonstrated. On off on off on off. "Works like a charm."

Pete left and Walt wouldn't leave her alone. He wanted her to tell him things she didn't want to tell. Pete was fixing the television and Walt had interfered and she'd gotten so confused and now she wasn't sure the set was fixed. She wasn't sure Walt was a good man. He kept pressing on her, his voice joining the others in her mind. She walked away from him, out of the kitchen, into the hall, but she couldn't go in the living room because she wasn't sure the set was fixed so she went upstairs and Walt followed her and she went in the bedroom and he followed her there saying tell me tell me. To the doctor next week new pills but she didn't trust the doctor or the pills and maybe not even Walt. She couldn't think straight with him there. Carole lay down pulled a pillow over her head made herself small. Walt offered her a pill but it was poison.

Maybe she slept. Maybe time just passed. The room was dark, the window lighter, silvery.

She sat up, pushed the hair from her face. The voices were quieter now. Murmuring rising and falling like the breath of a giant animal. She glanced at the clock: 5:16. She should do something, make dinner. Where had the children been all day? She could not remember, if she ever knew, and it frightened her.

Voices. Singing? The boys in their room. The television.

Carole got up and went into the hall. The sound wasn't coming from downstairs. She walked a few steps to the boys' room. No light under the door. She followed the sound to the attic door. Was Alison singing? It was her voice, Carole was sure now, as sure as she could be lately about voices.

The door was ajar. Carole opened it and started up. Alison's voice became clearer, her chanting merged with the voices in Carole's mind, amplifying them, sharpening them.

"Ancient moon, lend your power. Bring us peace this very hour. I call upon your strength and might . . ."

Strength and might. Might makes right as rain.

Carole paused a few steps from the top, her heart hammering. Her daughter sat cross-legged on the floor. Light from a candle shone on her face and hands as she held her index finger over a piece of paper with a drawing on it. In the other hand was a needle.

Needle and pins needle and pins trouble begins.

"Heal my—"

The needle went in. A drop of blood fell.

Blood fell. Blood will tell.

Bad blood.

Carole screamed.

32

Alison

She dropped the needle, startled by the scream, and turned to the door. Her mother, her face twisted, her mouth open. Before Alison could think what to say or do, her mother disappeared down the stairwell, her footsteps loud and fast. Her father shouted her mother's name from below. Alison put her bloody finger in her mouth, tasted the salty sweet.

Her father was in the upstairs hall. "What's wrong, Carole?"

Her mother was crying. Her father was asking her questions, soothing her.

Alison looked down at the blue box. Blood spells were the strongest. The drop of blood was supposed to hit the pearl, but it missed because her mother made her jump. Plus she hadn't finished the incantation. It wouldn't work, and now her mother was crying.

Her father was coming up to her room. She knew his feet. Alison stood, waited.

He flicked on the overhead light and glowered at her. "What the hell is going on?" His eyes fell on the magical things: the green construction paper with Satan's circle drawn in soapstone, the candle, the blue box with the pearl, the needle. "What in God's name is this?"

"I was trying to help Mom."

"Trying to help her? How?"

Alison knew he wouldn't understand. He wouldn't believe she had any powers at all. She shrugged and wound a curl of her hair in her fingers.

He pointed at the green paper. "What's that drawing?"

"A magic circle."

"Magic? Jesus Christ. Is everyone one in this family crazy?" He ran a hand through his hair. "Blow out that damn candle before you burn the house down."

Alison knelt and blew it out. She closed the lid on the blue box. A lump stuck in her throat. "I was only trying to help."

He let out a big breath. "You want to help? I'm putting you in charge of dinner. Should be some TV dinners in the freezer. Maybe make some mac and cheese, too. You know your brothers."

She pulled at her curl again and looked up at him. There were lines around his mouth she'd never seen before. Or maybe never noticed. "Sure."

The macaroni stuck to the bottom of the saucepan. Alison had been setting the table and had forgotten to stir it. She turned the heat all the way down, hoping it hadn't burned. She glanced at the clock. The TV dinners would be ready in five minutes.

Lester came in from the office, followed by Warren and her father. Her mother was upstairs, supposedly resting.

"Hey, Alison!" Lester peered into the pot. "I'm starving!"

Warren went to the fridge, pulled out the milk and set it on the table.

"It's done." She stepped away from the stove. "Daddy, can you get the dinners?"

He came around behind Lester, twisting sideways in the narrow space, took the oven mitts from the hook on the wall and slipped them on. He looked strange, like he was in a comedy skit. "Who gets which?"

Lester was guzzling milk and slammed the glass down, sloshing it. "Salisbury steak is mine. It's always mine."

"I don't care, Daddy," Alison said. "Whichever."

"Okay, then." He gave Lester his, and plunked the fried chicken dinner in front of Alison. Warren had loaded two cereal bowls with macaroni for him and Lester, and moved his to the side to make room for his turkey dinner.

Lester reached across and almost stuck his fork in their father's food. "You got Salisbury steak like me, Daddy."

"I sure did."

Warren spoke around a mouthful of food. "Where's Mom?"

"Resting upstairs."

"She sure rests a lot."

"You know she hasn't been well, Warren."

Alison picked the corn and slices of carrot out from among the peas and moved them over to the mashed potato compartment so she could eat them together. She took a couple of bites of a chicken leg and put it down again. She didn't feel very good. Even though she was practically touching her father's elbow, the kitchen felt too big without her mom there. The silence was awkward.

Finally, her father said, "Lester, what did you do today with Miss Honeycutt?"

His mouth was full of macaroni that almost fell out when he started to talk. Alison put a finger to her closed lips. Lester smiled and finished chewing. "She gave us some tests, except they weren't like tests at all. There were puzzles and games and stuff like that but you had to do them as fast as you could but not so fast that you messed up."

"Sounds fun," Alison said.

"Better than PE."

Lester hated PE because of all the rules and because he always got picked last if Warren wasn't there to threaten people.

Warren nudged Lester. "Miss Honeycutt's a real fox, isn't she?"

Their father had been bent over his plate, but that got his attention. He pointed his knife at Warren. "That's not any way to talk about a teacher, son."

"Daddy's right," Lester said. "You should treat her with respect. It's a class rule." He speared a chunk of meat. "Anyway, she can't like you, Warren, because she already likes Mr. Bayliss."

Alison was sure she didn't hear that right. "What?"

"Miss Honeycutt can't like Warren because she already likes Mr. Bayliss."

Warren said, "Likes him how?"

Their father cleared his throat. "This isn't the right kind of conversation to be having—"

Lester started giggling. "I saw them!" He had macaroni in his mouth and a yellow dribble ran down his chin.

Alison looked down at her plate. A creeping feeling started climbing her spine and was at the back of her neck before she could get out the words. "Saw them what?"

Lester couldn't talk from laughing so hard. Warren patted him gently between his shoulder blades. "Take it easy, man."

He took a long breath. "I forgot my lunch box. If I forget my lunch box then I don't have anywhere to put my lunch for tomorrow and I have to eat school lunch and it might be salmon pea wiggle or something else gross."

"Shit on shingles," Warren said.

"Warren!" Dad said.

Warren shrugged because that's what everybody called salmon pea wiggle. Pink goop with peas the lunch ladies poured on crackers.

Lester went on. "I'm gonna finish my story now. I forgot my lunch box. So I went back to Miss Honeycutt's room and Miss

Honeycutt and Mr. Bayliss were behind her desk all smooshed up together. I saw them. They were kissing!"

"For Pete's sake," their father said. "At school?"

Alison shut her eyes to block out the picture her mind was drawing of her teacher and Miss Honeycutt with their arms around each other. Miss Honeycutt as close to him as Alison had been last week when she'd hugged him. Blocking out wasn't working. A cord pulled tight in her belly. The tightness moved up into her chest, squeezing out the air. She opened her eyes. Her heart pounded with an anger that spread over everything in her sight. The pieces of chicken with soggy crust pulling off, peas with dimples in them, carrots cut with a stupid crinkle pattern. The table crammed with TV dinners and milk and macaroni and elbows and that ugly dolphin salt-and-pepper shaker. Her anger grew larger and hotter and devoured her family: Warren, who trampled on feelings and laughed it off; Lester, who didn't know any better and still made her mad; her father, who couldn't see the truth about anything, who didn't get that she'd been helping her mom with the spell. It all made her so completely furious. Her head was going to explode from the force of the unfairness of it—how she didn't matter, how she had to fight just to breathe.

Her fork was in her hand and she stabbed it into the fat part of the chicken leg, jamming it all the way through. She couldn't see very well through her tears, but she kept pushing the fork deeper, straight through the metal tray and into the table. Her palm hurt from squeezing the fork and she focused on the pain, making it bigger, as big as her anger, willing it to spread up her arm and across her chest and take over her whole body.

"Hey, squirt," Warren said, his voice dancing around like everything in life, but especially her, was a big fat joke. "What's your problem?"

She yanked the fork out, slid her hand under the foil tray of her dinner and flung it at him. It hit his chin and arm and knocked over his milk.

"What the fu—"

Alison was on her feet. Her father's arm shot out to stop her, the way her mom's arm flew like a human seatbelt when the car stopped short. She ducked around it and stepped back until she was almost in the hallway. The three of them were staring at her, but she could hardly see them. The kitchen was filled to the ceiling with her anger now, and it blurred them. Her dad pushed back his chair. He was going to do something, get her to stop, smooth things over, put everything back into place. Back to normal. It was too late for that.

Warren swiped mashed potato from his chin. "Stupid crazy bitch."

Her father wheeled around and slapped him, a move so fast she wasn't sure it had happened. He froze, half-standing, leaning over the table. "Don't you ever use those words in this house. Do you hear me?"

Warren nodded. His mouth hung open in shock, his fingers on his cheek. Lester looked back and forth between Warren and their dad and let out a low moan. Her father shifted his gaze from Warren to Lester to Alison, his face scrambled with confusion and rage and disappointment. "I don't know what's going on with this family. Honest to God, I don't."

Alison trembled, her emotions spinning in a thousand directions. Anger was the biggest, and the loudest.

Her father got up, motioned to her. "Come clean this up now. This was your doing, Alison."

"I won't! I'm not doing anything. Why don't all of you just leave me alone!" She spun away and ran up to the attic and slammed the door shut. If only she could lock it. She threw herself on the bed and buried her face in the pillow. Her rage had been holding back her tears, like a tall dam, but now she was alone and there was no one to show her anger to, no one to throw it against. The solid burning tower of it began to weaken, and her tears spilled over.

Her father shouted from the stairs. "Alison!"

She covered her head with the pillow and let the tears come. They poured from her in giant sobs that squeezed her chest so hard she could barely catch her breath. The sobs came in waves, washing over her, and she let herself be thrown against the shore again and again. She heard sounds from downstairs and pretended the people talking and opening and shutting things were strangers. It was true. They didn't know her. They didn't understand the first thing about her. She sank deeper into the pain. As far as her family was concerned, she might as well be someone else, or dead.

She wanted more than anything else to run away. It was so much worse to be here where the people she thought loved her were pretending or lying or stupid or crazy or just plain mean. She wanted to get away from them, not hide in an attic. She wasn't going to pretend the way grown-ups did. She wanted to be honest and have someone to trust. She wanted someone to love her for real. It didn't seem like such a lot to ask for.

Alison wiped her face on the bedsheet. Her breath came in painful chunks and her throat was raw. She hiccupped and it hurt. Every few seconds, another hiccup. She sat up, pushed wet hair from her face and dug out a duffel bag from under the bed. A lump in her throat made it hard to swallow. She did her best to ignore it. She crammed some clothes into the bag, enough for a couple of days. Flopsy's ear stuck up from under the blanket. Alison smoothed her ears, propped her against the pillow. No stuffed animals for this trip. She wasn't five.

Her bag was packed. She put on her jacket, went down the attic stairs to the landing and stopped to listen. Except for the television on low, the house was quiet, like it was holding its breath. If she was lucky, she could leave without anyone noticing. She passed the closed door of her parents' bedroom, felt a stab of guilt for leaving her mother, then tiptoed down the steps and slipped out the back door before she could change her mind.

The night air was sharp and cold. Alison moved out of the light falling from the windows, crossed between the shed and the house and headed for the road. The moon hung low in the cloudless sky, helping her find her way.

First she had to decide where to go. Delaney was closest but Alison couldn't imagine being this pathetic in front of her. She'd probably tell everyone about it at school on Monday. What about Aunt Janine? Her house was a long way, maybe four miles, and the last time she'd tried to talk to her aunt, she hadn't been exactly helpful. She'd probably just drive her straight home.

Mr. Bayliss? Even if what Lester said was true (and she didn't quite believe it), he was still her teacher and her friend. If she told him about how her whole family didn't think she mattered, he'd understand. He'd let her stay and give her a ride to school on Monday. He might even have ideas about what to do about her mother. And his house was only about a mile down the road.

She kept away from the edge of the auto graveyard, where the heaps of metal threw shadows so black and huge they could swallow anything, walked through the circle of yellow from the security light and onto the shoulder of the road. Even with the moon's help, she could barely see the ground, and what light there was made it easier to imagine what she couldn't see. The back of her neck tingled.

Alison shifted the bag to her other hand. Her feet crunched on the gravel. She walked faster and kept her gaze ahead, ignoring the pull of her house behind her, and thought about arriving at Mr. Bayliss's house, and him smiling at her when he opened the door. Alison got that feeling in her stomach like swinging too high, but it was mixed in with a sadness so thick and deep it was like cement oozing out of her pores. The swirling of her feelings was making her sick, as if she'd eaten ten hot dogs and jumped on a Tilt-A-Whirl. She rehearsed what she would say to him when he opened the door.

It all sounded ridiculous: "My mother hears things." "My father gets mad when I try to help." "Delaney was my friend and now she's not." The realest truth was too awful for Alison to say, except in the far corner of her mind, away from dictionary words and hurts and jealousies and tarot cards, away from everything she knew and felt, far away even from the magic of a wish: no one loves me.

Tears sprung into her eyes. She looked around her at the dark shapes and deep shadows, at the bright moon and scattered stars, and felt hollowed out. Alison stopped. There was no point to going anywhere.

Footsteps behind her, coming fast. She froze, too terrified to turn around. She dropped her bag, ready to run for her life.

"Hey! Squirt!"

Alison spun around. Warren was jogging toward her. Her fear disappeared and her anger flared. "Leave me alone!" She picked up her bag and walked off.

He ran past and stood in front of her. "What are you doing, squirt?"

"None of your business. And stop calling me that."

"I saw you out my window."

"So?"

He pointed to her duffel bag. "Running away isn't going to solve anything."

"It solves being with you, and everyone else."

His voice went soft. "No, actually, it doesn't."

Alison sniffed back tears but they ran down her cheeks anyway. "Just leave me alone."

"Mom and Dad don't know you left. If you come home now, you won't get into any more trouble."

"I don't care."

"What's wrong, anyway?"

Alison shook her head.

Warren waited.

She peered over his shoulder at the dark road. The bag was heavy in her grip. Worn out from crying and being mad, she wanted to be in her bed. She didn't want to see anyone or talk to anyone. She was done with her family.

Warren reached for the bag and she let him take it. And when he started down the road for home, she went, too.

33

Alison

The next morning, she hung out in the kitchen, her face sore and tight from all the crying she'd done the night before. Her grand-mother's present, wrapped in paper with balloons on it, lay on the counter near the office door. A couple of weeks ago, when her mother was almost normal, Alison had picked out the sweater from a store in town while her mother stayed in the car. The woman behind the counter had wrapped it, and now the stick-on bow was peeling off. Alison pressed it down. She hadn't asked her parents if she could go with Aunt Janine to visit her grandmother and she wasn't going to. She'd just ask Aunt Janine. Alison had already made a card, figuring it would be harder for her aunt to turn her down.

The door from the office swung open and her aunt marched in.

"Hi, Alison." She was on a mission and pointed at the present. "That for me? I mean, for my mother?" Her lips puckered like the words were sour. "Your grandmother."

"Can I come?"

"Oh, I don't know—"

Alison showed her the card she'd made with a vase of colorful flowers on the front. "I could give it to her in person. Please?"

"I'm not staying long. Just a few minutes."

Alison grabbed her jacket from the chair and picked up the card and present. "I'm ready!"

On their way out, she told her father where she was going. He gave her a long look, like she was doing this to make trouble again.

Aunt Janine said, "Don't worry, Walt. We'll be back before you know it."

"All right, then. Tell her happy birthday from me."

Aunt Janine didn't talk much on the drive. Alison had a lot of questions she might've asked, but her aunt's mind was on something else. That was fine with Alison, who was glad to get away from her parents.

The hills rolled by, the woods a collection of tree skeletons, the rivers muddy and swollen, the fields bristling with corn stubble. The sky was blue but not summer blue. It was deeper than that, as if the atmosphere had thinned and space had moved closer, bringing the stars on their midnight sheet to the brink of day. Alison, too, was at the edge of something. She fingered the blue box she'd stashed in the pocket of her jacket. Maybe her grandmother could tell her what it was for, and give her hope, because she sure could use some.

They wound into the village of Underhill. Alison peered out the window, reading shop signs.

"Look! There's a bakery. Let's get her something, okay?"

"Let's not go overboard."

"Did you have cake on your last birthday?"

"Well, in fact, I did. Your mother made a carrot cake." She sighed, pulled up to the curb and handed Alison her wallet. "Not an entire cake, okay?"

"Be right back."

She bought three cupcakes—chocolate, vanilla and lemon— figuring Grandma could choose her favorite. She guessed it would be vanilla, same as her. Holding the pink cardboard box by the string, she slid into the car.

They continued through the village, past the large, old houses that ringed a small green, and out the other side. On the right appeared a wide lawn stretched in front of a row of tall brick buildings. Many times, Alison had tried to remember what the hospital looked like and couldn't, but now it was familiar.

"Welcome to the loony bin," Aunt Janine said.

She parked the car and they walked to the entrance.

"We should've brought flowers," Alison said.

"It doesn't matter. She'll be happy to see you. If she remembers you." She turned to Alison. "Don't be upset if she doesn't, okay?"

"I won't."

Aunt Janine signed them in, and they flipped through old magazines in the waiting area.

Her aunt stuffed the copy of *Woman's Day* into the rack and sighed loudly. "I hate this place."

"Why?"

"Because it smells and it's depressing."

Alison looked around at the yellow-gray walls and the light pouring in through the high windows. "It's not that bad."

Her aunt shook her head and smiled a little. "Let's hope today it's not."

A few minutes later a man in white opened the double doors and waved them in. They followed him down a corridor to a lounge with a dozen people in it—both patients and visitors, Alison guessed from the little groups. She recognized her grandmother right away, sitting at a card table by the window, holding the arms of her chair as if she hadn't decided to sit or stand. Grandma smiled at her and Aunt Janine. Alison smiled back and went up to her.

"Happy birthday, Grandma." The skin on her face was like an eggshell, her eyes bleary but not frightening or unfriendly.

"Thank you, dear."

Aunt Janine came beside Alison and kissed her mother's cheek as if it were on fire. Her aunt took a seat across the table and made a commotion arranging her coat and her handbag and the bag with the present, acting kind of mental herself. Grandma peered at her daughter with her head sideways. Once Aunt Janine was settled, she caught her mother's look and frowned.

"I'm Janine."

From the look on Grandma's face, that didn't help a lot. "Where's Carole?"

"She couldn't make it. She's not well. Nothing serious, of course."

Grandma pointed a not-quite-straight finger at Aunt Janine. "Janine, you say?"

"Yes, Janine." She raised her eyebrows at Alison to say, *You see?*

"Pleased to meet you, Janine," Grandma said uncertainly. She looked at Alison, who stood holding the bakery box, not quite sure what was going on. "You've grown a lot since I last saw you, Alison."

"Great," Aunt Janine said. "Just great."

"I'm in sixth grade." Alison set the box on the table and sat down. "We brought you cupcakes and a present. The flavors are chocolate, vanilla and lemon. It's your birthday so you get to choose first."

"Oh, how nice. Vanilla, then."

Alison nodded, suddenly happier than she'd been in who knew how long. She untied the string, opened the box and offered her grandmother a cupcake. "No candle. Sorry."

Aunt Janine said, "They probably don't allow them here anyway."

Her aunt didn't want a cupcake. Alison picked the lemon one, and she and her grandmother ate while Aunt Janine stared out the window.

When they finished, Aunt Janine pushed the present across the table. "Happy birthday."

Grandma smiled at her like she wasn't used to taking presents from strangers. She unwrapped the box more slowly than Alison thought possible, folding the paper neatly before opening the lid, and removing an emerald green cardigan. "Oh, how lovely. Thank you both."

"And Carole," Aunt Janine said.

"Yes, dear Carole. Too bad she couldn't come."

Alison said, "That color is really nice for redheads like us."

Her grandmother nodded and a warm feeling of belonging surprised Alison. This was the perfect moment.

"I have something to show you, Grandma. To ask you about." She reached into her pocket, pulled out the blue box and displayed it in her palm.

"What is it?" Aunt Janine asked.

"A box," Alison said.

"I can see that."

"It's Grandma's."

Her grandmother's gaze was glued to the box. Alison didn't know what to make of her expression. It seemed to contain more feelings than Alison had names for.

Alison said, "It's special, isn't it?"

"Oh, yes." Grandma looked up. Her eyes were as green as the sweater folded in her lap. "My mother gave it to me." She pursed her lips and swung her head back and forth, like she was trying to get something moving in there. "To help me. At least that's what she tried to do."

Aunt Janine pushed back her chair. "I haven't a clue what either of you are talking about. We should be going anyway."

Alison ignored her. She cupped the box in her hands. "How, Grandma? How could this help you—or anyone?"

Grandma closed her eyes tight. Alison closed hers, too. Maybe if she linked her mind with her grandmother's, she could help her remember. She fell inside herself drifting, floating. A pair of white shutters appeared before her. She lifted the latch and a breeze blew the shutters open, revealing an empty space, cobalt blue, same as the box. Alison's heart rose in her chest like it might wriggle through her ribs and take flight. She opened her eyes.

Her grandmother was waiting for her. "It can bring someone back to you, someone who should've been there all along."

"Who? Who was your mother trying to get back?"

"Me."

34

Janine

The entire drive home, Alison chatted about her grandmother as if she was her new best friend. Maybe the girl was as relieved as she was that Solange had managed to be relatively sane for an hour. Janine would have appreciated being recognized by her mother, but she hadn't expected miracles. She had done her duty for her sister and that was that.

The excursion to Underhill had temporarily distracted Janine from the situation with Greg, but as they made their way to Adams, she began to turn over possible strategies for winning him once more. There weren't many. Maybe she should give up and move to some other low-rent Vermont town, find another Greg, one that didn't have an April Honeycutt barnacle attached. The problem was that she liked this Greg rather a lot. Too much.

"Aunt Janine?"

She hadn't heard a word the kid had said for a good five minutes. "Uh-huh?"

"I was saying how great it would be if Grandma could come have Thanksgiving with us, at our house. Just for the day."

"Oh, I don't think so."

"Why not?"

"I know she was okay today, but she's not always like that."

Alison stiffened. "Seems like lots of other people aren't okay, but nobody cares about that."

Janine didn't know what she was talking about and wasn't inclined to pursue it. The kid was getting weirder all the time. It might have been a mistake taking her to see her grandmother. All that nonsense over a little box.

"Your grandmother has been at Underhill a long time. Leaving, even just for the day, would probably upset her."

"Or maybe that's just easier for everyone."

Good lord, she was moody. Two minutes ago she was chirping away and now she was on a crusade to repatriate her nutcase grandmother into the family, pulling Janine into the middle of it. This was why she never wanted to be dragged to Underhill. And certainly not with a temperamental kid who couldn't be satisfied with a cupcake and a car ride. What a waste of time.

The garage and its charming auto graveyard came into view, and Janine breathed out a sigh of relief. The birthday jaunt was over. She pulled off the road and came to a stop alongside the pumps.

Alison swung the door open. "Thanks for letting me come along, Aunt Janine. I'm really glad I went."

Jekyll had become Hyde again. "Thanks for the company." Over Alison's shoulder, she caught sight of a light blue car on the lift in the garage. A Comet with Connecticut plates. She'd been stalking it long enough to be certain it belonged to April Honeycutt. "Tell you what. That visit to your grandmother put me in the mood for family. I'm going to pop in and say hi to everyone."

"Okay." Alison trotted off.

Janine parked next to Carole's car, got out and wound past the pumps to the garage. She had no plan, but if there was an opportunity, she sure as hell was going to take it.

Through the glass front of the office, she spied Walt conferring with a tall man at the counter. The waiting area was empty. Janine proceeded to the garage and stood behind the car on the lift. Lester was under it with his back to her. A VW station wagon with the hood propped open occupied the other bay, but no one was working on it.

"Hey, Lester." She spoke softly. He startled easily, and she didn't want tools flying.

He startled anyway, jerking around to face her, wrench in hand. "Hi, Aunt Janine!"

"What are you working on?"

His eyes lit up. "This is Miss Honeycutt's car. My teacher. She's not here now, though. Mr. Bayliss picked her up. They were both here, my teacher and Alison's. Isn't that neat!"

A sour taste flooded her mouth. "How exciting for you." She clenched her fists. Next to her was a bench with an array of heavy tools. She fought to keep her hands at her sides and not pick up one of them—the crowbar would do nicely—and smash the shit out of the car.

Lester waited, staring, thrilled to have her attention.

"So, Lester, what's wrong with this nice car?"

"Not too much. I'm adjusting her brakes."

"And you can handle that?"

"Sure can, Aunt Janine. Mr. LaPorte showed me how. It's not hard at all." He grinned, proud and eager. "Wanna see?"

"Absolutely." She had never been interested in car mechanics—other than what her husband, Mitch, had insisted she learn for safety's sake—but now she was rapt.

"These here are the brake pads, and when they wear down you have to move them closer."

"Makes sense."

"Cars always make sense, Aunt Janine." He pointed with his wrench to the adjuster on the back of the brake drum. "So I move the pads all the way in, then out a little bit."

"That's it?"

"Uh-huh. Except we always check the lines, in case they're rusted or something."

"The brake lines?"

"Yup. Them." He swept the wrench along a narrow metal tube running front to rear. "I checked them both already."

"No holes?"

Saliva flew as Lester burst out laughing. Janine curbed her annoyance at being laughed at by someone with an IQ near seventy, and concentrated on the job at hand. "What's so funny?"

"If the brake line had a hole, the brakes wouldn't work at all, Aunt Janine. We check them to see if there's maybe going to be a hole later."

Janine traced the brake line to where the metal linked to an S-shaped rubber hose. From there it went somewhere near the brake drum. She suppressed a gleeful laugh and smiled broadly at her nephew. "You're doing a great job, Lester. I'm impressed." She flipped through a flywheel of options for distracting him and settled on a simple one. This was Lester, after all. "Your mother's calling you."

"I didn't hear anything."

"Well, I did. You'd better go."

He frowned. "Okay, Aunt Janine."

"And please tell her I'll be there in a sec. I need to get something from my car."

"Okeydokey."

He lay the wrench down and sidled through the door to the office. Before the door closed again, Janine confirmed that Walt was still conferring with the customer, but probably not for much longer. He wasn't a big talker. Janine scanned the workbench for a blade, or something she could abrade the rubber with. The metal saw in front of her was too large, too crude. Why wasn't there a simple knife? Her heart thumped in her chest as she turned to the adjoining table. Screwdrivers, wrenches, other tools she didn't know the names for. The front office door chimed. The customer leaving? Someone else arriving? She hadn't heard a car drive up. In desperation, she yanked open a drawer. Boxes of screws. She opened another one. More screws. A third. An assortment of junk. She raked it aside and pulled the drawer out farther. A narrow, rounded piece of serrated metal with a wooden handle. A file.

In two steps she was under the right front wheel. Her heart pounded in her ears so loudly she'd have been deaf to anyone approaching. It didn't matter; she just had to be quick. She reached up, grasped the black rubber hose and ran the file back and forth along the top, close to where it joined the wheel, where the damage would be least noticeable. She pressed down, gently, wary of going all the way through. How thick was this hose anyway? Better too little than too much. Walt or Lester had checked for any weak spots, hadn't they? She slid the file across one more time, returned to the workbench, tossed the file inside and slammed it shut. Brushing off her hands, Janine hurried out of the garage.

The tall man was getting into his truck. Janine reached the office windows and slowed. A door closed behind her, maybe Walt going into the garage. She didn't look.

She retrieved her handbag from the front seat of her car. She leaned against the door, taking deep breaths, striving to quell the mixture of rage, fear and hope coursing through her. It was done. Whatever would happen, would happen. Soon, she hoped. It had to be soon, didn't it? Ah, well, it was out of her control now. She'd done everything she could.

Her stomach settled. She checked her hands for grease and, finding them clean, arranged a pleasant look on her face and walked casually across the lot. A short visit with Carole, then home. Perhaps an afternoon movie on the television and a glass of wine. With any luck she'd soon have something to celebrate.

35

Alison

Alison thanked her aunt for taking her to visit her grandmother and went into the garage office. Her dad was busy with a customer, so she wound past the counter and into the house. She didn't want to talk to him anyway. The chairs were upside down on the kitchen table. Her mother was on the far side of the room mopping the floor.

"Hi, Mom."

Her mother straightened and blinked at her. "Watch out. It's wet."

Alison tiptoed across the room in giant steps to the wood floor in the hallway. "Grandma said she was sorry you couldn't come."

"Oh. I wish I could have. I've just been so—" She stared out the window, studying the sky, as if the explanation for how she'd been was a weather report.

Alison felt sorry for her. Again. Still. It was like a toothache. "We brought her some cupcakes and she loved the sweater."

Her mom pulled away from the window. Her forehead was creased but she smiled a little, too. "I'm glad. I'm glad she had company on her birthday."

The smile opened a door of hope in Alison. The story of the blue box was on her lips, but she reeled it inside, worried about her mom freaking out about it for a reason Alison didn't understand or for no reason at all, and worried, too, about spoiling the special connection she had with her grandmother. She wasn't a little kid, and her mom didn't need to know everything. It was better that way.

Alison said, "I'm going to the river."

"Of course." Her mother blinked at her once, twice, then went back to mopping.

In the attic, with a layer of rooms between her and her mom, Alison shoved down her frustration. Part of her felt her mother wasn't trying to get better, that she'd given up. Alison wanted to shake her, wake her up, make her snap out of it. Her mother had been better for a month, maybe longer, before the television thing. And her mother took pills for it. How could pills work and then not work? Alison didn't want to be mean, but after so much worrying about her mother and wondering if she really had a mother at all, she was tired of it. Let her father take care of her, since he seemed to know everything.

There was only one person in her life she could rely on, one person she could trust not to hurt her or ignore her or misunderstand her: Mr. Bayliss. Alison hadn't known what to do when Lester said Mr. Bayliss had been kissing Miss Honeycutt. She hadn't wanted to believe it, but now it didn't matter, because even if it was true, Alison had the solution. She'd found out this morning what the blue box was for. The box's power had been obvious from the beginning; she just hadn't known what sort of power it contained. One question was bugging her though: should she use the blue box in a spell with the pearl and the soapstone, or should she just give it to Mr. Bayliss?

Maybe she could figure it out if she went to the river. She slid open her top dresser drawer and fished out the white sock with the objects inside. She unzipped her jacket pocket, took out the box and spilled the pearl and the soapstone into it. All set.

As she sprinted downstairs, Alison gripped the box to protect it and to feel the pearl leaping inside like the trout, as if the pearl had made the fish surface and take the bait, delivering itself to the light and coming to rest within the blue box.

Between having to go to school and the buckets of rain pouring down nearly every day, Alison hadn't been to the river in ages. She chose the longer path, tracing an arc past the Dalrymples', and gave only a passing thought to what Delaney might be doing. Delaney wasn't worth more than that. Alison entered the woods, the leaves underfoot a brown, soaking mess, sunlight hitting the ground head-on the way it never did in summer. The sun wasn't warm, though, and the woods didn't protect her from the stiff wind in her face. She tugged her jacket tighter.

She heard the river before she saw it, a rumbling like distant thunder that slowed her step. The trees thinned and the roar deepened. She came to the edge. The muddied water, not a yard from her feet, had flooded the shore. It surged past, slicing at the banks, the rapids foaming and churning.

How had she not noticed this, even from a car or the school bus? She searched upstream, toward the swimming hole, for something familiar, a reminder of her favorite place. There was nothing. On the opposite bank, a large maple tilted over the water with some of its roots hanging free. The tops of the rapids slapped the roots again and again. That maple might end up in the river. It was a scary thought.

Her river had changed from a playful, bounding puppy into a snapping, vicious dog. She hugged herself, shocked and sad and frightened. A gust of wind blew a spray of water into her face. She turned her back on the river and ran through the woods, as fast as she could, in the direction of home but not for it. She ran to leave the cruel river behind. If she could, she would run straight off the earth.

Monday morning, Alison packed her book bag and checked her bedside clock. Ten minutes before she had to go outside and wait

for the bus. She still hadn't made up her mind about what to do
with the blue box. Her great-grandmother had given it to Grandma,
so maybe that's the way it was supposed to go. But Alison had the
pearl and the soapstone, too, and refused to accept that they didn't
have their own power and were supposed to be used together with
the box somehow. A spell made sense to her, a love spell, of course.
It would work best if she had something of Mr. Bayliss's, something
personal.

With a little luck she'd take care of it today at school. If that
didn't happen, if she couldn't get the last piece for the spell, then
she'd do exactly what her great-grandmother had done: she'd give
the blue box away—to Mr. Bayliss. It might not be today or tomorrow, but it would be soon, and she had to be prepared.

Alison left the pearl and the soapstone behind inside the white
sock. She zipped the blue box into her jacket pocket. She might
need it anytime. Her inner voice would tell her when.

It took Alison all morning to realize that snatching something
personal from Mr. Bayliss wasn't simple. She couldn't just waltz
up to his desk and take his coffee cup, which she wasn't sure was
personal enough anyway. He kept his wallet in his pocket (not that
she would take his wallet—she wasn't a thief) and his car keys and
other stuff in the top drawer of his desk. The best thing to get
would be some of his hair, but she'd never seen him comb it except
with his fingers, when he was thinking. Blood would work, too,
but she couldn't exactly stab him. If she was lucky, he'd get a paper
cut. She kept a tissue in her pocket, just in case.

The lunch bell rang and she lagged behind, pretending to dig
in her book bag. She looked up and he was waiting at the door.

"Got what you need, Alison? I'm off to a meeting."

"Sorry." She grabbed her lunch and scurried past him. She shot
him a smile, but he was shuffling papers and didn't see.

During sixth period, the second to last of the day, Mr. Bayliss
handed back their social studies tests. Alison's stomach knotted

up when she saw her grade: a seventy-nine. She had never scored that low in her life. She folded the test in half and straightened the other papers on her desk. He moved on.

That low grade was a shock, but by the end of the day she had a plan of how to use it. The last bell rang and the kids scrambled out of their seats, grabbed their coats and bags and zoomed out the door. Alison went, too, then ducked into the bathroom and slid into a stall. A few seconds later, another girl came in, peed and left. Alison waited for the noise in the hall to die down, then waited several minutes more. She'd miss the bus—there was no way around that—but she didn't care. Either she'd find what she needed from Mr. Bayliss's desk or, if he was there, she'd use her test as an excuse for staying late to talk to him.

Enough waiting. She unlatched the stall door, crossed the bathroom and stuck her head into the hallway. All clear. In three steps she was across the hall. She turned the knob and stepped inside, glancing around, as if her teacher might be hiding under a table or in the closet. The skin on her arms tightened and her mouth went dry. Kids weren't supposed to be in classrooms without a teacher. She'd better be quick.

She closed the door behind her and crossed to his desk. Nothing on top. She moved the swivel chair and pulled open the top drawer. Her hands were sweaty as she shoved aside erasers and notepads and boxes of thumbtacks in search of something, anything.

The door latch clicked. Alison froze.

Miss Honeycutt stood in the doorway. Alison slowly closed the drawer. "What are you doing in here? Alison, isn't it?"

Alison's face was on fire. She moved out from behind the desk. "I was looking for a pen to write Mr. Bayliss a note. I wanted to talk to him about my test." She opened the flap of her book bag, pulled out the test and held it in front of her. The papers shook so hard she could hear it. She clutched them to her chest and stared at the floor.

Miss Honeycutt said, "Mr. Bayliss left for a meeting at the district office. Did you tell him you wanted to see him?"

Her voice was soft. She wasn't suspicious or mad. No wonder Lester liked her so much. And Mr. Bayliss. Alison wished she could sink right through the floor and disappear forever.

"No, I didn't tell him. I was embarrassed." It was true. Everything was embarrassing and awkward and painful.

Miss Honeycutt came closer to Alison, smiling. "It's only a test."

Alison shook her head. If only Miss Honeycutt knew. But Alison was too hurt and too tangled up inside to explain, or to hope that explaining would matter.

"Gosh, will you look at the rain?" Miss Honeycutt pointed to the drizzle outside. "You've missed the bus, haven't you?"

"Yeah."

"Tell you what. I'm done for the day. Why don't I give you a ride home?"

It wasn't raining hard but the air had a bite to it. Alison followed Miss Honeycutt to her car and climbed in, shivering. Miss Honeycutt started the car, and they sat there a minute, waiting for the engine to warm up. The windows fogged.

Miss Honeycutt grabbed a towel from the backseat and wiped the windshield. "Manual defroster." She rolled her window down an inch. "Can you crack yours, too?"

They left the school and drove through town. Cars coming the other way sprayed arcs of water from their tires. The sign at the Lamoille County Bank blinked "3:14" then "34°."

"Maybe we'll get our first snow tonight," Miss Honeycutt said. "I hope it won't spoil trick-or-treating Wednesday. Are you going with your friends?"

"Sure." In fact, she'd been avoiding all the talk about Halloween costumes, parties and plans, just like she'd been avoiding everything else. It was simpler.

As they passed the library and the last houses in the town, Alison began feeling something was out of place or pulled inside out. Or maybe the way she'd been looking at everything was messed up, like when she'd lie on her back and stare at the ceiling and imagine it was the floor. The windows were still windows but the world was upside down in them. She walked along the ceiling and stepped over the threshold at the door, because the top of the door in this world went all the way to the ceiling, which was actually the floor. She'd meander through the entire house that way, crawling along the sloped ceiling over the upside-down stairs, peering out into the green field, trees dangling into the blue sky at the bottom. It gave her a wide-open feeling. The world could be many ways at once, and she had it in her power to choose. She only had to decide what it was she wanted.

The houses were farther apart now and set back from the road. They passed Grantham's Dairy and began dropping into the valley, going pretty slow. Alison glanced at the speedometer. Not even forty.

Miss Honeycutt noticed her look. "It almost freezing, so it might be a little slippery."

"Okay."

The long bend of the river came into view below, blanketed in mist. Halfway down the hill, Miss Honeycutt moved her foot to the brake. She grabbed the wheel tighter. "Oh God."

"What?"

"The brakes! My foot's all the way down. They're not working."

Fear crawled up Alison's legs and arms. Miss Honeycutt pumped her foot up and down, up and down. The car was gaining speed. The road curved to the right just ahead, right before the bridge.

Alison's heart raced and a metallic taste filled her mouth. She pressed her hands against the seat, her insides turning slippery, her mind swallowed up with fear. Miss Honeycutt hit the brake again and again, staring at the road, her mouth open, but the bridge only got closer.

"I'm pulling into the field. Hold on!" She yanked the wheel to the right. The windshield filled with yellow grass. Alison squeezed her eyes shut and pushed against the seat, waiting to hit the ditch. Her stomach lurched as the car slipped sideways. She opened her eyes. A scream burst into the air. The guardrail, the bridge zoomed to her window, in slow motion. She threw her arms to cover her face. A massive crunch and Alison was knocked onto her side, the seatbelt tearing into her belly. The car jumped forward. A jolt from below threw her upright again.

The river.

Screams filled her ears. The car tipped nose down. Alison braced her feet on the floor and grabbed the door handle. A bump yanked it from her. Water rushed over the hood.

"Help!" Alison reached for the door again. "Help!"

The river swallowed them. An arm clutched at hers. The car swayed, one way, then the other, and leveled. Freezing water poured onto Alison through the gap in the window. Leaks sprouted everywhere: the floor, around the steering wheel, through the dash.

"Help!" Alison sputtered. She flailed in panic. Her hand hit the seatbelt. She groped for the buckle. The car tilted. She glanced at Miss Honeycutt. She wasn't moving. Water streamed through the window and sprayed off her. Blood flowed from a gash above her ear.

Alison pushed her shoulder. "Wake up! Wake up!"

She had to get out. Now. Alison's fingers found the seatbelt buckle, lifted the latch. She reached for the other buckle, Miss Honeycutt's. The world went black at the edges. Water rose to her shins. She reached again and opened the seatbelt latch. Miss Honeycutt fell against the door with a thud, water streaming over her face.

Alison grabbed her door handle, jerked it up and pushed. It

wouldn't budge. She threw herself against it, her breath cutting her lungs, her sobs choking her, water pouring onto her head and shoulders. She got ahold of the window handle and cranked it. The force of the water knocked her backward, but she held on to the handle. She grasped the window frame with her free hand, bracing herself against the river flooding in, pushing her. Alison took a breath, gave the handle another turn and thrust herself headfirst into the water. She squirmed through the opening, her knees scraping the window edge. Her shoe caught on something. She tried to kick it loose and her foot slammed into metal. Pain shot up her leg. Her lungs burned. She kicked again and her foot was free.

The river took her. The cold entered her. She clawed her way to the surface, sucked in the cold air. A wave threw water into her mouth. She was sinking. Her clothes weighed her down. She kicked and fought to stay afloat, carried downstream, the car somewhere beneath her or behind her, Miss Honeycutt inside.

Yelling. Someone was yelling. Her legs were frozen. She didn't know if she was kicking. She went under, swallowed water, grabbed for the air and surfaced. Her name. She turned to the sound. Her head snapped sideways, a searing pain shot through her skull.

Black.

36

Carole

The rain had eased to a drizzle. Carole rose from the office chair, pulled on Walt's quilted jacket from the stand by the door and went out to get the mail. She skirted the pumps and heard Walt's voice come from the open garage. At least she assumed it was Walt. She couldn't make out the words, and these days if she heard talking and there was a reasonable explanation for where it was coming from, she didn't investigate further. The crowd noise was always in the background, sometimes loud, sometimes soft, but always there, even in her dreams. It put her on edge, but it was soothing compared to the others. Others smothers. Smothers mothers.

She lowered the mailbox door, reached inside and pulled out the mail, hoping it wouldn't take long to sort through, hoping it was ordinary. Then she heard a different sound, not voices, but the whine of tires on the wet road; a car coming down the hill. Carole closed the mailbox. A loud crunch startled her. She oriented to it. A pale blue car, sliding sideways. A flash of red in the window. She stood transfixed as the car careened off the barrier and hurtled down the bank, toward the river, and fell out of view.

"Walt!" She glanced at the garage. No one there. She screamed with all her might. "Walt! The river!" He appeared, Warren beside him. "A car went in the river!"

She dropped the mail and ran up the road. The car. It was familiar. And in the window. Red.

Red hair.

She sprinted harder, gasping for air. A sharp pain stabbed her side and her foot slipped sideways on the icy road. She regained her balance and moved to the shoulder, shoes crunching, lungs burning.

She neared the bridge. Stumbling down the embankment, Carole pushed through shrubs, yanking her arms from entangling vines. She emerged at the riverbank, alarmed at the force of murky water rushing past. The car was gone. She glanced downstream. Something red. The back of her daughter's head. Carole raced along the bank toward her.

"Alison!"

Alison spun around, mouth open. A log floated in her direction. A wave tossed it at her head and she went under.

A surge of electricity shot through Carole. She stripped off her coat. Walt shouted her name from behind. She ignored him, stepped to the edge and dove into the river, the shock of the cold forcing air from her lungs. She opened her eyes but it was impossible to see. She searched with her hands, probing frantically. Out of breath, she climbed to the surface, stole a lungful of air and dove again. Carole kicked hard, grasping, reaching. Her hand hit fabric. She grabbed it and pulled it toward her. An arm. She wheeled herself upright and clutched her daughter tightly, scissoring her way to the surface.

Her head emerged from the water. She gasped for air and laid back, Alison on top of her, waves splashing over them. Carole sculled out of the faster current with her free arm.

"Carole! Alison!" Walt rushed down the slope and waded in. He scooped their daughter into his arms and laid her on her side on the grass, raking the hair from her face.

Carole fell on her knees beside Alison. "She's not breathing!"

Walt held Alison by the shoulder and hit her upper back with the heel of his hand. Her body convulsed and water spewed from her mouth. She coughed and gasped, her face contorted. Carole sobbed with relief. Alison coughed, again and again.

Walt patted her back. "Easy does it, sunshine." His voice broke.

Alison's gasping eased. She blinked her eyes open. "Mom?"

Carole gathered her daughter in her arms. Alison buried her face into her mother's chest, coughs racking her body. Walt touched the top of Alison's head and hurried off. Carole almost called out after him, but noticed figures upstream, under the bridge. Warren squatted, holding someone. Lester stood over them, flapping his arms at his sides, wailing.

"Put her on her side!" Walt shouted as he ran. "Smack her on the back. Hard!"

Carole bent over Alison, rocking her and smoothing her hair. Her daughter's chest heaved. Carole heard the voices of a large crowd at the edge of her mind. *Go away*, she told them. *Please.* She spoke over them. "Alison, are you all right?"

She nodded, lips quivering.

"Whose car were you in?"

Her daughter's body tensed. She jerked up and looked at Carole, her eyes wide. "Miss Honeycutt! The brakes didn't work and the car skidded—" She twisted around, scanning the river, the far bank, her eyes finally alighting on the group under the bridge. "Is she okay? Mom?"

"I don't know. Your father's there."

Alison wriggled out of Carole's arms and onto all fours. She placed a foot on the ground to stand. Her ankle crumpled and she cried out. Carole caught her under the arms and pulled her close.

A violent bout of coughing echoed under the bridge. Lester cheered. Carole and Alison watched as Warren and Walt helped April Honeycutt to a sitting position. Lester draped the jacket his mother had abandoned over his teacher's shoulders.

"She's okay!" Alison's teeth chattered and her lips were blue.

"Here, let's get you out of that soaking jacket."

Carole helped Alison take it off, then wrapped her arms tightly around her daughter, whose entire body shook.

"Mom, can I ask you something?"

"Of course."

"Something's wrong with you, isn't it? Something worse than what the doctor thinks, right?"

Carole started to shake her head, to deny it. The crowd noise rose, as if clamoring to be acknowledged. She had had enough of hiding. She was exhausted.

"Yes, there is. I've been pretending it's not serious. I've been afraid."

Alison grew very still. "There's something in the pocket of my jacket."

"We'll get it later."

"No." Alison paused to cough several times. "I want you to have it now."

Carole dragged the jacket closer, unzipped the pocket and removed a small blue box. It was familiar. She turned it in her hand, her memories pushing against the muttering crowd in her mind, getting louder, nearer. The box had been her mother's, she remembered now.

Alison watched her. Her eyes were red and brimming with tears. Her voice was rough from the river water. "It's for you, Mom. I was always supposed to give it to you."

"Why?"

Tears spilled down her daughter's cheeks. "To bring you back to me."

"Oh, Alison." Carole hugged her daughter with all the warmth and strength she could find. If only courage and love could be enough.

The voices in Carole's head roared, shouting down her simple wish. Each cry was a needle piercing her brain, one here, one there, another and another and another, dozens upon dozens of cauterizing pinpoints, sharp, searing.

"Stop!" she shouted.

"Mom!" Alison squirmed in her arms.

Carole squeezed her tighter.

A man's voice exploded in her head, a deafening thunder. *Blood will tell! Blood will tell! Like your mother! Blood will tell!*

Carole began to hum and rock, hum and rock. Alison twisted in her lap. Carole hummed and rocked. The man's screaming became unintelligible, painfully loud. Carole cringed and whimpered.

She'd heard this voice before and others just as overwhelming and terrifying. They came from inside her. She believed what they said about her selfish, disgraceful mother and her cowardly, unloving father. They were her. She was them.

She was trapped and could not save herself from the voices and the truths they told. She was guilty and wretched and ashamed. Drenched and shivering on the riverbank, Carole held on to Alison as if her daughter was the lifeline rather than the one rescued.

A different male voice bellowed inside her, steel-hard, a sword run through her skull: *Bad blood. Bad mad blood. You should have drowned. You should die.*

Carole clung to her daughter.

"Mom! You're hurting me!"

Carole released her and fell backward onto the soaking grass, her hands clamped over her ears. She screamed with all her might but could not drown out the voices.

37

Alison

Warren pulled Alison away from their mother and helped her into the truck bed, telling her to stay put while he and Lester lifted Miss Honeycutt into the cab. Alison couldn't take her eyes off her mother, thrashing on the riverbank, kicking and screaming at her father, who was trying to get ahold of her. Finally, he got his arms around her and she calmed down a little. He gripped her tight, as if she would fly apart otherwise.

Warren drove to the house and called the police. Lester dragged blankets down from upstairs and wrapped them around Alison and Miss Honeycutt. It was like a disaster movie. Their dad told Warren and Lester what to do while they waited for help, shouting instructions from the kitchen, where he stayed with their mother. Twice she tried to run out the back door, but he stopped her. Alison pulled the blanket over her head so she couldn't see the wild, scared look on her mother's face.

Miss Honeycutt's head was bleeding badly, and most of the time she had her eyes closed. The police and the ambulance crew showed up and took care of her first. Alison wanted to talk to her mother, give her a hug, calm her down, but Warren had been told to keep Alison quiet in the living room and he took his job seriously. The policemen, who'd both known their family for a long time, pulled their father into the hall for a talk.

After, her dad knelt beside her chair. There was mud in his hair and worry all over his face. "Listen, sunshine. I've got to take your mother to Burlington, to the hospital. She won't go otherwise."

"Okay."

"You'll go in the ambulance with Miss Honeycutt. I'll see you there."

"Okay."

He squeezed her hand.

"Dad?"

"What is it?"

"What Mom has? It's not the Change of Life, is it?"

"I don't expect it is."

"She thinks people on television can see her."

He nodded. "I know she does."

"Tell the doctors, okay?"

He kissed her forehead. "Don't worry. I'll tell them everything. It'll all be fine."

Alison's throat clogged with tears. She wanted to believe him more than anything in the world.

The emergency room doctor examined the lump on her head, took an X-ray of her foot and left her lying on the bed surrounded by machines and a white curtain. A nurse brought her an extra blanket but Alison still felt cold deep inside.

"Hey, you." Her father pulled the curtain to the side and sat in the chair next to her. "Doctor says nothing's broken, so that's good. We just need to keep an eye out in case you have a concussion."

"How's Mom?"

"Better. They gave her something to calm her down."

"Can I see her?"

"Not today. I'm going to take you home."

"Does she have to go to Underhill?"

He frowned and thought a minute. "Let's not get ahead of ourselves, okay? The doctor doesn't know exactly what's wrong yet. Said he'd know more tomorrow. I'll come back then." He scooted closer, leaned his elbows on his knees. "Your mother's in the right place now. I wished I'd listened to you better, wished I'd seen things more clearly on my own. I'm sorry."

The bridge of Alison's nose tingled and pressure built behind her eyes. "I just want her to be better, Daddy."

"I know, sunshine. You and me both." He picked up her hand and held it in his. Hers—small, pale and freckled—and his—broad and tanned, nails stained with grease—could have been from two different species. But they weren't.

Alison stayed home from school the next day, reading and watching television with her foot propped up on a pillow on the coffee table. "Keep it elevated," the doctor had said. Her ankle had blown up to the size of a cantaloupe and throbbed like it had its own heart. So did her head. She had a lump on the back the size of an orange. Basically, she was lumpy fruit. She hadn't slept very well because of her foot and her head, and because she was worried about her mother.

Her brothers came home from school. Lester brought her a snack and told her how everyone at school went bananas over Warren for his rescue of Miss Honeycutt. Not just for diving in and pulling her from the car, but also for smacking her on the back to get the water out of her lungs.

"I know, Lester. I was there. Dad told him to do it." On the way home from the hospital yesterday, her father had told her he'd learned the smacking thing when he was in Korea in the navy.

Lester said, "I told all the kids how Warren spotted the aerial sticking out of the water and dove right in. Like a superhero."

"He did. He was brave. Just like Mom."

"Only your head was the aerial." He burst out laughing. So did Alison.

Their father had assigned chores for her brothers to do while he was gone. Alison read for a while, then dozed in front of the television, bored out of her mind.

Warren came in from the garage and stood in the doorway. This was the third time he'd checked on her.

"Still alive, squirt?"

"You don't have to keep checking on me."

"Dad said every half hour. Lester's keeping track and won't shut up until I do." He plonked himself on the couch next to her. Sally was snuggled up on the other side of Alison and peered across to see what he was up to. "What are you watching anyway?"

"Reruns of *Love, American Style*."

"Beats cleaning up the body shop." He pointed at the bag of Lay's on Alison's lap. "Hand me those, will ya?"

Later, the three of them watched television together and waited for their dad to come back from Burlington. Lester groaned when the news came on and got up to change the channel. He hated the news. The door to the office opened and the smell of pizza floated into the living room. Their father came in, shucking his coat. He looked so sad. Alison's heart squeezed tight.

Warren got up out of their father's recliner. "How's Mom?"

"I won't beat around the bush. The doctors think your mother has schizophrenia." He dropped into the chair.

"What's that?" Lester said.

"It's when you can't think straight and you imagine things. They've started her on the medicine for it."

Alison said, "Is she better yet?"

Their father shook his head slowly. "That's the thing. It takes a couple weeks to work. They'll keep her in the hospital until they're sure she'll keep taking it."

Warren frowned. "Why wouldn't she?"

"The schizophrenia makes her suspicious of things."

"Oh. How long has that been going on?"

"A lot longer than it should've."

A huge weight pressed down on Alison's chest. She wanted her mom to come home, to be her normal self. She didn't want to wait weeks to find out if she'd get better. It seemed so unfair. Her mom belonged at home, with them. "What if the medicine doesn't work? It didn't work on Grandma."

Her father said, "They're different people. And from what I understand, they're not sick the same way." Her father looked at each of them, his blue eyes bloodshot. "I'm not promising miracles. Far be it from me. But I do promise to take care of your mother." He stood up and motioned to the kitchen. "Come on now, boys. Let's dive into this pizza before it gets cold. Alison, you want cheese, right?"

Alison nodded, then watched them go. Everything seemed different because of the accident. Some things were worse, like her foot, and some things, like her mother's sickness, were in that in-between place where they could go either way. Then why did things feel better overall? Maybe because the secret was out and they didn't have to pretend everything was hunky-dory. Pretending, it turned out, was a problem all by itself. If you didn't know the truth, how could you know the best thing to do, or what to hope for?

That was the trouble with magic. Omens didn't always mean what you thought they did, and magic spells, well, maybe they worked and maybe they didn't. Magic spells were concentrated wishes—she understood that much—but maybe the wishing part was more important than the magic. Maybe you had to wish that hard to find out what you really wanted.

. . .

After dinner, she was hobbling from the bathroom when the phone rang. It was Caroline. She'd heard about the accident and wanted to make sure Alison was okay. Alison pulled the phone around the corner for privacy.

"Yeah, I'm okay."

"You probably can't go out trick-or-treating tomorrow, huh?"

Alison glanced at her foot. "Maybe as a mummy." Caroline giggled. "You going into town?"

"Not sure. Delaney, Maggie and J.J. are going as the Three Blind Mice." Her voice trailed off.

"And you don't want to be the cat?"

"I wish I'd thought of that!"

"Well, I'm stuck here."

"You could come over, give out candy with me. Watch a movie."

"Really? You sure you don't want to go out?"

"I'm sure. Can your mom drive you?"

Alison stared at the ceiling. She could just say her dad or Warren would drive her—they probably would—but it didn't feel right. Everyone would find out about her mom eventually and she wanted someone to trust. She'd practice on Caroline.

"My mom is sick."

"Like the flu?"

"Not like that. You can't tell anyone, Caroline. No one knows yet and it's super important you don't tell, okay?"

"I swear I won't."

"She hears things that aren't there. It's really scary for her."

"Wow. That would be scary."

"She's in the hospital. In Burlington."

"Gosh."

"But they're giving her medicine that will probably help."

"That's good. Is she coming home soon?"

Alison swallowed. "I hope so."

"Me, too. I'd miss my mom if she wasn't here. But so far she always is. I'm going to ask her about tomorrow. Hold on for a sec, okay?"

Alison twirled the cord, remembering when she'd called Aunt Janine to ask her about the Change of Life. How Aunt Janine had laughed at her. Her throat closed remembering how awful she'd felt. Caroline was a much better person to talk to.

"Alison, I'm back. My mom says it's fine. And she'll take you home after. Can you get a ride here?"

They worked out the details of their plan. Alison hung up the phone and went into the living room, where her father and brothers were watching television. Her foot was aching and her whole body was sore, but the heaviness in her chest had lifted some. She sat on the couch next to Lester.

"Here, let me do it." Lester hoisted her leg onto the table and Sally jumped onto her lap.

"Allayed," that was the word. Her fears had been allayed.

Well, some of them. She stroked Sally and thought about her mother, alone in a hospital room. Maybe she could visit her the next time her dad went. Alison was afraid of what she might be like—strange things she might say or odd looks that didn't line up with anything real—but she wasn't afraid of her. If Alison could, she'd lie on the bed next to her. Her mom might even put her arm around her and they could stay that way for a while.

Alison handed her book bag to her father and hopped down from the attic on one leg. It took forever and her brothers were already outside waiting. Lester scrambled into the backseat of the Nova so Alison could have the front—first time ever. Her father put her bag in her lap and squeezed her shoulder. "Take it easy today, sunshine."

"I will, Daddy. See you later."

Warren stashed her crutches behind the seat and got behind the wheel. He put a Bad Company tape in the player and tapped his fingers on the steering wheel while he drove. Lester started singing and Warren told him to cut it out.

They pulled up to the curb near her classroom. Warren helped her with her book bag and crutches.

"Thanks for the ride," Alison said.

"Only until you can walk again, squirt. Don't get used to it."

It had only been a couple of days, but Warren seemed different, more confident, like he didn't need to keep pushing everyone around to make himself superior because he'd actually done something to be proud of. Alison wondered if it would last.

The tarmac was buzzing with kids, more hyped up than usual because of Halloween. They weren't allowed to wear their costumes until the parade after lunch, but some had taken hats and wigs and masks from their bags and put them on anyway. Alison went straight to the door to beat the stampede when the bell rang. Kids came up to her, girls asking if her foot hurt and boys asking if it was cool to almost drown.

Davey shouted as he ran past, chasing a ball. "Hey, Alison! Did you see the light?"

No one asked what happened because everyone already knew. A boy in her grade opened the door for her, and she limped down the corridor, the book bag over her shoulder hitting her hip with every step. Her armpits were killing her.

Mr. Bayliss was sitting behind his desk and gave her a big smile.

"Hey, Alison. It's really good to see you." He came over and pointed at her bag. "Let me help you with that."

"Thanks."

She moved her crutches to one hand. Mr. Bayliss slipped the bag off her shoulder and let it dangle at his side.

Alison didn't know what to say. The jumpy feeling was there

in her stomach, but she also felt shy and a little embarrassed, like she'd stepped over an invisible line that wasn't invisible anymore. Alison pretended her injured foot was suddenly interesting.

Mr. Bayliss said, "I heard your mom pulled you out of the river."

"Yeah, I got clonked on the head by a log, and she dove in and saved me."

"That's amazing."

She looked at him. "My mom is amazing."

He smiled. "You had to get it from somewhere."

38

Janine

The fuss around April Honeycutt's accident was ridiculous. You'd think the woman had been raised from the dead, and having the entire LaPorte family at the center of it made it that much worse. For a week no one talked about anything else: April this and Warren that and poor little Alison and her brave mother. To be honest, Janine hadn't thought her sister had the guts for that sort of stunt. And Warren. Why couldn't he just have been a little less heroic, or just a minute slower? That's all it would've taken to finish off April Honeycutt, or leave her a cabbage. No such luck.

April appeared in the school office ten days after the accident. The staff flocked around her. Janine stood—she couldn't very well sit there—and moved closer. Her mouth dropped open. April's hair was no more than a couple of inches long all over, except for the completely bald patch where they'd stitched up her skull.

April touched her head. "I know. It's drastic. But they shaved so much off, I decided just to go with it."

"It's very chic," another teacher said.

And, damn it, it was. It might have been the hairstyle—or the "brush with death," as that idiot Kawolski called it—but April Honeycutt had lost her sacred wholesomeness. She'd acquired the merest edge to her, a glint of tragedy, and it brought her beauty into sharper focus.

Janine couldn't stand to look at her.

As soon as Janine got home, she kicked off her shoes, poured herself a glass of Chablis, drained it and poured another. It was becoming an afternoon habit and she really didn't give a damn. Greg called partway through the second glass.

"Hey, Janine. You got a sec?"

"Sure. What's up? We still good for tomorrow?" They were going to hear a band at a bar in Burlington. She had gotten tickets while April was languishing in the hospital. Janine was dying to know whether Greg could dance.

"That's partly why I'm calling. It has to do with April. You know, the special ed teacher."

"I'm the secretary, Greg."

"Right. Well, I don't quite know how to tell you this."

Over the phone, like a coward. "Tell me what?"

"I've been seeing April."

"Seeing her?" Part of Janine was enjoying how awkward this was making him—she'd done her job—and the other part wanted to climb through the phone line and wring his neck.

"Yeah. I thought maybe you knew. In fact, I thought maybe you'd be cool with it."

She finished her wine and poured the rest of the bottle into her glass. "Where are we going with this, Greg? Are you playing eenie meenie miney mo?"

He let out a nervous laugh. "No, not that. I had an epiphany of sorts."

Janine hated epiphanies. And what was an "epiphany of sorts"? *This* was what was wrong with Greg. *This* was what she could fix if he gave her the chance.

He went on. "When April was in the hospital, I realized how much an accident, or anything out of the blue, could change a relationship. I mean, we were sleeping together, and she almost died, and it didn't matter as much as it should have."

"It didn't?" The words came out before she could think.

"No. And it made me rethink not just April and me, but you and me, too."

Hope fluttered in her chest. She drank some wine. They were finally getting somewhere. "Greg, I want to hear about us."

"Oh, Janine. That's just it. It's the same. Me and April. Me and you. I should take things more seriously, because, you know, sometimes life does get serious. I'm not saying I don't have feelings for you. You know I do—"

"Deep feelings take time."

"Sure. But here's the other thing. You both work at school. It's really not cool."

"We've been careful, haven't we?" Unlike that little blonde slut who allowed herself to be pushed up against the wall like a ten-dollar hooker.

"Yes, but that's not the point."

Patience was leaking out of her. Why didn't he spit it out?

An agonized sigh came through the phone. This epiphany was not sitting quite right with him, or else he would've said what he wanted to say and hung up.

Finally, he said, "Here it is, Janine. I'm not going to be involved anymore with someone I don't feel deeply about, especially not someone who works at school. That goes for April and it goes for you. I'm sorry."

Janine froze with her wineglass an inch from her lips. She waited for the next line, the one that would prove he meant it.

"You're such a great gal, Janine."

"Fuck you, too, Greg."

She slammed down the phone, threw the glass across the room and kicked the table leg with her bare foot. A jolt of pain shot up her leg. She cried out and tears flooded her nose, welled in her eyes and ran down her cheeks. She allowed herself to cry for ten minutes, or maybe a bit longer, then went to the bathroom to splash cold water on her face. She'd been a fool, a complete and utter fool.

The following Monday after work, Janine parked her car next to her sister's and entered the garage office. The door chime sounded. Walt was leaning against the front of the counter, rubbing grease cleanser into his hands. He picked up a rag and wiped his fingers one at a time. Something about his posture stopped her from speaking first, and she stayed near the door. Walt finished with one hand and started on the other. He was three fingers in before he spoke, and even then he kept his eyes on the rag.

"Afternoon, Janine."

"Hi, Walt. How'd you know it was me?"

"I think I know that car by now."

"Right." She approached him. Once she was in motion, the rudeness of his refusal to look at her registered. She was already irked by his attitude in summoning her in the first place, an annoyance layered on top of the injustice, the stupidity of what had happened with Greg. She wanted to punch someone. Not once, but again and again. Really pummel the crap out of them. Or cry. Both. She wanted to make someone hurt, make them hurt everywhere, then shut the door on them and cry. Again.

Instead, she walked past Walt toward the door to the kitchen. "Let's have some coffee, and you can tell me why I'm here."

He spun and grabbed her arm, stopping her.

"Walt!" Janine spun to face him. His expression was stony, his eyes cold. She drew back.

"This isn't a talk for coffee." He let go and lowered himself onto the swivel chair behind the desk. There was a chair behind her but she remained standing, out of defiance and so she could flee.

He read her easily. "I don't care if you sit or not, Janine."

"Walt, I don't know what's going—"

"Which is why I aim to do the bulk of the talking."

Janine sighed impatiently and took a seat.

Walt rested his elbows on the chair arms and interlaced his fingers. "The police have been going over Miss Honeycutt's vehicle, looking to see why the brakes failed. And yesterday they came over here asking about the service we'd done right before it happened."

Janine adjusted her handbag on her shoulder. "What's this got to do with me, Walt?"

"I'm getting to it. We stand by our work, that's what I told Bill. Bill Tuttle, he's the sheriff. We go back a ways. I told him we changed her oil and adjusted the brakes. He wanted to know who did the work." He leaned forward, forearms on his knees. "It was Lester. He's been doing simple brake work for a while now. Good at it, too. But I think you know all about it."

Her mouth filled with cotton. "Me?"

"Bill asked Lester about the job, whether there'd been any problems. Lester told him it'd gone just fine. After Bill left, Lester said he didn't have any problem remembering the job because you'd come around near the end and he'd showed you what he was doing."

"Well, sure I was here. I dropped Alison off after we went to see my mother at Underhill. And Lester—"

Walt raised a hand to stop her, his mouth a taut line. "That's plenty. This isn't a conversation. I can put together what happened. The brake line blew out on that car. She wasn't gonna stop until she hit something. Bill didn't think for a minute Lester'd done it—why would he?—but he did get it in his head that a mechanic ought to check the brake lines if they're in the neighborhood. Lester says he did. Said they were fine. Got right upset about it." He stared at her. "And I believe him."

She fought the urge to squirm in her chair. "I hope Lester's not in trouble."

"He doesn't appear to be. Line broke at the bracket. Not the easiest place to see a problem."

Janine forced a smile. "So Lester's fine, then. That's good."

Walt slapped the side of his thigh and Janine jumped. "It sure as hell is." He glowered at her. "Lucky for you. If it weren't for Carole, I'd point the sheriff in your direction, not that they'd have much to go by, other than Lester telling me you *asked* him about the brake line. Funny you asking him that. Never showed much interest in mechanics, far as I can tell. Maybe the police would find something else funny. I can't say and I don't rightly care. But I'll tell you this, Janine. You could've killed my daughter, and that teacher, too, and put Lester and the rest of us in an ungodly mess."

He wheeled the chair toward her until their knees were nearly touching. Her heart beat in her ears. The look in his eye was terrifying.

"Walt, I don't know what you are talking about. Honest."

"Honest? I think you need the dictionary for that one." He laughed bitterly and scooted back to the desk. He opened the top drawer, removed a pen and searched under the piles of paper. "Here's the deal, Janine, so listen up. I don't want you around, knowing what you likely did and not knowing what you might do next. I can't run you out of town, though, on account of Carole. She doesn't know a thing about any of this and she's not going to. Pretty quick, I need you to make up a story about getting a job— a good job—someplace else. Someplace far, you got me?"

"A job? Where?"

"I don't care. Ah, here we go." He plucked a checkbook from the mess and showed it to her. "Will five thousand set you up all right?"

Janine froze. "Where would you get that sort of money?"

"Remember when your Aunt Regina passed two years ago? Carole never said anything because she didn't want to upset you, but Regina left her a sum of money. It came down from your father, after he died in the war. Not as much as you might expect. I imagine Regina dipped into it whenever it suited her. Carole was supposed to have it some time ago but Regina held on to it like it was hers."

This was the first she'd heard of an inheritance. Every time she'd asked Carole about it—starting in her teens—Carole said if there was money, she didn't want it, which made no sense at all. Everyone wants money. And now Carole had some. "He was my father, too. It all went to Carole? That's not fair!"

Walt stilled. "I'll tell you what's not fair. Getting goddamn schizophrenia's not fair." He let that sink in. Janine looked at her lap. "Anyway, you're getting your share now. Another thing Carole doesn't need to know or worry about. As long as there's plenty for whatever Lester might need, and something for Warren, too, if he needs it, and college for Alison. Extra expenses maybe for Carole being sick. We don't need more than that. And we've got plenty." He opened the checkbook and held the pen over it. "So, five thousand it is."

It was a lot of money, more than she ever expected to have again, not counting what a husband might provide. It would get her away from Greg, out of Adams, out of Vermont.

"Make it six."

He gave her a long, steely look. She didn't flinch.

He wrote the check, tore it from the book and reached it across. She tried to take it from him, but he held on, stared her down again. "Carole will want you to visit. You'll be far away, you'll be busy. You'll call, send cards. Carole loves to get cards. You'll be goddamn happy. But you won't come back hardly at all. You got that?"

"Sure, Walt."

He released the check.

She folded it in half, slipped it into her handbag and stood, smoothing her skirt. A series of retorts, curses, promises and lies marched through her head, but she didn't waste her breath. "Goodbye, Walt."

Her back straight, she strode out of the office. As she approached her car, she admitted Walt had surprised her, rattled her even. He had more backbone than she'd credited him with. Carole was lucky; Walt would stick by her no matter how crazy she was.

But he'd gone too far in blaming Janine for what had happened. It wasn't her fault her niece was in that car. She had nothing against the kid, and like Walt said, there would have been serious grief for a lot of people if anyone had died. She'd have felt terrible about that. Except, of course, if it had been April Honeycutt.

Janine slipped behind the wheel and pushed all such useless thoughts from her mind. She had what she wanted, at least for now.

39

Carole

Walt got up from the kitchen table, refilled Carole's water glass and set it in front of her.

"Practically a full-time job." He winked at her.

"I can't believe how thirsty I am all the time."

She'd been taking the antipsychotic medication for more than a month now. Her mouth was constantly dry, and she felt dizzy and groggy much of the time. The doctor advised her to be patient, saying he would adjust the dose as necessary.

Alison's near drowning had set off a terrifying episode. She'd stayed in the hospital for more than a week. When she wasn't heavily sedated, she was confused and scared. The voices and paranoia followed her home, and she'd often refused to take the pills, sure they were poison. Walt, and sometimes Alison and the boys, would have to soothe her and reason with her before she would relent. Carole found out later Walt had twice resorted to putting the medicine in her food, which made the treatment take longer to work.

But, eventually, it did. Little by little, the voices receded, as if her mind were a train, underway at last, leaving unwelcome passengers stranded on the platform. She'd become so accustomed to the voices, the quiet in her mind was unsettling, her natural inner voice unfamiliar. Carole's paranoia abated, and she was restored to herself, but not completely. Her thoughts were like bricks she had to push around in her mind. Although she couldn't recall precisely how she had felt before this disease overtook her, she knew it was not like this, one foot poised on quicksand.

Walt took a swig from his beer and stabbed the last piece of pork chop on his plate. Carole sipped her water and studied him. He'd been unusually quiet the past week or so. She had a hunch about the reason, and tonight, with Alison at her friend Caroline's house and the boys at a basketball game, was as good a time as any to talk.

"Walt."

He looked at her, steady as always, but holding back a little, too. "What's on your mind?"

"I'm sorry."

"What for?"

"I should've told you. About the voices and the rest."

He pressed his lips together, considering. "Well, not trusting is part of it, isn't it?"

He was giving her an out. And it was true that shortly before the accident, her net of suspicion had widened to include him. But that wasn't the whole story.

"It is. But I had a lot of chances to tell you, and I should've." She reached for his hand, damp from the perspiring beer can. "I should've had faith that you'd do the best for me. You always have."

He squeezed her hand and smiled, the blue of his eyes deepening. "I like to keep my promises."

"I know." Her voice caught in her throat. "I was so scared."

Walt nodded. "Knowing something was wrong with you and keeping all of it to yourself. No one's that strong." He looked down and gently spun her wedding band between his fingers. "Not alone."

． ． ．

A week before Christmas, Walt took Carole to the medical center in Burlington to see her psychiatrist. After Dr. Friedman gave her a physical exam, he invited Walt to join them to discuss how Carole was faring.

Dr. Friedman jotted notes in the file. "I'm pleased the Thorazine is working so well for you. Usually an early positive response means it'll keep on working, but of course we'll be monitoring you closely." He flipped to another page. "I've been waiting for you to feel better before bringing this up."

Carole glanced at Walt, who lifted his hands an inch to say he was in the dark, too.

The doctor continued. "When you were first admitted, I asked your husband about any family history of mental illness, and he shared with me your mother's condition. Because it's an important part of your history, I requested her records from Underhill State Hospital. Carole, do you know why your mother was admitted there?"

"I never got a clear answer. Hysteria, I think."

"I see. In 1938, the term 'hysteria' was an umbrella term for all sorts of symptoms and conditions. Your mother's physical exam showed nothing of interest other than that she'd recently given birth and was very thin. Her history of mental or behavioral problems was vague and brief. Do you remember anything?"

Carole couldn't see where this was leading. "Only that she didn't leave the house much during her pregnancy. Once my sister was born, she became agitated." She thought about adding that her mother had run away, but since she'd only been going to her mother's, Carole wasn't sure. So much of what happened then still confused her. "I always assumed she had a breakdown—something more than what I saw, or remember."

The doctor pointed at his notes. "There was a notation on her admittance report saying 'Husband requests committal.'"

Walt said, "Maybe he was worried about her, that she'd hurt herself."

A sense of foreboding came over Carole.

Dr. Friedman shrugged. "It's possible. I can't say anything with certainty. But that phrase was often used when a man wanted his wife committed, not necessarily for her good, but for his. It was not uncommon and most doctors went along with it."

Carole stared at the doctor, stunned. "But why would my father do that?" As soon as she said it, she realized she knew. Because of her mother's betrayal. Her chest constricted and she struggled to breathe.

Walt leaned toward her. "Are you all right, Carole?"

She'd never told him about her mother's affair. She should have, she could see now, but she hadn't. Instead, she'd borne her mother's shame. "Yes. Of course. It's just all so upsetting."

Dr. Friedman said, "Mrs. LaPorte, I only bring it up because we should be aware of your mother's history. You suffer from schizophrenia while your mother, as best as I can surmise from her files, had a collection of memory and anxiety problems as likely to have been caused by early, misguided treatment as helped by it."

"I'm sorry," Carole said. "I must have misunderstood you."

"It's distressing, and of course it's only conjecture, but there's nothing in her files to suggest otherwise."

She pictured her mother in her room at night, screaming for her baby. Her stomach knotted and she clenched her teeth. "They made her this way."

He nodded. "It's possible. At that time, once patients were admitted, especially if no one advocated for them, they were unlikely to leave."

Walt put a hand on Carole's shoulder. She hung her head and squeezed her eyes shut. Her father did this. Her aunts had to have known, too. Had Aunt Bettina ever visited Solange as she claimed she had? By the time Carole saw her mother, ten years along, the damage had been done. Pity swept through her.

The doctor went on. "There's something else."

Carole straightened and tried to breathe normally. She felt Walt tense beside her.

Dr. Friedman referred to the file again. "When I asked for your mother's records, the clerk found two S. Giffords. I gave your mother's year of birth and your father's name, in case your husband had the date wrong. Osborn is an unusual name." He made a pyramid with his fingers. "The other S. Gifford was Osborn's mother."

Carole frowned. "I don't see how. My father, and my aunts, too, I think, told me she had consumption. That's tuberculosis, right?" The doctor nodded. "They sent her someplace dry, Arizona, maybe. But she never recovered. She died before my parents met."

Dr. Friedman said, "Her files are very complete. She was admitted for psychotic symptoms and diagnosed with schizophrenia." He tapped the files with his pen. "She committed suicide at Underhill in 1921."

The edges of Carole's vision went black. She was only dimly aware of Walt's arms around her, the murmurings of the doctor, the linoleum underfoot, the cold snap of the air as Walt led her to the car.

On the ride home, she cried, heartbroken that her mother might have been confined to Underhill for so long without reason, that her suffering and bewilderment and isolation might have been preventable and, worse, that Carole's father might have been the cause. Yes, Solange had betrayed him, but getting rid of her, locking her away from her children—from her life—was unspeakable.

Carole pulled a tissue from her handbag and blew her nose. She'd been keeping the secret from Walt for so long, but now it seemed a simple thing to tell him. It wasn't her secret. It wasn't her shame.

"On my eighteenth birthday I found out something from Grandma Rosemarie. My mother's mother."

Walt looked over at her then returned his attention to the road. "What was that?"

"My mother had an affair."

Walt let out a low whistle. "Well, I guess that happens."

"No, Walt. You don't understand." The urgency in her voice caused him to glance at her again. "Janine's my half-sister. We have different fathers."

"What's this?" Walt signaled and pulled into a small side road. He put the car in park but kept the engine on. He pushed his watch cap off his forehead and sighed. "Now, Carole, tell me again."

"I never understood why my father and my aunts didn't care for Janine—"

Walt raised his eyebrows and sighed. He didn't care for Janine, either. Carole must have understood this, because it didn't surprise her. He'd kept it to himself because he knew how much she loved her sister.

Carole wiped her eyes. "I should've told you. I was ashamed of my mother, and I didn't want Janine to know. She's had a hard enough time."

"You don't suppose I could've kept a secret?"

The sorrow in his voice pained her. How many times would she have to hurt him? He was right to be disappointed in her.

"I know you would've. But I didn't have anyone to talk to before I met you. I pushed all of that ugliness away. It was all I knew to do. And once I'd buried it, that's where it stayed."

She began to cry again, for the frightened girl she'd been, for her futile attempt to rid herself of her parents and for how she'd compromised her marriage in the process.

Walt unclipped his seatbelt, slid over to her and wrapped her in his arms. "You don't need to be sorry. None of it was your fault. None of it."

"But I should've told you."

He pulled back and lifted her chin with his fingers. "You told me now. And it doesn't matter a damn." He kissed her. "I love you, Carole. You. Everything that's worth a damn in my life starts with you, and nothing about your family will ever change that one least bit."

She smiled, despite everything. "I love you, too."

He slid behind the wheel. "Let's go home."

Carole dabbed her eyes dry and looked out at the bare winter landscape, turning over the doctor's revelations and trying to reconcile them with what she knew about her parents, especially her father. She had no idea whether he knew about the true nature of his mother's illness, much less that she'd been sent to Underhill and had taken her own life there. His sisters were more likely to have known, given that they were older, but that wasn't a certainty, either. Osborn's father might have lied to his children about their mother to protect them; that, at least, was more understandable, even laudable, unlike Carole's father's lies, which seemed to serve only himself. He sent his wife away because he could not cope with raising a child who was not his, or find some way to preserve the happiness of both his wife's daughters. The shame was more salient to him than his own life, which he sacrificed on the false altar of war. Only this fact softened Carole to her father at all, because she was only too aware of how powerful shame could be.

They arrived home before noon. Walt opened the office door and flipped the sign so the Open side faced out.

Carole removed her coat and folded it over her arm. "Will you have something to eat before you start work?"

"Sounds good."

They'd only had cereal that morning, so Carole set to work making fried-egg sandwiches. Walt poured coffee. Carole arranged slices of bacon in the pan and adjusted the flame.

Walt handed her a steaming mug. "We don't have to talk about this, but I'm wondering if you knew who Janine's father was."

"I don't mind talking." Carole sat at the table and Walt sat, too. "My grandmother told me the day I found out my father died. His name was Caleb Ploof. He grew up on the lake, like my mother did.

He died in the war." She sipped her coffee. "But Regina must've known, too, because she called Janine 'that pirate child' once. On that same day. I wonder if they'd have treated her differently if her father had come from their side of the tracks." She shrugged. "Maybe it wouldn't have mattered."

She got up to turn the bacon over.

Walt said, "I only met your aunt a couple times, and that was plenty. She was hard."

Carole smiled at him. "Well, you weren't good enough for me."

She'd said it lightly. It was a joke between them, as old as their relationship. But in the words now she heard echoes of countless slights and offhand remarks made by her father's relatives during her childhood. She heard the late-night arguments between her mother and father, and her aunts' pride in referring to Carole as her father's daughter, as if she'd escaped being tainted by the curse of her mother. She felt her sister's hurt at being pushed into a dark corner again and again.

Bad blood.

The idea had haunted her for so long, permeating her subconscious. The irony was that if she had bad blood, it came not from her "pirate" mother, but from her father, in the form of this disease.

Walt got up and slipped his arm around her waist. "That old biddy Regina might've had that right, you know."

Carole put down the spatula and faced him. A sly smile played at the corner of his mouth and his eyes drew her closer. She put her arms around his neck. Tears filled her eyes, and when she smiled at him, they fell.

"I doubt it," she said.

"Let's call it even."

Walt swayed her slowly, and leaned his hip against hers. She slid her foot back.

They were dancing.

40

Carole

Outside the office windows, snow fell in large flakes, far apart, sifting down like seconds. Carole tapped the stack of November's receipts on the desk to align the edges, fastened a binder clip to the top and set them aside. She'd reconciled the month's accounts. A humble enough feat, but one she knew better than to take for granted. The figures on the pages of the ledger obeyed simple laws when her mind was clear enough to see them.

Walt came in from the kitchen, followed by the boys. He pointed in the direction of the garage. "No funny business while we're gone. Do the oil changes and look after that carburetor. Remember Mrs. Tuttle'll be in for an inspection on that Saab of hers. That's it. Don't start taking apart someone's engine if they happen to pull up for gas."

Warren headed for the garage. "Yeah, Dad."

"Yes, sir, Mr. LaPorte!" Lester gave a small salute and trailed after his brother.

Walt held out her coat for her. She thanked him and slid her arms into the sleeves, aware the coat was snug. She'd gained fifteen pounds, a side effect of the medication. Her body felt awkward with the extra weight, but she didn't dwell on it. Walt settled the coat collar, rested his hands on her shoulders and kissed the back of her head.

Alison came through from the kitchen, a cake in a Tupperware container balanced on the crook of her arm. "I'm ready to go!"

"So you are," Carole said.

Walt grabbed the keys from the desk. "We'll take the truck. Haven't gotten around to putting snow tires on the Valiant."

Out front, Alison handed the cake to Carole and climbed in beside Walt. Carole passed the cake to her and got in, trying to recall the last time they'd had Alison between them. She hadn't known she'd missed it until now.

They turned onto the road and crossed the bridge. Alison craned her neck to see the river, tumbling gray and quiet. Carole couldn't picture what had happened there, having no clear memory of it.

She asked Alison, "Does it scare you?"

"Not really." Alison leaned back and adjusted the cake in her lap. "It's never the same two days in a row."

Carole nodded.

They followed the river valley out of Adams. The truck rumbled along, past small towns and through hills dusted in white, snow coming down so slowly it seemed winter might last forever.

Her father shook his head in wonder. "Will you look at that."

"It's like a snow globe," Alison said.

Carole took her daughter's hand and squeezed it. "It's beautiful."

She remembered driving along this road in August, when the world had been a feast of green. She'd been frightened then, by the mysterious scrambling of her perception, by the encroachment of ominous and unwelcome sensations. She'd been tipped upside down, and turned inside out, and now, as in a snow globe, the flakes were settling.

Still, she worried, not so much for herself, but for her children. The doctor had told her each child had a one-in-eight chance of developing schizophrenia. There was nothing she could do to alter the odds, to block the path of misfortune, nor would there be a remedy for the guilt she would feel if one of her children should inherit the illness from her. It wasn't logical, but it was true. What is in your blood matters, but not as much as what is in your heart.

They arrived at Underhill and walked toward the entrance along paths coated with snow. Walt carried the cake because Alison said she was worried about dropping it. Once inside, they stomped their feet on the mat. Walt signed them in and they took seats in the waiting area.

Carole studied the drab room. How fortunate she was to have medication that worked. Without it, her fate might have been the same as her mother's; she might have languished here with scant hope of improvement. A surge of compassion for her mother's misery came over her with more force than she'd ever felt. The terror and isolation she'd experienced at the height of her illness was fresh; maybe because their illnesses had different origins, her mother's internal world was less chaotic and frightening, but how could Carole know? She reined in her emotion by focusing on Alison, whose face shone with excitement.

An orderly appeared at the doors.

Carole said to Alison, "She may not remember you. Please don't be upset if she doesn't."

"She remembered me last time. Right away."

"All right. But it might be different today."

Solange was waiting by the French doors, as if contemplating a walk in the snow. She wore a deep green sweater and a gray skirt. As they approached, she furrowed her brow, perhaps searching for a plausible slot in which to place them.

"Mama. I'm so happy to see you." Carole kissed her cheek.

"Carole, dear."

"Walt's here. Isn't that nice?"

She smiled at him but her expression betrayed confusion.

Walt ran a hand through his hair. "Good to see you, Mother."

"And you, Walt." Solange's eyes brightened as she stepped closer to Alison. "And Alison, too. Well, this is a quite a treat."

Her daughter looked up at Carole, beaming, then addressed her grandmother. "I made a cake for you. It's vanilla."

"That's my favorite."

"Mine, too. I like your sweater."

"Thank you."

They moved to a table, and Carole served the cake. They talked about the snow, and Alison told her grandmother about her friend Caroline. Solange listened politely for a time, but her attention soon drifted.

Carole handed Alison the paper plates and plastic forks and pointed to a nearby trash can. She covered the remaining cake. "We're tiring you, Mama."

"Hmm?"

"You seem tired."

"I am a little. I haven't slept much. I've been so worried about the baby."

Alison had returned. "What baby?"

Carole stilled her daughter with a look. "Please don't worry, Mama. The baby is just fine."

"Is she? I was sure she was in pain." Her eyes glistened. She clutched Carole's hand, hanging on, knuckles white. "I couldn't bear to think of her in such pain. She was such a lovely baby. Such a good baby."

Her mother's face was a terrible, beautiful image of agony and love. Tenderness swelled within Carole. She pictured her sister as she'd first seen her, lying in her bassinet, fists wheeling, dark eyes wide, astounded at the bright, confusing world. Carole focused on the sweet innocence of the child, on all it could not suspect about life, the same innocence she'd marveled at in each of her children when she'd first held them and which she still saw, even now, if she looked. She hoped—no, she knew for a fact—her mother had reveled in her in the same way.

Solange's eyes beseeched her. Carole squeezed her hand and smiled. "Yes, Mama, she's perfectly happy."

Her mother's body softened in a shudder of relief. "Oh, I'm so glad."

Carole leaned to kiss her mother's cheek and stood. "See you next week, Mama."

"Good-bye, dear."

Carole looked on as Walt and Alison said their good-byes. How little it took, sometimes, to smooth the rough currents of worry and fear: a word, a look, a hand. How very little.

41

Carole

June 1973

Walt peeked through the driver's side window of the Valiant. "You ladies sure you've got everything?"

Alison didn't look up from her book. "I'm sure, Daddy."

Carole nodded. "And before you ask, I double-checked my pill case."

"All righty, then." He opened the door, slid behind the wheel and started the engine. He hung his elbow out the window and called to Warren and Lester in the Nova. "Remember, boys, this isn't Thunder Road. Five miles over the limit and no more."

"Got it, Dad." Warren revved the engine and gave Walt a sideways grin.

"Tell me, Carole. What was I thinking when I let him put a V-8 in that vehicle?"

"I believe you were proud he'd graduated high school with a B average."

"So I was."

Alison said, "I hope no one's thinking of getting me an engine for graduation."

Walt laughed. "What's your idea, then?"

"I'm not sure. I'll think about it."

"Well, you've got a few years," Carole said, wishing it were longer.

A month ago, Walt surprised her by insisting they take a family vacation after school got out for the summer. "High time," he'd said. He had never been one for traveling, and going anywhere with the twins when they were small had been inviting chaos. Carole wouldn't have minded going farther than Lake Winnipesaukee when the children were school-age, but Walt hadn't wanted to close the garage, and she'd been satisfied to stay where she'd always been.

He asked her to choose the spot, so she suggested Steamboat Springs, where Janine had been since Christmas, managing condominiums. The move had seemed sudden to Carole, but Janine claimed she'd finally recovered from Mitch's death and was itching for a fresh start. Walt said Colorado was too far for a five-day trip, so Carole proposed Cape Cod. He'd asked her why.

"Because it's the one place where I remember being happy with my parents. I'd like to see it again."

Clouds spit rain as they paralleled the Connecticut River Valley south. Walt was content to allow Warren to lead. "Better than having him on my tail." They crossed into Massachusetts, where mid-June seemed more like spring. Forsythia bloomed and the trees hadn't quite gotten used to their leaves. The mountains became hills then disappeared altogether. The land reached for the sea.

They curved past Boston and headed east. High winds scattered the clouds and yellow beams of sunlight shone on dark lakes, illuminating the marsh grass along their borders. Alison abandoned her book and stared out the window as Carole did, eager for a glimpse of the ocean. It would be Alison's first, and the twins'. Walt had seen too much ocean in the navy, but that was hardly the same.

Carole rolled down the window as they crossed the bridge over the Cape Cod Canal. "Alison, if you lick your lips, you can taste the salt."

"Oh my gosh, I can!"

They were staying in a motel in Wellfleet for five days, but had agreed to search for the cottage in Chatham on the way. Walt had asked if she remembered how to get there. "I doubt it. But the town's small, or it used to be, so maybe we'll stumble onto it."

A while later, Walt left the main road and pulled up to a diner in Sandwich.

"I could've packed a lunch," Carole said.

"Not on your life. Vacation's for everyone."

They squeezed into a booth. Carole ordered a tuna sandwich. Lester let loose a laugh and the waitress rolled her eyes.

"A Reuben, please," said Walt.

"Sandwich, Dad," Lester said, barely able to control himself. "You forgot to say 'sandwich.'"

Warren passed his menu to the waitress. "I'll have the same." He glanced at Lester. "The same *sandwich*."

Lester howled.

Alison bent over the menu, twirling a strand of hair. "I'll have the chili, please." She folded the menu, pressing her lips together to stop from laughing. "The chili sandwich."

Walt caught Carole's eye. Everything is right here, his eyes said. She smiled.

He was right.

They lingered over ice cream and set off once more along Route 6 and then south for Chatham. At the second crossroads, Carole instructed Walt to turn left. They passed several clapboard houses, one nearly engulfed by climbing roses, and rounded a corner. A half mile away was the sea, laced with rows of white wave crests, stretched taut to the horizon.

"Nantucket Sound," Carole said. "Just a little farther. I never dreamed I'd remember."

The road dipped. On the next rise, she asked Walt to pull over. Warren and Lester drove up behind them and everyone got out.

The cottage sat as she remembered it, nestled in the dunes, enclosed by a picket fence in need of paint. The flowerbeds were overgrown but as colorful as Carole's memory of them.

Walt pointed at the windmill, listing inland. "Hard push would finish that off."

"Doesn't look like anyone lives here," Warren said.

Alison said, "It's so pretty. I can't believe you lived here a whole summer!"

"It was lovely."

"Was Aunt Janine here, too?"

"No, before Janine. Just my mother and me. And my father."

Alison ran ahead on a path through the dune grass toward the shore. The boys followed, loping. Walt walked with Carole to where the grasses ended and the water spread out before them, deep and wide and sapphire blue. Her mother used to stare at the ocean, and now she understood why. Some things were easier to reflect on when there was nothing in your way.

Carole turned to look at the house. A memory came to her of sitting inside on the window seat, the sun warming her shoulders and spilling onto the whitewashed floors. Her parents were in the kitchen preparing a meal, conversing softly, passing by the doorway from time to time, where sunlight reached them, too, from another south-facing window.

That was all Carole needed to remember. She had harbored her mother and her father in her own dark space, cultivating their worst selves like mushrooms. The truth of her parents was larger than what she could hold inside. It didn't matter that she would never know how much fault to apportion to each, to the times they lived in, to their own parents and to fate. Here, at the edge of the ocean, light had fallen across the three of them for a time, a good strong light. They had shared love.

But Carole had come to recognize that an abiding love, one that would not give way to a hard push, depended on more than where light happened to fall. The truest, best love had nothing to do with luck. Luck was faithless, and worth little. True love wasn't fancy and it wasn't magical, but simply true in every sense: honest, loyal and sure.

Walt took her hand and led her toward the water. The boys had rolled up their pant legs and waded in the foaming surf. Alison raced across the smooth sand, arms outstretched, scattering sanderlings and sandpipers into the air. She was still a girl, Carole was relieved to see. The careless arrows of misfortune were tangents glancing off the pure circle of her dreams.

If the beach were long enough, her daughter would teach her feet to fly.

AUTHOR'S NOTE

Ploof v. Putnam was a real case. The inciting events and the trial occurred much as I've described, but nearly three decades earlier. The social and political tension between the French Catholic lake-dwelling families and the Protestant elite persisted through the first half of the twentieth century. Some would argue it persists today, albeit in altered form.

Henry Perkins, the driving force behind the eugenics movement in Vermont, was a real man. I used the true names of some of the public figures; others I fabricated. I relied heavily on Nancy L. Gallagher's excellent study of this bleak chapter in Vermont history: *Breeding Better Vermonters: The Eugenics Project in the Green Mountain State* (University Press of New England, 1999).

I portrayed the historical treatment of the mentally ill and mentally handicapped as accurately as I could. Mental hospitals in Vermont did have visiting days for the public to view patients, and treatments such as insulin coma therapy, colonics and submersion in ice-water baths were given to patients almost without regard to symptoms or diagnosis. Through the mid-twentieth century, people, particularly women, could be institutionalized on demand, or with the aid of a doctor.

Finally, the typical onset for schizophrenia is during young adult-hood. However, the disease also has a distinct adult-onset type, often marked by auditory hallucinations, thought confusion and paranoia, and is more responsive to antipsychotic medication than other types. Antianxiety drugs such as Valium are not used to treat schizophrenia; Carole's improvement after her initial visit to the doctor was due to the episodic nature of the disease. Schizophrenia can be intractable, and even patients who respond to treatment suffer from serious side effects, some permanent. That is still true today.

All the Best People

———❦❦———

SONJA YOERG

DISCUSSION QUESTIONS

1. The story is filled with water symbolism. Indeed, each of the main characters is associated with a body of water: Solange and the lake, Alison and the river, Carole and the ocean. What meaning do these places have for each of them throughout the story?

2. Carole is able to hide her schizophrenic symptoms for some time by withdrawing from her family and making excuses for her behavior. But the members of her family, with the possible exception of Alison, are not very perceptive. Everything is "right as rain," as Walt says. Do you think this is common? Are we at least able, or willing, to see problems in those we are closest to?

3. Carole's relationship with her mother changes several times throughout the course of the story. Significantly, on her eighteenth birthday, she learns about her mother's affair and her sister's parentage, and begins to despise her mother, rather than pity her. After Carole meets Walt, she softens toward Solange, then comes to resent her when she believes she has inherited her illness. By the

end of the story, do you believe Carole accepts her mother? Does she forgive her? Should she? Are there relationships you have had that have taken a similarly torturous path?

4. Class conflict is central to Solange's story, but it is also present in Alison's life, especially in her relationship with Delaney. How does it affect Alison? How did Carole sidestep this conflict in her life?

5. Given the disparity between the backgrounds of Solange and Osborn, was their marriage destined to fail? Who do you think was more at fault and why?

6. How does Solange come to have an affair? Was it a decision, an act of desperation or the inevitable unwinding of her fate as shown to her by the fortune-teller? How do you think she saw it? How did you?

7. When Solange becomes pregnant with Janine, she faces some hard choices. She eventually runs away to the dock with Carole's help, but is intercepted by Osborn and the police. Given her position, what were her alternatives? Should she have given up the baby?

8. What is the significance of the title? Carole's tormented childhood leaves her with a deep-seated self-hatred that emerges during her illness: her bad blood from her parents. How does this relate to "all the best people"? For Carole, what are "the best people" like? Are those your criteria, too?

9. Warren and Lester are fraternal twins, as are Walt's brother—Janine's late husband, Mitch. By contrast, Carole and Janine are separated by ten years and have different fathers. Thinking about the sibling pairs, how do the relationships add to the theme of

inheritance and upbringing, i.e., nature vs. nurture? How do the characters respond differently to misfortune?

10. Janine is callous and self-absorbed, to say the least. Most of her vitriol, however, is internal and her behavior is mostly acceptable—even charming. Is her anger and vengefulness a legacy from Solange and/or her "pirate" father, or the result of being spurned by Osborn's family? More simply, is she a sociopath, incapable of change, or could she become a good person?

11. Alison and her grandmother, Solange, both have red hair. They also share a belief in magic, as exemplified by the blue box. How is that significant in the story? Near the end, Alison thinks, "Magic spells were concentrated wishes—she understood that much—but maybe the wishing part was more important than the magic. Maybe you had to wish that hard to find out what you really wanted." Does this mean her belief in magic had changed?

12. Alison and Solange both receive tarot readings. Their cards are the same (the High Priestess, the Wheel of Fortune and the Fool), but the orderings were different. What meaning did Alison and Solange attach to the readings? Did that alter the course of their actions? If you have had a tarot reading, did it have any effect on you?

13. Alison is on the cusp of adolescence. What aspects of her feelings—about her mother, her friends and her teacher—are "normal" for her stage of development? If Carole had not become ill, what do you suppose Alison's relationship with her mother and the others would have been like?

KEEP READING FOR AN EXCERPT OF
SONJA YOERG'S NOVEL . . .

The Middle of Somewhere

Available from
New American Library!

1

Liz hopped from foot to foot and hugged herself against the cold. She glanced at the porch of the Yosemite Valley Wilderness Office, where Dante stood with his back to her, chatting with some other hikers. His shoulders shrugged and dropped, and his hands danced this way and that. He was telling a story—a funny one, judging by the faces of his audience—but not a backpacking story because he didn't have any. His idea of a wilderness adventure was staring out the window during spin class at the gym. Not that it mattered. He could have been describing the self-contradictory worldview of the guy who changes his oil, or the merits of homemade tamales, or even acting out the latest viral cat video. Liz had known him for over two years and still couldn't decipher how he captured strangers' attention without apparent effort. Dante was black velvet and other people were lint.

Their backpacks sat nearby on a wooden bench like stiff-backed strangers waiting for a bus. The impulse to grab hers and take off without him shot through her. She quelled it with the reminder that his pack contained essential gear for completing the three-week hike. The John Muir Trail. Her hike. At least that had been the plan.

She propped her left hiking boot on the bench, retied it, folded down the top of her sock and paced a few steps along the sidewalk to see if she'd gotten them even. It wasn't yet nine a.m., and Yosemite Village already had a tentative, waking buzz. Two teenage girls in pajama pants and oversize sweatshirts walked past, dragging their Uggs on the concrete. Bleary-eyed dads pushed strollers, and Patagonia types with day packs marched purposefully among the buildings: restaurants, a grocery store, a medical clinic, a visitor's center, gift shops, a fire station, even a four-star hotel. What a shame the trail had to begin in the middle of this circus. Liz couldn't wait to get the hell out of there.

She fished Dante's iPhone out of the zippered compartment on top of his pack and called Valerie. They'd been best friends for eleven years, since freshman year in college, when life had come with happiness the way a phone plan came with minutes.

Valerie answered. "Dante?"

"No. It's me."

"Where's your phone?"

"Asleep in the car. No service most of the way. Even here I've only got one bar."

"Dante's going to go nuts if he can't use his phone."

"You think? How's Muesli?" Valerie was cat-sitting for her.

"Does he ever look at you like he thinks you're an idiot?"

"All the time."

"Then he's fine."

"How's the slipper commute?" Valerie worked as a Web designer, mostly from home, and had twenty sets of pajamas hanging in her closet as if they were business suits.

"Just firing up the machine. You get your permits?"

"Uh-huh."

"Try to sound more psyched."

How could she be psyched when this wasn't the trip she'd planned? She was supposed to hike the John Muir Trail—the JMT—alone.

With a few thousand square miles of open territory surrounding her, she hoped to find a way to a truer life. She sure didn't know the way now. Each turn she'd taken, each decision she'd made—including moving in with Dante six months ago—had seemed right at the time, yet none *were* right, based as they were on a series of unchallenged assumptions and quiet lies, one weak moral link attached to the next, with the truth at the tail end, whipping away from her again and again.

Maybe, she'd whispered to herself, she could have a relationship with Dante and share a home if she pretended there was no reason she couldn't. She loved him enough to almost believe it could work. But she'd hardly finished unpacking before her doubts had mushroomed. She became desperate for time away—from the constant stream of friends in Dante's wake, from the sense of sliding down inside a funnel that led to marriage, from becoming an indeterminate portion of something called "us"—and could not tell Dante why. Not then or since. That was the crux of it. Instead, she told Dante that years ago she'd abandoned a plan to hike the JMT and now wanted to strike it off her list before she turned thirty in November. She had no list, but he accepted her explanation, and her true motivation wriggled free.

The Park Service issued only a few permits for each trailhead. She'd faxed in her application as soon as she decided to go. When she received e-mail confirmation, a crosscurrent of relief and dread flooded her. In two months' time, she would have her solitude, her bitter medicine.

Then two weeks before her start date, Dante announced he was joining her.

"You've never been backpacking, and now you want to go two hundred and twenty miles?"

"I would miss you." He opened his hands as if that were the simple truth.

There had to be more to it than that. Why else would he suggest embarking on a journey they both knew would make him miserable? She tried to talk him out of it. He didn't like nature, the cold or energy bars. It made no sense. But he was adamant, and brushed her concerns aside. She'd had no choice but to capitulate.

Now she told Valerie, "I am psyched. In fact, I want to hit the trail right now, but Dante's holding court in the Wilderness Office."

"I can't believe you'll be out of touch for three weeks. What am I going to do without you? Who am I going to talk to?"

"Yourself, I guess. Put an earbud in and walk around holding your phone like a Geiger counter. You could be an incognito schizophrenic."

"I'll be reduced to that." She dropped her voice a notch. "Listen. I have to ask you again. You sure you feel up to this?"

Liz reflexively placed her hand on her lower abdomen. "I'm fine. I swear. It's just a hike."

"When I have to park a block from Trader Joe's, that's a hike. Two hundred miles is something else. And your miscarriage was less than three weeks ago."

As if Dante could have overheard, she turned and walked a few more steps down the sidewalk. "I feel great."

"And you're going to tell Dante soon and not wait for the absolute perfect moment."

Despite the cold, Liz's palms were slick with sweat. Her boyfriend knew nothing of her pregnancy, but her friend didn't have the whole story either. Valerie had made her daily call to Liz and learned she was home sick, but she'd been vague about the reason. Knowing Dante was out of town, Valerie had stopped by and found Liz lying on the couch, a heating pad on her belly.

"Cramps?"

"No," Liz had said, staring at the rug. "Worse."

Valerie had assumed she'd had a miscarriage, not an abortion, and Liz hadn't corrected her. Next to her deceit of Dante, it seemed minor. Valerie had made her promise she would tell him, but when

Liz ran the conversation through her mind, she panicked. If she revealed this bit of information, the whole monstrous truth might tumble out, and she would lose him for certain.

"I will tell him. And I'll make sure I've got room to run when I do."

"He'll understand. It's not like it was your fault."

Liz's chest tightened. "Val, listen—"

"Crap! I just noticed the time. I've got a call in two minutes, so this is good-bye."

" 'Bye."

"Don't get lost."

"Impossible."

"Don't fall off a cliff."

"I'll try not to."

"Watch out for bears."

"I love bears! And they love me."

"Of course they do. So do I."

"And me you. 'Bye."

" 'Bye."

Liz put the phone away. She checked the zippers and tightened the straps on both backpacks. On a trip this long, they couldn't afford to lose anything. Besides, a pack with loose straps tended to creak, and she didn't like creaking.

Dante was still chatting. He glanced over his shoulder and flashed her a boyish smile. She pointed at her watch. He twitched in mock alarm, shook hands with his new friends and hurried to her.

"Leez!" He placed his hands on her cheeks and tucked her short brown hair behind her ears with his fingers. "You're waiting. I'm sorry."

She was no more immune to his charm than the rest of the world. The way he pronounced her name amused her, and she suspected he laid it on thick deliberately. He had studied at the best schools in Mexico City and spent seven years so he had little reason for sounding like the Taco

"It's okay." She rose onto her toes and kissed his cheek. "We should get going though. Did you get the forecast?"

"I did." He threw his arms wide. "It's going to be beautiful!"

"That's a quote from the ranger?"

"*Más o menos.* Look for yourself." He swept his hand to indicate the sky above the pines, an unbroken Delft blue.

Things can change, she thought, especially this late in the season. Her original permit had been for the Thursday before Labor Day. It could snow or hail or thunderstorm on any given day in the Sierras, but early September was usually dry. She'd had to surrender that start date when Dante insisted on tagging along, because he didn't have a permit. They were forced to take their chances with the weather, two weeks closer to winter.

And here it was, September fifteenth. A picture-perfect day. Dante's beaming face looked like a guarantee of twenty more like it.

When he'd first seen the elevation profile of the John Muir Trail, Dante said it resembled the ECG tracing of someone having a heart attack. Up thousands of feet, down thousands of feet, up thousands of feet, down thousands of feet, day after day.

"You're going to love Day One in particular," she'd said, pointing out Yosemite Valley at four thousand feet, then, twelve miles along the trail, their first night's destination at ninety-six hundred feet.

He'd shaken his head. "Impossible."

"Difficult, yes. But entirely possible."

He'd argued that since they would arrive at Tuolumne Meadows the second day, and could easily drive through the park and pick the trail there, they should skip that nasty climb.

"That would be cheating," she'd said.

"would be our little secret."

"ing the *whole* John Muir Trail."

He'd sent her a doleful look, but didn't bring it up again.

At least not until they'd been climbing for two hours. Panting, he undid his hip belt and slid his pack to the ground. Dark patches of sweat stood out on his green T-shirt. Liz stepped aside to let a group of day hikers pass. She leaned forward on her trekking poles, but did not take off her pack. They'd already taken two breaks and hadn't yet reached the top of Nevada Falls, two and a half miles from the start.

He plunked himself onto a boulder, took off his cap and wiped his forehead with his sleeve. "It's not too late to turn around and drive to Tuolumne."

She stared out across the valley. "Breathtaking" didn't begin to describe it. A mile away, the falls shot out of the granite cliff like milk spilling from a pitcher and crashed onto a boulder pile before being funneled into a foaming river. She could make out the tiny colored forms of people at the falls' edge. The tightness in her chest loosened slightly at this first hint of vast space. Above the falls was Liberty Cap, an enormous granite tooth, and beyond that, Half Dome. Its two-thousand-foot sheer vertical wall and rounded crown made it appear to once have been a sphere split abruptly by an unimaginable force, but Liz knew better. A glacier had erased it, bit by bit.

Her back to Dante, she said, "Let's keep going to the top of the falls. Then we can have lunch, okay?"

The trail leveled out after Nevada Falls, no longer as steep as a staircase. After a set of switchbacks, they passed the turnoff for Half Dome, where all but a few of the day hikers left the main route. The early-afternoon sun was a heat lamp on their backs, and by two o'clock they'd finished the three liters of water they'd carried from the valley floor. At the first crossing of Sunrise Creek, Liz unpacked the water filtration kit. She'd shown Dante how it worked at home—for safety's sake—but gadgets weren't his str⸺ suit. He might be inclined to coax bacteria, viruses and p⸺

out of the water with a wink and a smile, but she was the professional gizmologist. She designed prosthetic limbs, myoelectric ones that interfaced with living muscle. He worked for the same company, on the sales side.

Crouching on the grassy bank, she attached the tubes to the manual pump and dropped the float into a small current. It took five minutes to filter three liters. She handed Dante a bottle. He took a long drink.

"So cold and delicious!"

She disassembled the filter and carefully placed the intake tube in a plastic bag she'd labeled "DIRTY!" "And what's strange is that every stream and lake tastes different. Some are flinty, some are sweet, some are just . . . pure."

She zipped the pouch closed and looked up. Dante had that expression he reserved for her. His dark brown eyes were soft and a smile teased at the corner of his mouth, as if someone were poised to give him a gift he'd been wanting forever. She held his gaze for a moment—his love for her running liquid through her limbs—and got up to stow everything in her pack.

Liz had consulted the map when they'd stopped and knew they had to climb more than five miles and fifteen hundred vertical feet before making camp. Her feet were sore and her thighs complained as she hoisted herself—and her thirty-pound pack, nearly a quarter of her body weight—ever upward. She was fit, as was Dante, but this first day was asking far more of her body than it was accustomed to. Hiking would get easier as they got stronger, but there was no getting around it: today was a bitch.

They walked in silence, kicking up small clouds of dust. The creek stayed with them, then disappeared, and they were left with only pines, boulders and trail. After an hour or more, they came over a rise. The trail followed the crest for a short stretch, then dipped toward a creek bubbling down a seam between steep slopes. On the near bank two hikers were resting—the first they'd seen since the

Half Dome turnoff. Each man sat leaning against a pine tree. The nearer man was large, and imposing even while seated. He'd taken off his boots and socks, and his long legs were crossed at the ankle. His head was tipped back, and his eyes were closed. When the other, smaller, man swiveled in their direction and lifted his hand in greeting, Liz immediately noticed their resemblance. The same lank, sandy hair, the same square jaw and full mouth. Brothers. They even had identical cobalt blue packs.

"Hey," she said.

The big one opened his eyes and massaged his jaw. "Hello."

Closer now, she judged they were both in their twenties. The big one was definitely older. He had the swagger as well as the looks.

"Hello," Dante said, stepping off the trail to stand next to Liz. "How's it going?"

"Excellent. Just taking a breather."

"I hear you. I feel we've climbed halfway to God."

The big one gave an appreciative snort, and took a swig from the two-liter soda bottle that served as his water container. "Is that where you're headed?"

Liz glanced at Dante to see if he thought this an odd remark. He smiled good-naturedly and said, "Well, maybe eventually, if I'm lucky. But today, just to . . . what's the place, Liz?"

"Sunrise Camp."

"Yes, Sunrise Camp," Dante said.

The man nodded. "You on a short trip, or doing the whole JMT enchilada?" He raised his eyebrows when he said "enchilada," and gave it a Spanish pronunciation.

Liz frowned at the possibility he meant it as a slight on Dante, but checked herself. He seemed friendly enough otherwise. "The entire JMT," she said. "At least that's the plan."

"That's a lot of quality time for a couple."

Liz didn't know how to respond.

Dante stepped in. "How about you?"

The brothers exchanged looks. The younger one said, "Depends on how we feel. Could be a long trip. Could be a short one."

Dante nodded as if this were the sort of freewheeling adventure he wished he could join.

"Well," Liz said, anxious to leave these two behind, "have fun whatever you do."

"We always do," the younger brother said.

She started down the trail, with Dante behind her, and stopped at the creek's edge. On the opposite side, one path followed the stream uphill, while another led downstream for a while, before dissolving into the forest.

She turned to the men, and pointed at one path, then the other, with her trekking pole. "Do you happen to know which way it is?"

The older brother pointed upstream.

"Thanks."

Aware of the eyes on her, she gingerly crossed the creek, stepping on half-submerged rocks and using her poles for balance. The added weight of her backpack meant a small slip could result in a fall. When she arrived safely on the far bank, she waited for Dante to cross and turned left up the hill.

The trail followed the stream for a stretch, then cut steeply up the slope. Her pack felt heavier with each step. The footing became uneven, and she had to concentrate to avoid a misstep. She could hear Dante breathing hard behind her. Twenty minutes after they'd crossed the creek, she stopped, panting.

"Does this look right to you?"

His face was flushed with exertion. "You're asking me?"

"I don't know. The trail hasn't been this lousy."

"Maybe it's just this piece."

They struggled uphill on an ever-worsening trail for another fifteen minutes. And then the path disappeared.

"Damn it," Liz said, and jammed her pole in the dirt.

They retraced their steps to the junction. The brothers hadn't moved. They regarded Liz and Dante from their side of the creek.

She tried to keep the irritation out of her voice and pointed to the downstream trail. "It's this way."

"Really?" the older brother said. "I was sure it was the other way."

The younger one added, "Thanks for saving us the mistake."

"No problem," Dante said, waving.

They started off again. Before the trail veered to the left, Liz looked over her shoulder. The older brother stared in her direction. Given the distance, she couldn't be certain, but she thought she detected a smirk on his face.

Sonja Yoerg grew up in Stowe, Vermont, where she financed her college education by waitressing at the Trapp Family Lodge. She earned her PhD in Biological Psychology from the University of California at Berkeley and published a nonfiction book about animal intelligence, *Clever as a Fox* (Bloomsbury USA, 2001). Sonja, author of the novels *House Broken* and *The Middle of Somewhere*, currently lives with her husband in the Shenandoah Valley of Virginia.